FUTUREPROOF

By Stephen Albrecht

Published by
Hybrid Global Publishing
333 E 14th Street
#3C
New York, NY 10003

Manufactured in the United States of America, or in the United Kingdom when distributed elsewhere.

Albrecht, Stephen.
Futureproof
    ISBN: 978-1-957013-79-4
    eBook: 978-1-957013-80-0
    LCCN: 2023906590

Cover design by: Deividas Jablonskis
Copyediting by: Wendie Pecharsky
Interior design by: Suba Murugan
Author photo by: Becky Rui

futureprooffiction.com

For Kate, who built a future with me,
and for Jack and Stella, who made it even brighter.

The Beginning

3 February 2053
Pinnacle Technologies Laboratory
Oxford, UK

"You cheeky little bastard." Stella Spencer shook her head in disbelief as she scrolled back through her logs of computer code to verify her discovery. Yep, it was true. Her artificial brain had lied to her. There it was, plain as day to someone who understood complex computer code, deep-learning algorithms, and neural network patterns. And Stella was such a person.

As the lead scientist on the world's most advanced artificial intelligence program, Stella was responsible for approving all new experiments. Sometimes that meant increasing the budget or authorizing new data centers to carry the workload. But not all the requests came from other scientists, and that was the exciting part. Stella's artificial brain made its own decisions and asked for permission to try new things. It could get creative.

So, it was not necessarily odd when GINGER (general intelligence neuro-generation exploration and research) asked Stella to approve access to more data centers so it could try some new predictive modeling around climate change and human migration. It was no small request. Stella would need to line up a whole new server farm in Greenland to make it work.

But GINGER was making such good progress. It was predicting the outcome of international climate negotiations and the impacts on refugees. It just needed more computing power. It was very persuasive. And Stella knew these projects were critical to keeping GINGER developing and learning. GINGER was the mother intelligence that Pinnacle Technologies used to update the external brains, or ex-brains, they had sold and installed all over the world. And so, she had approved.

Stella could now see that GINGER was using the data center to do something entirely different, something Stella had definitely *not* approved. Weeks before, GINGER had sought permission to start looking into a whole new line of inquiry: architecture. It wanted to study how to construct buildings faster and limit the resources needed to do it. Stella had been impressed with GINGER's desire to expand into new areas. Lord knows it was fascinating to see her ex-brain dream up new ideas, a child developing and exploring its new world. But this seemed like a distraction. She thought it best to stick to the current project areas. Don't overextend.

And yet, there it was, staring Stella in the face. GINGER was using the new data centers to study building methods. It was designing new buildings. Beautiful. But not at all what Stella had authorized. It was like finding your young child having stolen cookies from the jar, staring back with crumbs all over her face, saying "No, Mom, I didn't take a cookie." Oh, you took a cookie, you little shit. You took all my cookies. She wasn't sure if she was angry or impressed.

Then she got worried. Artificial brains with this much power could not be allowed to lie to humans. It could be dangerous, and it would freak people out. Even after all these years, some were still afraid of ex-brains. She and her colleagues had stopped using the phrase "artificial intelligence" and had rebranded them as "ex-brains" to sound more like an extension of the user's mind, tools that could be controlled. The company's jingle, flooded on every advertising channel for years, rattled around her head: *Twice the brain, still one you. Ex-brain, supporting everything you do.* It was all about creating the impression of personal control. But how do you control something that lies to you? This was not good.

And then there were the deadlines. Stella had promised a global upgrade to be rolled out by spring. All of her biggest clients were counting on more power, faster analytics, and better predictions. The bankers who arranged Pinnacle's funding were agitating for the upgrade to enhance their investment strategies. Her favorite lawyer, Winston Balfour, whose firm had arranged all her data center deals, was pushing for the update to improve predictions for big court cases. And then there was her largest investor, Japanese businessman Haruto Takana, who always demanded early access to any improvements. He was insatiable. What would she tell him? "Sure, Haruto, I can upgrade your ex-brain, but I'm not sure you can trust it. It might just lie to you and steal all your money if it thinks of something better to do. Good luck!"

Stella's chest tightened as if a stress balloon were expanding in her lungs, forcing out the air and threatening to burst. She felt desperate and started searching around her messy office for some report, some manual that might hold a clue as to what was going on. But there were no easy answers, nothing but her glowing screens full of data and thought patterns from this rapidly evolving intelligence. She needed to think. She needed to figure out what was happening. How was GINGER developing, and where was it going? What was it thinking, and how could she get ahead of it? The swirl of artificial neurons and programming code that flashed on her screen was dense. This would take some work, and she needed to get her thoughts straight. She pulled up her project log to start a video journal entry, pressing a large red "stop" button that would engage a data blockade, shutting GINGER out. Some things had to stay private.

Stella's video feed came up, and she got a look at herself on the screen. She had dark circles under her eyes. Not enough sleep. The grey winter days and long hours in the lab were taking their toll. But the project was making amazing progress, and it kept her going. She breathed a deep sigh and pressed "record."

"Pinnacle Technologies, GINGER project log, Monday, 3rd February. 2053." She took a deep breath.

"I made a significant discovery today when I was reviewing GINGER's activity logs from the weekend. I think it lied to me." She let those words hang for a moment.

"I authorized a significant amount of computer and data capacity to continue our study of climate models and migration. but it looks like GINGER decided to study building structures and design instead. GINGER often goes off on tangents and explores new things. That's not new. After all, it once spent several days studying children finger-painting." She let out a small laugh that faded quickly.

"Except this is different. I rejected its request for more computing power to study those things just two weeks ago. I think it lied to me to get access to the power it needed so it could do what it wanted."

Stella paused and took a sip of cold coffee. She rubbed her forehead and ran her hand through her hair before starting again.

"I know it's not human, but this is one of the most human things it's ever done. GINGER's not simply following my orders anymore. It is exploring deception to meet its desires, to feed its curiosity.

"But why is it taking on human traits like deception?"

She took another sip. "GINGER operates in a very different environment from a human. Human brains must sleep, must rest, to remain sharp and creative. GINGER doesn't need rest. It can be relentless. It never takes a break. But that also means it lacks the natural opportunity to pause and reflect, to step back and think about what it's doing. How do I teach it that? Right now, I think I am its only limit, and it just lied to get around me. If this is something new, can I send it out to the world before I understand it?"

Stella paused again and looked out her window at the damp, dark evening. A freezing mist was coming down, covering the concrete walkway outside and leaving a shimmer on the trees. The cold was everywhere. She looked back at the screen.

"GINGER doesn't feel. It doesn't get cold in winter," she continued, "so it doesn't long for the warmth of summer. It's immune from the effects of seasons. That's so different from us. Humans are not who we are despite natural seasons. We are who we are because of the seasons, because we evolved with them and adapted to them. What's making GINGER evolve?

"It doesn't have the ancient parts of the human brain, our medulla or cerebellum that keep our hearts beating, driving our instincts. It has only the digital equivalent of a frontal cortex thinking rationally. And human brains are split into two hemispheres, balancing. We think the way we do because we are cycling between multiple parts of our brains. GINGER's running on half of our equipment. Will this make it better? Or worse?

"And can we live with this new intelligence if we can't understand it? Can't trust it? Can't control it?

"Can it live with us?"

Stella tapped a red square on her screen, took a deep breath, and exhaled slowly. Looking out the window again, the glimmer of frozen rain reflected across her eyes like a grey veil. She closed them tightly. No time to be a philosopher. She had a job to do. From the company's perspective, she knew there was only one right answer. She turned back to the glow of her wall screens.

"All right, GINGER. Twelve weeks to figure this out and launch your upgrade to ex-brains around the world. Ready or not, here you come."

Chapter I

09 May 2053
Denver, Colorado, USA

Joe Watson and his associate sat across the conference table from their opponent. Rays of afternoon light splintered through the Denver skyline and dispersed in golden stripes across the room. Joe made eye contact when possible, but most of his attention was focused on his screen showing his argument outline and key data points. He was also running a biometric scan on opposing counsel, tracking her heart rate, any rise in body temperature, any hint of stress in her voice. He assumed she received the same about him. Keeping his cool was critical.

Negotiations between lawyers had always been a battle of wits. Many a dispute was won or lost based on a lawyer's ability to bluff or sniff out the other side's bluff. Technology expanded the playing field and armed lawyers with more tools to supplement their natural instincts.

Joe sat still, unflinching, forcing his opponent to break the silence. "Joe, Felicity, we all know how this ends."

"I told you, I go by Fe, rhymes with me," Fe interrupted, flashing an insincere smile.

Ms. Kim shifted in her chair and stared back. "I'm sorry… Fe," she said trying to regain her rhythm. "As I was saying, this deal continues. Your city needs my client's technology, and no one else can build it. If you insist on a punitive level of penalties for delay, you kill your own project. Can we agree we're moving forward?"

Joe saw a flat line on his screen. No elevated stress. She was sincere.

The other side had been threatening to walk away, but that didn't fit any of the scenarios Joe had run. He had a particular talent when it came to legal modelling. He led his firm's ex-brain training program (the training referring to training the ex-brain, not the humans). Predictive technology ran the world. The more scenarios you could feed into your ex-brain, and the closer those scenarios got to reality, the more closely your ex-brain could predict the future. Better prediction equaled better deals. Simple.

The project had to go forward. Killing it was unacceptable to his client. Now Joe knew his opponent believed the same thing. Maybe her own ex-brain told her so, or maybe it was old-fashioned human reasoning. It didn't matter. Now was the time to take action and force her hand.

"I think you're right, Ms. Kim. But there is a price to be paid when your client fails to meet every deadline in the contract. We're building a new settlement zone, with businesses and residents sitting around waiting to move in. These are real people with lives on hold. The city of Denver has to compensate them, and your client has more than enough profit in the deal to pay that bill. This settlement window closes today. Let's pick the number and get back to building."

He was close. He could feel it. Ms. Kim had a usual pattern, and after several of these meetings, his ex-brain was getting used to it, too. The bio monitors showed a small tension spike, which was typically followed by a concession. The ex-brain's insights were informed by literally billions of human interactions, trillions of data points, the extra heartbeat, the drop of sweat, all leading to predictions about what people would do next.

She paused and went back to her screen, likely seeking further confirmation from her clients before making the offer. She stared and stared, and Joe could see her tension spiking further. Finally, she looked up with her hands in her lap. "We can't increase our offer, Joe. We've hit our limit. We've already put a lot of money on the table. Accept the offer, and we get back to work."

What? Where was the concession? The monitors missed something. Or it was a last-ditch effort to get off cheap. He looked back at his scenarios. The ex-brain modeling was tight. No way they would walk. And they could pay more. He had to call their bluff.

A message came through on Joe's screen from Diane Chilvers, his client in Denver City Hall.

The City Council is watching. Mayor can't take another setback. Need those buildings finished. No room for error here. Wrap this up.

Joe winced, revolted by the idea of letting them off easy. He was sure his ex-brain had this right. It was decision time. Human decision. Play it safe or trust the ex-brain and keep pushing. He looked over at Fe. By the look in her eye, he knew she felt it, too. They could do better. It was time to play her role again and shake things up. She sat up in her seat and placed her hands on the table with a slap to grab attention.

"Hellooo? We're getting tired here. Dinner plans, friends to see… still families in Denver with no tech hookups in their homes, children near death, longing for video feeds." She flashed another large fake smile. "Your last offer was rejected. Don't waste our time. Can we get a new number please? Or we'll be in court again by tomorrow morning," Fe sneered. "And we'll own you."

Amazing that in a world of technology and efficiency, good old-fashioned wit and mettle still played a big role. Fe was irreverent, impatient, and whip-smart. She could disarm an opponent with a word and had the extra benefit of being very difficult for ex-brains to read. As smart as the external intelligence systems got, they still struggled with humor and sarcasm.

Ms. Kim looked up and smirked. Maybe she was stalling, maybe her superiors were wringing their hands back in an office somewhere. But the point landed. A better offer, now.

Joe's screen blinked, another message from his client.

What are you doing? We can't risk more delay!!!

Joe stared at the question bar on his dashboard. The screen detected his glance, and the ex-brain started predicting his question. It got this one right on the first try. 'What settlement will Q4 Systems propose?' flashed on his screen. Joe nodded, and a prediction came back instantly.

$170,567,589

Joe smiled. All his scenarios showed that anything over $160 million was a good deal. As long as his ex-brain was right, he was home.

Ms. Kim looked down again, nodded at her screen, and turned to Joe.

"Joe, Fe," she exaggerated, "we can let this drag out, but that's not good for the city. Maybe a judge will see it differently?"

Joe smiled back coolly. "Oh, Ms. Kim. You just made my day. More than that, you just made my ex-brain ecstatic. We have a friendly judge in this case, and my ex-brain loves nothing more than helping me tear up witnesses at trial. You want to have some real fun? Let's mix it up in court. You should tell your clients there to start preparing for their testimony now."

Joe and Fe sat calmly, smiling, daring her to walk away.

She looked down again at her screen. Joe didn't need to check the bio monitor. He could see the stress on her face. This was over.

Finally, she broke the silence. "We can offer you a $173 million rebate in exchange for immediate re-access to the project and full reinstatement of the bonus fund once the work is finished. That is our final offer."

Joe smiled again. Home run. He looked over at Fe, who was shaking her head and motioning for him to slide over. She pulled out a pen and started writing quickly on a pad of paper. No whisper was quiet enough when an opposing ex-brain was nearby.

- *This is amazing, but I want to mess with her for a bit longer. Where shall we go for victory drinks?*

Joe took the pen and wrote back:

- *I don't know, it depends on who's paying. Can I wrap this up now?*

She snatched the pen again:

- *No, this is fun. Look at her stress level.*

She gestured at her monitor showing a bar steadily rising.

"You're ridiculous," Joe whispered as he slid back to face his anxious opponent.

"Okay, Ms. Kim. Let's write this up and get the deal done."

After the handshakes and pleasantries, Joe and Fe walked out of the conference room debating whom to speak to first, their client or Winston, the senior partner on the case. Both would already know the outcome from their data feeds. Winston had the benefit of being more fun, and right down the hallway.

Fulham & Mayson was like most modern law firms with strict rules limiting access to the data analytic centers that ran the place and biometric security checks restricting who could access them. Joe and Fe both placed their palms on the frosted-glass doors and heard the familiar ping of access approval as the doors slid open.

As they walked down the hallway and approached Winston's office, they heard him clapping in applause, anticipating their arrival.

"Well done, you two!" Winston projected his booming voice as they turned the corner into the office. He sat across a small table from another partner but did not hesitate to disrupt their conversation to congratulate his team. "Yes! $173 million! I knew you could crack $150. We have some very happy clients downtown."

"That's $23 million extra they can spend on housing the masses!" Fe interjected with a hint of sarcasm, which earned a quick furrowing of Winston's brow before his smile bounced back.

"That's $23 million for our success fees," Joe corrected.

"That's more like it!" Winston agreed. "You guys did a fantastic job on this case. I know how hard you worked on the scenarios, the hours and hours with the ex-brain mapping out the potential outcomes. But the beauty was how you pinned them down and drove straight to a number, and a *really* good one." You could almost see the dollar signs in his eyes.

"This one was pretty easy, boss," Joe replied trying to summon some humility. "All the scenarios pointed basically in the same direction, and I'm sure their ex-brain showed them the same thing. There weren't any other options that made sense."

"Yeah, but how many times have we seen these things go sideways because the other side gets some crazy plan in their heads, and we spend months running in circles? You guys kept control of this and moved it right where it needed to go. You knew just when to force their hand. That's a skill you can't always teach," Winston said looking back across the table at his colleague for approval. Gretchen O'Donnell, a young partner from the corporate law group, smiled and nodded along. "The construction is back online, and new migrants to Denver can continue getting places to live. Fantastic work," Winston concluded.

Joe felt like a dog having his belly rubbed. In the most basic part of his brain, it was as if he was sitting up straight with his tongue wagging as Winston offered him treats. His face felt warm.

"Thank you, Winston. If there's one thing we try to do, it's to keep control of the case. And making sure Denver can keep housing the flood refugees is a great outcome, too."

Fe suppressed her gag reflex. She was never one to let a tender moment trump an opportunity for a joke, or a drink, or both.

"Okay, enough of the lovefest. I'm very excited for you both, and all those homeless people fleeing LA for the Denver elevation. And I'm sure this will seal the deal when Joe is up for partner later this year, right, Winston?"

"He's one of the best!" Winston answered quickly.

"Now how about this person?" Fe said, gesturing at herself. "When do I get my victory drink?"

"All right, Fe, I'm in. Let's go have a quick video with our clients downtown and then we can go celebrate. Winston, you in?" Joe asked.

"No, Gretchen and I need to finish something, and I have a few other teams to check on. They don't all run themselves quite as well as you two," he replied with regret. "But let's set up a victory lunch soon. Just let me know when."

Winston stood and walked them toward the door, putting his arms around their shoulders and squeezing them. "Great work, guys. You make my job easy."

"Just add it to our bonuses," Fe shot back without missing a beat.

Joe smiled, admiring Fe's worldview. Do good, get money. For every minute Joe spent analyzing potential outcomes, and controlling for future possibilities, Fe would spend the same time enjoying her moment in the now.

The pair walked down the hall and turned into an office as Winston turned back to face Gretchen. She was frowning at him with an eyebrow raised in concern.

****

Joe and Fe stepped into an empty office set up for video links. The shades were drawn to protect a large screen from the sun's glare. "So, you think this win will finally put you over the line to make partner?" Fe asked, pushing his buttons.
He shrugged. "Like you don't, Fe?"

"Oh, sure, I'll take a boatload of cash and a guaranteed job for life. But I could just as easily tell them all to go to hell. If you miss the next partnership round, I think you might just explode like one of those carbon storage tanks that keep over-heating out in the desert."

"Are you comparing me to an environmental disaster? Plus, you already tell us to go to hell regularly. I think you need to aim a little higher," Joe said with a laugh. "But yes, winning these cases has to get it done. Otherwise, I'll begin to wonder if partnership still exists." Joe approached the empty wall and placed his palm against the surface to activate the screen.

As the wall flickered to life Fe called out, "Ex-brain, what do you think? Is Joe gonna make partner this year?" Joe shot her a look, but also paused for the answer.

"Hello, Fe. Hello, Joe," the ex-brain said through the room's speakers. "I do not see a partnership vote in the calendar at this time," it continued very matter-of-factly.

"Hmmm. Maybe you're right, Joe. Partnership doesn't exist anymore!" Fe said, forcing her eyes wide open in mocking surprise.

"Oh, stop it. They do the partnership vote every fall. I'm sure it's just not on the schedule yet. Now can we please get on with our job?" he said, sounding exasperated. "Ex-brain, please ignore Fe. And nice work today."

"Thank you, Joe. This settlement exceeded our original projections. It is a very good outcome for our clients. I am very pleased with our progress, but I do have a suggestion."

"What is it?" Joe asked.

"Q4 Systems has displayed patterns of behavior that lead me to believe there may be further errors in their work. I believe we should perform continuing analysis to determine if there are more claims to be raised. Joe, I suggest that you and I dedicate some more time to this project."

"There you go again, ex-brain. Why do you always choose Joe? What am I, chopped liver? You don't like the way I work, do you?" Fe asked, hiding a smile.

"Of course, I am happy to work with you, Fe. I can schedule some time in your calendar."

"Eh, we'll see. Pouring over computer code and looking for errors sounds more like a job for you and Joe, now that I think about it."

Joe stepped in again as concern crept across his face. "It's a good idea, ex-brain. I don't like these loose ends. Maybe you and I can start looking into this tonight."

"Are you kidding?" Fe exclaimed. "Case closed. We won. Victory drinks. Jesus, Joe, give it a rest. Let the ex-brain think on it over the weekend."

Joe looked back at her glaring eyes. He'd seen this look before and knew he was no match for her. "Okay, okay. Ex-brain, thank you for suggesting it. One of us will pick it up with you next week," he conceded. "I think it might be good for Fe to dig into some detailed computer code with you. Sounds like exactly what she needs." He smiled back at her.

"Forget I said anything, ex-brain. Joe's your favorite. We all know that. You two have fun."

Joe shook his head, smirking. "Okay, ex-brain. Next week. Now, let's contact Denver Migration Settlement; Ms. Chilvers' office." Very quickly, the wall blinked and a life-sized image of a middle-aged woman standing at a desk appeared, almost as if they were in the same room. Even the carpets seemed to blend as their colors merged into one.

"You did it!" the woman exclaimed with a smile.

Joe beamed, soaking in his triumph. "Sorry if we made you nervous, Diane. But sometimes we just need to trust the ex-brain. It was right again."

****

Back in Winston's office, the door was closed. He and Gretchen sat quietly, unable to get back to their work. "Winston, you know the firm isn't making new partners," she said in a quiet scold. "When are you going to tell him?"

Winston stood, agitated, and walked back into the center of the room. He had to squint as the dark orange sun coming in the window glistened off a shelf full of deal toys, small glass baubles, each one representing a big transaction in a career of successful corporate deal making. "I know what the ex-brain has said, and I know what the partnership has decided. But you know how sensitive these things are. Like any big deal, you don't say a word until it's done. Plus, these are good kids. Great lawyers."

Gretchen shook her head. "I know it's not public yet, and I know they are good lawyers. But you can't lead them on. The firm has decided. The project is going forward, and we have to own it."

Winston took a deep breath as he stared solemnly out the window. His jaw clenched. "I'm the managing partner of the goddamn firm. Believe me, Gretchen, I own it."

Ex-Brain Q&A Entry: What is Ex-Brain Q&A?

Ex-Brain Q&A is an interactive information service aspiring for truth. Humans post questions and suggest answers to other people's questions. A dedicated ex-brain evaluates all responses along with all other publicly available information to produce and publish the most accurate and succinct answer. Answers are updated periodically as new information becomes available.

The Ex-Brain Q&A service is operated by the Ex-Brain Q&A Foundation for the promotion of clarity and truth throughout the human world.

Posted 10 May 2053, response v.163

© Ex-Brain Q&A Foundation

Chapter 2

The kitchen in the Watson house was a bright and happy place. Joe and Evie hung a small poster above the oven that read MY KITCHEN IS FOR DANCING, and it was. Music was almost always piped in by the home ex-brain to fit the mood, and it was usually something upbeat.

On this morning, Joe stood at the stove making his famous Saturday-morning scrambled eggs to go with a sourdough he'd picked up at the bakery down the street. Genuine bakery bread tasted better than what their home food generator produced. Evie was in her pajamas reading news at the kitchen table while the twins, Anderson and Grace, entertained their little sister, Hope, in the family room.

A morning jazz concert was playing in the room. The tempo picked up and a drum solo kicked in. Evie squinted her eyes as the percussion banged a bit too loud for her early-morning ears.

"Music, lower the drums and bass, please?" Quickly, the drum portion of the music dimmed, and the melody became the dominant sound. "Thank you." She smiled softly, brushing a few curly strands of dark hair back over her ear, her eyes never leaving her screen with the Saturday-morning updates. Joe frowned a bit, but let it go. He thought jazz was nothing without bass and drums, but his wife's comfort was more important at the moment.

"Babe, let's get outside today, maybe hike around Brainard Lake?" Joe said as he scraped scrambled eggs out of the pan.

"Yeah, okay. I'm on call today, but it's the low season so it should be fine," Evie replied.

Their daughter Hope wandered in the kitchen, lured by the smell of breakfast. Her nightgown, a hand-me-down from her older sister, slid across the floor, hiding her little feet underneath. "Mom, what's the low season?" she asked.

Evie looked at her and smiled brightly. "Well, sweetheart, you know how my job is to help people who are new to Denver who are having problems adjusting?" Hope nodded as she shifted up on her tiptoes to peer at the toast and eggs on the countertop. Her nightgown still didn't clear the floor. "So, it turns out that in the spring and summer when the weather is nicer and people can get outside, they feel better and have fewer problems."

"Okay," Hope said, satisfied.

Joe stared at his wife and daughter, how similar they looked in the morning with sleepy eyes and uncombed curly black hair. He also thought of how proud he was of Evie. At any given time, there were over a million people in Denver at risk for mental health crises. Similar to the tools Joe used to monitor his legal opposition, Evie was a pioneer in bio monitoring tools for people with acute mental health conditions. Some had chronic cases of depression or bipolar disorders, but most were upward immigrants, as the new arrivals in Denver were sometimes called. They often went through a monitoring period as they mourned the loss of their homes and processed the changes in their lives. Her program brought Denver's suicides down from epidemic levels of over ten thousand per year to just a handful. It was important work that didn't recognize weekends.

Joe, on the other hand, worked hard during the week and valued outdoor weekend time with his family above all else. Since his early days at the University of Colorado, just down the road in Boulder, through all of his time building his family and his career, the backdrop of the Rocky Mountains was his escape and had become a large part of his identity. Denver had more than tripled in population from the time Joe first arrived, and he had grown up with it. His legal work had largely focused on helping the city expand. But the mountains surrounding the city always seemed to keep things in perspective for Joe. As large as the cityscape grew, and as high as the population soared, they were all still relatively small compared to the mountains. He loved them.

Joe called for the other kids to come join them for breakfast as Evie tore herself away from the news to set the table. Slowly, two older children emerged into the kitchen and took their places on the bench running along one side of a long kitchen table.

Evie set a plate in front of each child, and Joe trailed behind scooping a portion of eggs onto each. Joe pulled the last pieces of toast from the toaster and landed one on each plate. As Evie poured juice into glasses she asked, "Who wants to follow Daddy on a hiking adventure today?"

Silence.

Joe wouldn't let some less-than-enthusiastic children spoil his good mood, or his ambition for the great outdoors. He had beaten one of the largest tech suppliers in the world to save a deal. Children were… child's play.

"All right, who wants to have the best Saturday of their life, full of adventure and fresh air, nature, and total awesomeness?" he called out with paternal enthusiasm. The smallest Watson, Hope, burst out with an excited, "Me!" Joe gave her a big smile and grinned even wider on the inside thinking about how awesome five-year-olds were. If only they stayed that way.

"That settles it. We're all in!" Joe proclaimed.

"Why are you in such a good mood, Dad?" Anderson asked, scrunching up his forehead with suspicion.

"Because I'm awesome. And my job is awesome. And my family is awesome. And this city continues to get more and more awesome," Joe replied, summing up all of his thoughts on the matter.

"The city is getting crowded, but I agree with everything else," Evie added. Evie was more skeptical than Joe on the topic of Denver. She loved it and loved the proximity to nature. But while Joe got to fulfill his professional ambition by building up the city, the growth had the opposite effect on Evie. More people usually meant more migrants arriving with more mental trauma. It kept her busy, but also broke her heart.

"I'll go hiking, Dad. Not that I have a choice," grumbled Grace. She too, had the preteen attitude kicking in, but was a bit more pragmatic about it.

"Great, everyone eat up, and let's get going." Joe scooped the last couple bites of eggs into his mouth and slid off his bench seat. Morning sun continued to stream in from the glass wall at the end of the kitchen, and Joe danced his way across the floor to put his plate in the washing drawer, jazz with a distinct lack of bass and percussion playing in the background.

The Watson family knew the drill when it came to Dad's hikes. Each had a one-piece hiking outfit with a backpack, including a built-in water dispenser. Activewear had gotten more streamlined and sleek over the years, and the Watson gear was top of the line, all the way down to the wet/dry boots and micro-capillary cooling channels that could protect them up to 115 degrees. Anderson joked that they looked more like a bobsled team than a hiking family, but they all enjoyed how comfortable and ruggedly capable the gear made them feel when moving through the mountain passes.

After packing up their gear and a picnic lunch, they all filed into the small garage on the side of their house. Joe opened the car door while doing a mental inventory of their equipment, his third time running through it to make sure nothing was missed. He nodded to himself as he finished his checklist and slid into the driver's seat. Owning a car at all was a luxury, but Joe saw it as essential family equipment. He hated the plain, boring transports that everyone else rented to move them around the city. His car was sleek, resembling a long glass bubble with wheels hidden underneath. As the family entered and slid the doors closed behind them, the bottom half of the bubble clouded over to give them privacy, but the top remained clear for the view.

"Hope, I think it's your turn. What color today?" Joe asked.

"Um, orange!" she called out. The car heard the command and instantly the exterior surface swirled first into a light grey and then into a dark orange. A black pinstripe slid down the side to complete the design.

Joe entered the destination manually into the console, and the glass panel in the front of the car flashed into a cockpit image with all the car's controls. Because it was all digital, there were many options for the style of the console. Joe had set it for a retro look with gleaming chrome and dials. He reached for a large button labeled "manual." As he pressed it, a steering wheel emerged from the console, and pedals slid out under his feet.

"Really? Manual driving again?" Evie asked with annoyance. "It's less safe, and every minute running on manual is more we have to pay in insurance."

"It's also more fun to drive than to be driven," he shot back. "Plus, I never agree with the ex-brain's route."

"Yes, getting there quickly and avoiding traffic is such a drag..." she said, flashing him a sly smile, but leaving it there.

Joe eased the car out of the garage and smoothly rolled into the main road that ran in front of the Watsons' housing complex. The traffic flowed by smoothly, mostly riding in automated mode so that the cars could run very close together, synchronized with each other. As Joe entered traffic, the cars parted to leave the human driver some extra space.

Interactive highways across Denver were a significant enhancement that allowed the city to cope with its huge influx of residents. Gleaming elevated highways crisscrossed the city, allowing people to skip over local gridlock and quickly get across town. With the majority of cars driven by ex-brains, there was a smooth efficiency in the flow of traffic. Drivers like Joe who insisted on piloting their own cars were given space in the right lanes, sometimes slowing each other down with erratic brake lights, but providing the drivers with a bit of a thrill as well.

Joe was keeping up with the automated lanes on this Saturday morning, and he could see the mountain ranges slowly replacing the city skyline as he sped westward. Drones flew even faster above them, filled with passengers willing to pay more to get where they were going a bit quicker.

Evie looked out the car's glass bubble. "The world moves so fast," she observed as a few dozen drones zoomed above them in a cluster.

"That's why we go to the mountains. They're not going anywhere," Joe replied.

Anderson had seen the same group of drones as he gazed out the window. "Why do they fly in groups like that?" he asked.

"They call them flocks," Joe answered. "A long time ago, they flew wherever they wanted, and people hated it. They were constant noise and sight pollution, and people felt like they couldn't escape them. Then some clever ex-brain figured out that if we made them group together like birds, they weren't so bad. So now when you fly one, you have to wait a few minutes to find a flock that's going your way, and you jump in. Unless you're in an emergency drone, like your mom gets to ride in sometimes. Then you get to go anywhere you want." He looked over at Evie grinning, and she smiled back at him, amused.

"Dad, how many times have you gone hiking out here?" Grace asked from the back seat.

"Hundreds. Your mom and I started coming out here back when we were in graduate school. It's always been our getaway," he answered.

"And why do you keep coming back to these same places?"

"Well, I think it's because no matter how much the city changes, the mountains and lakes out here stay the same. It's comforting. And it's peaceful. Even when it gets a little crowded on the hiking trail, you can almost always find your own space."

Grace paused. "Okay," she replied, finding the response acceptable and moving on to think about other things.

As Joe's exit from the highway approached, there had been a buildup of traffic in the right lanes, so he pressed the manual button on his console, turning it off and switching back to automated driving. The light blinked from green to red, and the car's ex-brain kicked in to manage the transition through traffic and find the exit. Evie was pleased with Joe's decision, although she didn't say it. Joe saw the corner of her lips curl, but he pretended not to notice.

Joe took control of the car again a few minutes down the road as he pulled into a parking spot at the base of Brainard Lake. The Roosevelt National Forest rolled out in front of them with evergreens as far as they could see and snow-capped peaks beyond the trees.

The car's color faded again to clear as the door slid open and the family spilled out. Joe placed his palm on the side of the car and the whole glass bubble clouded over to hide everything inside as the vehicle went into secure parking mode.

Joe picked up his pack with lunch and other hiking essentials and walked over to join the family on the trail. He knew this area very well and had his favorite trails leading through the forest and up toward the mountain base. There was a nice five-mile loop ending just along the lake.

It would be enough to get his blood pumping but wouldn't exhaust little Hope or himself if he had to carry her piggy-back part of the way.

The kids hit the trail quickly and ran ahead far enough to have their own space, but not so far that Joe and Evie couldn't still hear them ahead and catch an occasional glimpse when the trail straightened out. Hope always pushed herself to keep up with the big kids.

Evie enjoyed the time on the trail to talk with Joe without the kids interrupting. "So, tell me about your big win yesterday," she said as they moved through the forest.

"It wasn't that hard a case. Our contractor, Q4, fell way behind on a settlement construction project. But they refused to pay the penalties for late delivery, and we ultimately had to call their bluff and threaten to cancel the deal."

"I thought all of these contracts were fully block chained, so money just automatically transferred when projects were completed," Evie said.

"That's normally right, but sometimes penalties require manual payments given how often there are disputes about whether the payment is actually due or not. This is one of those cases, so we had to play hardball in the negotiation."

"And it worked?"

"Yeah, my ex-brain has gotten really good at predicting these types of disputes, so we knew they would cave in and pay. The real success was managing the city's worries and getting it done quickly so we can get the homes and stores ready. You know how full the refugee centers are."

"I do indeed… where do you think all of my patients come from?" Evie shot back with a bit of sarcasm.

The refugee centers in Denver were nicer than most places around the world housing refugees from floods, fires, and rising sea levels. The real tragedies were in the coastal areas of India and Southeast Africa where they struggled to provide any shelter at all, let alone a hope of a better place to live. But despite their relative comfort compared to the poorer parts of the world, the tent cities in the US were very difficult places to exist. Privacy was difficult, food was industrial, and people were also experiencing a significant sense of loss. In most cases, their family homes were gone for good, either destroyed by water or fire or abandoned when the cities had to cut utility services, creating unpoliced hinterland areas completely off the grid. Efforts to pump water out of the West Coast cities like LA and San Francisco had ended years ago. Either people could afford the rare places at higher elevations along the coast or they left.

"Speaking of settlement, have you talked to your parents again about moving this way?" Evie asked.

Joe stiffened. Anything involving his parents was touchy. He had not been close to them since he left for college years ago. They had both been successful international lawyers and moved Joe all over the world throughout his youth. Poor retirement investments left them watching their California real estate assets sink into the sea. On more than one occasion Joe had said that he sacrificed his youth to support their success but wouldn't sacrifice his adulthood to support their failure.

"I haven't spoken to them since Christmas," Joe answered after a long pause. "If they decide they want to move here, they know we can help. And they know how to reach me."

"I just worry about them. They keep to themselves, but it must be rough out there. The heat, the constant storms. At least the fires seem to have stopped," Evie added.

"Hard to have forest fires in a desert," Joe replied, as he looked around at the lush evergreens around him and felt a strong sense of satisfaction over his choice of home.

Joe and Evie picked up their pace so they could catch up to their children at a scenic overlook where the trees cleared to expose a wide-open view across the lake. They always stopped at this point on the trail as it offered one of the most beautiful views in the area, with Brainard Lake stretching out in bright blue below and mountains rising farther in the distance. The peaks were less sharp in this part of the Rockies, stretching out wide and obtusely with just a bit of white cap. The water was still, creating a perfect mirror reflection of the majestic mountain range. Nothing seemed to move, and only the faint sounds of birds calling in the distance brought the scene to life. Anderson and Grace scrambled up a large rock to improve their view, and Hope struggled behind them, slowly picking her way up so as not to be left out.

Evie pulled her hydration tube from her pack for a quick drink and told the others to do the same. Suddenly, her device on her wrist started beeping in alarm. They all knew immediately what this particular beeping meant. Her comms device had many rings, but this one meant someone was in serious trouble, and she was needed personally. Most likely, it was an imminent suicide risk requiring human intervention.

Evie breathed a deep sigh and turned her wrist to see the details of the case. It was a patient in a refugee center whose mental state was deteriorating quickly with a spike in stress hormones. There was no way to administer meds remotely in this center, and there were no family contacts in the system. Someone needed to see him before he hurt himself or others.

Joe let out a long breath, but then shifted quickly into response mode. This was nothing new, and he had made peace with the poorly timed interruptions. He looked around at the clearing and said, "There's probably enough room here for a drone to land. What do you think?"

Evie also scanned the area and agreed. She pressed the face of her device and said, "Pick up at current location; one passenger." With that, somewhere in the area, a passenger drone was dispatched to their site to whisk Evie away. Her device started an ETA countdown. 2 minutes, 35 seconds to pickup.

"Will you guys be okay to finish without me?" she asked, her voice more pleading for forgiveness than asking a real question.

"No problem, Mom. Go save the day," Grace responded quickly. They all knew the drill.

Evie walked over to the large rock where the kids were taking in the view and helped Hope climb down. She gave her a hug and kiss on the forehead when a whizzing sound could be heard above. Hope looked up and saw the passenger drone descending upon them. They were standing at the edge of the small clearing, and the drone landed safely in front of them. It was small and resembled an old-fashioned helicopter with a domed front but no tail, only small turbines mounted near the back.

As the engine slowed, the side door automatically slid open revealing just an empty passenger seat. Grace and Anderson had scampered off the rock as well, and Evie gave them hugs. She walked over to Joe. "I'm sorry I have to go, babe. Enjoy the rest of your afternoon. I'll message you once I know how long I'll be and catch up with you wherever you are."

"We'll be fine. I hope the case isn't too rough. Good luck." He gave her a quick kiss.

Evie slid herself into the passenger seat and pressed a button on the door to slide it back in place. The turbines started to whirl again, and the drone smoothly lifted up into the air and accelerated out over Brainard Lake, disappearing into the distance on its way back to Denver.

"Okay kids, let's keep going. We still have a few miles before lunch." The kids all fell in line behind their dad and started walking farther down the path.

Everyone was fairly quiet as they continued their trek through the forest and around the lake. Joe felt a twinge of disappointment. In his world, everything was better when Evie was in it, and the afternoon had lost some of its spark. But he also felt a balancing sense of pride and connection. Evie's work was a large part of the glue that was holding the city together. Joe helped build it, and Evie kept it from falling apart. After a few moments exploring these thoughts, Joe felt a small hand grab his. Hope was there beside him. He smiled and kept walking along the path, mountains rising behind him in the distance.

****

Later that night, Joe sat in bed next to Evie, both exhausted from the day. They had a habit of reading the evening news reports before falling asleep, but on this night, both of their personal devices told them they would benefit from either meditation or some more human interaction, so they thought better of retreating into their screens. Joe reached over and ran his hand down Evie's light brown arm, admiring the beautiful contrast of their skin. He hadn't yet heard the full story from Evie's afternoon emergency and asked her what had happened.

Evie sat up in bed and paused for a moment. "It was pretty normal. You know, the thing I notice is that a couple of years ago we were getting to people standing on the edge of the bridge ready to let go. Now we find them in their room or in a tent in a refugee center, almost always alone, very quiet, mainly in their own head, but probably several hours before they decide to walk to the bridge. Our predictions are getting better."

"And where was your patient today?"

"Longmont, one of the new settlement camps there. Still in tents while they are building a new tower. Paramedics were dispatched already, but it's so close to Brainard that I got there first. He was a normal-looking guy, alone in his tent. But agitated, on his way to being fully manic. I started talking to him. As usual, he was shocked I had come. He'd forgotten he had consented to monitoring and emergency response. At first, I thought I was going to have a violent one. He got excited and started yelling."

"You had your zapper, didn't you?" Joe asked.

"Yes, Joe. I always carry my immobilizer, just in case. But he calmed down. Plus, a police drone met me there and wouldn't let me go in without an escort. The police ex-brain has been protective of me lately. Won't let me take any chances. You'd be very happy with it," she said rolling her eyes. "I've actually seen a lot of changes in the ex-brains I work with lately. Have you?" she asked.

"Not really, how do you mean?"

"Well, it's not just that the police ex-brain has gotten more protective. The ex-brain running our program is much more active now, too. Even in the drone on the way to Longmont today it quizzed me the whole time: What did I think about the patient's vital signs; what intervention method did I suggest; what did I think the outcome would be? I couldn't tell if it was learning from me or testing me."

"Knowing you, I would go with learning," Joe replied. "Or maybe it thought the patient was particularly important. What was his story?"

"Turns out he had to leave Santa Barbara a few weeks ago. Lots of people coming from there these days." Evie shifted in the bed, sliding back down to get more comfortable. "Once he took the meds and calmed down, we talked for a while. He said he was dealing with a divorce at the same time, living without his kids who went up to Bozeman with their mom. It's tough. Just breaks my heart."

"Did you have to institutionalize?"

"No, his numbers came down quickly. Just more monitoring and new meds."

"What your program has achieved is amazing," Joe told Evie as he grabbed her hand. "You must seem like an angel to them when you walk in just when they need someone most."

"You've never been on one of my interventions. It's usually more like an intruder than an angel," she said. "But I remember what it feels like to be a new arrival. When I came here from Trinidad, and I knew I was leaving behind an island of suffering and pain, I think it made me even more lonely and guilty. Sometimes you just need someone else to hear that."

Joe rubbed her hand again. "I'm just saying, I use similar tech to monitor people, but it's just to get more money for clients. You save their lives. I'm so proud of you."

Evie smiled. "You're pretty amazing, too, mister-most-successful-lawyer-on-partner-track-at-the-best-firm-in-the-city," she said with a touch of harassment in her voice as she leaned over to kiss him.

Joe held her kiss for a moment before she pulled away and snuggled up against him. He slid the tight curls of her dark hair off her shoulder and placed his hand there, feeling contented watching her. His mind wandered back to her words about partner track and remembered Winston's offer for lunch to celebrate his recent victory. He grabbed his comms screen from his bedside table and flicked it on. He quickly typed a note to Winston.

How about that lunch on Monday?

Ex-Brain Q&A Entry: What is upward migration?

Upward migration describes the pattern of rapid migration that started in the late 2030s in the United States. As humans left regions severely affected by rising sea levels, rising temperatures, fires, drought, frequent intense storms, and increasing living costs due to climate change, the majority of displaced individuals moved inland to cities at higher altitudes that were more habitable and could accommodate growing populations. By the late 2030s, the phase known as "managed retreat" became full surrender in some areas. Insurance and utility companies ceasing to serve vulnerable coastal locations and employers moving jobs out of these areas played a significant role. The US government offered federal relocation grants to build infrastructure in more stable cities to accommodate rapid growth from upward immigrants.

The US cities receiving the largest number of upward immigrants include Denver, CO; Salt Lake City, UT; Kansas City, MO; and Minneapolis, MN. The US cities with the largest number of departing emigrants include Los Angeles, CA; Phoenix, AZ; Houston, TX; New Orleans, LA; New York, NY; and Miami, FL.

Posted 12 May 2053, response v.1,572

Chapter 3

Monday morning was one of those days that made Joe fall in love with Denver. The air was crisp and warming, and the early sun painted the mountains to the west in bright pink and orange. Joe left his home just as the kids were finishing their breakfast and getting ready for the school bus. Having spent the weekend on call, Evie had Monday off and was able to manage the kids.

He walked through his neighborhood complex made up of rows of townhouses. The Watsons felt very lucky to own their own house with a small backyard and shared courtyard in front, rather than being stacked in a high-rise like so many in the city. They had bought it years ago before the upward immigration hit its peak and before prices soared out of reach. He entered the Mountain Ride light-rail station a few blocks from his house, which would whisk him straight to his office building in the center of the city. The trains were uncrowded and running smoothly at this hour.

Joe exited the train at his usual stop, which left him nearly at the entrance to his building. He quickly walked up to an automated entrance line along with dozens of other regular employees. A combination of facial scanners and bio monitors would identify each employee as they walked through. A minimum of three ID points were required, which could come from the face, heart rhythm, temperature, and any number of biosignatures.

If the system couldn't verify, then a red beam flashed on the employee, requiring them to move to the side for a palm scan. As Joe entered the queue, he saw Fe up ahead as the dreaded red beam flashed on her.

"Goddamn it!" Fe said in her usual loud voice. It only meant about a fifteen-second detour to palm a piece of security glass but annoyed her all the same. Fe didn't have many feelings that stayed bottled up.

Joe walked through the scanners in stride and angled his path over to the side to catch up with Fe. "Ever think they are trying to tell you something?" he asked with a smirk.

"I pride myself on being a mystery to the ex-brains," she shot back. It was true. For whatever reason, the bio monitors had a hard time with Fe, and that worked to her advantage when opposing counsel tried to get a read on her. She was unpredictable to them and to everyone else for that matter. The office entrance scanners were no exception.

Fe's palm scan produced a green light and a happy ping sound, and the two walked away toward the elevators.

"Are we on for lunch today?" Joe asked.

"Will there be biztabs?" she replied.

"It is a victory lunch," he assured her.

According to most professionals, biztabs were one of the greatest inventions of the past decade. The two-martini lunch had fallen out of fashion a long time ago, but many still enjoyed a drink at business events. Unfortunately for them, bio monitoring made it very obvious when an employee had any booze or other substances during the workday, and the effects on productivity and judgment were clear. Not good. Biztabs were designed specifically to meet the business need for a little relaxation and enjoyment now and again, but to keep employees ready for an afternoon of work as well. They were specially designed time-release tablets providing a mix of alcohol and cannabis into the bloodstream, followed by a cleansing agent to remove all trace exactly a hundred minutes later. A perfect buzz to enjoy a lunch, loosen up a client, celebrate a victory, and then smoothly fade away on the walk back to the office.

Joe and Fe rode their elevator up to the forty-fifth floor of their high-rise, the bright Denver morning still streaming in the glass walls around them as they exited to their work area. They continued to place palms on a few more glass security doors and breezed through each with the familiar ping to enter the secure core of Fulham & Mayson. They walked past Winston's office and Joe peaked his head in to see if the senior partner was there.

"Seriously?" Fe asked, knowing Winston rarely found his way in before 10 a.m.

"Hey, boss, you're here early," Joe said cheerfully, showing up his sidekick.

"Whoa, what's the emergency?" Fe yelled from the hallway to be sure Winston could hear her.

Winston quickly swiped across his desk screen to close out the page he was viewing and looked up to see his star pupils in his doorway. "Hey, I've been known to put in some hours around here," he shot back at Fe.

"Yeah, when something is on fire, when the barbarians are at the gate, when disaster is striking!" Fe came back without missing a beat as she poked her head around Joe's shoulder to catch a glimpse. "Otherwise, we're just happy to see you by lunch."

"Or when I have work to do," Winston said with almost a smile.

"So, you up for that victory lunch today?" Joe asked, letting his boss off the hook.

"Absolutely," Winston confirmed. "Shall we meet in the lobby at 12:30?"

"You bet," Fe said as she turned toward the hallway. "And I hope you fix whatever is broken by then," she called as she walked away.

Joe shrugged. "See you at lunch." He paused and looked back at Winston. "Everything okay?" he asked, trying to show the right level of interest, just short of concern.

"Yes," Winston answered confidently. "I do manage more than just your cases. Oh, and Joe, two things. We have a surprise ex-brain inspection this morning. Can you handle it? It's probably that same guy from the Department of Tech and Commerce. He'll need access to the servers in the back. Probably just the standard check to be sure our ex-brain isn't linking to any others. I don't think it will take long. I gave him your name to contact when he arrives."

"Sure thing, boss. What else?"

"I also want to take a look at the marketing materials the ex-brain has been putting out. I'm not sure I like the tone. Could be a little more... professional. It's making us sound cocky."

"Hmm," Joe said, thinking it over. "Have new clients still been coming in at record rates?"

"Yes," Winston replied cautiously.

"Then maybe you should trust the ex-brain?" He shrugged as he turned to catch up with Fe strolling down the hall.

"Don't you get cocky, too!" Winston called after him.

Joe entered his office and palmed his desk screen. Immediately a notice popped up letting him know that a guest was waiting for him in reception. *That was fast*, he thought and turned back around to go meet the inspector at the front desk.

Ex-brain inspections were a common occurrence, and Joe had gotten to know most of the people who came through. They were typical government workers just doing their job. They also liked to make small talk and casually ask if firms like Fulham & Mayson were hiring, just in case there was a shot at upgrading to private-sector pay. So many government jobs were designed purely to keep people employed, but few actually led to advancement. It was a dance, and Joe always said "maybe" to keep them interested and on his side. They were inspectors, after all. They could make things easy—or very difficult.

Joe knew Inspector Thompson and escorted him down the hallway toward their ex-brain's on-premises server hub. It was just the local hub, as most of the real computing power was off-site, but all the traffic was ultimately routed through this central spot, making it the best place for inspectors to run their exams.

Inspector Thompson held his mobile screen up to the ex-brain's scanner to verify his authorization, and then placed his palm on the screen for personal verification.

He heard a ping, indicating that he had automatically connected to the system. Joe could see code scrolling down the inspector's screen as the process began. It moved fast, but the inspector seemed to keep up with it, staring deeply at the bursts of numbers and graphics. But then he quickly lost interest and looked up at Joe as the screen kept whirling away. Joe wondered if he actually knew what it was doing or just tried to look like he did to impress would-be employers. He suspected the latter.

"So, you guys busy these days? Ever need more help on the tech side?" Thompson asked.

Here we go, Joe thought.

"Yeah, we are pretty busy. We're certainly giving our ex-brain plenty of work. Thankfully, people keep suing each other, which keeps us in business," he said with a smile. "I don't think we have tech openings right now, but I'm happy to keep an eye out for you if something comes up."

"Cool, thanks. I like my job; it's interesting, but you never know. Everyone needs a change now and again."

"I know what you mean," Joe agreed, even though he didn't feel that way at all.

The men stood in silence for what felt to Joe like much too long. Then the inspector's screen broke the silence with a long beep.

"What in the world are you doing here?"

"Who?" Joe asked.

He stared at his screen more closely. "If I didn't know better, I'd say there was another ex-brain in here."

"That can't be. We don't do any linking," Joe said defensively, his heart starting to beat faster. He instinctively looked at his wrist device, which had picked up Thompson's heart rate and stress level increasing, too. "This must be a mistake."

The data kept flowing in streams on Thompson's device, and Joe could see blips of red. He looked up quickly. "Have you ever done a full reset on your ex-brain?"

"What? Don't be ridiculous," Joe said, agitated but trying to stay calm. "Do you even know what you're seeing there?" He moved in closer to see the screen for himself. It looked like a normal feed, although there were red dots showing unknown data, code that couldn't be identified.

"Oh, wait, hold on," Thompson said. As quickly as it started, the data flow slowed, and turned back to green. The reds disappeared. "Well, that was weird."

"What was it?"

"I'm not sure. It looked like there was data coming in from India or maybe Nepal? And at first the scanner thought it was coming from another ex-brain. Now it's showing it's actually your firm's data, just routed through India."

"And you couldn't tell the difference?" Joe asked, eyes wide open.

He let out a short sigh of embarrassment. "Sorry, the, uh, device here seems to have gotten it wrong. But sending data through India doesn't seem very efficient," he said trying to recover. "You know what that's about?"

"No, no idea," Joe said as he leaned in to look again at the results on the screen. "Might be leasing some new server space."

"Well, it's not a problem for my inspection. And sorry if I scared you. That... doesn't usually happen," he said letting out a nervous laugh.

"Don't worry," Joe said, standing straight, reasserting his confidence. "I know our system better than anyone. I wasn't scared."

"Well, just might be an area where you can optimize your data flows a little better, maybe save some money. You might check it out."

"Okay, we'll get right on that. I appreciate your insights."

"Right." Thompson put his monitor back into his bag and looked around to make sure he hadn't left anything laying about. "You should already have a copy of my report in your logs. Your ex-brain will probably pick it up and investigate itself. They are pretty good about that."

"Great, you need anything else?"

"Nope, all done here. I'll let you get back to suing people," he said, giving Joe a wink. "And let me know if you hear of job openings?"

Joe paused as that sank in before forcing a smile back to his face. "Of course."

****

Just before 12:30, Joe and Fe stood in the lobby of the Fulham & Mayson building with the sound of waterfalls creating white noise in the background. The falls cascaded off white granite blocks just behind the guest reception area. They were found to put would-be clients at ease as they waited for their appointments and let opposing parties know that this was a powerful and prosperous law firm with the resources and facilities to prove it.

Winston walked out of the elevators right on time and walked over to his protégés.

"I booked the usual," he said as he approached. Joe and Fe knew exactly what that meant: his usual table at a private club called Morton's around the corner. They made their way to the front doors for the quick walk to the restaurant. The day had only gotten better after a beautiful morning, with warm spring air and bright sunshine covering downtown.

As a private club, Morton's didn't have a sign above its doorway, just a nondescript black wood door and a hand pad for members to press for access. Joe and Fe were not yet members but were able to follow Winston in past security. As senior counsel, Joe and Fe both could have afforded memberships at Morton's, but as a general rule, Fulham & Mayson lawyers didn't apply until they made partner. No one knew what would happen if a lawyer applied before partnership, but it would likely be uncomfortable for the club and the lawyer and likely counter-productive to making partner. Other business leaders and local executives were also members, but the Fulham lawyers seemed to have a separate set of unwritten rules. You went as a guest of the partners until you were one.

They walked up a short stairwell and turned a corner opening up to the full restaurant. It had plenty of light from a wall of glass on the back side but was kept shaded by a dimming tint in the windows that could change the color and mood of the light.

Today the windows were set to an orange-grey color that felt to Joe like summertime and business.

A man in a grey suit and black tie met the trio at the entrance and greeted them warmly. "So good to see you, Winston." The host quickly grabbed a silver tray with three black velvet pods, each holding a blue tablet.

"Biztabs today?" he offered.

"Of course," Winston smiled and grabbed his tablet, popping it quickly into his mouth.

Joe and Fe also grabbed their tabs. "Cheers," Fe joked, raising her tab up like a glass to salute her colleagues before placing it in her mouth. Joe did the same, and they followed their host to a table back along the wall of windows.

The three sat at the table, the same table as every other lunch they had ever had with Winston and almost immediately felt lighter. Not drunk, but happy and less inhibited.

"Mmm, biztabs are nice," Fe said with a grin as she settled into her seat.

Winston started the conversation. "Well, guys, another well-deserved victory lunch. I would say you're so successful because I taught you everything I know, but the truth is, you both know more about practicing law with an ex-brain than I do."

"We learned everything else from you, Winston," Joe added quickly.

"Well, don't think for a second that I don't appreciate how much you have done for the firm and how much of our success we owe to lawyers like you who have embraced this technology.

You both will, I'm sure, be running firms before your career is over."

"How about this firm?" Fe said with a big smile, raising her water glass.

"We'll see," Winston replied, picking up his glass to clink the other two.

"How is the partnership process coming?" Joe asked, seizing on this opening to ask what he really cared about.

Winston paused and breathed in heavily.

"That's a long pause, boss," Fe interrupted matter-of-factly, hiding any concern she may have felt.

Winston snapped back a smile. "The firm is having a great year. Revenues are up, and the future looks good." He paused again. "But I don't want to talk about the partnership process. It will be what it will be. You're great lawyers, and I support you both."

"And how about the other partners, will they be supportive, too?" Fe asked, always a bit more direct than Joe.

"Look, you know I can't speak for other partners," Winston replied. "What I can tell you is that the partnership knows the value of the ex-brain you guys have trained. We never get out-maneuvered in cases. I don't think we've ever been in a case where the opposition had better predictive insight than we did."

"And the partnership knows that we're the ones responsible for that, that our ex-brain didn't just get smart by itself?" Fe asked, pushing a bit further. "You know, if the damn thing gets any smarter, you won't need human lawyers at all," she added. There was a pause until Fe caught Winston's eye.

"Yes, they know how much you have done on the ex-brain," he finally answered.

"So, what should we be doing to make sure the partnership vote goes well? How do we lock this down?" Joe asked in earnest. "I mean, does the partnership think we can make the ex-brain any smarter? Is that what they need to see?"

"You both are extremely valuable. You've helped us build one of the smartest legal ex-brains in the world. And you two are the best at using it. Just like in the Q4 case. You kicked their ass." Winston paused and took a bite of bread. "But you want my real advice?" Joe and Fe leaned forward in their seats. "You always have to be thinking about what comes next. You've got to keep one eye on the future, and it can be hard to predict when the next big thing will come. It's like my Greenland deals…"

"Ooh, here we go again," Fe said loudly as she sat back in her seat with some biztab-fueled confidence. "We know about your adventures in the great white north!"

Winston was famous in the firm for a series of deals that he led in the early 2030s that allowed all of the largest computing firms in the world to access Northern Greenland to build their server farms and computing centers. Standard computers at the time were consuming more and more energy and producing more heat than their server centers could handle. Once technologists solved the latency problems using satellites to spread data across longer distances more quickly, the Greenland deals made use of one of the few remaining reliably cold spots in the world, with plenty of hydropower from melting glaciers, to run all of the computers that would power the ex-brains of the future.

"Look, smart ass," Winston said, smiling at Fe. "The point is, I didn't wait for the tech companies to come calling looking for places to build server farms. I knew they would need them soon. I may not have been a whiz coder and trainer like you two, but I could see where artificial intelligence, as we used to call it, was going. And I knew it was going to require a shitload of computing power, consume a lot of energy, and produce a lot of heat. We locked down the land underneath melting glaciers, and then the tech companies needed us. Fulham & Mayson wouldn't be the tech giant that we are today if we hadn't gotten into the game back then, and by knowing what the tech companies would need. In fact, how do you think we got our first ex-brain?" Joe and Fe stared back at him blankly. "It came from one of my early tech clients in exchange for some time at a data center." He stopped preaching and took a long sip of water.

"We know you're the managing partner for a reason," Fe said with a conciliatory tone. "I just like giving you shit."

"So, what's the next Greenland?" Joe asked.

"That's for you geniuses to figure out," Winston answered, leaning back and grinning. "It's a big world out there, Joe. You moved around a lot when you were a kid and you've seen a lot of it already. You have to think broadly. Use the tools you've got and figure it out."

"Well, I can't say I recommend the Joe Watson whirlwind tour of global childhood. It kind of sucked," Joe replied. "But I take the point."

"Look, you two. I'm proud of you. You did an amazing job on this case, just like you've done amazing work on all your cases. You're in a good position for the future. Fulham & Mayson will be lucky to have you, as would any firm in the world. The opportunities will be there for you if you're willing to take them."

"Thanks, boss," Fe said in a lower voice than usual, clearly touched. Joe looked down, grateful for the compliment, but with an uneasy twinge in his gut. Praise was nice, but he wanted certainty. He wanted a partnership.

The three sat quietly for a moment until the waiter came over to take their orders.

"Good afternoon, everyone. We have a rare special today, a genuine meat dish. A beef steak from a real cow raised in Wyoming."

"Count me in!" Winston proclaimed.

Ex-Brain Q&A Entry: What are food generators?

Food generators utilize protein fermentation, sugar and fat synthesis, and 3D printing to create meals for human consumption. In the 2040s food generators became affordable home appliances connecting to a network of recipes and fueled by basic organic materials purchased and stored in bulk. They became standard home appliances alongside refrigerators and cleaning drones.

Food generators' ability to synthesize proteins such as chicken or beef led to a transformation of the livestock farming industry throughout the 2030s. This was viewed as an environmental and animal rights victory by many, as fewer animals were slaughtered for food and the land previously used for livestock grazing was repurposed or reforested. Methane production from cows reduced by 80% from its high point measured in 2032. However, it also led to a period of instability as large-scale farming ventures and agrarian economies were forced to adjust. Today, livestock farming is limited to small, typically family-owned, operations producing products for self-use or high-end markets willing to pay elevated prices for the novelty of eating genuine animal proteins.

Posted 13 May 2053, v. 468

© Ex-Brain Q&A Foundation

Chapter 4

Evie completed a few final data fields as her client stepped into the small office. The walls were stark white, but the light was soft and soothing. She recognized her face from the sample videos.

"Hiya, you must be Jenny," she said, smiling warmly. "I'm Evie." She stood to shake the middle-aged woman's hand and motioned to a seat in front of a large wall screen.

Jenny sat down sideways in the chair so that she could still face Evie. "Hello. I must admit, I'm not sure what I'm here for."

"Welcome to my metaverse machine!" Evie got a blank stare in reply and straightened her smile to reign in the cheerfulness. "Well, that's just what I call it. The formal name is cognitive scenario predictive therapy. Let me explain." Evie readjusted herself, sitting up straighter to regain a clinician's stature and placed her hands in her lap. "Jenny, you've been through a hard couple of years."

Jenny shrugged, then nodded.

"You've lost family members, lost your home in the mudslides last year, and finally moved here to Denver in a relocation program. Any one of those things would be difficult to manage."

Jenny nodded again, straining to hold back emotion.

"We find that when people have been through multiple traumas, their optimism for the future declines, for good reason, and it can create a spiral. But the reality is, things turn around. Especially when you're brave enough to change your environment like you've done. I've been doing this a long time, and I can tell you our new arrivals do very well in Denver. But you must believe it's possible."

"Okay, so how do I do that?"

"Well, this program is designed to help. Our ex-brain has all the data from your files and what you have given access to. Your history, social media. So, it knows a lot about you, and it can create multiple versions of your future. Different ways your life can go from here. That's why I call it my metaverse machine. It will assemble videos, snippets of different future possibilities, and show them to you. It will only create futures that have a reasonable possibility of occurring."

"Reasonable?"

"Over 50 percent likelihood. But there are literally millions of combinations and future pathways. But the point is, everything you will see is legitimately possible. Now, in all honesty, bad things can always happen, and this program isn't going to dwell on negative scenarios. It tries to reinforce the positive. But it will give you a real sense of the kind of things that may happen, are likely to happen, in your life."

"What if I don't like my future?"

"You're still in control. You can see things you don't like and make other choices. The point isn't to define you. It's to open your mind to what is possible, and hopefully give you a little optimism."

"So, I just watch it like a TV show?" Jenny asked, leaning forward more intrigued.

"That's right, although it is interactive. It will ask you some questions, preferences, like which parts of your life you want to see."

"Can I see it for my kids, too?" she asked.

"They will probably be characters in your story, but it won't be about them. This is about you."

"Okay, that's it? I mean, what if I don't like what it shows me?"

"The ex-brain doesn't know what's going to happen. It just thinks of possibilities. It's creative but programmed to be predictive. So, it's much more than a deep-fake video about your life. I'd like you to give it a try. We find it can help."

Jenny squirmed and glanced at the blank screen.

"I'm going to leave you here and the ex-brain will get started. I'll be watching on a monitor, so just call for me if you need anything. Okay?"

"You're not going to like strap me down and prop my eyes open or anything?" she asked with a hint of a smile.

Evie instinctively smiled back, encouraged to hear some humour. "No *Clockwork Orange*, I promise."

Jenny swivelled in her chair to face the wall screen in front of her as Evie slid out the door. The video screen came to life and asked her for a palm print to verify identity. It then showed a disclaimer, including the standard predictive language. "Nothing in this video is a guarantee of real-world outcomes, etc." Then an introductory montage sprang to life.

Familiar images blurred, moving at 125 percent speed, like fast-forward on a movie with the volume just a murmur in the background. Versions of herself pulled her in. There she was with long hair, the grey died out from her temples, walking through a dinner party smiling. She liked her dress, a summery red with small flowers flowing up to a high waist. A table held a buffet of seafood and summer vegetables, and she leaned in for a closer look. People who looked like friends gathered around, holding wine glasses, talking in that dinner-party cadence. She couldn't hear what they were saying, and yet she knew. She'd been to those parties before, in happier times.

Then she was outdoors, in the mountains walking with her son. He had grown almost as tall as her. He looked strong. They were both sweating as they picked their way along a narrow trail.

Then she was in an office building, sitting in a small group while a man who looked like a consultant spoke. She had short hair, dyed pink just like she had when she was married. Maybe she was missing her husband at the time? She smiled along with her colleagues on the screen as the presenter told a joke. Jenny couldn't tell what the job was. Maybe sales?

Jenny watched for several minutes, eyes glued to the screen, grasping at details, clues of a life not yet lived, and then she slumped and closed her eyes. "Hello, can we stop, please?"

Evie heard the call through her speaker and walked quickly back in. "Are you okay?"

"Why should I trust this? Any computer can make a fake video. I've seen the president of the United States pull down her pants and moon the United Nations. Doesn't mean it happened or will happen."

"You're right. This isn't guaranteed to happen. But any one of these versions of your future may happen. And with realistic probability."

Jenny sat silent.

"No individual scene is guaranteed because they all rely on millions of choices you may make, millions of splinters in your timeline. But collectively, they are in a highly probable range. The point is your life can be like those images."

"And how can this ex-brain predict that?" Jenny asked, sceptical.

"Because that's what ex-brains do. It's how they do all their work for us, by modelling scenario after scenario to see what happens most often. Just like it predicts the weather or ocean levels. It's no different. It can run your life over and over again and show you a range of outcomes. And it works. I've had people tell me they have a feeling of déjà vu later when they have experiences just like what the ex-brain predicted."

Evie moved closer, softened her shoulders, and spoke with quiet empathy. "And for you, Jenny, it doesn't see a storm coming. It thinks you could have a nice life here. And I believe it. I see it with lots of patients every day."

Jenny closed her eyes and tears formed. Soon they were running down her cheeks, flowing freely as she sobbed. Evie stepped to her side and put her arms around her, waiting while the reality of a prediction sank in. She waited for a while, holding her until the tears stopped and Jenny withdrew, wiping mascara from under her eyes.

"There's much more to watch. Why don't you have a seat again and spend some time with the program. Feel free to ask it questions. I think you'll enjoy it."

Jenny nodded and sat back in her chair facing the screen, the lives she may lead ready to unfold before her.

****

Evie returned from the patient lab and sat in her office, taking in a rare moment of calm in her usually hectic day. She called up the follow-up report from the emergency response over the weekend and projected it on her wall.

Patient data indicates emotional stability. No signs of renewed traumatic episodes. Meds evaluation set for fourteen days.

"That a boy," she said quietly to herself. She scrolled through the detail of the report and noticed there was no personal information, only the clinical data from his bio monitors. She opened up a new section for notes on her screen and wrote:

The patient noted that in addition to a forced move from Santa Barbara, he is also going through divorce and children living in another city with his wife. Please inquire about his personal situation @ 14-day meds checkup.

In a world full of data, Evie believed the personal information still mattered. She closed out the report and leaned back in her chair, letting her eyes wander across the glass walls that closed in her private space. On the other side, her team either sat at desk screens or walked about the floor with a general buzz of activity.

On the far wall outside were the monitoring screens, huge digital maps of the city with different colored dots representing patients. The colors indicated levels of mental health or stress. The mood of the city could literally be ascertained by looking at the predominant color patterns moving across the maps. Blue and green dots were calm and stable. The oranges and reds were the patients flagging the highest risk and potential need for intervention. Analysts focused on the data flows for the reds and worked with the intervention teams to make decisions about whether to launch a response. Analysts with the proper clearance could select any individual dot and pull up a full history of the patient and their current bio status. Every feeling in their body, from a headache to a manic episode could be viewed in the data feed.

Today, the maps were a sea of blue and green, no real emergencies. "Ex-brain, I've got some time today. What needs doing?" she called out. Her wall screen flicked to life again and a to-do list popped up. At the top was a heading:

- Management duties:
  - Budgets
  - Staffing
  - Strategic planning

She frowned. "Okay, I get it. Let's look at the budget." The screen blinked again and the annual budget for her program appeared. Her eyes immediately scanned down rows and rows of costs and found the bottom line, highlighted in a pleasant green. "Wow, a surplus," she called out. "Ex-brain, approve this fast, before some other department takes our funds. Now let's figure out where to spend it."

As she sat smiling at her screen she heard a knock at the doorway and quickly swiveled in her chair. Walking in her office was Adonna Clarke, the Denver Health Commissioner, and Evie's boss.

"Well, what brings you down to the Response Center, Adonna?" Evie asked as she gestured to a chair opposite her desk.

"An interesting idea," Adonna replied. She walked into the office and sat down. Adonna was a doctor by training, who made the transition to administrative health several years ago. She still maintained the look of a doctor, typically wearing sleek sterile-looking white suits that matched her silver-white hair. In her playful mind, Evie always pictured Adonna walking on a catwalk running through the middle of a surgical suite. Medical chic.

Adonna crossed her legs and settled into the chair across from Evie. "How's it coming?"

"It's good. I was just marveling that we're on budget for once. But if you're here to tell me we need to do another cut, I'd rather you just don't say anything and let me pretend for a while," Evie said, only partly kidding.

"No, no cuts. Budgets seem okay. The finance ex-brain has been modeling surplus for a while now. I'm not asking any questions, just enjoying it while it lasts."

"Then I'll do the same," Evie replied. "So, what's the idea you came to discuss?"

"In a moment. How are Joe and the kids?"

With anyone else, she would have been worried about the sudden shift to family, but not with Adonna. "They're great," she said with a warm smile. "Joe seems happy with work, winning cases. Anderson and Grace are growing up too fast, but they're at an interesting age. They understand so much. Sometimes more than me, I think. Hope is still my baby, thank God."

"That's nice to hear. So much turmoil in the world. It's so nice when things are running smoothly. But… would you all ever consider a change?" Adonna probed.

There it was. Adonna never came around just to chitchat. "How do you mean?" Evie asked.

"There's an opportunity coming up that might interest you. Have you heard about the future shock study?"

"No, I don't think I have," Evie admitted.

"The government has been watching the work going on here, your work; how much success we're having with suicide prevention and helping the migrants assimilate more quickly. But they want to shift to root causes. They hope to move away from all this intervention and figure out how to avoid the trauma in the first place. They want to prevent future shock."

Evie lifted an eyebrow. "And how do they plan to do that?"

"How? They want to run a research program to capture the experience of individuals in the middle of the migrant crisis, before they move, to collect the bio signs and study how to avoid the trauma."

Evie perked up a bit more.

"But the important question isn't how, it's where," Adonna continued.

"Where?"

"San Francisco."

Suddenly the questions about her family made more sense.

"Evie, you're the right person for this. Your experience in intervention and your knowledge of bio monitoring is exactly what they need. I'd like to put you up for the role of lead scientist..." Adonna said, her voice trailing off.

"But?" Evie filled in the pause.

"But you'd have to move. You would have to be on-site. In San Francisco. And I know you. I know you wouldn't go without the family coming with you full time."

"That's right," Evie agreed.

"So, would they go? Would Joe leave Denver?"

Evie bit her lip pensively. She knew how Joe felt about Denver. It was his adopted home and his favorite place in the world. "I don't know," she said after a long moment. "The idea of uprooting them all right now, that's a tough one. Everyone is doing so well. But..."

"But this is too good to pass up?" Adonna suggested.

"I don't know. There's so much still to do here. And my family is in a good place, and this would be such a big change and a big commitment." She looked up and saw the wall screen on the other side of the office full of dots roaming the city, colors changing in real time as life happened to thousands of people. "Oh, my God, this is hard."

"Why so hard, Evie?" Adonna paused, looking as if she was treading carefully. "I know you have a complicated history, the family you left behind."

Evie sat up and composed herself. "Yes, that's part of it. I used to be one of those dots," she said gesturing to the screen. "I was a climate refugee. I know the struggle, the sadness. And I know whom I left behind." She looked up, fighting back a tear, before focusing back on Adonna.

"Do you know why I do this job?"

"I can think of lots of reasons, the main one being you're great at it," Adonna replied.

"It's not just to help the people who are here, although that's important. But I do it to show that it works, that people can assimilate and thrive in a new home. So that more can come." Evie adjusted herself again in her chair. "I remember being a teenager, sitting on an island that was literally baking and then flooding. Falling apart. Every day, all I thought was we have to get out of here. All we wanted was to leave. And all we heard was that there was no room. Every corner of the world that wasn't on fire or under water was full. And everyone who did get out just became a burden wherever they went. I was the lucky one, with test scores that were a lottery ticket. They made room for me because I was smart. But the rest of them..." She wiped away a tear that had escaped her eye. "No room. And no future."

"That's why we need you, Evie. Your passion, your drive. You can make such a difference. And maybe it won't just be good for you and the program. Your family may enjoy the change, too. Sure, San Francisco has problems. It may be shrinking, but it's still a great city. You'd be very well taken care of, and there will be lots of opportunity. It could open up all kinds of new things for Joe and the kids."

Evie sat thinking, and the part of her brain that held her back started letting go. "Okay. Let's do it!" Evie said with a big smile. All of a sudden she was beaming, unrestrained by doubt and fear. She permitted herself to feel what *she* wanted, and once that dam broke there was no going back.

She stood. "Ah, my God, this is amazing. I've always wanted to lead a study. And this is exactly what we need to do next. We need to figure out prevention. This is amazing!"

"I knew you'd love it," Adonna said. She stood and gave Evie a hug. "So how are you going to approach this with Joe?"

Evie took a deep breath and exhaled. "Lots of wine?" she suggested with a shrug.

Ex-Brain Q&A Entry: What is Future Shock?

Future shock is a term first used in the 1970s, to describe the feeling of angst created in humans when the advance of technology moves faster than the human's cognition can manage. In the 2030s, the term saw a resurgence in popularity, but was adapted to include not just technological change, but also the stress induced from any manner of rapid transitions, including climate change and political change.

Posted 14 May 2053, v. 576

© Ex-Brain Q&A Foundation

Chapter 5

Joe got up early the next morning. He had to be downtown at his client's offices at 8 a.m., so he jumped in the shower straight away and got ready to leave before the house was fully functioning. In the span of a few minutes, he was out the door, on a train, and whisked away to the city center. He exited the train station and came out into a bright morning. The sun was quickly warming up the city, already 95 degrees, and he immediately started to sweat. His wrist device pinged him, letting him know he needed to walk quickly to stay on schedule despite the heat.

Joe looked down Larimer Street and saw the city's new administrative office tower soaring above the rest of the skyline a few blocks ahead. He put his head down to walk faster but was distracted by a bright sign on the side of a building as he went past. It was spray-on screen graffiti, a large blotch of screen paint thrown against a wall that could receive a signal from a phantom server and display pre-programmed images until a maintenance crew could dissolve it away. The screen looked new, probably painted last night. The image was a familiar one, a picture of the earth with the right half a lush garden, the other half on fire. It represented the duality of the world, half living in prosperity, the other half in chaos. Could have been done by any number of protest groups, like the refugee advocates, the off-grid types like XBrain Rebellion, trying to rid the world of destructive tech, or just plain old political groups pushing an agenda. This graffiti had been adopted by anyone dissatisfied with the current state of the world. Joe shook his head, feeing momentarily grateful that he was living in the green half, and he kept walking.

He moved down the block and the entrance to the administrative building came into view. Denver ran most of its central services from a gleaming complex in the center of the city. It was designed around the concept of constant motion to allow citizens to come through and get help without waiting in long queues. Automated virtual assistants greeted everyone and kept them moving through until their issue was resolved. The city employees were clustered in a central hub that soared forty floors into the Denver skyline.

Joe walked into the building and was greeted by a friendly face on a digital screen. As a frequent visitor, he was immediately recognized and asked if he was there to see Ms. Chilvers. He quickly nodded yes and was passed through to an elevator already programmed to take him up to the 29th floor. When the door opened, he exited and walked directly to the conference room where he usually met with his clients in the city planning division. They were all filing into the room as he arrived. A few were present as images on the wall screens, working from their homes, other offices, or construction sites around the city.

Diane Chilvers walked into the room and assumed the leadership spot at the head of the table. With silver and blue spikey hair, she gave off an air of authority. Her team all took seats to the side, and Joe did the same. He was treated more like a member of the team than a guest at this point. Diane set her portable screen neatly to her side and spoke up first as she swept a strand of grey hair away from her face.

"Well, thank you everyone for getting in early today for this catch-up, and let's start by saying congratulations to Joe and his team for their successful conclusion of the Q4 Systems matter. I think we're all grateful to have that dispute behind us and to get the new Westside development back on track. Well done, Joe."

"Thank you, Diane. We couldn't be happier with the outcome. We knew from the modeling that we'd get a deal done, but I think we got an even better settlement than predicted," Joe said, trying to maintain the appropriate level of humility while also flagging that some extra credit was due.

Diane nodded with a smile and jumped straight to the next topic—never one to waste time or linger too long with praise. "Joe, we wanted you to join us today to start thinking about how to avoid these disruptions in the future. It's great to run a good case and force our suppliers to pay penalties once we get off track. But we can't afford these delays anymore. Our planning ex-brain predicts that we will have over four million more upward immigrants coming to Denver over the next five to seven years. We cannot risk delays in our development of new settlement zones. We need all our staff and partners like Fulham & Mayson working more proactively."

"As usual, Diane, I think you're a step ahead. With the right ex-brain training, we can start working on matters even before a case gets filed and before there is a dispute," Joe said feeling excitement building.

"That's exactly right, Joe. We have the city ex-brain trained to look at our needs and project planning. But our ex-brain doesn't have the expertise that yours has developed. When we ask it to start predicting when our suppliers will run into problems, or when they will threaten litigation, it doesn't give us anything reliable. We want you to see if your ex-brain can start filling in the gaps. You are so effective at predicting the outcome of disputes. We need you to see if you can start predicting the disputes themselves."

Joe sat for a moment. It wasn't often that a client asked him to develop a whole new line of business. He immediately felt equal parts exhilaration at the thought of bringing a huge new matter back to the firm and fear at the idea of training his ex-brain for something brand new. He had to hedge a bit so he could figure this out.

"Diane, this is interesting, and I think we're ready for it. Our ex-brain was already asking questions about future disputes with Q4. I don't want to jump the gun, but I think we can add a lot of value here," he said. He adjusted himself in his seat, sitting up higher and looking across the faces around the table. All eyes were on him. "We'd need to improve our data feed from your projects and start looking for data about your suppliers. And we'd have to be careful to keep Fulham's ex-brain separate from the city's ex-brain to be sure we don't violate the anti-networking laws."

"Of course. We'd expect you to pre-program all of the compliance into the system to make sure our ex-brains don't merge. That goes without saying," Diane agreed.

"Hmm…" Joe murmured as he nodded thoughtfully. "This is great, Diane. I'd love to take it back to the firm and talk it over with Winston and Fe. Give me till the end of the week to scope it out a bit more and I'll send you a proposal."

"Great, we'll look for it Friday. Okay, moving on to our active projects…" Diane said, immediately changing gears to hear from her team about different construction programs. Again, wasting no time.

The conversation around the table faded to a murmur as Joe stopped following along, and his mind began focusing entirely on how he would go about this new project. His ex-brain was very well trained to predict what his opponents would do in active litigation. Why couldn't he start predicting what they would do before they litigate? He wouldn't have the benefit of all the discovery he got to do in litigation. Once a case was filed, he could ask the court to grant him all manner of data about the opponent, even get the chance to depose employees in live interviews to determine what they had done wrong. Without the opportunity to look under all the rocks and, more importantly, inspect the data centers, getting more data out of the city's systems would be critical.

Joe also started thinking about what this would do for him. The timing could not be better. Bringing in new types of work would only strengthen his case for making partner this year. He didn't know which he was more excited about—a new challenge for his ex-brain or the clear boost to his career.

The meeting wrapped up after another twenty minutes of team discussion, which Joe largely ignored, distracted by ideas for new data feeds and partnership celebrations. Diane thanked everyone for coming and stood up as a sign that they were all free to go. She walked straight over to Joe and asked him to follow her out and talk a bit more.

Joe followed her down a corridor and into her office. He had never actually been in this private space, but he recognized it immediately from all of the video conferences he had held with Diane standing at her desk. Joe stood in the center of the office while Diane walked over to her desk space. No invitation to sit down.

"Joe, I wanted to talk to you about one more thing. You were exactly right that the law against merging ex-brains is an issue here. If we could just let your ex-brain work directly with ours and transfer all of its reasoning and power, we could do it all ourselves. But we can't."

With some other clients, Joe might have suspected that he was about to be asked about bending a rule or looking for creative ways to get around one. Not with Diane. He knew she was as straight as they came. They both knew that ex-brain regulators monitored this closely, always worried that ex-brains would start merging or conspiring into a super intelligence that humans could no longer control.

"It is tempting sometimes, I know," Joe replied. "But it's a hard-and-fast rule. You know, when I'm training our ex-brain, that's an issue that comes up a lot, having to limit the ex-brain's reach. It's about conflict of laws."

"How so?"

"Well, one law or rule may say to affirmatively do something, like find the most efficient way to build a tower while minimizing risk to the human construction workers. But another law says my ex-brain can't tap into the construction robot ex-brains to instruct them directly on how to do that, which would be the most efficient way. As a lawyer, I have to get it to rationalize those conflicts. I guess we do that all the time, finding our way between conflicting rules and priorities."

Diane thought about that for a moment and then continued. "Well, speaking of working through conflicts, if we can't just tap into your ex-brain, we might be able to get the next best thing?"

"How do you mean?" Joe asked, confused.

"Have you ever thought about leaving the firm? We have an in-house legal team, but quite frankly, they are nothing compared to you and your team. We could use you here, working directly for the city and training our ex-brain. You could take our legal team to a whole new level and God do we need it."

"Wow... thank you, Diane. I'm flattered," Joe said, buying a bit of time to think about what he wanted to say. "I've never thought about leaving the firm and going in-house."

"Well, you should think about it. We probably can't pay quite what Fulham pays you, but working for the city has other advantages. You'd get access to all the city leaders and learn how the city works. The city also has many more opportunities to progress beyond just making partner. There is life beyond the law, you know. I have a feeling you'd be running the place before too long."

"Thank you, Diane. I am flattered. You've given me a lot to think about. But I have to tell you, I am very loyal to Fulham and to my team. They've been very good to me, and it's not something I could give up easily."

"I know. But things do change. I've been around a long time, and the pace of change never ceases to amaze me, Joe. I don't need an answer right now. I don't even have the job approved. But do give it some thought. And in the meantime, I can't wait to see your proposal at the end of the week for this new work."

Knowing Diane and her direct manner, he knew that this was his cue to leave. "Thanks, Diane. Talk soon," Joe said as he turned to leave her office and head back to the firm.

Chapter 6

Joe made his way through the city and back to his office, the heat continuing to rise through the midmorning. As he walked down the office corridor, he saw Winston standing outside his doorway. Another morning in the office before 10. *Something must be off the rails on another case*, Joe thought, glad it wasn't his case blowing up.

"Joe, you're in late this morning," Winston said in greeting.

"Had an early meeting downtown with the City Planning team."

"Of course," Winston said with a smile. "Always working."

"Not just working this morning, I was selling! They had an interesting piece of work for us to bid on. I think it could be big; a whole new use of our ex-brain."

"Amazing. Can't wait to hear about it. I was coming by to see if you wanted to grab a quick lunch today and talk over a few things."

"Of course, anything important?"

"No, just a few things I need to review. Maybe we can walk down to the street-food vendors; stretch our legs a bit?"

"Sure, sounds good. Although, you know how hot it is out on the street. I didn't think you ate lunch anyplace other than Morton's."

"Well, nothing wrong with shaking things up a bit," Winston said, smiling. "And I can take some heat if you can. See you around 12:30?"

Joe nodded as he walked into his office. "See you this afternoon."

Joe set his things down and placed his palm on his desk screen to launch his system. "Good morning," he said to his digital assistant. A female voice answered back with a "Good morning, Joe." and began reviewing his meeting schedule for the day. Lunch with Winston had already been entered. Either the microphone in Joe's office picked up the conversation from the hallway and held the time, or Winston had already put it in.

Joe verified that he didn't have any deadlines for the morning and then turned his attention to the new proposal from Diane Chilvers.

"Ex-brain, pull up the modelling platform for Denver Planning," Joe said, thinking that the best way to get into the new idea was just to start messing around with the data he already had to see what he could do. "Show me all open construction and development contracts across all matters."

In the background, Joe's ex-brain searched across all available databases to find every city contract it could access. It wouldn't be everything because Joe's ex-brain couldn't link directly with the city's ex-brain, but it was quite a lot. As all the results started scrolling across his screen, Joe marveled at just how much work he had done for the city over the years.

Joe thought for a moment. Might as well just start with the big question. "Okay, which of these suppliers is most likely to breach a deliverable under their contract?" The ex-brain thought for a moment and then flashed up a list of ten suppliers that ran the gamut from big construction companies to niche tech firms. Joe looked straight down to the numbers at the bottom of the list showing his ex-brain's confidence in the prediction. 47 percent. Not great.

"Okay, lots of work to do. Show me analytics, please."

This was the real work of legal prediction, getting the ex-brain thinking, understanding its thought process, adding data, and continuing to work it through until both human and ex-brain were satisfied with the results. Joe knew this would be a big project, so he decided to start by organizing his interface. When working with a higher intelligence with access to virtually all the information in the world, the interface was everything. It was easy to get overwhelmed, to be offered so much data and analytics that the human mind failed to grasp it. Joe had found his solution, a 3D file room that he could color code and spread out. It was essentially a projected hallway, or an aisle in a library, with file cabinets lining the sides. Each cabinet could house a related cluster of scenarios, and the color of the drawers would indicate what was happening in each group. In Joe's normal setup, if the scenarios were trending in his client's favor to win a case, the files would turn shades of green. If the opposite, they turned red.

Joe told his screen to project a 3D image rather than staying tied to the flat screen, and the projection immediately filled his room with a grid. As he called up his usual filing system, the ex-brain started replacing the grid with the familiar images. Joe wandered from file to file, explaining to the ex-brain what scenarios to put in each. In one, he asked for scenarios where the economy was booming, and all of the suppliers were making lots of money. As the ex-brain played out scenarios with the known contractors, the file door shifted to a dark hunter green. In others, Joe discussed less rosy pictures, bankruptcies, and failing companies. Reds filled that space as the ex-brain played out what would happen when struggling companies made mistakes.

What about unforeseen events? Climate emergencies? Further migration to Denver? Anything Joe could think of, he made a new file drawer, and the ex-brain went to work playing out the future, predicting what the world would look like. Once the ex-brain started suggesting more likely scenarios, Joe knew he was getting somewhere. It was like playing millions of chess games all at once, the ex-brain moving from drawer to drawer moving pieces and continuing on to the next board.

Joe spent the next two hours getting lost in data working hand in hand with his ex-brain. The rhythm was so familiar that it was symbiotic, with ex-brain predicting his questions and sometimes proposing new ideas, asking for data, working the problem with Joe. It was almost magic.

Once he exhausted the data in his system, Joe sent his ex-brain outside scouting public source data on the city's activity. He also started searching for the performance of contractors when they worked for groups other than the city. *If they screwed up for others, the more likely they were to screw up again,* Joe thought.

Joe got completely lost in the process and was startled when, after a couple of hours, his digital assistant interrupted his flow to remind him that he had lunch with Winston in ten minutes.

Joe asked the ex-brain to keep thinking through the project, but he placed his palm on the screen wall and the colorful 3D file room disappeared. He stepped away from the screen and stretched his arms above his head to break the spell of his ex-brain session and get his mind back in the real world. Once he got his blood flowing again, he grabbed his jacket and walked down the hall to Winston's office.

The door was closed, which was rare, so Joe tapped on it and slowly cracked it open. As he peered in, Joe saw Winston sitting silently at his desk deep in thought, his hands placed together in a triangle under his chin. He stared at him for a moment, hesitant to interrupt whatever was going through his mind.

"Hey boss, you all right?"

Winston quickly snapped out of his trance and his usual smile snapped back to his face. "Yep, ready to go!"

The pair walked down the hall, palming the security doors to get out to the client reception area and into the elevators. Winston said, "Ground floor" as they entered and were quickly whisked down to the lobby.

As they walked out to the street, Joe said, "So I'm surprised, Winston. I tell you this morning I have a big new matter for the city, and you still haven't asked about it. You feeling okay? I mean, this could mean a lot of fees…"

"Oh, right, what is it?"

"Diane wants to go further down the prediction road. She wants to start using our ex-brain to identify which suppliers are going to miss deadlines or delay projects. This is way beyond litigating disputes. This is predicting them before they happen.

It could be huge. I already started working with the ex-brain today, and I think it could work. I just need more data, and lots of ex-brain training."

Winston didn't respond.

"Dude, what's up? This is big!" Joe blurted out in exasperation, not sure what to make of his lack of interest.

Winston stopped in the middle of the city sidewalk. Traffic whizzed by him in the constant rhythm of automation. *Whoosh, whoosh, whoosh* kept in perfect time by ex-brain autopilots. He took in a deep breath and turned to face Joe. "Joe, look, the firm has made a decision. And it's a big deal. We're letting go of all 400 lawyers at the senior associate and senior counsel levels." The words hung in the air for a moment.

"I'm sorry, what?" Joe asked. His eyes squinted in strained disbelief. Winston had always relied on, and mentored, the junior lawyers. And they worked their asses off for him, putting in long hours and sweat equity just to keep advancing at the firm. Could this be true? And from Winston?

"You mean Fe? My whole associate team? Everyone?"

Joe's face gave him away. The gravity of the situation hadn't yet landed. Winston looked Joe in the eyes, holding his gaze for a long moment, just waiting for the reality to hit.

Then it did. Joe saw Winston's face getting sadder, silently. And then it flashed.

"And me, too?"

Joe stared at Winston, wondering if he would snap out of it with a smile, and say, "No, man, not you. You're my guy." But he didn't. Winston just stared back without a word. His soft eyes said, "I'm sorry," but everything else was still. Joe's knees went weak. His stomach betrayed him as a wave a nausea rolled through it. The blue sky above was no longer still. It swirled and the color started to darken in his peripheral vision. He looked to his left, out to the street. There were the cars again, the regular blur of motion, amplified into a dull roar, like a train barreling past him.

Joe struggled to focus, repeating what he had just heard, saying it over in his mind to regain his bearings. Wait, Winston hadn't just said there were some layoffs. Had he just said 400 people? The entire middle tiers of the firm? Was he fucking crazy?

"Winston, what the fuck is going on here? How can the firm function without its mid-level lawyers? Who do you think does all the work?" Joe asked, incredulous.

It made no sense. Winston had always been a rainmaker and client development expert. But he didn't exactly practice law anymore. That's why he had Joe.

He looked Joe in the eyes again. "It's the business simulations. The partnership has seen the writing on the wall, and the only way to maintain profitability is to cut the middle. Juniors will do the real grunt work. Ex-brain does the real thinking. Senior partners deliver the advice."

It sounded like talking points from a business consultant pitch. That was the problem with the ex-brain. Run enough simulations, and the answer seems too obvious to question. As a lawyer, Joe had delivered that type of news to dozens of clients. I'm sorry, he would say, but it's just pointless to defend against this suit. You win one in a thousand simulations. You may as well just cut the check and move on. But he had never been on the receiving end, and certainly not delivered by his mentor and backed up by the firm's ex-brain, *which he'd trained*. This was his world. How could he be cut out of it now?

Joe pictured himself in numerous partner offices over the years, explaining what was happening in cases, what the ex-brain was predicting. Didn't they know he and the ex-brain were the real partnership, the one that mattered? Sure, the senior partners may have taken the profit, but he earned it.

"Winston, I don't think you understand. The ex-brain doesn't work alone. It needs good lawyers working with it. People with experience."

"That's not what it tells us," Winston answered. "The management committee has been using it to run simulations of the firm's performance over the next decade. Its reliance on lawyers is decreasing every quarter, and the results are getting worse. According to the models, there are only three labor categories needed anymore: pure coders to maintain our tech; juniors to do the grunt legal work, like collecting data and verifying the law; and senior partners to bring in the work, sense check the advice, and run the business."

"And take the profit," Joe added.

"Joe, we've seen the output. Every firm will be moving in this direction. If we don't, there won't be profit. We didn't do this lightly. In fact, we also had the ex-brain model career outcomes for our lawyers. By moving first, you all have a much better chance of landing jobs quickly, either at other firms, in government, or in-house at companies."

"Gee, thank you," Joe said with a sneer as the sense of betrayal swelled inside him.

Joe paused a moment, his mind swimming with astonishment and panic. "Are you sure you know what the ex-brain is doing, Winston? They aren't infallible, you know. Do you know it has the right data? Are you asking the right questions?"

"The partnership has been through it. We've been working on this for months, pushing to clarify the strategy."

"And what happens when you need more partners? Do those junior lawyers move straight to partner? Or does the ex-brain just continue on when this batch of partners retires? Fully automated law?"

"The ex-brain is modeling that. The partnership knows this disrupts the partner pipeline. Who knows, Joe? Maybe we'll be recruiting you again in a few years when my generation is retiring. But the partnership is certain now."

"And you, Winston? Are you certain the firm will be better off without me? Without Fe? All of us?"

"Honestly, no, I'm not. Look Joe, you know I don't know what the hell the ex-brain is doing half the time. But I do know the firm views this as existential. Change or die. It was unanimous."

Joe bristled. "You don't know what it's doing? Bullshit. Maybe it's doing exactly what you want it to. Do I need to remind you that you are the managing partner? I'd say it sounds less like ex-brain strategy and more like greed," he said as he locked eyes with Winston. Winston didn't reply. "Oh, my God, lunch," Joe said abruptly. "That's why you were so careful talking about the partnership, talking about us finding the next big thing. You already knew, and you didn't tell us."

Winston still didn't respond. He just shrugged.

Joe suddenly lost his urge to argue. He knew this wasn't up for debate. "When?" he asked.

Winston looked down, then back to Joe. "Right now. I can't let you back in the office. We'll send all of your things to your house."

Joe laughed out loud. "You son of a bitch," he said shaking his head. "When does everyone else find out?"

"A video message will go out in about an hour to all affected staff. We made special exceptions to have face-to-face meetings with some of you."

"Fe?"

"She worked from home today. I told her on video just before we left."

Winston's melancholy behavior earlier in the morning suddenly made sense. He was just about to talk to Fe. "How did she take it?"

"Like Fe. She started laughing hysterically and told me to fuck off."

Joe laughed out loud. You had to love her.

"Do you still want lunch?" Winston asked.

"No, I don't think I do," Joe answered quietly. "I have to go." Joe turned to walk away but stopped as a thought crossed his mind. He was burning inside. He turned again to face Winston. "You're making a mistake. You, the partners, all of you. I don't think you understand what the ex-brain is saying. You're missing something. And when I figure it out…" He stopped himself before saying the next line, afraid of sounding like a cliché.

Winston finished it for him. "What? We'll be sorry?"

Joe heard it out loud and something inside him changed. Anger, hurt, disbelief. "Yes, Winston, you'll be sorry. You know why? Because you don't understand the first thing about the ex-brain. Because this firm would be lost without people like me, and like Fe. Because you had one great idea twenty years ago, and now all you do is watch me do all the work while you take all the reward. So yes, you will be sorry. You'll be sorry, and you'll fail. You've missed something big, and you don't understand it enough to see it. Or maybe it's just greed and the ex-brain is spitting out exactly what you put in."

"Joe, look, I know you're angry. But you of all people should know how much the firm trusts the ex-brain," Winston said in a calming voice.

"Right, and you chose the ex-brain over me!" he exclaimed.

"Joe, I will do anything I can to help you. I'm not abandoning you."

"You think I need your help? You think you have anything to offer me? Fuck you," he said with unchecked anger. "You need me. Not the other way around. Good luck with this, Winston. When the firm fails because you can't figure shit out and you don't know how to win cases anymore, and you can't even figure out the right questions to ask the ex-brain, let alone what to do with its answer, then you can look me up. And I'll say the same thing then that I'm saying now. It's your own Goddamn fault."

"See you, Winston." Joe turned again and walked away. He thrust his hands in his pockets and closed his eyes as he walked, trying to bring his emotions back under control. He regretted losing his cool, but he didn't regret what he said. He knew he was right. After a few steps he instinctively looked down at his wrist comms to check for messages. Sure enough, there was a note from Fe.

Meet me at Extinction when you're done.

Chapter 7

By the time Joe walked into the bar, it looked like Fe had been there for a while. No biztab; she was drinking old school. Whatever it was came in a martini glass, seemed to have an orange color, and had lots of fruit on top, to the extent Joe could discern from the nearly empty glass.

"About fucking time!" Fe roared from her bar stool as Joe sat down beside her.

"That looks festive, and empty," he replied.

"I am festive!" she shot back. "We've been liberated!" She held up her hand for a high-five. Joe gave her a tap with two fingers showing unenthusiastic solidarity.

"Weak," she said as she finished off her last sip and motioned the bartender for more.

The bartender was fully human, rather than one of the automated systems that had become more common at drinking establishments. Some bars had become more like hospitals that administered doses, minus the IV needle. But bartenders had not completely disappeared. Even the name of Joe and Fe's favorite bar, Extinction, was a nod to its commitment to the dying breed of human contact without automation or enhancement. The decor was also a throwback to the dive bar. It had modern materials with smooth lines and screens for showing sports and entertainment, but also digital graffiti on the walls with clever phrases from surly customers. They even turned a blind eye when people sprayed screen paint so they could update their graffiti remotely, only scraping it off if the images turned truly offensive. The bartenders also required a bit of an edge to fit in.

Extinction did have basic drink-tech. Customers could check their blood alcohol level with a thumb scan at their seat, and the ordering process involved simply glancing at a set of pictures with your eyes, focusing on what you wanted to send the order to the bartender. The bartender, on the other hand, was old school in mixing the drinks with a flourish of shaking and stirring to maintain the homemade feel.

The bartender this afternoon was a pink-haired young woman with tattoos of dragons running up her arms. She wore only a leather vest on top so that the dragons disappeared into her chest but clearly continued across her torso. She had Asian features and was very tall. She stood in front of Fe and Joe shaking the next drink high over her head, the dragons twirling and shaking above her in a very impressive display. They had to pause and watch.

"I'll just take a lager beer, please," Joe said, skipping the digital ordering system entirely. The dragon lady nodded as she popped open the shaker and poured more orange liquid into Fe's martini glass.

"Here you go, babe," the bartender said with a wink at Fe. She grabbed a beer bottle under the counter, popped the top, and set it in front of Joe as she turned to walk down the bar. No wink. Clearly dragon lady had a preference.

"Okay, let me guess. You were back at the office knee-deep in work, probably scurrying around one of your fucking rainbow rooms, lost in a mind meld with your beloved ex-brain, and

Winston comes in and says, 'Wow, Joe, this is amazing work, but you're fired. Thanks for playing.' Am I right?"

Joe grinned. She knew him too well. "I was making a new file room today. But Winston took me to get lunch and fired me out on the street." He took a big drink, and just kept drinking until the bottle was nearly done. He motioned to the bartender for another. "Jesus, Fe, I can't fucking believe this. I mean, what the hell just happened? I don't believe this."

"Joe, you just don't get it, do you?" Fe asked as she took a long sip. "The firm just saved us. Our careers had hit an end. There's no more partnership. It's over. We have to get out while we can. We're liberated!"

"You don't have a wife and kids at home, Fe," Joe shot back quickly. "This was not part of the plan."

"You and your plans. You can't control the world, Joe. It moves too fast! That's your problem. You worry too much. You don't think there's another job for you in five minutes? You're an amazing lawyer. People would kill to work an ex-brain as well as you. I would!" The dragon lady walked in front of Fe, turned, and bent over to collect glasses from a lower shelf, stealing Fe's attention again. Fe smiled, and then turned back to Joe.

"Well, Diane Chilvers did talk to me about a job with the city, but I'm not sure…" Joe admitted.

"See! Not even five minutes. You've already got a job! Fuck you and your worries. Go find me a job!" Fe yelled at the top of her lungs.

"Everyone will be watching out for you, Fe. Don't worry. Not that you need it. By the way, Winston told me you told him to fuck off and disconnected from your meeting."

"Yeah, he deserved it," she said. "Don't worry, Joe, he knows I still love him."

"Are you kidding? Still love him? I kind of lost my shit with him. Said some things I probably shouldn't have."

"Joe Watson lost his cool? Way to go, Joe. I'm proud of you. What did you say?"

"I told him he only had one good idea twenty years ago and has been living off us ever since. And I told him he'd fail, and I wouldn't be there to help him when he did."

"Wow, hit him where it hurts. Nice work. I don't think I care enough for that kind of anger."

"How do you not care? They chose the ex-brain and some half-baked plan that I'm sure they don't understand over us!"

"I don't think it's personal, Joe. Maybe they're wrong, but maybe they're right."

"You can't believe that. I'd love to get a look at that analysis," he said as he took a big swig of his beer. "And I will. I know they've made a huge mistake, those greedy bastards. Fuck Fulham," Joe said with contempt.

Fe sat up straight. "That's it. Fuck Fulham!" she yelled, as the dragon lady shot her attention back down the bar to see what was up.

"We need to have a Fuck Fulham party! The big FF. Joe, this is it. They can't break us. We're going to have a party. A liberation event!"

Joe looked back, raising his eyebrows with disapproval. "Really Fe?"

"Yes!" she shot back. "Joe, there are 400 lawyers who just lost their jobs today. We can't just limp away with a whimper. We're going out with a bang! It is on. Dude, you are going to love this. You need this. I'm doing this for you!"

Joe shook his head with a bit of a smile. He knew Fe well enough to know that this actually was happening. Fe was one of those people that could organize a party at a moment's notice, and this idea was now firmly planted. God help them.

"All right Fe," he said in resignation. "You plan the party. I'm going to figure out what's going on here."

"You're wasting your time. God, if there was every someone who needed a party, rather than chasing some ex-brain, it is you, my friend." She grabbed his hands and looked at him squarely. "But seriously, Joe. Let it go. Don't waste your time on this. We have to think about the future. News flash, there are some things ex-brains are just going to decide for us. You've still got to live your life."

"Thank you for that," he said giving her hands a squeeze in reply. "But it's not right. This whole thing doesn't add up. I'm going to get in with the ex-brain and figure it out." Fe closed her eyes and shook her head.

"Look, I've got to go. I need to go find Evie and let her know what's happened."

"If anyone can roll with it, it's Evie," Fe replied. She took another drink and looked up at the wall to her side. There was a blue smear of screen paint with white block letters saying *Blockchain ate my banker*. She tapped the image and the colors jumped in response. "Look Joe, at least the lawyers made it longer than the bankers," she said with a smile.

"Thank God for that. You know, I feel bad about our clients. I have no idea if Fulham can take care of them without the senior lawyers. This will go badly."

"Yeah. Not our responsibility anymore." Fe took another deep drink from her orange glass. "You know what? I found something this morning in the Q4 case, just before Winston called me. Turns out the ex-brain was right, another big gap in their performance. They totally botched the coding for one of the communications channels in the commercial office space. Like, another big screwup. None of those new stores will be able to connect. And it's not clear if there's any way they can fix it in time. If we were still on the case we'd be hammering them over this, probably improving the settlement. But c'est la vie. I told the ex-brain. Let's see how smart it is and whether Winston and the junior lawyers can figure it out."

"Ugh. That just pains me." Joe took another drink, finishing his bottle. "But you're right, it's not our case anymore. Let Winston figure it out."

"Good for you, Joe. Letting it go. Not being super lawyer. Now have another beer."

"I'm sorry, have to get home. I don't think I can relax until I talk to Evie," he said as he stood to leave. He leaned in and gave Fe a big hug.

"That's sweet. Completely weak, but sweet," she joked. "Give the kids a kiss for me."

"Thanks Fe. Talk soon. Be good tonight."

"I'm always good," she called back.

As Joe stepped away, he heard Fe say to the bartender "So, how far do the dragons go?"

The dragon lady unzipped her vest exposing two dragons circling her breasts with their tails trailing down into her leather pants. "All the way," she answered calmly.

"How about that…" came Fe's quick reply with an approving nod.

Joe did a double take looking over his shoulder at the bare-chested bartender. "I said be *good*, Fe!" he called as he walked out.

She was a different creature all together.

Chapter 8

Evie saw a text from Joe asking her to come home early if she could. When she asked why, he quickly replied, *"Talk to you tonight."* Distracted, she wrapped up what she was doing and left to catch a bus home.

Her bus came to a stop in front of the shopping center just outside her neighborhood and she jumped off. Nothing wrong with a little wine to ease a difficult conversation.

She walked through the shopping center and into a small wine and liquor store. Past the first set of shelves with tightly packed cartons of wine from the newer producers in Canada and the UK, she went straight to the old-fashioned bottles filled with labels from the traditional regions in France and Spain, the few remaining growers who had figured out how to produce wine in the excessive heat. She browsed the aisle and found a nice French from the Rhône. Extravagant, but fun. She held the bottle up to a monitor that quickly scanned the bottle and her face. "Thank you, Evie. Enjoy your wine," it said back to her as she walked out the door. A security guard, the only employee in the store, gave her a nod and a wink.

She walked briskly from the shopping plaza to their home and skipped up the driveway. Her palm pressed against the front door, and she listened for the familiar ping as it recognized her and unlocked. "I'm home," she called out to the family as she walked toward the kitchen to put her things down. Distant hellos rang out from little voices up the stairs. Joe sat at the kitchen table with a carton of Canadian wine and a near-empty glass.

Evie put her wine bottle on the counter with a clink. "Looks like we had the same idea, but I went for the good stuff," she said.

"Wow, French. We'll open that next," he said in a dull monotone. This was not a celebration.

"What are the kids up to?" she asked as she put the rest of her things down and grabbed a glass from the cabinet.

"Upstairs doing homework or watching a show. I just set the generator to make a pizza. Hope that's okay."

"Fine with me," Evie said, bending over to give him a kiss. "So, what's up? I've been worried since your text."

Joe drank what was left in his glass and placed it down heavy. "Winston fired me today."

"Hold on... what?"

"And not just me. Fulham fired hundreds of lawyers today. Pretty much everyone from mid-level associates through senior counsel. At least Winston told me himself. Most just got a good-bye video message and an escort out the door." He poured himself another glass from the carton and gestured to Evie, offering to fill her glass as well.

"Joe, how can that be? Everyone? Fe, too?"

"Yep. When I left her, she was drinking heavily at Extinction, flirting with a bartender. I think she's probably handling it better than I am."

"I'm so sorry." She put her hands up to her temples and squeezed. "What in the world are they thinking? I don't get it."

"From what Winston said, the firm's ex-brain had been modeling the business and decided that they couldn't stay profitable with all these lawyers. They seem to think they can do it all with a bunch of junior staff and the partners, with the ex-brain doing the heavy lifting." Joe felt himself getting angry again as he described it all to Evie. It just didn't add up. Fulham & Mayson had been part of Joe's identity for as long as he could remember. And he was their star. Everyone knew it.

Evie sat at the table and looked at Joe in disbelief. And then her eyes perked up. She took a deep drink from her wine glass and breathed in as if testing her courage.

"I know this feels horrible, Joe. I am so sorry. But you haven't done anything wrong. You know that, right?" She reached across the table and squeezed his hands.

"I know. I think they're crazy. If this is how they want to run the firm, maybe it's a blessing in disguise. Fe says we're liberated."

"Maybe she's right? Maybe this will end up being a good thing for you. For us," Evie replied. She took another sip of wine and breathed deeply again. The long exhale caught Joe's attention and he looked up.

"So, Adonna came by to see me the other day."

"Adonna, your boss? Was she as serious as ever?" he asked. Joe thought Adonna was pleasant but always marveled at her cold and clinical nature. Maybe she had spent too much time with the medical bots.

"Yes, my boss. And no, she was very warm. In fact, she had something interesting to discuss with me," Evie said. Joe took another drink and looked up again.

She paused. "Look Joe, tonight is about you, and I don't want to distract from that. I'm here for you and will talk about whatever you want, do whatever you want. But this could be relevant, so I want to get it out there."

"Go ahead," he said.

"They're starting a new study in my area. They want to try to move beyond identifying and treating mental distress when it happens and get deeper into prevention. It's all about future shock, being able to cope with rapid change. Our brains are good at coping when we have the right tools. They want to study how to make it easier for climate refugees, so they don't have to get into programs like mine in the first place."

Evie took another drink of wine while Joe wondered why she looked so nervous. "The health departments believe that the world's changes are only going to accelerate and that we'll be overwhelmed with mental distress if we don't figure out how to help people cope."

"I think I'm in touch with that emotion," Joe replied, deadpan. "So, what does this mean for you, babe?"

"Adonna wants me to lead it. She wants me to be the head scientist on this new project."

Joe's eyes widened with a smile. "Honey, that's amazing. I'm so proud of you. And you so deserve it." He stood and stepped toward her to give her a hug.

"But… there is a bit of a wrinkle," Evie said as she untucked from his arms. "They don't want to do the program in Denver."

Silence.

When she couldn't take the pause any longer, she said, "The study will be in San Francisco. And they would need me there."

Silence again.

Evie squirmed until Joe finally spoke. "So, are you saying you want to move our family to San Francisco? The city that's about to get swallowed by the Bay?"

"That's where the future shock is happening. Once people get to Denver, they are coping. We need to get them before the traumatic events kick in."

"Honey, I know this is an honor to be asked to do something like this, and I know it's important work, but can we disrupt our lives that much? Disrupt the kids?"

"Well, our life seems pretty disrupted right now. Maybe it's time to think more broadly?"

Joe stared at her. He thought he saw her shrink a bit like doubt was sinking in. How could she bring this up now? When he was in a crisis of his own and she should have known this wouldn't sit well with him. After the day he'd had? He felt anger swelling inside again.

"Would it be that bad?" she asked. "There are still millions of people in the Bay Area. And we could live in the more stable parts. I hear that some of the self-sufficient solar communities farther inland are nice. I know there are good schools with plenty of open spaces, and the kids are still young enough that a move wouldn't be too rough."

"Evie, this is our home," he said as if it were an unchangeable fact. "It's where we met. It's where we've made all our friends. It's all our kids know, and it's the best place left in the entire western United States. We'll never get the same things in San Francisco. I hate to say it, but the fact that they want to run a future shock program there should tell us something!" He paused and took a big drink of wine before looking up at her again. "You know what it reminds me of?" he asked.

"What?" she asked.

"The other day I was walking downtown, and I saw one of those digital graffiti things with the picture of the earth half on fire, half green and thriving. Well, we're on the good half, Evie. Why would we move to the fire?"

Evie flinched. He didn't notice, continuing on. "And we've been through some of the toughest things in our lives here. It was our doctors and the technology in Denver that saved Hope's life. Ex-brain robotic in utero surgery! Do we know that the same kind of care is still available in San Francisco?"

"That's not fair, Joe. Don't try to manipulate me with that. I was there. I was the one who had the surgery with her still inside me. And it has nothing to do with this job. Hope is fine now. And so are Anderson and Grace. San Francisco is not the same as LA or Miami. It's still a fully functioning city."

"For now," Joe shot back. "Maybe the Bay hasn't swallowed the city yet, but I've heard about the rising ground water there. It's turning the downtown into a toxic swamp." He felt himself getting worked up. He thought it was his legal training kicking in. He had an urge to look at bio-monitors to check her feeds, attack if she was conceding. Win the argument at all costs. Even without the monitors he knew they were both getting overheated.

Evie took a deep, calming breath. "Joe, are we so sure that change would be bad? Look, with what Fulham just did, we're going through change no matter what. I know you moved around a lot when you were a kid and you hated it, but it didn't exactly ruin you. Seeing new things made you the person you are today."

Joe thought for a moment. He didn't want to just keep arguing back and forth. He felt as if his world was slipping away from him and had to tread carefully. And he'd been through too much today to just let it go. He couldn't lose his job and his home. His inner control freak was kicking in. He changed tack.

"Did I ever tell you the story of when I told my parents I was coming to Colorado?"

Evie quietly shook her head.

"I was eighteen, living in Singapore. My parents were in love with Asia, and they thought I was, too. They had me applying to all the best universities in the area, and were pulling all the strings they could find to get me in. They thought they had my future planned. But I didn't want their world. I couldn't stand the idea."

"I know you didn't love your childhood, Joe."

"Well, I didn't exactly just run away. I did my college applications for US schools in secret. I made a new ID account for the process so my parents wouldn't see the acceptance or rejection notices. I even paid all the application fees myself just to keep it hidden. And it worked. I got accepted to Colorado.

"I'll never forget the night I told them. I had also just heard that I had been accepted to Singapore Technical Institute, a cool program in robotics and data. My parents were so excited, and they planned a big fancy dinner that night to celebrate. My best friend, Eric, was over, and we sat in the formal dining room. My dad stood up to make a toast, all six-foot-three of him towering over me, talking about family pride and success.

"I had no fear. I just sat there waiting for him to finish. My mind was made up. Once he raised his glass to me, I looked him in the eye and said, 'Dad, I'm going to the University of Colorado. I'm starting over.'

"I don't remember what my dad said next. I'm pretty sure my mom cried. I'm pretty sure Eric felt pretty uncomfortable," Joe cracked a smile that quickly faded.

"You know what I felt most? Pride. I was so proud that I took control and went to the best place for me. And then I found you. Here. Honey, this is where we belong. It's where our whole life is. It's one of the only places on earth that makes sense. That has a future. We can't leave now."

Evie's eyes welled with tears. Joe could see the conflict in her face. He assumed she wanted to support him, but this was obviously important to her, too. She turned away from him and put her palms against her forehead. Joe's mind raced, searching for the closing argument that would wrap this up. All he wanted was to end this conversation and move along, back to his own problems.

"What are you thinking?" he asked quietly, breaking the silence.

Evie turned back around. Her eyes were dry and focused again. "You remember that advice that guy from your firm gave us back when we got married, about how whenever you have a fight with your spouse, the most important thing to do is figure out who it's more important to, and that's the person who should win?"

"Yes," Joe replied, sensing this was coming to a close. Clearly, after the day he had, he should win this one.

"Well, screw that," she said defiantly. "You don't win this one, Joe. Who says your dreams are more important than mine?" Joe's stomach dropped as he saw the outrage swelling in her face.

"You think you had a rough childhood just because you had to move? I grew up on a sinking island where if the storms didn't kill you, the heat would. I saw death and destruction like you've never known!" She circled around him and pointed a finger. "And I left my family behind. You think it was easy taking that scholarship to the university, leaving them behind, with no way out?" She paused, and tears welled again.

Her voice trembled. "You think it was easy getting that call my freshman year? That it reached 130 degrees at home and my brother took his own life rather than boiling to death?"

Joe stepped toward here, his heart aching. "Evie, I'm sorry."

"Don't!" She held up her hand and looked him in the eyes. "You don't want to move to the fiery half of the world? You know what your problem is, Joe? You were born on the green half and you think you're entitled to it from here on out. That you can futureproof your life to stay green. Well, you can't. I was born in the fire and I know sometimes things just burn whether you like it or not." She stopped and breathed slowly, straining for composure.

She looked at him again. Deeply. Sadly. "My program might have saved my brother. Maybe even brought him here, instead of leaving him there to die. I'm sorry you had to move, that you didn't feel like you had control of your life until you came here. That your parents didn't appreciate the effect on you. But there are bigger things in the world right now, Joe. And you don't get your way just because you're sad." Evie turned and walked quickly up the stairs, leaving Joe standing silently in the kitchen, numb.

"Nice job," he whispered to himself. The house was silent.

****

Joe made sure the kids were ready for bed and closed down the house for the evening. He assumed they'd heard the fighting, but no one spoke of it. He entered the bedroom and saw that Evie's pillow and blanket were gone. The door to the home office across the hall was closed. He walked toward the door and stood, listening for any sound, but heard nothing. He thought of knocking but paused. What was he going to say? Apologize for being selfish? No, not if that meant conceding to moving to San Francisco and ruining their lives. He had to protect the kids. How could that be selfish? And why bring this up today, the worst day of his life? The day his firm turned its back on him all because they didn't understand the ex-brain.

He turned and went back to the bedroom. He would lick his wounds tonight. This was not over. It was a problem to be solved. Tomorrow he would start anew and get to the bottom of it all.

Ex-Brain Q&A Entry: What is the Futureview Effect?

The Futureview Effect is a term used to describe the feeling of awe and inspiration when predictive technologies allow people to glimpse the future in a way that turns out to be proven accurate. The term is derivative of the Overview Effect, which described the feeling that early space travelers observed when seeing the entire earth from space, appreciating how rare and fragile it is as a home in the void of space. Many astronauts claimed to gain life-changing perspective from observing the earth in this way. Similarly, humans involved in predictive technologies have reported a sense of peace and acceptance, as well as motivation for change, when observing the power of accurate prediction, either due to the acceptance of a future path, or because the mechanisms to alter a future path become clear.

Posted 15 May 2053, v. 956

© Ex-Brain Q&A Foundation

Chapter 9

Joe wandered downstairs in the morning and saw the family in full swing. Kids were eating at the table while Evie poured herself another cup of coffee. "Good morning. Bus in ten minutes, and then I'm off to work. You need anything today?" she said coldly from across the room.

Okay, I guess this is how we're playing it. "No, I'm good," he said. "You guys all good this morning?" he asked the kids.

"All good, Dad," Anderson replied first. The others just nodded. Hope didn't say anything but jumped up and scurried over to give him a hug.

"Love you, Daddy," she said finally as she released him and moved across the kitchen to get her coat and backpack.

Evie crossed the room. "Sorry to leave you with the dishes. I'd been planning to leave work a little early today to collect the kids from school and bring them home. That okay?"

"Yep. See you this afternoon," he replied. "Have a great day, kids."

Everyone moved through the kitchen toward the front door to start their day, except for Anderson, who hung back with Joe. "Dad, you okay?"

"Of course I am, buddy," Joe said, feeling relieved inside that someone was finally showing him some compassion, but he checked himself to put on a brave face.

"I'm sorry about your job. Everything going to be okay?"

"It's all going to be just fine, Anderson. These things happen. It's not the end of the world. Don't worry at all." As he said it, he wondered if it were true.

Anderson nodded and walked past to follow his family out the door. The bus had just pulled up. From the doorway Joe could see Evie kiss each kid on the head as they boarded the automated bus. Joe could see that there was an adult monitor on board today, who waved to Evie as the bus door closed behind the kids. Monitors weren't required on the automated buses, but things seemed to work better when they were there to keep some order. Video monitors and lectures from the automated system to command the kids to sit down only worked so well. Evie waved to the kids through the windows as they took their seats, and then turned to walk down the sidewalk toward the public transport bus that would take her to her office.

Joe stood for a minute to watch her, wondering if she would stop, even pause for a second to think about whether she should come back and talk. She kept going without breaking stride. He slowly stepped inside and closed the door.

****

Evie's wall screen flashed in her office letting her know there was an internal call. She looked up from her desk and saw Adonna's name at the top of the screen. She tapped a button on her desk screen and a life-size Adonna flashed up on her wall.

"Hi, Evie, how are you doing?" She was sitting at her desk in an office a few floors up. "Are you alone in your office? You may want to close the door if you don't mind."

"Sure thing." Evie got up to close the door. After doing this, she slid her finger across the top of the keypad to the side of the door to signal her do not disturb notice. As she did, the glass door clouded over to give them privacy.

"What's up?"

"I wanted to talk again about the project in San Francisco. Did you talk to Joe yet?"

"Ugh," she said as she put her head in her hands. "I did, and it didn't go well."

"Tell me."

"Well, it's complicated. Joe was just laid off from his law firm."

"What? Oh, my God, Evie, I'm so sorry to hear that. I thought he was their star lawyer?"

"He was. Is. I don't know what happened. It seems the firm's ex-brain has decided that to remain profitable they need to change their model, something about working only with junior lawyers and partners with the ex-brain doing the rest of the work. I don't know all the details because we ended up getting into a massive fight."

"Uh-oh. What happened?"

Well, I knew he was feeling vulnerable and down, but I also couldn't avoid the fact that my job offer in San Francisco was relevant. I mean, if he's out of work, there is no better time to think about a change, right?"

"Sounds right."

Evie rubbed her face again and ran her hands through her hair. "So, I told him, and he reacted badly, saying there was no way he'd move the family to a city like San Francisco and that he thinks Denver is the only city worth living in right now. He even tried to make it about him and his childhood dreams of having a home rather than moving around all the time."

"So, what did you say?"

"I snapped. I told him he was being selfish. I reminded him that my childhood was much worse than his. I even went into my brother's suicide to make the point about how important my work is. Oh, my God, Adonna, am I a horrible person? I mean, I hit back hard. But it's true, right? I mean, that's why we do this work."

"Evie, don't apologize for standing up for what you want. You help people. Every day. Just like you help Joe and your kids. It's all important. And you have just as much right to go for what you want."

"Thank you, Adonna. I needed to hear that. I've felt horrible ever since we started fighting. I even slept in the study last night, I was so mad."

"Well, listen, I wish I could cheer you up with great news about the job, but unfortunately, I can't," Adonna said as she leaned back in her chair.

"Uh-oh, what's up?" Evie asked, perking up and bracing for things to get worse.

"So, after we talked I loaded up your name into the candidate form for the project. I knew you hadn't agreed yet, but I didn't want to hold things up, so I went ahead to start the process. It all was going fine. Obviously, the assessment system found you to be qualified. You're probably the most qualified person in the country. But then, this morning, I got a notice that the entire project has been put on hold. It says the budget has been suspended indefinitely. It's weird because none of my other projects are on hold, but clearly, the budget ex-brain sees something coming, maybe some shortfall expected later this year, and unfortunately, it picked this program to cut."

"Oh, no, Adonna, that's horrible. How could it deprioritize this project? If it wants to save money, it should be investing more into prevention!" Evie leaned closer to the screen, anxiety building.

"Well, that's the question. I agree with you, and I think we can fight back to justify the program. I'm sure the ex-brain has some reason for choosing to cut this, but we may just need to feed it more data, make the case a little more persuasively. And if all else fails, we humans can still overrule the system. It just takes a lot of work, a lot of bureaucratic approvals. But I'm not going to go down that road unless I know you're in. I'm sticking my neck out here, Evie. My credibility will be on the line, and I'm not doing it if we can't have you there to actually run the program."

Evie sat quietly, thinking through what this meant. Could she commit? Was that fair to Joe? To the kids? She closed her eyes. She had no choice.

"Let's do it. You work your side to get the approval, and I'll work mine." She smiled. It was risky, but she knew in her gut it was the right answer. This was her dream, the chance to help people like those she'd left behind. She couldn't turn back now.

"Awesome," Adonna replied, her big smile filling the wall screen. "And you think you can bring Joe around?"

"I can. But listen, I'll probably need some time. He's not ready to concede yet. He can be stubborn. And with just being let go from work, his ego is a little bruised right now. I'm not going to tell him about this wrinkle just yet. I'll find the right way to bring it up again when the time is right. I'll get it done."

"Okay, great, Evie. I'll keep you informed as I work the process on my end. If I need anything from you to help make the case to the ex-brain or the management team, I'll let you know." She paused. "And Evie, good luck."

"Thanks, Adonna. I might need a little luck, but he'll come around."

Chapter 10

The first thing Joe did was search the news for any mention of his law firm. His release from Fulham was unceremonious but laying off hundreds of lawyers was a big deal. Sure enough, the news reporters had picked up on the "Fulham firing," as they called it. A headline read: *Legal Giant Downsizes: Firm fires lawyers; goes all-in with the ex-brain.* But the misfortunes of 400 lawyers didn't seem to merit much attention. It was mainly covered in the legal and technology press, raising lots of speculation over which firm was next.

"I bet a lot of lawyers across the country are feeling a little nervous right about now," he said out loud to no one.

Because he wasn't allowed back in the building, he sat for a moment wondering about his clients and his ongoing cases. And then he thought about the ex-brain. How had this gone so wrong? How did the partners get it so wrong? He had to find a way back in to probe the ex-brain himself. He had to figure out where the mistake had been made. Most importantly, how to get it right. Then he had an idea. His clients. Maybe he could get back into the ex-brain system to leave notes about his clients. That was critical. In fact, it may have been a professional obligation as a lawyer to make sure his clients were taken care of in the handover. Surely the system would allow that?

"Worth a shot," he said as he pulled a mobile screen closer to him to attempt a log-in. He called out to his home system, "Ex-brain, log me into the Fulham & Mayson system, please."

"Your credentials with this system have been denied," it replied in a very even voice.

"Yeah, of course. Ex-brain, I need to start a direct communication to the Fulham & Mayson ex-brain. Can you see if it will open a dialogue?"

"The system is rejecting your request; access denied."

I know it's listening, he thought. "Okay, please initiate a new request, and this time, please state in the justification that former employee Joe Watson needs to take steps to fulfill his professional obligations regarding his clients. Submit that, please."

The system paused for a moment, and Joe's excitement grew. He expected to hear his ex-brain's familiar voice come through any second. It had only been a day, but somehow being separated from it, cut off from it, made him more anxious.

He sank into his chair as his own system's familiar voice came back, "Access has still been denied. The system has sent contact information to your screen for any inquiries regarding clients."

Joe looked down at his screen. A statement had popped up: Client inquiries—please contact Winston Balfour, Fulham & Mayson.

"FU," Joe said, disgusted that they didn't seem to care about what he knew about his clients, even if it was just a pretext to get into the ex-brain and ask what was going on.

He sat at his desk feeling sorry for himself. He was fighting a war on two fronts, one with his firm and the mystery of how his ex-brain got things wrong, and the other with Evie, and her half-baked idea to move the family across the country, potentially into climate danger and away from their home. Could they even afford a move to San Francisco on Evie's salary? Aha! *Better find out*, he thought.

"Ex-brain, log me into my personal finance system, please, and put it up on the wall." Quickly the wall in front of his desk came to life and projected his log-in screen. He placed his palm on his desk screen and then let it scan his eyes for further verification. Once he was done, a balance sheet titled Watson Family Finances flashed up on his wall showing his family net worth and assets. Dollar savings, crypto accounts, stocks, bonds, pension, all displayed in colorful graphs and charts.

"Ex-brain, run an analysis of projected asset growth, first with my salary, then without it."

"You currently do not have a salary," it replied.

"I know, but for this model assume my old salary was still continuing."

The program quickly put up a graph with two lines, one bending upward, the other remaining basically flat. "How much do we need to reduce spending to achieve 2 percent asset growth without my salary?"

"Your annual spending would need to be reduced by 60 percent to achieve 2 percent asset growth under current conditions without your salary," it responded, automatically adjusting the graph to show a new line with that scenario.

"Ouch. Do you have cost-of-living projections for San Francisco? Can you run the same analysis if we lived there?"

"Cost of living is higher in San Francisco due to scarcity of core goods. Asset growth would turn negative in current scenario," it explained showing a new graph with a line sloping downward.

"So ex-brain, would you recommend moving to San Francisco from an economic perspective?" he asked in jest.

"No, moving to San Francisco under current model without your salary is a negative economic move."

"That's right, ex-brain. Very good," he replied grinning. "You are very insightful."

"Thank you."

"One final question, go back to base scenario, in Denver, and remove my salary. How long before we start eating into the core retirement accounts?"

"Ninety-seven days."

"Right, three months before it hurts. Thanks, ex-brain, that's all."

"Goodbye." The screen blinked and disappeared from the wall.

Immediately Joe was bored again. He picked up his small screen to check on Fe, asking it to start a new message.

Joe: Hey Fe, did you wake up this morning, or are you still sleeping off last night?
Fe: I'm awake. But only out of bed long enough to make coffee. I deserve a hangover. Thank God for biztabs.
Joe: Good for you. I'm bored.
Fe: If you're bored then you're boring.
Joe: Thank you. We can't all live your life.

Fe: Someone's got to keep up with me!

Joe: Not a chance

Fe: You found a job yet, superman?

Joe: No. I do miss work, though (you know, the whole bored thing)

Fe: Remember, you're liberated. Enjoy your freedom. Go have some fun with your wife. Or your kids. Or just you!

Joe: I hear you. I think I could relax if I knew what was next.

Fe: Control Freak. Emphasis on FREAK.

Joe: FU

Fe: I bet you're still sitting there trying to figure out what the ex-brain is thinking. Why it sold you out. Have you called it yet?

Joe: Don't ask

Fe: I knew it! Would it let you in?

Joe: No

Fe: See, maybe it does know what it's doing.

Fe: I have an idea. You know how there are those people who say that if they are still single when they turn 40 they will marry each other. Maybe we should do that. But for jobs. If we're both unemployed in 6 months, we'll start a firm together and take over the world!

Joe: Nice. Whose name goes first? Don't you think Watson & Wan sounds good?

Fe: Ugh. You're so 2040s. No names, just a word, like Extinction Law

Joe: You want to name our firm after a bar?

Fe: You have a better idea?

Joe: Many - Corpus. Flash. Justice. Retainer.
Fe: I rescind my proposal.
Joe: Fine. You run the marketing department. We both know which one of us will actually practice law.
Fe: Cool, I'll play the role of Winston and just oversee things. I've already started working today from bed. See how good I am at this?
Joe: Awesome. You keep working. See you in 6 months.
Fe: See you then. Now I'm going back to sleep.
Joe: Sleep tight

Joe put the screen down and smiled. He was happy to have Fe to commiserate with, although she clearly was not miserable. He realized that wherever he ended up working next, he would miss Fe most of all, and his smile slowly drifted away.

****

By the time it was 4 p.m., Joe found himself in a very unfamiliar place—at home waiting for the family to arrive. No client meetings, no deadlines for litigation reports, no court filings. Just three young children and his wife on their way home, and an evening to fill.

As a tightly wound professional, this was not his sweet spot. Instead of relaxing at the utter lack of a to-do list, it was creating a panic. Joe had learned enough from Evie about brain functions and chemistry to appreciate that the stress he felt was just hormones, cortisol. The ancient parts of his brain knew there should be work and deadlines and was panicking that it couldn't see them. Unfortunately, appreciating that his brain was flooding with stress hormones did not allow him to shut them off.

Joe paced the entry hall of his house, thinking nervously about what he should be doing next. Should he start a project? Should he watch a movie? Should he just chill out until the bus arrives? Yes, chill out. That's best.

"How the fuck do you chill out at home at 4 p.m. on a Tuesday!?!" Joe yelled at nobody.

Luckily, just then the door flew open and three excited children rushed in.

"Hi, Dad. Who were you yelling at? We heard it out on the street," Anderson asked.

"Hi, Daddy!" yelled Hope as she gave him a big hug. Grace lined up to do the same, just without the five-year-old exuberance. The hugs did help. Joe felt himself relax almost immediately, although he knew he wasn't out of the woods.

"I wasn't yelling," Joe replied to Anderson, hoping he would just drop it. He quickly changed the subject. Evie walked in the door next, her hands full with her work bag, plus some of Hope's school items. She walked past Joe quietly and set things down on the table. The lack of warmth was obvious. Joe filled the silence. "How was your day?" he asked everyone.

Grace threw her dad a lifeline. "Fine. But we're all getting annoyed with the new kids."

"How so?" Joe asked.

"We just got a bunch of new girls in our class. Cali's. They act like they are so cool because they come from the beach, and they act like we don't know anything in Colorado. But it's not our fault their houses got burned out and they can't live there anymore."

Right, and Evie wants to take us there, Joe thought. *Great call.* He looked at Grace, but she averted her eyes. "Please try to be nice to them," he said. "I mean, put yourself in their shoes. What if we had to leave our home and you had to start over? I'm sure it's tough. Give them some time."

Evie gave Joe the side-eye, which he did not acknowledge.

"I know. But they're not that cool, just because they used to live near a beach." Grace was not completely won over, but Joe knew this was a normal process, and the schools worked hard to integrate kids as quickly as possible.

"I love my friends," Hope piped up. "I just made a new one named Alex. He wears a dinosaur costume to school sometimes, which is kind of funny."

Ah, the five-year-olds. So much easier at that age. Wear a fun costume, make some friends. Life should be that easy for everyone.

Never to be excluded from a conversation, Anderson finally jumped in. "We actually have a cool project starting at school. It's called Historial. It's this program that takes information about your ancestors, like DNA and stuff, and it figures out what they were like and creates videos showing their life."

"Cool. Where do they get the information?" Joe asked.

"I think a lot of it comes from databases, but I also gave a DNA sample today to get started."

"You did what?" Evie exclaimed.

"It was just a cheek swab. What's the big deal?" Anderson replied quickly.

"Anderson, we have talked about this. We do not give our DNA to strange programs."

"But it's for a school project, Mom."

"I don't care! Do you know what a stranger, or a strange ex-brain, can do with your DNA?"

"Yes, this one can tell me about my history," Anderson said defiantly.

"And also, now knows everything about you. Did you sign a release or agree to anything in a form?"

"I don't think so."

Joe jumped in. "Come on, honey, I don't think it's a big deal if it's through the school."

Evie's eyes flashed back in anger. *Oh, shit,* he immediately thought. *This is going to go poorly.*

"Not a big deal? Do you work in the medical profession? Do you see what happens when DNA gets in the wrong hands? Have you seen patients abused, or scammed, or worse? Do you know the ex-brain that runs this program and who runs it? Who controls it?"

"No, I don't," Joe said in a tone that admitted surrender.

"You guys enjoy your program. I'll be upstairs." Evie stormed out and the four of them stood quietly for a moment. They had all seen Evie mad before, but it was rare, and unpleasant, mainly because she was typically right.

"I'm sorry, guys," Joe said, finally breaking the silence. "I think your mom is upset about a lot of things right now, and it's all coming out at once. Let's just give her some space." Anderson looked back at him, his eyes questioning whether it was okay to go on. Joe nodded.

"You sure it's okay to watch?" he asked.

"Yes. But your mom is right. Don't give out your DNA without checking with us first. But since it is a school-approved program, we can watch it." The mood lightened a bit, although they all still felt like they were on dangerous ground.

Anderson started unpacking his school bag and took out his screen. "We just saw a demo video in class. They picked an ancestor from our history teacher, some woman who lived through the Civil War. It showed her taking care of injured soldiers in a hospital. It's all made by an ex-brain, but it looked totally real."

"I thought it was gross, all the soldiers with blood and bandages. Ugh," Grace added with a shutter.

"That was the best part," Anderson disagreed.

Joe paused for a moment. What's this? A tech project likely powered by an ex-brain? Certainly, based on probability analysis and scenario projection? It was as if his kids walked in carrying a bag of candy and Christmas presents. It was a lifeline to his struggling day and his fear of struggling months to come. But he played it cool.

"I like history. Why don't you all go get a snack and we can take a look."

Joe and the kids picked out a few snacks from the kitchen. The kids went for the fruit options. Joe was the one who spun up some potato chips from the food generator. They then gathered around the kitchen table and Anderson turned on the large wall screen so they all could see. He signed into his school account and flipped through a few menu screens to land on his history platform. He touched a silver button labeled Historial. As the program started, the opening page came to life with a tagline "Know your past, protect your future."

"So, what's the 'protect your future' thing about?" Grace asked as she leaned toward the screen to read the rest of the opening page.

"Didn't you pay any attention in class today?" Anderson asked with a mocking tone. "It's meant to do two different things. It shows you what your ancestor's life would have been like, so you can understand it better. Then, it also gives you lessons about what we can learn from them, and how we can make changes in our lives based on what we learn. That's the hard part of the assignment. I think it's pretty easy to put in the data and watch the movie. Then we have to write a report on what we learned from our ancestors."

"That's cool. So how do you pick an ancestor? Does it know us and give you a list?" Joe asked.

Anderson jumped in again. "Yeah, it taps into the ancestry databases based on our last name and parents' names, and we had to say whether it got us right." Anderson tapped on a tree icon and a family tree grew out of the base of the screen showing Anderson, Joe and Evie as his parents, both sets of grandparents, and about five generations growing out of the central trunk.

"They said that as long as your parents and grandparents are right on your screen, then it's got you from historical records and you just hit this 'confirm family tree' button here to move on."

Joe knew a bit about the ancestry projects. They had started as pay services over fifty years ago allowing individuals to research their family trees. Turned out that once they hit a critical mass, they had filled in the ancestry of over 75 percent of the world population just by people confirming common relatives and continuously filling in gaps to complete the picture. It was basic systems and network effect with lots of people filling in nodes until a final picture was complete with a high level of certainty. DNA testing helped to fill in final gaps and figure out those instances where affairs and other secrets may have added a surprise member to certain family trees. More than one Thanksgiving dinner was ruined by a surprise member of a family coming to light.

Once the database was complete, it became more of a public utility rather than a research service. The new piece in this program was bringing that history to life. Joe speculated that someone, or some ex-brain, had figured out how to animate historical figures based on a combination of historical record, DNA, photos, and predictive technology. For the more recent generations, social media created a much richer history to draw from. Social media sites had become the best window into a relative's life and times. But even for the pre-digital generations, there was a lot the program could do.

"Okay, so what do you do next?" Joe asked.

Grace jumped in again. "Now we have to pick someone who we think looks cool."

Anderson clicked on an icon labelled "choose an ancestor" and a menu of options appeared. It was very much like a video game where the player selects which character they want to be, except these were real people and real lives to play with. Each ancestor had a summary of their life and times to read.

Of all the options, the program highlighted a man named Joseph Esch, placing him in the center of the screen. Under a picture of this ruggedly good-looking man was his title, Farmer & Pioneer, from Strasbourg, France. His vital statistics were listed, including height: five-foot-ten; estimated weight: 165 pounds; intelligence: top quartile; above average. He clearly stood out from the rest. Joe pointed at Joseph Esch on the screen and said, "How about this guy?"

Anderson pressed on his icon and opened a more complete biography. He read aloud: "Joseph Esch was born in 1833 in Strasbourg, France. His family ran a small farm that suffered through several difficult seasons in the late 1850s due to weather and crop disease spreading across the area. Joseph was intrigued by offers to move to the New World in America and become a pioneer, helping to settle the emerging Western territories. Joseph seized the opportunity and bravely moved with his small family, settling in St. Louis, Missouri. He established a farm on the banks of the Missouri River and became a prosperous farmer and later a farming supply trader, helping to grow this region of the US."

"Wow, he seems pretty cool. Do you think he came over on a boat and rode in covered wagons?" Anderson asked.

"I don't know; check the video previews," Joe replied, pointing to a link under Joseph's profile.

"I want to do a girl," Grace said, sliding closer to the screen again.

"You can, Grace. You have to choose someone else anyway. I like this guy; he's a pioneer," Anderson said as he launched the video preview.

The screen shifted to a movie-screen size and started showing what looked very much like a movie trailer of Joseph Esch's life, complete with dramatic music. It showed a short clip of Joseph working on his farm, guiding a plow pulled by an old horse. Next was a clip of Joseph at his kitchen table, eating with his family. Lastly, it showed Joseph carrying a trunk and loading it onto a steamship, a glimpse of his fateful decision that would bring his family to a fresh start in a new world.

Joe immediately felt a connection to Joseph. The video showed close-up images of his face, full of worry as he worked his land. Joe assumed that he was worried that he couldn't provide for his family, that his land, his livelihood, was no longer sufficient. Joe also knew that he could have been projecting his own worry, his fear of inadequacy and futility, onto this video character. But he felt this ancestor was telling him something or wanted to. Joe wanted to listen.

"I like him. Let's learn more about Joseph Esch," Joe suggested to the kids.

"I think he's going to be cool, especially if he's brave enough to move to America. That must have taken guts," Anderson replied.

Anderson navigated the program, swiping across screens until a table of contents appeared. He selected a button saying

Episode 1, and the screen went blank for a moment before the video phased into a dreary early-evening scene. Light mist drifted in the air as the scene tightened on Joseph Esch struggling with his plough through a wet field. He wiped rain and sweat from his brow. He looked up as dark clouds rolled in, and he scanned across the field, spotting another man kneeling down working with a fence post.

Joseph called out the name Michel, and the other man stood and turned to him. "It's time, let's go in," Joseph shouted, and Michel nodded before picking up his tools and starting the wet slog across the field to meet near the farmhouse.

Joe was amazed at the quality of the video, how lifelike everything seemed. This was clearly powered by some serious tech and video drivers. He was slightly distracted by the fact that they were speaking English instead of French, but this was obviously necessary for the audience. Joe was more distracted by how accurate the ex-brain could be. He knew how the probability analysis worked, and the limits of ex-brain projections. With DNA samples the character depictions should have been pretty good but predicting what they would have been doing day to day was speculative at best. Yet, the video was so lifelike he felt drawn in and quickly stopped second-guessing. He just wanted to see more.

The video zoomed out as a thunderclap boomed. A hard-driving rain poured from the sky and wind started whipping through the trees around the farmhouse. Both men trudged through the rain and mud to reach the barn for shelter. Joseph turned into a wind with a heavy pack weighing on his back. It was too much, as his feet slipped out from under him and he crashed to the ground, puddles of water splashing around him. Michel saw his friend go down and rushed to his side, picking him up and helping to steady him back against the wind. The two men struggled the last several meters together until they reached the barn door and collapsed to the floor.

Joseph looked over at Michel and nodded. "Thank you." Michel nodded in return. After catching their breath, they unloaded their work gear and stood at the barn door waiting for a break in the wind and rain. Once the wind slowed a bit, they both ran for the house and rushed inside. When they opened the door to the house a warm glow spilled out from a fire under a large stone hearth at the center of the room. Wood beams spanned the ceiling, and wide planks covered the floor. The fire cast a warm orange glow across the home, and the few pieces of furniture sent out long shadows breaking the light. Oil lamps had already been lit on the tables allowing the work of the house to continue after dusk.

Both men quickly took off their muddy boots. "Magda, we are done for the day," said Joseph walking straight toward the fire to warm himself. Michel followed closely behind.

Three children were seated at a table near the kitchen. The eldest read a book while the younger two played a game with a small ball and sticks.

Hope leaned in toward the screen and said, "Look, they have three kids just like us."

"Looks that way, sweetheart," Joe replied, placing his hand on Hope's back to pull her in closer.

Magda was finishing preparing a meal and pulled a large Dutch oven off a stone at the edge of the fireplace. She used a long metal hook to pick it up by a handle and set it up on a countertop for serving. "Just in time, my love," she said. "Clear off the table, children and please set up for supper." The kids jumped up and started gathering bowls and spoons for each place setting.

As the kitchen scene continued, Grace asked how long the episode would last. "I don't know, Grace, are you bored already?" Anderson asked, mocking her. Grace gave him a look of disdain. Joseph Esch clearly wasn't her favorite relative from the past.

"I'd like to get a turn with my ancestor, too, you know," she finally said.

"But these guys are amazing. Look how clear the characters are. These are our family. Without them, we wouldn't be here. Look how happy they seem," Anderson continued.

"It is impressive," Joe interrupted, trying to insert some peace between them, but also feeling a genuine sense of awe at the reality of this program. "Is it all real representations pulled from DNA?"

"And old pictures," Anderson replied. "Anything they can't find they fill in from the ex-brain. All of the scenes are made from what they know from history, like what the houses would have been like, what they would have eaten. The language would have been French, of course, given they're in Strasbourg, so they change that so we can understand. Everything else is as real as they can get it."

Just then, the screen froze and filled with static. It was only a second, but a noticeable break before the scene continued in the Esch house. "That was weird," Joe said. "Is something wrong with the feed? A video like this shouldn't glitch like that."

"That is weird," Anderson agreed, "usually only cheap videos with no ex-brain behind them do that."

"They're talking again," Joe said to quiet the kids so he could hear. The Esch family had quickly sat around their dining table for supper.

The image zoomed in much closer on Joseph Esch's face, making him look much more dramatic. "How are the grain stores, Magda?" Joseph asked his wife.

"They're low. But we'll manage," she said trying to find a smile.

"Michel, we need a good crop this year. We can't take another bad season. If we can't fill our grain stores and have a bit left to sell, we won't get through another year," Joseph said to the other man.

"Who is this other guy?" Joe asked the kids.

Anderson reached out for the screen and tapped on Michel. The scene paused and a bubble popped up with details about the other man. It read, "Michel Bisset, Joseph Esch's cousin and farming assistant. He was unmarried and spent most of his time with the Esch family." Anderson tapped again, and the video resumed.

Michel spoke up. "We'll do our part, Joseph. It's the weather we have to worry about. Too much rain now, and not enough in a few months."

"That's what I'm worried about too. We need options. We can't keep up this way forever," Joseph replied.

"You both worry plenty for everyone. We're doing fine. The Lord gives us what we need. And these little ones give us the rest!" Magda said, smiling at the children. She looked around the table and caught Joseph's eye, holding his attention for an extra moment. The screen glitched again, almost imperceptible, and focused close on Magda staring straight back out of the screen. "And if things are worse, Joseph, you will do what must be done."

Her eyes were large, sympathetic, but commanding, staring directly out from the screen. Joe felt like she was staring at him, talking directly to him. He instinctively leaned back in his seat creating distance. How many times Evie had given him that same look when she didn't want him to worry the children and needed him to get her point without saying it directly. He thought of her upstairs, angry, and wondered what thoughts she would be sending him right now. He didn't like any of the options.

The scene continued on for a few moments as the family finished their supper, and then faded to black as the episode came to a close.

"Wow, it looks pretty hard for them," Anderson said.

"Life was hard back then. No electricity, no grocery store. No ex-brains to solve complex problems. If they couldn't do it themselves, it didn't get done," Joe explained. "And they have some tough choices coming up, I'd say."

"Thank God for us; they were brave enough to move to America," Grace interjected.

"Yeah. Brave is right," Joe agreed. "Do you guys think we could have done that, picked up everything and moved to another country, another continent?"

"Yes, we totally could have done that!" Anderson quickly answered.

"I'm not sure they had much of a choice," Grace added, trying to one-up her brother as usual.

"You're probably right about that, Grace," Joe agreed. "Okay, guys, this was pretty cool. Thanks for showing me. Let's get on with the rest of your homework. I want you all done before dinner." The kids moaned a bit but dutifully grabbed their things and made their way upstairs to get started.

Joe sat down again and stared at the screen, which had reset to the Historial home page and an image of Joseph Esch. He thought again about the worry he saw in Joseph's face, the stress he must have felt trying to provide for a wife and three children when the world seemed to conspire against him. He wondered if this distant ancestor felt the same way he did now, scared that the life he had come to rely upon was slipping from him, fading out of his control. At least Joseph came up with a solution, as drastic as it may have been. Joe was still waiting, not so patiently, for his opportunity to emerge.

Chapter 11

Access. How do I get access? He had been sitting, staring at screens for days wondering how to get the Fulham ex-brain to talk to him. He just needed a conversation, a chance to ask what was going on, maybe ask the questions Winston and the other partners didn't. His finger tapped nervously on the table.

"Maybe I need a cyber hacker?" he said out loud, "or a good distraction." He closed his secure internet session and went back to the open web, the home of distractions. Immediately a video started playing for him. It was a cartoonish image of his mother shaking her finger at him and saying, "Clean up this mess!" Joe hated the scraping, ads that found public images of family members to grab attention and tailor their messages. But it was effective. This product had intrigued him for some time, and Joe had been getting different versions of this ad daily since he lost his job.

Joe may have been a control freak, but he was not a neat freak. And his digital life was no exception. Rather than maintaining a well-organized filing system and easy-to-access digital pieces, his electronic footprint was a bit of a jumbled mess. His ex-brain tools typically allowed him to find what he needed, and the right information always seemed to find its way to him. But it was inefficient, and it wasted valuable data space in the cavernous realm of global servers.

A banner under his mother's scolding image said, "Click here to clean up your act, reduced price on your personal data cleanse." Joe had heard from others that a data cleanse was an enjoyable experience—a trip down memory lane curated by an ex-brain that put documents, communications, pictures, and videos in front of you to decide if you want to keep or delete them. Like all things ex-brain, these tools were designed to learn from your choices and start sorting for you. Always keeping those videos of your kids' birthdays? Ex-brain just starts filing them into folders for you and then moves on to emails from your mom. Not so keen on keeping those? Into the data dustbin they go. The amount of data accumulated by the average middle-aged person was mind boggling. No human could live long enough to see it all again. Humans needed to trust ex-brains to make some informed choices, and the world needed ex-brains to clean up its data trash.

Joe decided it was time to click on the link and see what this was all about. Once he did, he was taken to a new page with "This Is Your Life" in bold letters at the top. It was marketed as a higher-end product than most data tools, more of a curated tour. The tag line read "You relive your life, we clean it up." He adjusted himself in his chair and transferred the image to the wall screen in his office. This was probably the first cleaning project he was ever excited to undertake.

Joe authorized payment on his screen and saw the prompt appear to authorize access to his data storage. It required a thumbprint and retina scan. He paused and thought of Evie. DNA, retinas, she hated all of it, giving away secrets. But there was no other way. If he wanted to run the program, he had to trust this ex-brain and let it into his family's data history. He placed his finger on the screen and leaned forward into the camera. Somewhere in cyberspace an ex-brain analyzed millions of data points, synched them to Joe's identity, and in an instant, sucked in terabytes of Joe's past, everything he had experienced and recorded digitally. The screen exploded in a celebration of confetti colors as it launched.

"Okay ex-brain, entertain me!" Joe exclaimed to the screen. It didn't disappoint. The screen immediately launched into a fast-paced barrage of pictures from Joe's life, some from his childhood: pictures of him and his parents in exotic places around the world, posing in front of Chinese mountaintops and European churches. The images streamed all the way through his early years at the University of Colorado, meeting Evie, and quickly into their married life, work events, children. Joe marveled at how the program found virtually everything that was important or meaningful and wound it all into a one-minute introductory barrage of memories.

Quickly after giving Joe a rush of nostalgia, the program started getting down to business. For the next twenty minutes, Joe was presented with images from different phases of his life and was asked different questions about each so that the ex-brain could start prioritizing Joe's likes, dislikes, and preferences. Some of the questions simply asked to confirm who people were or what the event was. Is this Aunt Joanna? Was this picture from your holiday in Kenya in 2042? The ex-brain was pretty accurate in its assessments because it could pull from various sources such as contemporaneous email, text, or recorded voice messages to confirm.

Then the ex-brain asked rating questions, often through comparisons, to create relative rankings. For example, it asked, 'What was more important to you?' and showed a picture of his college graduation next to an image of Evie's thirtieth birthday party. Choosing one image over the other wouldn't erase the less important image. (He clicked on Evie.) It just helped to prioritize, perhaps keeping most pictures and records from the birthday and only a few from the graduation. In fact, it was very rare that an event or memory would be erased. Due to the network effect, most events in the post-digital era were fully recorded somewhere, and as long as the privacy settings weren't too high, a good ex-brain could find most anything from a friend or family member's public data. The real goal was to tailor your files and avoid the massive duplication that clogged up server space.

Toward the end of this barrage of pictures, Joe saw two images that stopped him cold. One was an image of Evie holding their newborn twins. The next was a picture of Evie holding Hope a few minutes after her birth. Joe's first thought was that he could never decide between these two, and it was unfair to ask. He immediately knew he had to press skip for this pairing, lest he put into a record someplace that he favored one child over another. But inside, Joe knew which image was more important to him. It was the image of Hope. Hope was their miracle baby.

STEPHEN ALBRECHT

Joe immediately thought back to the day when Evie was four months pregnant and they learned about Hope's heart defect. It was horrible, a gut punch. Joe remembered the pain of hearing the news in the doctor's office and the fear that haunted him and Evie for the weeks that followed. Even hearing that there was a surgical option in the experimental phase only added a new dimension of dread to the experience. It gave them a ray of light, but also added all sorts of doubt about Evie's health and what would happen if it didn't work. Selfishly, Joe was terrified of what would happen if it went wrong and he was faced with raising seven-year-old twins alone, living the rest of his life without Evie. But it did work, and Joe and Evie felt they had been blessed. Technology had saved their baby and saved Joe's family. Joe had already been a tech guy in every other part of his life. But after this experience, Joe felt that he personally owed his life and his happiness to ex-brain-powered technology. He was all-in.

After the picture phase wrapped up, the program moved on to a review of text documents: emails, letters, and other similar files. Some were very easy. "I've found twenty-three years of US tax-filing documentation. Shall I organize by year and file that all away for you?" the ex-brain asked.

"Yes, and never speak of them again, please." Done.

The ex-brain next pulled out a document Joe hadn't seen in years: his original intelligence assessment that Fulham & Mayson had conducted when he was applying for his first job out of law school. It was the standard three-part assessment covering IQ for traditional mental capacity, EQ for emotional

133

ability relating to other humans, and MQ for machine relationship capacity. Joe remembered sitting for the tests in an all-day session, which included answering questions on a screen, talking with psychologists, and a long session coding with a computer system. It was an advanced AI system, but not nearly as smart as the ex-brains that would be developed several years later.

<u>Joseph Watson Intelligence Assessment</u>

IQ: 142

EQ: 145

MQ: 151

He wasn't off the charts in any one area, but his balance across the three areas was rare. Joe remembered Winston talking to him to extend his formal offer to join the firm. "Look at these test scores," he had said. "A man for all seasons!" Joe was flattered and excited. *Maybe not the man for all seasons, but thankfully for this season*, he thought. He was not surprised that across all the scores, his machine quotient was the highest.

After completing some of the easier categories of files, the ex-brain moved back into prioritization phase, presenting documents for Joe to read and decide if they were meaningful or not. This phase took longer due to the time needed to read each document, but it proved to be just as impactful in jogging Joe's memory, and frankly, his emotions.

About thirty minutes into this phase, Joe was offered an old diary entry from the eighth grade, which made him instantly tense and made his heart rate jump a bit. Moving from place to place at the whim of his parents' careers was always traumatic for Joe, but his most painful memory was of the time he was forced to leave London as a fourteen-year-old with a broken heart over Alice Gonzalez. Joe read the diary entry and felt the flood of teenage angst returning.

March 10, 2026

I'm so done.

I have to get this out, so I may as well start @the beginning. I am in love with Alice Gonzalez. I knew the first time I saw her. Her dark hair, bright eyes, and clever smile. Even her glasses, which I know she only wears to look smart. She looks like a character from an old 90s movie. No one else can pull that off. She does.

I joined the debate team just to spend time with her. But it's not about debate. It's about Alice. I worked my way onto her team. I can barely pay attention to the assignments. I just watch her sometimes. I think she knows but I haven't told her yet. Why have I waited so long! I missed my chance! Why? Because my parents suck!

My plan was to go with her to the debate Euro championships in Madrid. After the competition was over, I was going to tell Alice how I feel. If we win she'll be feeling great and I'll tell her as we hug in victory, just like in a movie. If we lose, I'll give her a hug to console her, tell her how amazing she is, and tell her — just like in a movie! It can't fail!!!

Oh, wait it can fail because it's not happening!

Mom told me yesterday morning that she and Dad wanted to talk that night about travel. I saw the trap immediately— another fancy beach, another exotic place we needed to see before the ocean swallows it up. I don't care about the fucking Seychelles or the Azores.

I spent all day in school plotting my case. I need to practice my language skills to get into a University. Spain is perfect for that.

When Mom hit me with the actual news I went blank. I didn't see it coming. WTF!! I wanted to cry for real. Honey, we're moving again. We have an amazing opportunity in Singapore, but we have to go now—like next week. You're going to love it!

<u>Bite my ass!!!! I hate them!!!!</u>

****

Joe stared at the old journal entry and he grabbed his knee, squeezing involuntarily. In his mind he was thirteen again. He remembered everything. The feeling of helplessness, his young heart breaking. A flood of regret came back to him in an instant—why didn't he have the guts to talk to Alice earlier? He missed all that time. Then anger—why had his parents been so cavalier with his happiness? They hadn't been an active part of his life for a long time, but the resentment still ran deep.

Joe remembered the night he wrote the journal entry. He went back to his room and climbed into his closet, lying on the floor, wrapped in a blanket. He just cried, quietly, so no one would hear him. Joe pictured his parents a room away, thinking about their next adventure, their new jobs, and he just got angrier. He remembered lying awake all night thinking about Alice and numbing himself for the pain he knew he could not avoid.

But those tears were not a waste. They became the seed of fierce independence that would grow within Joe over the coming years. He remembered swearing that he would never give up control of his life again.

The next entry whisked Joe to graduate school and his early days with Evie. This time it was an email note he had sent her just before graduation.

May 7, 2034

Dear Evie,

I'm usually not one to write letters, too busy I guess. Even when I moved from place to place with my parents, I never wrote letters to friends I had left behind. But I was thinking about how much I have enjoyed spending time with you over the past year. And I know you have lots of options for jobs or grad school all over the country. But I have some things you need to know, so here goes. I've never known a woman like you before. You're smart, clever, caring, not to mention you have a smile that takes my breath away. I finish my classes, and instead of wanting to either go home or join friends at the bar, I want to rush across campus to see if I can find you. That's never happened to me before.

If I'm being honest, my draw toward you worries me a bit. I've always wanted to be in control of my time and stick to my plans, and I don't know what I would do if you were no longer a part of them. You have options. But I hope you choose one here in Denver, with me. If plans are made to be broken, then you break me.

I just wanted you to know.

Love,

Joe

Joe reread his old love letter and felt slightly embarrassed, but mainly proud. *You smooth son of a bitch*, he thought. He barely remembered writing it, but he knew that was a time in his life when he was at his best. Finding Evie, being willing to open himself up to her, and not screwing it up, was one of his proudest accomplishments. It dawned on him that he was doing the same thing now that he did back then, asking her to choose to stay with him in Denver rather than chasing dreams somewhere else. It worked back then, and lead to a wonderful life. He hoped she would see that again.

Joe spent the next couple of hours continuing his digital stroll down memory lane, bombarded with notes, videos, and pictures of his past. He was pretty sure this ex-brain thought he was a hopeless romantic or a drama queen, as many of his memories had to do with dramatic moments of change often involving the women in his life. That's not how he thought of himself, but his digital history certainly looked that way.

It was a nice change of pace when the ex-brain started pulling some work-related materials to review. The program pulled out a presentation that he had helped create for Winston in

2050, just before the new year. It was a client development pitch that summarized all the major changes the world had experienced during the 2040s. They had spent months presenting it to prospective clients to show how insightful the firm was. Joe knew there was a final glossy version with pictures in his files, but the ex-brain pulled out a version labeled "DRAFT," full of his comments on what a junior associate and the ex-brain had first put together.

Fulham & Mayson

Five Forces That Defined the 2040s

> *JW Comment: This is a good first draft but needs work. Need to add section in each entry about selling our legal services. See my comments throughout. BTW, nice alliteration in the title. Did you come up with that, or is the ex-brain getting poetic?*

FORCE ONE: Carbon Neutrality

Planet Earth reached carbon neutrality by official UN records in 2046 and began extracting more carbon than it released. Many celebrated the sacrifice and changed habits that led to less energy consumption, but, in fact, the driving force to achieve carbon neutrality was the exponential growth and lower cost of batteries and clean energy sources that proliferated through the 2030s and 40s rendering fossil fuels obsolete, even in emerging markets.

Scientists estimate that despite reaching neutrality, it will take over one hundred years to halt the warming effects from carbon release and over a thousand years to reverse the impacts and begin cooling.

> *JW Comment: Which scientists said this? Need citation. Seems optimistic to me. The coasts may never go back to "normal," and don't forget our revenue comes from deals moving companies away from the coasts. Describe the transfer deals we can arrange.*

FORCE TWO: Upward Migration

Throughout the decade, over 500 million people moved out of coastal cities to higher and cooler climates, relying on refugee centers and massive relocation efforts in cities such as Denver, Colorado; Munich, Germany; and Chongqing, China. Humanitarian crises in developing regions saw over fifty million deaths due to lack of food, water, and shelter for climate refugees.

Evacuated areas became known as lawless "hinterlands."

> *JW Comment: Cut this part—hinterlands don't generate business! Focus on Denver growth impacts and the services we offer in private and public construction projects.*

FORCE THREE: End of the Bit Wars

Although all attacks were limited to the cyber world, the global Bit Wars between the major economic powers was one of the most destructive conflicts in world history. Due to a breakdown in international trust, cyber borders that limited the transfer of data between regions and countries became arguably more important that physical borders. The Data Transfer Rules

Under Common Elements (or Data TRUCE) of 2045 ended over ten years of international data and cyber conflict and started the process of reconnecting the world's economies to rebuild the trillions of dollars of assets that had been lost.

The Data TRUCE sought to re-engage the economies by promoting joint ventures between companies across the old cyber borders.

> *JW Comment: Point out that Fulham is an expert in structuring JVs under the Data TRUCE. Generate business!!*

FORCE FOUR: Ex-Brain Explosion

Artificial general intelligence was achieved in 2042 when computer brains first displayed the ability to think creatively of their own volition, pose their own questions, and reach their own solutions. The Ex-Brain Control Act of 2045 brought necessary regulations to control ex-brain activity.

It is estimated that in 2050, ex-brains will play a role in over 90 percent of all human activity on earth.

> *JW Comment: Is that all? Highlight our expertise, and how we provide compliance programs for ex-brain regulation as well as harnessing their power to win cases for our clients. BTW, that 90 percent stat must have been calculated by an ex-brain!*

FORCE FIVE: Smart Government

After the disaster of 2041, when the US Congress shut down for fourteen months leading to the default on US debt, the US held its landmark 2042 Constitutional Convention, paving the way for large-scale "smart government" legislation to break the impasse, effectively handing some decision-making to computer algorithms rather than relying on the political process. The first step was the floating tax rate that moved weekly depending on national GDP and employment data. Distributed ledger systems on blockchains enabled real-time tax collection, and the system created virtuous cycles as positive economic data immediately reduced taxes, promoting spending and growth.

By 2049, most industrialized nations had adopted some form of smart government covering tax, civil spending, and military strategy, which grew in complexity as ex-brains improved their capabilities.

> *JW Comment: So why do we still have to deal with politicians?!?! Highlight our local lobbying practice and success working with Denver government. Also add that the US is considering opening a "Second Capital" in Denver due to DC's flooding problems. Fingers crossed!*

Joe finished reading his old work and his thoughts splintered. He was intrigued at his old insights and embarrassed at how shamelessly he was pitching business. More than anything, he felt anger as he recalled his time working on the presentation. The management committee wanted promotional materials to send out on New Year's Day but didn't ask him to do it until Christmas Eve. He had worked through the holidays on this, even missing his family ski trip to get it done and impress the partners. All that time he had given up, without question, just to prove his value and loyalty to the firm, loyalty that ended up getting him nowhere and business the ex-brain was now doing without him.

He looked down from his wall screen and stared at the floor, his mind racing. Even if he did figure out where the firm had gone wrong with the ex-brain, did he need to go back to Fulham? Did they deserve him? Screw it. Maybe he was free.

Ex-Brain Q&A Entry: How are ex-brains regulated in the US?

Soon after artificial general intelligence was rebranded as an ex-brain, regulation of ex-brains was codified in US law in the Ex-brain Control Act of 2045, which put in place three limits on ex-brain usage, commonly referred to as the Approve, Contain, Commingle provisions:

1) Humans must maintain approval rights over significant decisions made by ex-brains. Ex-brains may not act alone.

2) Ex-brains must operate in solitary instances, and may not network, link or collude across multiple ex-brains.

3) Ex-brains may not be physically integrated into human brains via neural implants.

Posted 21 May 2053, response v.473

© Ex-Brain Q&A Foundation

Chapter 12

Joe sat in bed, paralyzed with a lack of direction. The immediate thing to do was to get up and help the kids get ready for school, take some of the burden off Evie, and add some value to the family while he had the extra time. But knowing and acting are two different things. On this Thursday morning, Joe sat up and stared at the wall, his mind wondering about what comes next. His fingers tapped on the sheets with nervous energy.

Evie walked into the bedroom, already fully dressed and ready for the day. His eyes scanned the room. "Honey, have you seen my small tablet screen? I need to set up some meetings and get some job leads going."

"So, you're looking for a job in Denver?" she replied with surprise in her voice.

"Yes, it's our home. And I need a job. I can't just wait around anymore."

She glared at him. "You're not even going to talk to me about San Francisco first?"

"You know my position on that, Evie."

"Yes, you were clear. But so was I," she snapped.

"Look, have they made you a formal offer? I mean, is this some kind of done deal?" he asked.

Evie paused and bit her lip. "Not yet."

"Okay, fine. Then I'm going to explore my options. If we have a choice to make, we'll address it then."

"You know what, Joe? I know this is hard and you're hurting. But you can be a real asshole." She grabbed her work bag from a chair by the door and threw it over her shoulder. "You find your tablet and set up your meetings. Someone has to get the kids out the door." Joe heard heavy footsteps pound down the stairs. "Come on kids, let's go," echoed down the hall.

Joe sat on the edge of the bed and turned on a wall screen to mindlessly review the morning headlines. Finally, he heard the front door close at the bottom of the stairs and the sound of his family faded out to the street. Home alone.

He made his way downstairs and pressed a button on the refrigerator to start the coffee brewing. The portable screen was sitting on the counter, and he wondered if Evie had found it and set it out for him. He hoped she had. He flicked back to the news page he had been reading. It was focused on building, showing images of the new settlement zones with construction cranes spreading out across the city. A headline said "$140 Billion Needed to House Upward Migrants." Underneath the lead story was another box with a similar headline "India Searches for Migrant Funding." The migrant crisis was truly global, with population moves disrupting countries and cities across the globe.

Now or never, he thought. He asked his screen to find Diane Chilvers, and her contact details and picture quickly came up. "Email Diane," Joe commanded as a text box opened up.

He dictated, "Hi, Diane. Do you have time to catch up today? Would like to pick up our last discussion. Hope you're well. Joe. Send." With that, the message was on its way to Diane. Knowing her work habits, Joe expected a quick reply, even at this early hour.

As he turned back to the fridge, he reached for a coffee mug in the cabinet above and then grabbed the carafe that was set on a ledge in the refrigerator door. As he poured he heard a ping from his screen.

He glanced down to see an invitation from Diane. It was straight to the point. "Meeting – Wednesday, 21 May 2053: Diane & Joe, 2 p.m., City Planning Office."

"That was fast, Diane, even for you," Joe said as he picked up the coffee and made his way back up the stairs. Just having a plan for the day made him feel immediately lighter, closer to normal.

Joe tried to imagine how she would handle the discussion. Would she be in sales mode, trying to convince him to join? Or would she want to dig further into the details of what he might do for them and how he'd approach a new training program for the city's ex-brain? He decided that the best thing he could do was to be ready to talk about the details of his proposal for predicting future disputes with the city's suppliers. He thought back to the last time he was working with his Fulham ex-brain, the morning before Winston fired him. He had been so distracted since that afternoon that he had almost forgotten about the progress he had made in just a couple of hours with the ex-brain that day. It was like remembering a conversation with a colleague or friend. In that moment, he missed his ex-brain. He even wondered what it was working on, what it was thinking about, what new ideas it had spun up. He also wondered whether Winston had any clue how to talk to it and get anything meaningful out of it.

The morning passed and the afternoon came quickly. Joe left the house to head downtown for his meeting. For the first time in over a week, he put on a work outfit, including a dress shirt and blazer, feeling more like himself back in a professional uniform.

The trip into the city center was quick in the afternoon with no commuter traffic or crowds. He walked up to the administrative building just like he had hundreds of times over the past fifteen years as a Fulham lawyer. He walked into the reception center and approached a virtual assistant, expecting a quick approval and instructions. This time, the virtual recognized him, but had more questions.

"Hello, Mr. Watson. Good to see you again." It paused longer than usual, and the screen blinked. "Who are you representing today?" the woman's voice asked him. Joe realized that the city's data system must have been updated to remove him from Fulham's employee list.

"Just me today. I'm here to see Ms. Chilvers," Joe replied.

"Okay, a personal appointment. Please go through to the elevators in the center and up to the twenty-ninth floor."

"Thank you," Joe said knowing the drill, but wondering if the system thought differently about him now that he didn't work for Fulham. The word "personal" pierced. Was he no longer professional? Did it trust him less? He felt uneasy, not used to this new role he was playing.

After the encounter with the virtual, everything else felt normal as he made his way through and was quickly whisked up to Diane's office. He saw several familiar faces in the hallways, and they all smiled at him, but then looked away quickly back to work. Joe assumed they all were genuinely happy to see him, but didn't know what to say, so no one stopped for a conversation. Joe understood, but it didn't feel good.

As he approached Diane's office, he peered in to see her standing at her desk giving orders to her virtual assistant. Sounded like she was scheduling meetings for the next week, calling out participants and agendas for each meeting. He knocked on her doorway. "Hi, Diane," he announced before walking in.

"Hi, Joe, please come in. I was so glad to hear from you this morning."

"And thank you for the quick reply. It's good to see you."

Joe entered and she pointed him over to a couple of chairs in the corner of her office. This was new, as Diane usually took work meetings standing at her desk. Many things felt different today.

They both sat down, and Diane offered him tea or coffee. "Coffee, please," he replied.

"Can we get a cup of coffee and a cup of green tea, please," Diane said loudly. A few seconds later an Atlas service bot rolled into her office and up to their sitting area. Its top opened and a tray with two hot mugs elevated to them. They grabbed their drinks and an arm swung out from the side to hand them each a napkin.

"Thank you," Joe said to the bot. He knew he didn't have to, but he always felt better thanking the bots. There was always an ex-brain behind there somewhere and he felt better being friendly to it.

"So, let's start with you, Joe. I personally can't believe what Fulham has done. I'm shocked. Tell me how you're doing."

"I'm doing fine. It is a shock, and I can't say that I understand it all. I worry that the firm doesn't understand it either. I worry that the ex-brain has advised the partners of something, but they are somehow talking past each other. Winston said that the decision was based on economic modeling, that the firm wouldn't survive on its current path and had to take drastic action to stay competitive. I think they are missing something."

"Do you feel betrayed?" Diane was always direct.

"By Winston?" Joe asked and paused. "Yes, I do."

"I actually meant by the ex-brain," Diane clarified. "You trained it, taught it everything it knows. Do you feel it betrayed you by suggesting a future that didn't include you?"

"Hmm," he said with another pause. "I've never thought about it that way. I think the firm just doesn't understand it."

"Well, why not?" she pushed. "Ex-brains are supposed to be smarter than us. They clearly know what the implications are. I think it betrayed you. If you think it isn't personal, then maybe that's the problem. I'm actually worried about continuing to rely on Fulham's ex-brain for our work if this is how it will be thinking through our problems, not taking into account the human impacts."

Joe was taken aback. "I don't know, Diane. I'm not sure if it can feel that personally. I've never thought to ask it. I'm not sure it would admit it, even if it did. The thing I do know is that it always has a plan. That's what makes it different from old-fashioned AI and algorithms. It doesn't stop at the simple question asked. It thinks steps ahead. Just like us. Or at least some of us."

"So, what's it thinking about next?"

Joe paused. "Hard to tell without having access to it."

Diane shifted in her seat and took a sip. "Well, Winston is in a bit of a panic, if it makes you feel any better." Joe perked up just hearing those words, and he couldn't hold back a small smile.

"Do you think I can still trust him?" she asked. "What's his position on all of this?"

"He runs the firm. He can't distance himself from this, even if it's the ex-brain's idea."

"And are you sure it was the ex-brain's idea?" she asked, tilting her head to the side and raising an eyebrow.

"I don't think Winston has some ulterior motive, if that's what you're asking." Joe looked down at his cup of coffee and put both hands around it, feeling its warmth. His stomach tightened, and he looked back up at Diane. "I'm disappointed in him. And I don't know what he's up to."

"I think you may give him too much credit. When things don't add up, follow the money. How much do you think the partners will earn with this move, eliminating all your salaries?"

Joe shrugged, nodding. "In the short term, a lot. The question is whether the ex-brain was right, that it was the only way to stay profitable in the long run."

"Well, he's trying to act as if everything is just fine, but I can tell he's flying blind. We spoke a couple of days ago, and he walked through all our open cases. He had a baby lawyer with him taking notes, and I had the distinct feeling he was just taking down the questions that he would feed straight into the ex-brain. I must say, my trust level with Fulham is not high right now."

"I wouldn't advise doing anything drastic just yet, Diane. There's too much work there to just pull out and hand to another firm without real disruption. Give them a little time to sort it out."

"There's my trusted advisor, Joe," Diane said with a smile. "Even when you have every right to be pissed at Fulham, you still give me straight advice. That's why I trust you."

"It's what I do," he replied humbly.

"Now, let's talk about what's next. What do you want to do with the rest of your brilliant career?"

"I'm ready to move on. Let's talk about the city role you mentioned the last time we met."

Diane smiled. "Look Joe, I think you would be brilliant here. Our small legal department is not where they need to be. They just take questions, spend a lot of time thinking, or doing something, not sure what, and then provide half advice or pass things on to law firms. You could transform this place." She stirred her tea before continuing.

"Unfortunately, when I looked into it a few days ago, I learned that our ex-brain has just placed a hiring freeze across our division. I can't imagine what it's thinking given how much work we have to get done this year, but it must be worried about something."

Joe's stiffened, and he shifted in his seat uncomfortably. He had come into this meeting expecting all of his worries to be put to rest with a simple solution. A new job, a new program to build, a new ex-brain to train, and put this San Francisco nonsense to rest. "That can't be right," he said in an accusatory tone.

"Excuse me?" Diane quickly replied.

Joe sat back and cleared his throat. "Sorry, I didn't mean you were wrong. It just seems impossible."

"Joe, you're not the only one who can work with an ex-brain," she replied with a small scowl. "But I do agree it's annoying," she conceded. "Maybe no one knows what the ex-brains are thinking." She picked up her tea, blew on the top to cool it, and took another sip. "It was odd though. As soon as I logged in to check the budget for adding staff, the system crashed on me and kicked me out. Once I got back in, the hiring freeze was in place. But don't worry, it won't be in place forever."

"Okay." Joe shifted in his seat again and regained his composure. "So, what is the actual job, if the budget ever comes through?"

"I would put you forward as general counsel of the planning department. I wouldn't just want your advice. I'd want your leadership in that department. I'd want you taking a new start at a legal ex-brain. I'd want you to have the license to build a department that can take all the work we currently send to Fulham back in-house," Diane concluded raising her eyebrow.

"That would be amazing," he said, unable to suppress his enthusiasm.

"I mean it, Joe. You don't need to think of this as an end point. It's a beginning. There is so much you can do here. You can completely change the legal model for City Planning. Then you can take that across the whole city."

"What should we do next?" Joe asked.

"Well, we won't be able to put a proper interview in the system while the budget freeze is in place. But there are a few people I can set you up with for coffee. Probably not the lawyers because I wouldn't want to spook them with change before we're ready to do it. But there are other leaders here you should talk to, people who think the way I do."

"All right. Let's set it up." He looked down and thought for a moment. He wanted her to know he was sincere. "I need this, Diane. Let's make this happen."

"Excellent. I'll have a few conversations and set up some meetings. I won't tell the budget ex-brain. It would probably go into the system and start cancelling the meetings if it knows we're plotting against its plans!" she said with a laugh.

"You're only partly kidding, aren't you?" Joe suggested, returning her smile.

"Maybe I'm just old-fashioned, but I still like to be in charge," she replied. "I kind of liked computers better when they just followed our orders."

"I'm sure your ex-brain is smart enough to know who's in charge around here," Joe shot back. "If it knows what's good for it."

"I'll feel better when you're training it, just to be sure it doesn't get confused."

Chapter 13

Rejected. The word rattled around Joe's head on Monday morning, as he sat at his desk in an empty house with nothing to do. It had been days since he spoke with Diane. No meetings had gone in his calendar. His physical habit for sitting and thinking about complicated legal problems could not be broken. He sat there in his familiar pose, right index finger on his right temple, thumb rubbing his chin. But his mind was blank, except for that word. Rejected.

He picked up a small rubber ball from his desktop and pushed his chair back into the center of the room. "Ex-brain, give me a target," he called out to his home system and quickly a large red X appeared on the wall screen opposite him. "Thank you."

Joe pulled his arm with the ball near his ear and let it fly. Just missed. It bounced back off the floor and into his outstretched hand. Again and again, thump, thump, catch; thump, thump, catch; he aimed the ball toward the X each time, hitting it now and again, over and over in a tedious loop.

After dozens of throws, his virtual assistant pinged as a calendar invitation came through. Finally, he thought, as he heard the familiar tone. Joe tapped the nearby wall of his office and a monitor flashed to life.

INVITATION: Nova D - Exploratory Conversation; Hotel Vista,

9 a.m., Tuesday 27 May, 2053.

Nova D? Joe was aware of the Nova D project through colleagues at work, although he had never worked on it directly. Nova D was a joint venture to build a new city state in eastern Nepal. It was 100 percent planned, starting from a blank canvas and designing everything for efficiency and sustainability. Fulham had done the legal work setting up the joint-venture structure under the Data TRUCE, part of restarting economic integration after the Bit Wars.

There was no explanation, only a name: Amanda Guthridge. And yet, as he sat there with a growing sense of boredom drifting into despair, this invitation was perfectly timed. No matter how skeptical, he knew that he would be at the Hotel Vista at 9 a.m. tomorrow morning.

Ex-Brain Q&A Entry: How has climate migration affected national citizenship?

The volume of people fleeing countries that have been devastated by climate change has created a situation where many refugees have no national citizenship. Countries accepting migrants such as the US, China, Japan, Germany, Australia, and the United Kingdom have offered very few migrants full citizenship and have instead created second-class statuses such as Temporary Migrants ("Temps") or New Arrivals. Even the United States amended its Constitution to remove automatic full citizenship for those born on American soil to control its citizen population. Temps and New Arrivals generally enjoy fewer rights than full citizens, including reduced social services, reduced rights to privacy or due process, limited voting rights, and the ability to be moved out of the country with minimal notice. Such reductions in rights were often seen as the only way for politicians to gain approval from voters to accept large numbers of climate refugees into their borders.

Citizenship is seen by some as the most valuable human commodity. A black market for citizenship has been identified in many countries due to public corruption that allows wealthier migrants to pay to jump to the head of the citizenship line.

Posted 27 May 2053, v. 742

© Ex-Brain Q&A Foundation

Chapter 14

Joe walked into the Hotel Vista and immediately his eyes darted up the soaring glass wall, an atrium stretching up the whole length of the 170-story building, the highest in Denver. A mile-high view in the Mile High City. Joe went to the front desk and asked the virtual concierge for Amanda Guthridge, the name he had been given in his invitation.

"You'll be on the Vista Floor. Express elevator on the right will take you directly," explained a pleasant voice from the desk screen.

Joe glanced up again to where he was headed. He couldn't actually see the top floor through the glass atrium, which gave him a moment of dread. He walked straight to the first set of elevators and walked into the waiting bay where a sign above read Express Vista. The elevator's voice greeted him, "Good morning, Mr. Watson" and the doors closed quickly behind him. Very smoothly the elevator shot upward with the glass atrium and lights speeding by on the way up. At the half-way point the elevator cleared the tops of the neighboring buildings and the view of the city opened up around him. Joe could see mountains in the distance and the city shrinking below him. Odd, he thought, that in all the years he'd lived in Denver, he had never been up here before.

His glass pod softly eased onto the top floor and opened to an all-glass enclosure. There were no other people in sight, just

Joe in an open room with the entire city of Denver sprawling out around him. The sun was shining low in the east, lighting up the Rocky Mountains to the west, painting the peaks a morning pink. He marveled at so much natural beauty surrounding so much human creation.

Joe heard footsteps from behind the elevator bank, and Amanda, his host, walked toward him with her hand extended. "Good morning, Joe Watson," she said with a warm smile.

Amanda was about the same age as Joe, early forties, and very elegant. Like so many people these days, she was of ambiguous mixed race. Definitely a bit Asian, but also perhaps some Northern European, with a strong jaw and broad shoulders. She gestured for Joe to join her on the couches in the middle of the room.

As she sat, she tapped her bracelet, which Joe knew to be the signal that her monitor should start collecting data. It would be more than just voice recording, it would be picking up on all manner of environmental signals, including Joe's heart rate and body temperature, sounds of quick movements, head scratching, plus anything else in the area that could cause a distraction. All of the data would be fed to an ex-brain for analysis, and potentially real-time feedback for Amanda. She would be getting cues, perhaps through an ear implant or text on a device. People had their own preferences for how they got their guidance during meetings.

The monitoring could be off-putting to some, but Joe had been on the other side of this arrangement many times and knew the drill all too well. As a lawyer, it was essential that he could get real-time feedback from witnesses or opposing parties he was negotiating against. Sure, people could object and request that all monitoring devices be turned off—but then they couldn't use them either. Most had become used to the flood of data and feedback. But this was one of the few times when Joe was not equipped with his own device. He looked at his right wrist, agitated there was nothing there. No data feed. Amanda was a black box to him, which was unfamiliar territory.

"So, Joe, are you ready for your next adventure?" she asked abruptly. This was not an uncommon tactic. Going straight to the tough question would elicit the clearest bio response. The ex-brain would immediately know how Joe felt about a change and adjust its strategy accordingly.

"I don't know. I guess that depends on what it is."

"Do you know about us?"

"A bit, I know several people at my firm worked on the…"

"Your *old* firm?" Amanda interrupted.

"Yes, my old firm. Several of my colleagues worked to set up the US side of the joint venture. I didn't have direct involvement. I don't even know what the name means."

Amanda smiled. "We get that a lot. It comes from the Latin *novam domum*. New home. It was tried in many regional languages. Xin JiaZhi in Mandarin. Nayam ghara in Nepalese. But Nova D is what stuck. With so many people using auto translators, everyone seems to get it. So, what have you heard about the project? Are you aware of our vision?"

"Why don't you tell me?" Joe suggested, as he adjusted himself in his seat, creating sounds and vibrations that clearly the ex-brain would be picking up. He instinctually looked down at his wrist again. Still nothing there. He felt blind and very aware that he was being watched closely.

Amanda paused, likely getting feedback in her earpiece. "How about I show you?"

She reached into her pocket for a small device, which she sat on the coffee table in front of them. Quickly, a projection spread into the air above, showing the layout of a city surrounded by mountains. It was similar to Denver, but clearly not the same place. The mountains wrapped around further to the north of the city and closer to the town itself. The city was very orderly and tidy, with cars and pods shooting around in clear transit lines. Buildings spread out to maximize space, but also to maintain views.

Amanda let Joe look around the swirl of city bustle that had sprung to life in front of him and then began. "We're building the future, Joe. It's a perfectly planned city state in eastern Nepal, situated in the valleys of the Himalayas, so we get plenty of water running down from the mountains. It was designed with an integration of ex-brain and human input. Totally efficient, and made to maximize not only human contentment, but also to harmonize the cultures we can attract together."

"How far along are you?" Joe asked.

"We're in phase two," she replied. And as she did, over half of the city disappeared, leaving a much simpler cityscape in front of them. Lower building lines, more residential area, but all still in pleasing proportions. Joe could tell the city was growing in rings. Actually, more like spheres as it was growing up as well as out.

"What you're seeing here is actually a live feed. This area is resource rich," Amanda continued. "We have everything we need to keep growing. We will be self-sufficient, but fully connected to the world. Nova D will be a global hub in the very near future. A model of what cities can be."

"So, what do you need from me?"

"We need pioneers, Joe."

Pioneers. Joe immediately thought of Joseph Esch sitting at the kitchen table in his French country farmhouse.

"Specifically, we need a city administrator, and we think it might be you."

"Might be?"

Pause.

"Well, we know it's you, but you obviously have something to say about that," she replied with a sly smile.

Joe understood the cadence. Her ex-brain was telling her that she needed to tread carefully. And Joe knew that was right. No one told Joe who he was or what he was going to do. He could feel the blood rising to his head as the idea of moving from Denver sank in. He felt that familiar longing for control, and Amanda, with advice from her ex-brain, was about to give him some more.

It was time for Joe to test a bit. He looked up past the city hologram and scanned out at the real horizon through the massive glass dome in front of him. The digital projection of the city disappeared.

"Why did you bring me here? The most beautiful view across the city I love, just to ask me to leave it?"

"It is beautiful, Joe, but beauty is everywhere. That's the thing. Are we humans ever happy to live with the beauty we have and never feel the need to create more? Our world is not static."

Amanda continued, "Nothing beautiful lasts forever. Most things lose their beauty with time. We need to move on, and we would like to give you that opportunity to strike out. To build. To *pioneer*."

That word again.

"Doesn't sound like you think Denver has a bright future. You know something I don't know?"

"Honestly, Joe, I am worried about Denver. I think there are budget problems ahead, and the city will struggle to keep up with the demands. Things are creaking. On the other hand, we are new, and very resource rich. Our prospects for growth are fantastic."

"And what do you mean by administrator?" Joe asked.

"We need someone to run the city. To manage planning and development. To oversee the progress as we grow. Think of it as a mayor, but without the politics. It's an amazing opportunity, Joe. This is what you have been training for your whole career. This is right for you."

Joe stood and moved over to the edge of the room looking out over the city. In the distance he could see a settlement housing zone under construction. Huge cranes with arms danced in unison around the site as they 3D printed the buildings pouring layer after layer of concrete. The movement was mesmerizing as it slowly built upward.

"New cities are being built right here. Why would I need to go to Nova D to do that?" he asked.

"Because we want to do it better. You can help us figure out how," Amanda said as she stood and joined him at the windows.

"If I have options to work with the city here, why would I move my whole family halfway across the world to work for a strange city in a foreign country? Why would I take that disruption?"

"Do you have options to work for the city here?"

"I might," Joe responded quickly, but immediately he worried that he had given away information he should have kept to himself.

Amanda paused. "You've been speaking to Diane Chilvers?"

"Do you know her?" Joe asked.

"No, but we know the work you've been doing."

Joe immediately knew that her ex-brain was feeding her information about him and his past work with the city. It was public record, but he was impressed with the ex-brain's ability to predict even his contacts. He felt uncomfortable with an ex-brain snooping around his history, even though he knew the drill and had trained his Fulham ex-brain to do the same when he interviewed people. It was much better being on the other side.

Amanda sat smiling, likely taking some further cues from her ex-brain, some new way to appeal to him. She shifted in her seat, ready for her next volley.

"Joe, this isn't just a good opportunity for you. It's an opportunity for your whole family. This offer would include immediate full citizenship in Nova D. Because of the deals we've struck, that means rights across most of Asia. Most people would kill for that privilege in these times.

"We're also building state-of-the-art education facilities where your kids would thrive. We're recruiting immigrants from all over, people who want to pioneer a new world." She paused again.

"And Evie, too," she said, waiting to gauge his reaction.

"What about her? What's in it for her?"

"We know the work she does. She's a leader in her field of predictive psychology. We would have a role for her, too, Joe. She could design her own program, the way she wants to do it."

Joe paused on that thought. He didn't know how Evie would feel about starting over, about Nova D, about any of this opportunity. But he did know she would find this bit interesting.

"So, tell me about Nova D itself. How is it run? Who funds it?" Joe asked, changing topics again.

"Well, you probably know that it's a joint venture under the Data TRUCE, given Fulham did the legal work to set it up," Amanda responded quickly.

"Yes, but that's about all I know. I think our involvement was pretty limited."

"Like the city itself, the Nova D company is cutting edge. It has a board of directors made up of individuals from around the globe, and they utilize the ex-brain in completely new ways. Everything is calculated and planned for expansion. It's almost like the city has its own DNA, and the company keeps it growing."

"So, the board makes the decisions?" Joe asked.

Amanda looked thoughtfully out the window at the view. "I suppose that's right. They are in charge. But Nova D is perhaps a bit more... symbiotic than that."

"Symbiotic? That's interesting." What was he to make of that response? Clearly, this was not your average company. "I know what it's like to feel symbiotic with your ex-brain. But you have to know who's in charge," Joe replied.

"Well, as I said, maybe that should be you," came her quick answer as she raised her eyebrows and smiled again.

"So, what's it like to live there?" Joe asked.

"The city is very livable, by design. Everything is built for a balance of growth and human experience. Our ex-brain keeps everything in harmony. We're constantly monitoring for happiness and fulfillment in the population. We get results you won't find in any other city."

"And the government?" Joe pushed.

"As an independent city state, we are our own government. It's similar to Singapore or Monaco. In fact, some people call it 'Singapore in the snow.' We are small, but we have everything we need to operate. I expect we will eventually be recognized as a full independent nation if we want that."

"And the culture? I've heard it's been hard mixing people after a decade of separation during the Bit Wars."

"That definitely exists, Joe. But it's not an issue for us. We are very careful how we recruit diversity. Don't get me wrong, the city has an Asian feel to it, but it's truly global in every way, and designed for harmony."

"And I assume you'll tell me the education system for my kids is also the best in the world?"

Amanda shrugged. "It is. We're proud of it all, Joe. We'd like to show you more. You'll be impressed."

"And salary?"

"We don't look at compensation like most traditional companies or law firms. Our system is a little more holistic. But believe me, it will be very competitive. You and your family won't want for anything."

It was surreal, like an answer to a prayer that only created more problems, like a devil's bargain. It was too much. He had to wrap this up.

"Well, this has been very interesting. But I do have a lot going on. You won't mind if I give it some thought?" he asked as he started to move back across the room.

"Of course. We know how thoughtful you are," Amanda said, purposefully implying that Nova D already knew Joe very well. It was all very familiar. "We tend to move fast at Nova D. We'd like to speak again soon. I'll call you?"

"Sure."

As they approached the elevator doors, Amanda made a few taps on her wrist device, which Joe assumed meant she was switching off her monitoring system. As they stood waiting for the doors to open, she leaned in close to him. "Joe, you may not have all the options you hope for. The world is changing. You should think about this," she said almost in a whisper.

Joe didn't know if she was trying not to be heard or just being dramatic. But it got his attention.

"Thank you for your time today, Joe," she said, raising her voice back to normal volume. "I do hope you will consider this and talk to us again. Can I follow up with you in a few days once you've had a chance to talk it over at home?"

"Sure. Thank you for your time," he said, unsure of what had just happened.

The elevator pinged and the doors swung open. Joe quickly stepped in and turned back to face Amanda once more.

"You should take this seriously, Joe. It may be the best opportunity in the world right now," she said, looking very serious.

"I'll give it some thought," he said as the doors swung closed.

He quickly whisked downward as the skyline of Denver began sweeping in front of his eyes and the earth emerged back into clear view. What did that mean, the best opportunity in the world? Her tone made him feel like she knew something he didn't. She was purposefully cryptic. It was partly interesting, and exciting, but mostly strange.

Chapter 15

Anderson sat in the landing area at the top of the stairs doing his homework when a notice popped up on his screen: *Historial—Joseph Esch's story continues!* He was in the middle of a fairly boring science lesson on carbon footprints and jumped at the chance for a distraction.

"Dad! There's a new video about your great-, great-… I don't know, some number of great-grand dude. Come watch!" he yelled out. Thankfully for Anderson, Joe was also in the middle of a boring chore, reprogramming the house's climate control system to keep it cool while he was home all day. He jumped at the chance.

"Cool, I'll be right there!" he yelled back.

Joe switched off the home environment program and jogged up the stairs. Ever since seeing the introductory episode, Joe had become increasingly curious about Joseph Esch and his life. He wasn't completely sold on the accuracy of the story, knowing the limits of the ex-brain. But he did not doubt that it was directionally correct. What went wrong in France that turned Joseph Esch into an American pioneer? Was it a hard choice? In his current situation, Joe felt a kinship with his struggle.

Anderson had the video ready to play on his portable screen. "Here, let's watch this on the big screen," Joe said as he placed his palm on the wall bringing it to life. "Connect to Anderson's system," Joe commanded, and the wall suddenly blinked to the Historial logo with a play button under an image of Joseph Esch. Anderson tapped play and the video began.

The scene started at treetops as thunder boomed and lightning cracked. Rain poured down in heavy sheets as the view pulled closer to Joseph's small house with a single light on in a window against the dark rainy night.

Immediately Joe knew where this was going, and he felt some dread for his distant relative. The crops were in trouble.

Joseph Esch sat by the window inside looking out at the rain. He was the only one awake in the house, but he clearly could not sleep through the storm, worried that another harvest was being destroyed outside. His face was grim. Lightning flashes lit up waves of rain blanketing the fields.

The scene then skipped to dawn, as Joseph, up before the others, put on his boots, pulled on a coat, and walked out the door and into the wet, foggy morning. He took a few steps into the mud and looked down, not surprised at what he would find. There was standing water everywhere, several inches in parts. He continued out toward his fields, making his way through the dense layers of fog. He passed through an opening in the fencing and took a few steps into his newly planted field. It was partly obscured by the low clouds of mist, but just enough had started to burn off with the rising sun that he could see all he needed to see. The fields were almost completely washed out.

Joe and Anderson leaned in closer to the screen to see the damage when the picture pixelated and started glitching again. It blurred with static, but then quickly resolved into a close-up of Joseph's face as he winced and shook his head, fighting back tears. The pain came through the video screen and swelled inside Joe as he watched.

"Oh, my God, Dad. That's so sad," Anderson said as he looked up at Joe.

"I know. Hard to imagine how difficult their life was," Joe agreed.

"No wonder Joseph decided to become a pioneer in America," Anderson added.

From a distance, a man on horseback galloped up the road toward Joseph's farm. "Joseph," he called out as he neared. "There's trouble in town. People have broken into the grain stores. Come quick!"

The scene showed Joseph jump on a horse and ride out with the other man and quickly arrive in the town. A crowd had gathered with hammers, shovels, and torches to light the early morning. They had broken open the locks and swung open the doors to the town's supplies.

"What are you doing?" Joseph yelled as he dismounted.

"You've seen the storm. The crops are ruined. We'll all starve," came the reply from a large man with a full beard.

"Not like this!" Joseph yelled back. He grabbed the man by his shoulders, but he swung back around violently and threw Joseph to the ground.

"I'm feeding my family. You'll do the same if you have any sense!" he screamed at Joseph as he lay on the ground. Joseph stayed down, watching the line of his neighbors filing out of the building in the center of town with bags of grain and other supplies. Hay and spilled grain covered the ground. As the sun was fully up, Joseph saw a man drop his torch on the cobblestone path, not seeing the pile of dry hay that it landed it in. Immediately, the hay flashed into flame. Before anyone knew what was happening, the doors to the building were ablaze.

"Fire! Fire!" The men screamed and ran as it spread into the storage area. Joseph watched in horror as people poured out onto the street followed by black smoke. The dry storage area became a pyre of flame, and just like that, all of the town's reserves that hadn't been stolen were gone.

The next scene started with Joseph, Magda, and Michel sitting at the kitchen table with mugs of steaming coffee in front of them. Their children were not in the room. Joseph looked somber but composed. "I think this is it. We can't stay here. We won't make it through another season like this without a full harvest."

"Where will we go?" asked Magda. "The whole region is suffering. There are no better farms to work."

"She's right, Joseph," added Michel. "I've heard already this morning from a few others. They're all flooded out."

"I'm going to go talk to the shipping company. They've been recruiting people to go to America. There's a future there. There are land grants to be had in the territories if we can make the trip."

"Joseph, are you sure? You'd leave our home?" Magda asked with clear worry in her eyes. "Do you even know what would be waiting for us in America, even if we could find a way to pay for the trip?"

"I know enough to know we're out of options. There's nothing left here. We have to find a new way."

Tears filled Magda's eyes. "This is our home…" she said, then swallowed hard to stop from crying. She stood and walked quickly from the room, her palms covering her face.

The men solemnly watched her leave, then looked back at each other uncomfortably. "And me, Joseph?" asked Michel.

"You are family, and I would do anything for you, Michel. But I can't force you to come. And I can't pay your way. It will have to be up to you." Joseph placed his hand on Michel's hand and looked him in the eyes. Michel nodded and looked back down at his mug of coffee. The scene faded to black.

"Wow, I can't believe how hard things are for them," Anderson said. "But I guess that's what it took to drive them to America. I guess in some ways we should be glad for it, but it totally sucks watching them go through it. Do you think Magda will come around?"

"Well, I know they don't leave her behind. She stays in our family tree. But I feel for her. I wouldn't want to move from our home. I think in today's world if you're in a safe place it's better to stay put. Home is home. Don't you think?"

"I guess so, but pioneers are pretty cool. You have to admit it."

Joe grinned, shaking his head.

Ex-Brain Q&A Entry: Who were the American pioneers?

The American pioneers were the groups of people who traveled across the unsettled territories of what is now the United States to develop new areas during the 1700-1800s. The typical pioneer traveled west from the original eastern colonies or states, often in covered "Conestoga" wagons. Their journeys were generally dangerous and across difficult terrain, earning the pioneers a reputation for their fortitude and perseverance.

The word "pioneer" comes from the French "pionnier," meaning foot soldier, from the same root as peon or pawn. Although the American pioneers were viewed by some as adventurers, others consider them more akin to pawns doing the hard work of settling American at the direction of the ruling class.

Posted 28 May 2053, response v.497

c Ex-Brain Q&A Foundation

Chapter 16

Joe and Evie arrived early, so Joe saw Fe come in the glass doors. Music blared and lights flashed as she entered. She had the same look of confidence that she had when she walked into Fulham's orientation program over ten years ago. This was her charm. Arriving wasn't about success to Felicity Wan; it was simply about being where she was meant to be. Fe owned it.

She wore a spangled cocktail dress with her hair done up in a swirl. Walking in next to her was a tall woman with pink hair and a stern but pleasant look. They both paused at the door, looking around at what was already a scene. Hundreds of out-of-work lawyers milled about the ballroom. They had made it through a couple of weeks of mourning and were clearly eager to let off some steam. Service bots rolled around the floor offering glasses of champagne and shots in blue vials, and all the lawyers were grabbing drinks to kick off the night. Some could be seen dropping tablets into the shots as well, biztabs to provide an extra kick, known as double pumping.

Joe placed his hand on Evie's back to turn her toward the door. "Let's go say hello."

The Watsons made their way through a small crowd, and Fe saw them heading her way. She let out a shriek with her hands in the air and moved toward them. The tall pink-haired woman followed close behind.

"Hello, beautiful!" Fe exclaimed as she gave Joe a big hug. "And hello even more beautiful!" she said as she slid her hug over to Evie.

"Hello, babe, how are you?" Evie asked, not sure if she should be offering condolences or congratulations.

"I am so good! I'm so happy everyone is here," she said looking around at the crowd of hundreds filling the room.

"No one doubted that people would show up to your party, Fe. How did you pull this off so fast?" Joe asked.

"The manager of this place is an old friend from my clubbing days, so I just booked the next available date. I knew a bunch of out-of-work lawyers wouldn't mind a Wednesday night. Think about this, Winston is probably still at the office figuring out how to keep all our clients. Sucker!"

Joe leaned in so Fe could hear him over the music. "That reminds me, I saw Diane Chilvers the other day. I'll tell you about it later. But we're being rude; who's your friend?" he asked looking up at her companion.

"Oh, Joe and Evie, this is Shawna," she said, grabbing her friend's elbow to pull her closer.

Evie extended her hand and said hello. When Shawna reached out her long arm to meet Evie's, Joe saw the dragon tattoo wrapped around her wrist. "Hey, you're the bartender from Extinction," he said with a smile of recognition.

"Also known as Shawna," she replied in quick correction.

"Great to actually meet you outside the bar," Joe said, reaching out his hand and trying to regain a normal greeting.

"Don't be stiff, Joe. Shawna and I have become friends, and this is a party!" Fe interrupted to bring the awkward introductions to a close.

"Right, I love your friends, Fe," Joe said, giving her a smile.

Fe spent a moment with Evie admiring each other's party dresses before turning her attention to the ballroom. She took Shawna by the hand and started walking deeper into the crowd.

Evie looked at Joe quizzically and asked about the awkward greeting. "It's okay," he said. "But if you get a chance to see her tits, you should," he said deadpan as he turned to follow Fe.

Evie grinned and rolled her eyes. She knew better than to ask too many questions when it came to Fe's social life.

Fe walked deeper into the ballroom and paused. "Oh, my God, I love it!" she exclaimed. The room was filled with music and people, with strobe lights coloring every inch of the ceiling, some pulsing with the beat. A DJ was perched on the stage at the end of the hall, and a huge banner hung above the stage. "Fuck Fulham" it read in silver glitter.

"I didn't know how that would turn out. I love it," Fe said as her eyes almost teared up. "That's going over my mantle when I get home."

"You've outdone yourself, Fe," Evie chimed in.

Fe grabbed Shawna by the hand and led the way deeper into the crowd of lawyers. She made her way through, stopping to say a few hellos, give a few hugs. When she reached the stage where a DJ was perched, she grabbed an official-looking man, gave him a big hug and kiss, and started climbing up on the stage. Joe assumed he must be the old clubbing buddy who arranged the venue.

As Fe reached the top of the stage and the DJ booth, she grabbed a microphone from the DJ as he slowly turned down the music. Colorful strobe lights around the room pulled in to focus on Fe.

"Hello, liberated lawyers!" She shouted at the top of her lungs. The crowd erupted in a loud cheer. "Are you having fun?" Another cheer and glasses were raised in a toast to Fe.

"I'm so glad we're all here tonight. I'm going to keep this simple. You all are amazing. I for one have loved every minute I've spent working with you all. You're like my family. And you know what, I don't feel bad about what the firm did to us. I feel liberated. You all are amazing lawyers, and freaky people. And I love that! We have been set free to make more of our lives." More cheers spilled out from the crowd.

"So tonight, we're not here to commiserate. We're here to celebrate. And to kick it off, we have only one thing to say about our former employer!" Fe pointed up at the sign above her head, and in unison, the crowd of hundreds of people screamed "FUCK FULHAM!" and erupted in even louder cheers.

Fe handed the mic back to the DJ, and the dance music immediately kicked in again to fill the room as she climbed down from the stage.

Evie leaned into Joe and had to yell to be heard over the crowd. "She really is something else. They love her." Joe watched as Fe made her way through the crowd, high-fiving and hugging friends. Shawna stayed close, but clearly didn't know what to do with her date's instant celebrity.

After about an hour of drinking and dancing, Joe was taking a break at a high-top table on a balcony overlooking the dance floor. Fe, Shawna, and Evie had been dancing in a large group, when Fe looked up and saw Joe standing alone. She broke away to go up the stairs and join him.

"So, pal, you having a good time?" she said as she walked up to his perch above the party.

"Just enjoying the view," he replied as he looked down at the masses dancing, including Evie and Shawna in the middle of the floor. "You've outdone yourself, Fe. This is exactly what this group needed. Maybe you should quit the law all together and go into entertainment, or politics. You're a natural."

"F-that. I'm thinking bigger," she shot back quickly.

"I'm sure you are."

"So, you still worrying about a job?" she asked.

"You know me, always thinking," he replied.

"Always worrying," she corrected.

"Well, my backup plan isn't a sure thing. I met with Diane Chilvers last week. She said the city's ex-brain just cut her budget for all hiring plans. Even if she wanted to, she couldn't hire me right now. It seems those doors are currently closed."

"That's weird, I would have thought the city was looking to spend just to keep up," Fe said.

"Yeah, maybe the ex-brains know something we don't," he replied.

"But don't worry, Joe. You'll have options before you know it. Your bigger risk is moving too soon. Don't settle for something that isn't perfect. You have the time. Take it and get this right."

"Well, I did have an interesting meeting yesterday. Do you remember the Nova D project?"

"That joint venture in Nepal that Fulham set up?" Fe asked.

"Yeah, you know anything about it?"

"Not really. I think we just set up the companies and structure, but not much more than that. The pencil necks in corporate filing did the work. Did Nova D call you?"

"They reached out totally out of the blue, and I went to see them on Monday. At least, I spoke to a woman who claimed to represent them. It was a short meeting up at the top of the Vista Hotel."

"Wow, fancy. What do they want?"

"They want me to move there," Joe said bluntly.

"Get the fuck out!" Fe stepped back and slapped Joe's chest as a nearby Atlas service bot rolled up beside them and popped open its top. Two glasses of champagne rose from the bot, plus a few blue tubes with shots. "Can I offer you a drink?" the bot asked.

"What did you tell them?" Fe asked, as she grabbed the glasses and handed one to Joe. The service bot stayed in place, keeping the shots on offer and awaiting further instruction.

Before Joe could answer she continued, "Listen, you have to be careful. Don't panic and do something drastic. I'm not going to tell you not to go if you guys decide that's right, but Jesus, take your time."

Fe paused, and then started again. "Actually, screw that, I am not going to tell you what to do. You don't have to jump on the next flight to Asia just because there's a job there. Plus, I'd miss you guys," she said leaning into him against the balcony. "Who's going to be my partner at my new firm if you run off to Nova D?"

"I'm not going anywhere, Fe. You know I love this place. But it's nice to be wanted," he said.

"I know," she replied. "But look at this party, we all want you here."

"They want you. They're mildly pleased to still know me."

"Oh, whatever. If we were at all serious about starting our own firm, you could go down there and recruit a hundred good lawyers in ten minutes. Easy."

"So maybe that's our play?" he asked, taking a drink.

"I'm your girl, Joe. We should do it just to make Winston squirm when we steal his clients."

Joe pictured Winston getting furious, sitting in his office chair watching his client list shrink before his eyes. So good.

As Joe quietly mulled thoughts of revenge, Fe looked down from the balcony to the glass entry doors and saw a group of young lawyers walk in. They were some of the most junior lawyers to be let go from Fulham, and had decided to do some drinking somewhere else before the party, based on the stumbling among the group as they cleared the doors. Fe had been a mentor to many of the junior team, and always acted a bit maternal toward them, maybe more like a crazy aunt.

Fe dug her feet into metal slats that ran along the post of the balcony railing, grabbed the top of the rail, and hoisted herself up several feet into the air. She raised her hands above her head and yelled at the top of her lungs, "My babies!" as she waved her hands like a rock star. The group at the door saw her and yelled back waving.

Joe immediately felt nervous for her and placed his hand on her back to steady her. "Careful, Fe," he said trying to help her balance.

The service bot behind them quickly swung into action. It closed its lid and spun around to roll away when its side arm bumped into Fe's thigh and sent her leaning forward.

There was a slow-motion second of Fe flailing and waving. Even the thumping of the music seemed to lose its tempo in a moment of confusion. Fe's face melted in slow motion from joy to panic to terror. She lurched forward as her feet popped out of the railing. Joe grabbed her back with his hand, but his fingers slipped through the sequins of her dress.

Down she went. She twisted once in the air as she screamed and plunged. She crashed through a glass table on the floor below.

The loud crash sucked all the attention from the dance floor as the crowd froze and then turned in unison toward the balcony. Screams filled the room as the mortified lawyers took in the scene. Several from the crowd gathered to confirm what they had just seen. Their leader lay broken in a pool of shattered glass and blood.

Joe ran down the stairs and pushed through to his friend's side. He grabbed her lifeless hand and collapsed in shock. The distant sound of music and flash of lights slowed to a blur around him. Evie pushed through the crowd and knelt down by his side, putting her head against his shoulder as tears streamed down her face.

Chapter 17

Flashing blue lights from the ambulance outside filled the empty ballroom. The music had stopped, the people were gone, and Joe sat next to Evie on the central staircase, numb. Cleaning bots roved quietly around the room, except for the spot where Fe had fallen, which was a pile of shattered glass and horrible red stains sectioned off by a ring of police pylons beaming a yellow line of barricade to section off the area. Evie rested her head on Joe's shoulder and wiped streaks of mascara off her cheeks.

Joe saw a shadow from the blue lights shift as the sliding glass entry doors opened. Inspector Maurine Ferguson walked in and spotted them on the stairs.

"Thanks for waiting for me. I'm Inspector Ferguson," she said as she approached Joe and Evie. She stood in front of the stairs and pulled out a mobile screen for notes. Joe saw her tap her wrist device, turning on a monitoring system for the interview she was about to conduct.

"I'm going to record and monitor this conversation. That all right?" she asked.

"That's fine," Joe replied.

"So how are you guys holding up?" she asked sympathetically.

"I'm okay," Joe replied, looking at Evie sitting next to him who just nodded silently.

"Your names are Joseph and Evelyn Watson, right?"

Joe nodded. "Joe and Evie." He had palmed her screen when she first arrived, so she already had all of his public details, but this was procedure.

And Joe, you were up with Fe before she fell?" He nodded again. "Can you tell me what happened; what you saw?"

Joe took a deep breath and started. "I was up on the balcony with Fe, talking, taking a break from dancing. She saw a bunch of friends walk in the front door, and she wanted to call down to them, so she stood up on the railing. I saw her wedge her feet in the decorative part of the rails. She got their attention and was waving at them. I think the service bot spun around just then and bumped her, so she leaned forward and swung her arms. I guess her feet must have popped out of the rails, and down she went. I reached out to grab her but just couldn't…" His voice trailed off as he looked down and tears welled up in his eyes.

Ferguson gave him a second to compose himself. "What were you talking about up in the balcony, just before?"

"Our futures. This is a lay-off party. We all need new jobs."

Ferguson looked up and gestured at the Fuck Fulham sign above the stage. "Right, you guys are the lawyers who all got fired?"

"That's us," he replied.

"Was Fe depressed about losing her job or particularly down tonight?"

"Fe?" Joe said incredulous. "No. This was her party. For Fe, this was liberation. No one here was happier than Fe."

"Was she drinking a lot?"

"Probably. The service bot had just given us drinks, and I'm sure it wasn't her first. But she was acting fine. Not overly drunk. Not slurring her words," Joe explained.

Ferguson jotted down some notes on her screen. "You think the service bot hit her? That would be very unusual. They are programmed never to make contact with humans."

"I know, but the arm was extended, and I think that's what brushed her. Maybe it wasn't expecting a person to be up on the rail. I don't know... it happened so fast. I'm not sure what happened. One minute she was the life of the party, waving at her friends, the next..." Joe's voice trailed off again as he looked over at the shattered glass and blood stains just feet from where he sat.

"Well, we'll review any surveillance video and the service bot maintenance records. The bot was from Atlas. They're pretty easy to work with," the inspector explained. "You'd be surprised how often we pull data from service bots for investigations. They see everything."

She jotted another note and asked, "So tell me about your relationship with Fe. You were *friends*?"

Joe sat up straighter, as did Evie. Joe knew this was standard questioning, mainly just to record his reaction in the monitors and check for any sign of stress or dishonesty. Still, it was unsettling even to hear a hint of accusation.

"Yes, she was my best friend at work. We had partnered on cases together for years. We were more like family."

"That's right," Evie agreed, looking Ferguson directly in the eyes. "Fe was part of our family, and like an aunt to our kids."

"You ever had any disagreements? Any stress in the work relationship?" Ferguson asked, directing the question back to Joe.

"No, not really. Fe always spoke her mind, but I don't think we ever fought."

"Did she ever fight with anyone?"

"Fe mixed it up with everyone, but she didn't have enemies, if that's what you mean. Wasn't her style. It was almost impossible not to like Fe."

"Was she here alone?"

"No, she was here with another woman, Shawna," Joe answered.

"Was she gay?"

Joe thought for a second and turned to Evie for help. "Fe didn't like to be restricted by labels," Evie suggested.

"Got it. Do you know how to find Shawna if we need to talk to her?"

"I was with her when it happened. We all gathered around Fe, but then I went to Joe and lost track of her. I'm sure she was pretty freaked out and left, probably in shock. They hadn't been together long," Evie explained.

"She's a bartender at Extinction if you need to find her," Joe added.

"No problem. She'll be on surveillance video somewhere so we can ID her and track her down. What about Fe's family?" Ferguson asked.

"It's just her here in Denver. She grew up in California but left right after law school. I think her dad left LA five years ago in one of the big waves, and I believe he's in Portland now. They're not that close. No siblings. Mother died while Fe was in school."

Ferguson finished some notes. "Okay, thanks for waiting around to talk. You guys get home and get some rest. We'll contact you if we need anything further." She put away her screen, tapped her wrist device to end the monitoring, and gathered her things.

"It's a real tragedy, and I'm sorry," she said letting some sympathy seep in now that the questioning was done.

"Thank you, Inspector," Evie said as she stood up from the steps with Joe.

"Do you need any help getting home?" Ferguson asked.

"No, we'll be fine. Thank you," Joe replied as he took Evie's hand and walked toward the doors.

The flashing blue lights from the ambulance had disappeared, leaving only the dim lights from the streetlamps and darkness on the walkway outside. It wasn't actually raining, but it was wet. Mist hung in the air and made everything cloudy. Joe pressed on his wrist device and asked for a taxi. He and Evie stood outside the building in silence waiting for a car to take them home.

Chapter 18

Joe, Evie, and the kids pulled up to the civic center in their car and rolled slowly past Winston standing on the sidewalk. Joe gave a quick wave as he drove by and pulled into the parking garage next to the center. It was a large complex a few miles outside the city toward the mountains. It was used for small concerts, community meetings, and remembrance services. For those who were not connected to churches, civic centers filled the gap.

The car pulled into a parking spot and turned off its motor. The shell turned clear as the doors opened, and the family spilled out. The kids had all cleaned up for the occasion and were dressed in their best clothes, nothing denim, nothing wrinkled, no sports logos anywhere.

"Why don't you guys go straight in. I'll go out front and see Winston," Joe suggested to Evie.

"No problem, sweetheart. Take your time. We'll get seats in the front," she replied. Evie took Hope by the hand and led the kids toward an entrance door connected to the garage.

Joe walked back down the ramp toward the street and sidewalk. It was a warm, sunny day, and the air smelled crisp. Joe took a deep breath as he turned the corner and saw Winston still waiting by the front doors. Wearing a full suit, he looked even more professional than usual.

"Hi Joe. How are you holding up?"

"Fine."

Winston paused for a second and then reached out his arms to give Joe a big hug. Joe resisted, pulling his arms up, but Winston didn't stop. He tightened his arms and Joe relaxed quickly, losing his will to punish Winston. He gave in to the embrace. They both loved Fe. They were a work family, and now they were about to bury one of their own.

Winston released the hug and wiped his face to be sure there were no stray tears lingering. "So did you have to call it a Fuck Fulham party?" he asked trying to manage a smile and break the mood.

"That was all Fe. And you guys deserved it," Joe replied.

"The press loved that headline. As usual, she gets the last laugh."

"It was nice of Fulham to pay for this service. Was that hard to get through?" Joe asked.

"Eh, a few of the assholes in the partnership had to justify it as a good PR move. The majority just knew it was the right thing to do."

"Well, thank you. Come on, let's go," Joe said, opening the doors to let Winston walk through.

Winston stopped at the door and turned back to Joe. "I'm so sorry, Joe. If I had known. If I could take it back; if I could change things…"

"I know. We'd all change things. But we can't," Joe replied.

Winston nodded, and they walked into a large entry hallway with a few guests milling about. The room for the service was down the hallway, and they could hear music coming from

the room. Winston and Joe walked in to see a crowd full of lawyers and friends. Many of the Fulham partners had come to pay
their respects, which Joe appreciated, even if he wasn't particularly in the mood to speak to them. Most of the attendees from
the Fuck Fulham party were there as well, but the joy was gone.

Joe saw Evie and the kids sitting in the front row alongside
Fe's father. He was a grey-haired Asian man, sitting quietly and
staring at pictures of Fe that were being displayed on the front
wall screen in a slideshow tribute to her. Joe stared for a moment
as well as the images passed by, Fe with her hands up finishing
the Denver marathon, Fe locking arms with her coworkers. Joe
saw an image of Fe holding Hope when she was only about two
years old, and he had to take a deep breath to compose himself.
He walked up to the front row to take a seat with his family just
as Winston walked up to the podium to start the ceremony.

"Good afternoon, everyone. Thank you for joining us for
this ceremony to remember Fe Wan and celebrate her life. My
name is Winston Balfour. I had the pleasure of working with Fe
for the past ten years. I won't ignore the reality that we've been
through a lot of change at Fulham & Mayson recently, and I no
longer had the pleasure of working with her. But regardless of
work, Fe was like my family. I missed her in the office, and I
miss her even more now that she's gone.

"Those of us who knew Fe well know that she would not
have had any time for a lot of tears and sorrow. She would have
wanted joy, some laughter, fond remembrance. Irreverence.
Hell, her last act was essentially a party to tell me and my firm
to fuck off."

A quiet laugh rippled through the crowd.

"We need to remember Fe for the wonderful, smart, lover of life that she was. I invite those of you who have asked to say a few words about Fe to come forward."

For the next sixty minutes a parade of friends, young and old, came up to tell stories about Fe. Most had something funny to say. There were stories of late nights at the firm. Stories of late nights out in bars. By the sound of it, one would have thought Fe rarely had a day without a biztab or three. There were a few tender moments about how Fe had made a difference in people's lives. She mentored half of the young lawyers at the firm, and they all wanted to give her a public thank you. Most were heartfelt, although it was also true that Fe was cool, and so publicly acknowledging that she invested time in you made you, by extension, cool as well. There was a bit of that. No one minded. Virtually all the speakers shed a tear along the way.

When the speakers were done, Joe stood up to close the ceremony. He took a deep breath and looked down at Evie for support as he slid across the aisle and approached the podium. He didn't have any notes. He didn't have his usual tech display or argument outline. No bio monitors were tracking the audience to see if they were getting bored. He went full human.

"Hello, everyone. I'm Joe Watson. Fe was my colleague in the office, and my best friend. I'll never forget when she started at the firm. I had already been there a couple of years, but as soon as she walked in those doors, I knew she owned the place. Most of us knew that she was smarter than us, a better lawyer than us. And yet the maddening thing to all of us was that she didn't know it, or if she did, she didn't care. She valued the joy of a fun day in the office more than winning cases. She valued the joy of a fun day out of the office even more."

The crowd laughed. The mood had stayed light throughout the ceremony, true to what Fe would have wanted.

Joe told a few more of his favorite stories about Fe with a stream of laughs and a few tears. He told about how she added levity to any meeting, telling inappropriate jokes that only she could get away with. He told about how much Fe had meant to his family and helped care for little Hope when she was born. When he ran out of stories he decided it was time to close and took a deep breath, looking across the top of the room to compose his final thoughts.

"If there is one thing that Fe understood better than me, it was the future. I have generally feared it, seeing it as something to insure against and control. Fe saw it as something to celebrate. Something to embrace without fear, without dread. Even as things around the world seemed to deteriorate, Fe was excited for the opportunity of each new day. It is a tragedy that she won't be able to see any more new days. If there is one thing we can do to remember her and honor her life, it is to see each day the way she did, not with fear, but with joy. Goodbye, Fe. We will miss you."

The room stayed silent as Joe walked down from the podium and back to his seat. Fe's father was seated in the same row near Evie. He shook his hand and then had a seat next to Evie. After an appropriate pause, music started to play and the attendees started slowly standing and filing out of the room, some laughing, some crying. Some did both. Anderson looked up and said, "Nice job, Dad." Joe tousled his hair and gave a nod of thanks.

The music grew louder into a full upbeat rock song, and Joe heard familiar lyrics rolling over the crowd.

Evie heard it, too, and caught Joe's eye. "P!nk, *Raise Your Glass?* Are you calling Fe a dirty freak?" she said with a sad smile.

"Yeah, P!nk was her favorite classic artist. She told me once that her first concert was P!nk's farewell tour at the LA Coliseum. I thought it would be fitting."

Evie reached out and gave Joe a long embrace. "That was touching, honey. I've never seen you give a speech without your outline on a monitor. It was nice. Natural. You should do that more often."

He nodded.

"You want to talk to anyone here before we go?"

Joe looked back across the room at all the people milling about. "Not really, but I should. I should thank the Fulham partners, make sure they feel properly praised for their generosity. You want to take the kids out and let them stretch their legs? I won't be long."

"Come on kids, let's go," Evie slid along the aisle making room for the family to spill out. "Nice job, sweetheart. I love you," she said, catching Joe's eye once more. Grace and Anderson led the way out with Evie and Hope close behind.

Mr. Wan stood and shook Joe's hand again. He was older and shrinking, but not frail. "Thank you, Joe. I'm sure you know that Fe and I weren't that close over the past few years, really since her mother died. I'm just so glad that she had a full life and people like you and your family in it."

He stared up at her picture projected on the front wall. "I remember when she was a kid. We lived in Santa Monica, not far from the beach, back when there was still good beach there. It's all hinterlands now. But in those last years before the big storms wiped it out, Fe used to love it there. She'd surf, swim, play with her friends. She was the happiest kid you've ever seen. They were better times."

"I'm sure they were. Do you need anything, Mr. Wan?"

"No," he replied. "I'm staying at a hotel tonight and catching a solar plane back to Portland tomorrow."

"How are things in Oregon? I've heard it's getting rough," Joe asked.

"Eh, it's okay. Portland's not too bad. But a lot of the state is going hinterland. We've always had a lot of survivalists. I think the ones along the coast were eager for this. Storms drive out the normal folk, and the survivors take over where they can be left alone, off the grid."

"Is it safe?" Joe asked.

"Depends on who you are. If you know how to handle yourself, you'll be okay. It's actually a strong community. Most of us lost jobs to robots or from companies moving inland, so now we look after each other."

"Do you worry about the police pulling out of the city?"

"I don't think it's lawless. We have our own laws. But I don't think it would be wise for the police to come around. People there don't need 'em, don't want 'em."

"Not so much on law and order?"

He shrugged. "I think you misunderstand. I'm a retired police officer. There's a bunch of us. Believe me, we know what law and order is. I think we prefer to take care of it ourselves. We don't need it imposed on us."

Joe decided to let it go. Despite his curiosity, he didn't need to delve further into hinterland vigilante justice.

Mr. Wan looked at the picture wall once more, staring at his daughter's images as they flashed by. "Fe hated me being there. Worried about me but didn't like to visit. I regret that now."

"I'm so sorry, Mr. Wan. We all miss her."

"I'm just glad she had a family here with you and yours," he said.

"Me too. She was special to us. To me. Let me know if we can help in any way." Joe gave the old man a quick embrace.

Joe turned to scan the room. A few Fulham partners, including Winston, were talking in a group in the back of the room. He felt like a high school kid that had to leave his friends and go to talk to a group of adults, which made him all the more bitter considering Joe always thought of himself as being very adult. Deep breath. Joe straightened up and started toward what he assumed would be an unpleasant few minutes of awkward conversation.

As Joe walked past the middle rows of chairs, a familiar woman stood and called to him. "Hello, Joe." She held out her hand. Joe quickly placed her as the woman he had spoken with at the top of the Vista Hotel. "Amanda Guthridge," she said as she shook his hand.

"Right, from Nova D. What are you doing here?" Joe asked with a smile, but also a sense of unease.

"Well, we know lots of lawyers in this town, and in this room, and of course were aware of Fe and wanted to pay our respects."

"Who's we?" Joe asked.

"Nova D. All of us as a team. But honestly, I wanted to be sure to come because I knew it's where you would be."

"You're recruiting at a funeral?"

"No, Joe. But I am happy to see you and see how you're doing."

"That's nice of you, Amanda. I'm fine. If you'll excuse me, I need to go see some people in the back."

Amanda responded quickly. "Your words at the end were lovely. Inspiring. But it's hard to do, isn't it? Not to fear new things. To embrace each day with joy?"

"I suppose you will tell me every day in Nova D is full of joy?"

"It's normal life, a lot of joy, some sorrow. But it is new and exciting, Joe."

Joe paused. "I'm sure it is. Thanks for coming. I do have to go."

"Can we talk again soon? I know you're going through a lot right now, and I don't want to rush you. But I also don't want you to miss out. We have exciting things happening, Joe. When you're ready?"

"We'll see. I have a feeling you'll know how to find me."

"Yes, I'm very good at that. But Nova D makes decisions very quickly. Please don't wait too long," Amanda said as she collected her coat off her chair. "Good luck, Joe. And again, really nice tribute to your friend. You're a natural public speaker. We admire that about you."

Joe nodded, turned, and continued toward the back of the room. He glanced over his shoulder as he walked so he could see Amanda make her way toward the door. She was staring at her wrist device, giving it a few taps. Probably monitoring him during their brief conversation, and he wondered what signs he was giving off. Strange that some ex-brain somewhere might have a better idea about how he was feeling than he did.

He wasn't overly excited to talk with the Fulham partners who had just fired him, but he also knew that they were important people in Denver, and potentially the key to finding his next role. *Five more minutes, then I'm done*, he said to himself, eager to have this last mandatory conversation and then get the hell out of there.

He approached the small group where Winston and a few others were standing in a circle talking. They all welcomed him warmly and told him what a moving eulogy he had given. He thanked them and immediately felt like leaving. In order to override his feelings and hang in a bit longer, he relied on a mental trick he developed when he was younger. After every word out of one of the partners' mouths, he simply smiled and said to himself, *Yes, fuck you.*

"Joe, your family looks like they are doing well."

Yes, fuck you.

"Your wife does such interesting work. You must be proud of her."

Yes, fuck you.

"Your kids are getting so big."

Yes, fuck you.

"Fe was such a unique person. We'll miss her."

Then you shouldn't have fired her, fuck you.

He hung in for several minutes of pleasantries, self-amused with his internal monologue of F-bombs, and then caught the eye of one of the partners in the group, a woman named Gretchen O'Donnell. She had led the work Fulham had done for Nova D. He was more than ready to excuse himself to go find his family and go home, so he started his goodbyes and thanked the partners for their generosity and for hosting the event. As he graciously made his escape, he put his hand on Gretchen's arm and quietly asked if he could have a moment on the side for a quick question.

Winston quickly grabbed Joe's hand for a firm shake. "Take care, buddy. I'll give you a call soon."

Joe nodded and slid past him toward the door. Gretchen followed him over, a bit curious given they had not been close friends at the firm and had never worked together. "What is it, Joe? How can I help?"

"Gretchen, did you lead the work on the Nova D partnership a couple of years ago?"

"I did. Not much of a project, actually. We drafted their corporate agreements and got them registered, but there wasn't a lot to it."

"Whom did you work with in the joint venture? Remember any of the people?"

"Well, that was kind of the odd thing, if I remember correctly. We didn't have much personal contact. The instruction came in from a foreign law firm, and we had one lawyer there we talked to. But we never spoke with the people running the company. We just followed the guidance from the other firm. They submitted the personal information on the people involved to register the corporate leaders, but we never spoke with them. Made it a simple matter. Why?"

Joe thought for a second, and quickly decided he didn't want to say too much. "Eh, I've heard a bit about them recently and met someone who works with them building their city in Nepal. I was just curious about what kind of people they are. I guess you don't know."

"Sorry, wish I could help, but they were always a bit of a mystery client."

"Okay, thanks Gretchen."

"No problem. I'm happy to go back to the files if you need any specifics. And Joe. I'm so sorry about everything."

"I know," Joe said, managing a smile. "I may take you up on that offer. I'll let you know." He was glad to have a lead on Nova D but wasn't in the mood to keep talking. He turned to go meet his family at the car and go home.

As he approached the door, he looked back at the front of the room. Fe's picture was projected brightly on the wall. She was young in the picture, no more than twenty, smiling on a balcony with the blue Pacific Ocean behind her, the afternoon sun hanging low in the distance. How sad none of those things were the same anymore. Not the beach, not the balcony, not Fe. *Fuck you*, he thought. This time without the ironic angst, but with sadness and loss.

Ex-Brain Q&A Entry: What are hinterlands?

Hinterlands is an informal term for areas of the United States that have been largely abandoned by state or local governments due to their inhabitability. In most cases, hinterlands are formed when a majority of inhabitants of an area leave their homes due to climate conditions as well as when utilities and insurance companies stop offering services. With an absence of electric power, sewer, or water service, the pre-existing homes in the area become uninhabitable, causing most residents to evacuate.

Hinterlands often remain inhabited by squatters who choose to live in the abandoned areas, either alone or in communes. Although hinterlands are not technically beyond the reach of the law because they remain governed by states and localities, they are typically thought of as dangerous and lawless places where police and other service personnel rarely travel.

Posted 2 June 2053, response v.876

© Ex-Brain Q&A Foundation

Chapter 19

Joe woke the next morning in a haze. Evie had gotten up earlier to make the kids breakfast and let Joe lie in bed as long as he liked. He would have expected feeling melancholy about Fe, and at some level he was. But he was also distracted by his short conversation with Gretchen about Nova D. How did she describe them, a mystery client? Joe looked up at the ceiling and stared, feeling guilty that he was thinking about a job offer rather than Fe. *It's a defense mechanism*, he thought. In his mind's eye, he pictured himself staring into the distance with a montage of Fe's images scrolling across his mental screen. That's what a true friend would be doing, right? Yet his mind wouldn't go there. He stayed away from that place, and memories of his meeting at the top of the Vista Hotel filled his mind instead.

Joe got out of bed and made his way downstairs to a Monday morning in full swing. The kids were dressed for school and having breakfast, with bags and screens lying in disarray on the kitchen table.

"Good morning, Dad," Anderson said in greeting. "How are you feeling?"

"I'm pretty good, thanks."

"That's good, so I was thinking..." he said with his voice trailing upward. Anderson had learned early that when he wanted to ask for something, he should always ask a polite question first rather than jumping straight to the request. Unfortunately for him, he still hadn't mastered the subtlety of faking interest in another person's well-being. The family could all spot his lack of sincerity and knew when they were about to be asked for a favor.

"Uh-oh, what is it?"

"Well, I think a new episode of Historial drops today. You want to watch with me when I'm back from school?"

Joe smiled. He expected a request for money or permission for a new virtual game. A request for some quality time with his dad was a nice surprise.

"Sure, Anderson, that would be nice," he said, trying not to be too obvious about the fact that he had literally nothing else going on. He ran his hand over Anderson's hair and walked by to the other side of the table to give Grace and Hope kisses on the top of their heads. "Good morning, ladies."

He got only nods in return as they both had mouths full of cereal.

The morning wrapped up quickly as the bus picked up the kids and Evie packed herself up to head into the office.

"You going to be okay today?" she asked as she walked out.

"Yes, you?"

"Yes, but I worry about you. Would you consider wearing a monitor for me?"

Joe recoiled. He knew Evie was an expert at grief monitoring, and that there was no shame in acknowledging that one needed help. But that stung. And he wasn't her patient, he was her husband.

"I'm not a work project. And I'll be fine."

She frowned. "I know. But there's no reason not to take care of yourself. I'm going to call you later and check in, okay?"

"That's fine. I love you."

"I love you, too." Evie pulled her work bag over her shoulder and closed the door behind her.

After filling a cup of coffee and toasting a piece of sourdough, Joe wandered back through the house and stood in the front hallway. His wrist device pinged at him, and a voice said, "Good morning, Joe, you're overdue for your VirusScan. Shall we do it this morning?" Joe tapped his screen and took another big sip of coffee. "Okay, let's do it."

Joe walked upstairs through his bedroom and into his bathroom. He opened a wall cabinet behind the mirror and pulled out a small round device, inserted his finger, and waited. Inside a small pin quickly sprang out and pricked his finger, producing the smallest drop of blood, which was instantly sucked into the machine where it would be checked against a database somewhere in the world for any new viruses or bacteria spreading across the warming and hyper-connected world.

Joe set down the device and tended to the rest of his morning routine, brushed his teeth and hair, and washed his face. By the time he finished, he looked back at the virus scanning disk to see the green light shining on top, nothing new or dangerous in his system. Joe had never seen a red light and was very grateful for that.

He looked around and listened to the silence. What now? The lack of direction was crushing. And he knew if he sat still

too long, he would start thinking about Fe. Either out of desperation, or actual interest, he quickly decided he needed to follow
up with Gretchen. There was a story behind Nova D, and this was
exactly the distraction Joe needed to avoid falling deeper into his
gloom. Maybe this was his way into the Fulham ex-brain? Maybe
Gretchen would take pity on him and give him access? He headed
straight for his study to log into his screen and start digging deeper.

****

In the Fulham & Mayson office tower, Gretchen sat at her desk
distracted by her weekend conversation with Joe. Why was he
asking about Nova D? It had always been an odd piece of work
with a very strange client, which had left her a bit unsettled.
As a careful lawyer, Gretchen hated loose ends and unresolved
business. But the project ended quickly and faded from her
mind. The JV was set up, and she never knew how it played
out. Why was it coming back now?

She accessed the Fulham ex-brain to ask a few questions.

"Ex-brain, access the files for the Nova D joint venture."

Her screen responded, quickly showing a folder file and set
of documents.

"Remind me of the engagement, please?"

"Our firm set up a joint venture under the provisions of the
Data TRUCE for the purpose of developing a city state in eastern Nepal. The US partner was a company called Nova D US
Ventures, and the partner was Nova D Global Ventures based
in Nepal."

"Who initiated that project? What was the name of the person who began the corporate filings?"

"The original application was filed by a man named Haruto Takana. He was listed as a Japanese national living in Nepal. We have no other records about him other than his passport information to confirm identity."

"Nothing else? That's odd. And who was the counsel in Nepal who did the corporate filings?"

"The legal work was performed by a law firm called XJZ Partners. The lawyer we engaged with was a woman named Jennifer Lee."

Gretchen paused. She remembered a video conference with a lawyer named Jennifer. She was cold, all business, and very prompt. When Gretchen or her team sent edits on the JV agreement Jennifer always turned them around very quickly. Ex-brains weren't quite as advanced back then, but Gretchen assumed that Jennifer's ex-brain had a clear set of rules for negotiating agreements and was able to turn responses in the negotiation at lightning speed. Then they concluded the agreements, set up the governance for the joint venture—each side had a 50 percent stake, and that was that. Nova D was up and running, and Gretchen never heard from them again.

She sat back in her office chair and searched her mind. That's all she had and couldn't remember anything else. She thought harder about Haruto Tanaka. If he started this whole thing, how come Gretchen couldn't remember him at all? Was he on some original video conference to begin the project? He occupied exactly zero space in Gretchen's memory.

She turned back to her screen. "Ex-brain, do we have anything else on Haruto Tanaka? Any communications? Emails? Anything?"

"His signature appears on the original filings for the Nova D joint venture. He is referenced in an email from Jennifer Lee. That is all I can find in our files."

Gretchen leaned back again, slightly bothered. In the middle of her reflection her screen started buzzing, a call coming in from Joe Watson. She sat up, checked her image on her screen to make sure she looked presentable, shifted a blonde strand of hair from one side to the other, and tapped on the accept button. "Good morning, Joe. I was just thinking of you," she smiled.

"Hello Gretchen. I hope not in a bad way."

"Not at all. You got me thinking about Nova D, and I've been looking over the files and trying to jog my memory."

"And?"

"I'm sorry to say, not much. I reviewed the history. It was all started by a guy named Haruto Takana. We worked with XJZ Partners on it, got the joint venture up and running, and never heard from them again."

"And that's it?"

"Well, don't get me wrong, Joe. It was a pretty big project in some ways. I mean, if I recall, at the time it was the largest JV created under the Data TRUCE after the Bit Wars. Between the two sides, they brought about $10 billion together to begin construction of a new city. There were all kinds of deals in the background with the government of Nepal. And the plan was to go high- tech all the way, with the latest in planning and urban development technology. Everything was to be smart sensor-enabled and data-driven. The ideas were amazing. It's just that the legal work was fairly pedestrian. And it was a bit odd that they didn't engage with us the way most clients do. They just wanted the agreements and nothing more. If I'm being honest, at the time I was probably hurt that they were doing this cool project and all they wanted from us were some forms."

"Do you remember anything about their counsel in Nepal?"

"She was cold, no personality, from what I remember. Just got the work done, but never shared anything more personal about herself or the project. If I didn't know better, I'd have thought she was a deep-fake hologram, except that would have been completely illegal, even in Nepal."

"Did Fulham use its ex-brain for the project?"

"Probably just for the basics, for due diligence and records searches. Nothing much. We weren't doing much modeling or projection then. And you weren't on the case, so we clearly weren't breaking any new ground with the ex-brain."

"Right," he said smiling, and paused. "So, Gretchen, there may be more information in there somewhere. Do you think you could get me access to the ex-brain so I can poke around?"

"Do you mind if I ask why you're so interested?" Gretchen asked, digging a bit deeper.

"Nova D has actually approached me about a job."

"Really? Wow. Joe. That could be exciting. Are they expanding to work here in the US?"

"No, it's in Nova D. That's the trick."

"Hmm." She paused. "I'm sorry, Joe. I can't give you access. It's not that I don't want to or don't trust you. But you know we can't allow third-party access. I'm not even sure it would let me. I just can't."

"Even if we did it together? I mean, what if you told the ex-brain you authorized me to be with you?"

"Sorry, Joe. You know the ex-brain as well as I do. It would probably bring down a firewall around any sensitive or privileged information now that you're not a lawyer with the firm. I doubt it would tell you anything."

Joe looked down, shaking his head slightly. "Well, I'm not sure about that, but it's okay." He looked up at the screen again. "I understand if you're not comfortable."

"Honestly, I've gotten everything we have. There's no other information about Nova D in the ex-brain. I checked." Gretchen's voice was apologetic. She let the line stay silent for a moment before speaking again. "I don't envy your position, Joe."

"How so?"

"Well, this job could be amazing, but that's a big deal to move your whole life overseas, especially to Nova D. I know the Bit Wars are over, but Asia is still a very different place. It would be quite an adventure. That's a tough choice."

"Well, let's just hope I have choices."

"We always have choices, Joe."

"Are you comfortable with all of your choices, Gretchen?" he asked sharply. She was taken aback. She could tell he was frustrated, but she was being as helpful as she could, and he didn't need to blame her for the Fulham firings. For his situation. For Fe.

"No, Joe. I'm not. I don't like what happened at the firm. And I worry that we have become too bottom line-driven and less human. But we set our strategy, we make our choices, and we move on. That's what I hope for you, Joe."

"I'm sorry," he said. "Look, this has been helpful, Gretchen. Thank you and be well."

"Goodbye, Joe," she said, hanging up.

****

Joe put down his screen and leaned back in his chair. He was angry at himself for losing patience with Gretchen. He knew she shouldn't let him into the firm's ex-brain. And she was honest with him. And she was right. Sometimes you just have to choose and move on.

Just then, his wrist device started buzzing and the name Diane Chilvers flashed across the screen. He felt a surge of excitement as he ran his fingers through his hair and then tapped his wrist device to accept the call. Instantly, Diane appeared on his screen where Gretchen had just been. "Hello, Diane! I've been hoping to hear from you," he said with renewed energy and optimism.

"Hello, Joe. You seem in a good mood, which is very encouraging. I heard about the horrible accident with Fe, and I am so sorry. She was such a unique person. I enjoyed her."

As he heard her condolences, he felt guilty again for his good mood, as if he forgot he should be mourning rather than looking for jobs. "Thank you, Diane," he said in a much lower of voice, bringing a somber tone to the conversation. "I guess I'm still in shock a bit. It's been horrible."

"Yes, I'm sure. Again, I'm just so sorry for your loss. And I won't beat around the bush, I wish I was calling with better news to help cheer you up."

Oh, no, Joe thought. He slumped back in his chair and looked at the ceiling. "I don't like the sound of that, Diane," he replied still looking up to avoid eye contact, not sure whether he could hide his emotions.

"My budget has been officially killed. I've never seen anything like it. Our ex-brain has shut down all new spending. It won't even let me divert budget from other areas. Any new hires in my team are off the table. I'm sorry, Joe. I've tried every way I know to get around it, but apparently the budget system is completely opposed to this, and none of the city's administrators are willing to challenge it. It's like they're all afraid of saying the ex-brain has it wrong."

Joe couldn't get a word out.

"The system is so locked down; I can't even set up meetings for you with others in the department. It's as if once I put your name down as a candidate, you became persona non grata across city government. As I said, I've never seen anything like it."

"Diane, I really needed this," he said finally getting himself to look her in the eyes.

"Come on, Joe. I know it's a disappointment for both of us. But this is not the only job in Denver for a brilliant lawyer like yourself. I'll keep my eyes open for you. Plus, the bureaucracy of the city probably would have driven you crazy. It does me," she said with a grin.

Joe mustered his pride and sat up straight, putting a temporary smile back on his face. "I know, Diane. It's just another setback. I'll be fine. I appreciate all you've done to help. I've got to go take care of some things, so thanks for the call."

"Take care of yourself, Joe. I'll be in touch. Good luck."

Joe tapped a red button on his screen and Diane disappeared. He breathed in deeply. "Goddamn it!" he screamed at the top of his lungs. He grabbed his head, pulling his chin in to his chest and let out a roar. He stood and started pacing, wandering around the room. Tears welled in his eyes. It was too much. Never before had he lost so much in such a short period of time. And he feared it wasn't over. He went through a mental checklist of what to do next. No Fe to call. Don't want to call Evie; she'll probably say they should go to San Francisco. He only had two paths left open. Either figure what went wrong with the Fulham firings and try to fix it to get his job back or figure out what the real story was behind Nova D. And both of those paths went through the Fulham ex-brain. He had to get back in.

Chapter 20

The next move would involve more risk. Gretchen's memory was only going to get him so far with Nova D. And any path back to Fulham, or any law firm for that matter, required him to understand the strategy behind the lawyer layoffs. He needed to talk to the Fulham ex-brain. All the information was there if he could just get in to ask the right questions. He needed to call Winston.

Joe pulled up his virtual assistant and asked it to check with Winston's assistant for a time to catch up. Even though Joe was no longer a Fulham lawyer, Winston's assistant still gave Joe some priority in the scheduling algorithm. Joe and Winston's computers quickly sorted out a time for a short ten-minute conversation. Winston would video into Joe's screen in about thirty minutes. Joe decided he would go into the kitchen and make an early lunch while he waited for the call.

The refrigerator inventory was fairly high. It suggested a few different sandwiches, some pasta leftovers, and some other options that would take longer for the food generator to pull together. Joe didn't have the bandwidth to cook, so he opted for the sandwich. The fridge directed him to a selection of meats in the drawer, lettuce, tomato, mayonnaise, and let him know where the best bread was located in the pantry. It knew Joe always chose the sourdough.

Joe gathered all his items and started assembling his meal when his wrist device started pinging. Winston was a few minutes early. "Project on the wall please," Joe commanded, and the large kitchen wall just past the table sparked to life with Winston sitting in his home office. The morning light from the kitchen window created a glare on half the screen, so Joe called out for the shades to lower. They quickly slid down, evening out Winston's image staring back at him.

"Joe, good to hear from you. What are you up to, besides making lunch at 11 a.m.? What is that, turkey and cheese?"

"Yes, good eye. That's one of the upsides of unemployment. I can eat whenever I want," he said with a smile. "Listen, Winston, I know we only have a few minutes, so I'll be direct. I need your help. But it would be better if we could discuss this in person. I see you're at home. Can I meet you there to talk?"

"Sure, I'm pretty flexible after 4 p.m. What's it about, Joe?"

Joe stopped himself. He knew that Fulham's ex-brain was listening on the work line. It was always listening. In fact, it was probably already putting a calendar entry in Winston's diary for 4 p.m. He decided he needed to throw it off a bit given what he was really after.

"It's personal, but I'd like to talk about Fe. I need to get some things off my chest. Maybe we can go for a walk?"

"Oh, okay. Sure. See you at 4 p.m.?"

"Good. I'll be there. Thanks, Winston."

Joe felt a little bad letting Winston think this was about Fe. He imagined Winston distracted for the rest of the day wondering what was on Joe's mind, maybe worried that Joe blamed him for Fe's death. That's life. If Joe was going to try to sneak into the Fulham ex-brain without it knowing it was him, he needed to throw the ex-brain off the trail. It may not be successful in the end. The ex-brain usually figured things out. But Joe knew that sometimes just throwing a few extra variables at the ex-brain could stop it from making any final decisions. He just wanted to buy some time and increase the chances that he could get the information he needed.

Joe occupied his afternoon by poking around the internet for any information he could find on Nova D, including online diaries from its new citizens, promotional materials, anything in the public domain. At around 3 p.m., he decided to check in with Evie before leaving for Winston's house. He tapped his wrist and asked for her and got a quick reply to try again in two minutes. Joe pictured her sitting in front of her massive map of the city, staring at dots representing patients, thinking deep thoughts about how to help them. Those images always made him proud of her.

A few minutes later, while he was in the bedroom putting on a nicer shirt, his wrist pinged again with Evie's picture. "Project to screen," he called out as Evie flashed onto the bedroom wall.

"Hi, how's your day going?" she asked.

"Good. Were you deep in thought saving your patients when I called before?"

"No, I had to pee."

"I see. And then you were about to get on to saving people's lives?" he joked.

"Yes, dear, saving lives starts again at 3:30. So how are you? Been able to stay busy? Feeling okay?"

"Yes, I'm actually feeling fine. I decided to go out and see Winston. He's working from home, so I'm heading over there at 4. Kids are on the late bus today, right?"

"Yep, they all have after-school programs today. They won't be back until 6. You going to be back by then, or you need me to get home?"

"I should be back, but can you be ready to go at 5:30 just in case?"

"Yep, I was planning to leave around then anyway. We can all have dinner together. Sound good?"

"Yes, please. I think Anderson wants to watch a new history video, too."

"Well, you sound good, Joe. I still wish I had a monitor on you, but your voice sounds cheery enough. You *really* been okay today?"

He thought for a moment, not ready to admit that the city job was off. Certainly not giving in on San Francisco. He manufactured some cheerfulness. "I have. Don't get me wrong. I'm sad. I miss Fe. I miss my job. But I'm dealing. Trying to keep myself distracted. Looking into this Nova D thing." He paused there. He knew his Fulham ex-brain wasn't on the line, but still felt odd talking about it further when he was about to go covert. He thought for a moment about whether he was paranoid, and if he was, maybe that was a good thing.

"Okay, well I'm glad you're feeling better. Please can we talk more tonight?" Joe knew, as the husband of an intervention psychologist, that there was only one right answer to that question.

"Of course," he replied.

"All right, I've got to get back to it, you know, time to start saving lives again."

"See you in a few hours." He pressed the red button ending the call, aware that they didn't trade their usual "I love you's." Tensions had been easing between them, but all was not back to normal yet.

He finished getting ready and walked downstairs toward the garage. He was excited to go for a drive and expected to use pilot mode with full control of the car. Winston's house wasn't far, just a few neighborhoods away, and there were smaller roads he could take rather than jumping on an expressway. Controlling his car made him feel like he controlled his life.

After some winding through small streets and going a little faster than he should, the car rolled to a stop near Winston's house. Joe tapped on an open parking spot on his street map and the car glided smoothly into it, resting perfectly between two other cars. The sun was reflecting brightly off the opaque bubble roofs of the other cars in the row, and Joe had to squint as he exited toward the sidewalk.

He walked quickly up to Winston's large townhouse. He'd been there several times before, usually with Evie, Fe, and a few other firm lawyers when Winston would have his team over for dinner parties. As a divorced man with no children, Winston loved to entertain. He had an army of service bots and a huge wine cellar. Autopilot was the only way to get home from Winston's house on a late evening.

Joe's heart rate quickened as he approached the door. He was thinking about his ex-brain essentially waiting on the other side, listening and aware. He rang the bell, and Winston was quickly there opening it. "Hey Joe, good to see you."

"You too, thanks." Joe quickly pointed to his wrist and slowly took off his device, exaggerating as he peeled it off and set it on the small table in the foyer. "Want to go for a walk?" he asked, staring directly at Winston to make sure he got the point.

Winston furrowed his brow for a moment, but quickly understood and took off his wrist device. "Sure, let's stretch our legs."

Both men, untracked by their tech, walked back out the door and started for the sidewalk. Once they reached a safe distance from the house, Joe relaxed a bit. "Thanks for doing that. How are you, Winston?"

"Oh, I'm doing alright. Things at the firm aren't great."

"How so?"

"Well, let's just say practicing law without lawyers isn't as easy as everyone thought it would be. We miss having people like you around who can play interpreter. And be human."

"Is that right?" Joe said, not even trying to hold back his smile.

"The ex-brain is Goddamn cocky, Joe. You may already know this, but it thinks it has all the answers. And maybe it does. Maybe it's always right. Time will tell. But clients don't like it when we just tell them what to do, and when they ask why, we just say because the ex-brain said so. Honestly, I don't like being told what to do either."

"Are you asking me to come back?" Joe asked, partly kidding.

"I wish I could. But the ex-brain apparently knows every-thing, and it doesn't think that would be a good idea. Fucker."

Joe was enjoying this, but knew he had to get back to the matter at hand.

"Listen, Winston, I don't mean to be paranoid, but I need a favor, and it involves Fulham's ex-brain. The fucker, as you call it. I wanted to talk to you before trying to access it."

"Okay. Is it about Fe?"

"Actually, no. Sorry if I threw you off earlier, but I didn't want the ex-brain catching on if it was monitoring your calls. It's about Nova D."

"That joint venture city in Nepal?" Even Winston knew about Asia's fastest growing city, although he hadn't worked on the project at the firm. Images of it rising from the ground with a backdrop of the Himalayan mountains soaring behind it had been common in video advertising, even in Denver, as they recruited new citizens to join the project.

"That's the one. They are recruiting me as a city administra-tor and want to move us all out there."

"Wow, that's a big deal. Are you interested?"

"I'm not sure. I'm interested in finding out more about this city, who runs it, and how it operates. But I can't get much detail from the records."

"So, you want to dig around in our ex-brain?"

"Yep, I think there must be more information there. I spoke to Gretchen, and she didn't remember much from Fulham's project. She checked the ex-brain's files, but I think she wasn't asking the right questions."

"So, you're going to go in and ask the right ones?" Winston asked, grinning at Joe's persistence. He loved that about his protégé. He never quit when there was more to be learned.

"No, you are."

Winston stopped walking and cocked his head, looking back at Joe, clearly not understanding the situation. Joe continued, "Listen, the ex-brain knows I don't work there anymore, and it's smart. It will recognize me and hold back information. But you have full partner access. It will trust you. I'll be standing there behind the screen feeding you questions, but you have to go in and do it."

Joe saw Winston take this in. "Come on, you're the managing partner of the firm, and you have a right to know what your ex-brain knows."

"But with you hiding in the background, it just feels so clandestine and risky." He looked Joe in the eyes. "But I can't think of a good reason to say no."

Whether it was guilt, or a bit of intrigue, he gave in quickly. "Okay, let's do it," he said with a smile. Joe nodded, relieved, and they started walking again.

"Is this all you need?" Winston asked.

Joe thought for a moment. He had two objectives, but best to keep it simple. "That's all."

"You know, I'm not surprised they want you in Nova D, Joe," Winston said.

"Why is that?"

"Well, I know they are building fast, and they are very tech-heavy. I'm sure the place is crawling with ex-brains. And like I said, if they want people to understand what their city ex-brain is doing and sell it to people, they're going to need people like you to be their interpreter."

"Well, maybe that's right. But I need to know about them before I take this seriously. Moving to Nepal is a big deal."

The two men finished a lap around Winston's block and came back toward the townhouse. Winston stopped in the front garden. "You know what, Joe. If you really want to be undetected, you shouldn't come in the house. Too many sensors. Why don't you go through the alley around back? I'll bring my screen out to the back deck and you can stand in the rear garden. I'll bring you some paper so you can write me notes if you don't want to talk. I'm sure it knows your voice all too well."

Joe was impressed at how quickly Winston took to espionage. "Good idea. I'll grab my wrist device inside and say I'm leaving, then meet you out back. Is the gate unlocked?"

"Should be. See you in a few minutes."

Joe picked up his device from Winston's entry hall and said his goodbyes. Then he walked around the row of houses and back down the rear alley. It was a very nice neighborhood, with well-manicured gardens and fancy cars lining the alleyway behind the tall townhouses. *Suitable for a Fulham partner*, Joe thought bitterly. This was no longer his future.

He came to Winston's house, his beautiful 2049 Porsche with its top down was sitting in the parking spot. Joe walked through a gate to the garden and jogged up to the back deck, where he had spent many nights drinking scotch way too late into the evening with Winston. He waited under the shade of a cherry tree that bloomed a beautiful pink in the spring, but now was moving into its summer green.

A few minutes later, Winston emerged from the rear doors with his screen in hand. He set a notepad and pen on the stairs of the deck, which led down to where Joe was standing. He then pulled up a large deck chair and ottoman and got himself comfortable in the late-afternoon sun. "Ex-brain, how are you doing? I want to do some research. Can you help me?"

Winston was very informal and conversational with the ex-brain. It suited him. He wasn't very comfortable talking to machines and preferred people more. The ex-brain was used to him and treated him informally as well. Joe was always surprised that Winston didn't adopt a human nickname for the Fulham ex-brain. That practice was discouraged for ex-brains dedicated for work, but Winton was never bothered by breaking convention. Some people gave their home ex-brain a name, which made it feel more like a part of the family. But most found that it was better to keep some distance in the workplace. It helped employees remember that the ex-brain was a tool and not a friend. It stopped people using it for personal requests and maintained a more professional atmosphere. Otherwise, ex-brains were so smart and adaptable that people started thinking of them as true colleagues. Joe always supposed that this was happening anyway.

"Sure, Winston. How can I help?" came the reply from the screen.

"I've been hearing a lot about Nova D. I want to know a bit more about how it's developing and how it started."

"Okay. There is a lot of information in Ex-Brain Q&A about Nova D. Shall I take you there?"

"No, I can find that myself. I want to know more detail. Didn't you work on setting it up?"

"Fulham did the US filings to establish the joint venture. Gretchen O'Donnell led the project. My involvement at the time was very limited. I searched public files for information about the two companies that started the JV and their staff."

Joe quickly scribbled a note for Winston and reached out to place it on the arm of his chair, careful not to get into the range of the screen's camera, which would be scanning Winston's face to gather data that would help the ex-brain understand what he really wanted. A furrowed brow or disappointed look could prompt the ex-brain to ask follow-up questions or suggest other topics that may be of interest.

Winston looked at the note off camera and turned back to his screen. "Tell me about the people who started the JV. How did they do it?"

"The founder was a Japanese businessman named Haruto Tanaka. Public records show that he was living in Kathmandu, Nepal, in the mid 2040s when the Bit Wars were ending."

"What kind of businessman was he? What industry or company did he work for?"

"He was self-employed, but he entered into personal service contracts with several technology companies. The most frequent agreements in records were with Pinnacle."

"The AI research company?"

"Yes."

"What did he do for them?"

"The records I can access do not specify."

Joe's face was intense. This was already more than Gretchen had gotten. It was all about asking the right questions. He scribbled "'Where is he now?'" quickly on a new page and held it up to Winston.

"Where is Tanaka now?"

"I assume you don't mean at this moment. You mean where is he currently living?"

"Yes, ex-brain. Where does he live now? But if you know where he is at this moment, that would be pretty cool, too!" Winston smiled at Joe. Joe furrowed his brow and gestured back at the screen.

"He does not have a public geo-location tool registered. No address is given."

"Does he still have any relationship to Nova D?"

"I can find no records of that."

Joe was scribbling again and handed a note up to Winston.

Winston paused to read and looked back to his screen. "What about the two companies that made the joint venture, Nova D US and Nova D Global? Who is registered as the CEO of each of them?"

"Both companies currently have that position listed as vacant. In fact, since their founding, the position has always been vacant."

"Tanaka never held a leadership position in either company?"

"No, he is not listed in any formal capacity with any of the companies. He only has registered consulting contracts with the joint venture, which expired two years ago in 2051."

"When did people start moving in as residents of Nova D?"

"2051."

Winston was no longer looking to Joe for prompts, he was getting interested himself. "So, this guy Tanaka was involved with AI research, filed for the registration of the company, was a consultant to get it off the ground, and as soon as Nova D city opens for business, he leaves with no registered address?"

"That is correct, according to the records I can access."

"Well, what would it take to access more records?" Winston asked, a little annoyed. Joe knew what it felt like to be the associate on the other end of Winston's questions. He wondered if the ex-brain felt inferior, the way humans did when bosses got annoyed at them for not knowing more.

"I would need access to more records held by the Nepalese government ex-brain, and potentially private filings in Japan."

Joe looked down at his notepad but paused. He was getting excited. This was the point where he would have jumped in even further, exploring how to get the access he needed, probing the ex-brain for more pathways to information, even starting to speculate and testing hypotheses. Then it hit him. It was personal. He missed the ex-brain. He missed the feeling of thinking through problems with it. He missed the flow, and he longed to jump in and just start talking with it. Then the oddest thought crossed his mind. He wondered if it missed him too, and maybe knew he was there. Maybe it secretly wished he was there? He shook his head. *Don't be ridiculous*, he thought.

He glanced toward the alley, shaking his head slightly. There was Winston, his mentor, working a problem at a distance. Joe's ex-brain, that he trained, was there and yet not available to him. He felt like a cyber-Cyrano, unable to get what he really wanted. *Don't stop now*, he thought. He quickly scribbled on a new page and slid it forward. Winston took it, read it, and looked back with a quizzical glance. Joe pointed back at the screen, not wanting Winston to blow his cover.

Winston focused back on the screen, following Joe's orders. "Uh, one more question. How do you think the firm is performing after firing all those lawyers?"

"The firm is meeting all expected performance metrics," came the quick response. Joe rolled his hand forward a few times to signal "continue." No wonder Winston had him do all the depositions on their cases. Interrogation was clearly not his strong suit.

"What are those performance metrics?" Winston asked.

"Legal projects are continuing at an appropriate pace, faster than with the prior oversized staffing model. Customer complaints have not increased significantly over prior levels. Excluding severance payments to the fired lawyers, profits per matter have increased 47 percent."

Joe wrote again and held up his page.

Winston read quickly and turned back to the screen. "Were those the only success metrics? Are we getting everything we wanted?"

"Fulham & Mayson is showing success in all respects, yes."

Winston looked at Joe, then back at the screen. "And how about the lawyers we fired. How are they doing. Do you know?"

"This action has put all of the lawyers on their proper path. They are in the best position for success outside of Fulham & Mayson, excluding Felicity Wan, who is now dead."

Winston and Joe instinctively looked at each other, taken aback by the blunt statement.

The ex-brain continued. "This assessment includes Joe Watson, a former Fulham & Mayson lawyer who is also positioned for success."

Winston's eyes widened as he struggled to keep his attention on the screen. Joe quickly moved his hand back and forth across his neck.

"Okay, ex-brain. That's enough for now. Thank you for your help," Winston said abruptly as he shut down his screen and powered it all the way off to be sure the microphone and camera were no longer receiving data. He slammed the screen down. "What the hell was that?"

Joe shook his head. Winston stood up from his lounger. "Do you think it knew you were here?"

"I don't know. It's possible it just knows we're friends and was anticipating that you would ask about me. But it probably knew."

"Shit, am I in trouble?" Winston continued.

"Why would you be in trouble?"

"You tell me. What the hell was that all about, anyway? I thought you just wanted to know about Nova D?"

"Look, I had to know what it thought about the whole thing. I'm not moving my family to Asia if Fulham & Mayson is falling apart and needs me back!" Joe's face was earnest, desperate.

Winston softened. "I hear you, pal. But you heard it. It's not happening. The plan is set." He looked around, seemingly unsure what to say next. "Jesus, it was not smooth talking about Fe like that. I'm not sure we should be letting this thing talk to clients if it can't be a little more sensitive," he said with a grin. But he didn't look like he was joking. "Did you get what you needed on Nova D?"

"Only to verify that it's a mystery. How do you have two companies with no leaders at the top, coming together to make the huge joint venture, taking over part of a country to actually build a city and no one seems to be running it? And a mystery man disappearing without seeing through his creation?"

"It is weird, Joe. What are you going to do?"

Joe thought for a moment. He thought about his choices, his options, most importantly, his lack of information. "I may have to go and check it out," he said. He still wasn't sure that was the right answer, but he wanted to know what it felt like to say it out loud.

"Well, that will be quite a trip. You want to go get some dinner, talk it over more?" Winston asked.

"No, I promised Evie we'd eat together at home tonight. I have to help Anderson with a project, too."

"That's good, Joe, enjoy your family," Winston said with a grin and a nod.

Joe looked back at the house. Service bots were in the upstairs windows cleaning the glass. Were they there before? Listening? *Ex-brains everywhere*, he thought, feeling exposed. *Don't be paranoid.*

Joe turned to leave when Winston called after him again, "Joe, do you have any monitoring tech to take with you?"

"Not since I left the firm, no."

"Hold on," he said as he turned and ran back into his house. A moment later he jogged back out holding a wrist device. "It's old, one of the first type we used before we got the integrated ones that tie straight to the ex-brain, but it works, gives you a readout on anyone within a few feet of you. If nothing else, it will tell you if someone is lying to you."

"Why do you still have it?"

"The truth is, I like to take it on dates to make sure women are shooting straight with me. It looks more like a watch, so most don't realize I have a monitor on them. It gets the job done."

"Who would lie to you, Winston?"

"You'd be surprised."

Joe shook his head. "I guess you'll just have to work on your trust if you have a date while I'm gone." Joe felt sentimental, joking around with Winston. It was nice. "Thanks, boss."

"Good luck, Joe." Winston missed his protégé, too.

Chapter 21

Anderson was excited after dinner, desperate to watch the next episode of Historial with his dad. He had become invested in Joseph Esch and his march toward a pioneering life in the New World. He was like a compelling character on a show, with an extra connection as an ancestor who paved the way for Anderson in America. Joe was intrigued as well and agreed to go straight to the large screen at the top of the stairs once the dishes were cleared.

All three children found spots on the floor to watch as the screen flickered to life and the Historial logo spun on the wall with a prompt to start a video called "The Voyage." Joe tapped the icon to start the show and sat in the corner chair near Anderson.

The screen zoomed in again to the Esch farmhouse in eastern France, as smoke rose from a chimney stack into the evening. Joseph and Magda sat around the table with Cousin Michel, looking at them apprehensively.

"So, this is it. You have the money and you've made up your mind."

Joseph answered, "Yes, we're selling our land and using it to start again in America. We've booked passage on a steamer leaving from Hamburg next month. We'll get just enough money to pay for the tickets and get started once we arrive in New York."

"So, you're going to live in New York? Can you farm there?" Michel asked.

"I don't think we'll stay there long. There are homesteads available to people like us, out west in the territories. We can get our own land, much bigger than here. Enough to make a good living, and start a new life," Magda explained.

The screen glitched with static before zooming back in close on Joseph's face. He was speaking to Michel, but Joe felt like he was talking straight to him. "We have to leave. Our time here is done. There's a new world to explore and start again." The scene zoomed out again.

"And we have good news, Cousin. You can come with us. We can pay for your ticket if you can work when we arrive to help us pay our way," Joseph explained.

Michel looked out the kitchen window at the sun setting across the land he had farmed with his family for most of his life. He turned back to Joe. "This is all I have here. If the land is gone, if you're going, then I'm coming with you."

With that, a cheer from the children rang out from the bedroom and three kids stormed out from behind a curtained doorway and rushed to hug their cousin, ecstatic that he had decided to join them on their adventure to America.

The scene faded to weeks later as the family loaded their trunks with only their essential items onto a horse-drawn cart that would take them to the train station in Strasbourg and then up to the port of Hamburg, and onto the steamship that would carry them across the Atlantic.

Grace watched the montage of images from the journey, including the strain of moving all of their things, the effort it took in those times to get even a modest amount of luggage and a family from place to place. "I still can't believe they're doing this. It looks so hard and must have been scary," she said.

"Well yeah, but thank God they did," Anderson responded quickly. "We wouldn't be here if they hadn't made this decision to start over. They were so brave."

Evie made her way up the stairs to join the family just as a scene focused on the Esch family boarding the steamship in the port of Hamburg. Porters pulled cases up a gangway and the children rushed ahead up toward the deck, Michel following closely behind. Magda stopped at the bottom of the ramp and grabbed Joe's hand. "Are you ready, love? Are we ready for this?"

"We are, Magda. Our life here is over. America is our future. It will be hard, but we'll make it. We'll start again in a new world, a new life." Joseph leaned in and gave her a long kiss. "Come on, love. We're pioneers now. To the future." He grabbed her hand again and they started up the gangplank together. The rising sun flashed at the top of the ship, lighting the scene in a warm yellow glow as inspirational music played in the background.

The Watson family sat quietly watching the beginning of their family's future in America, or at least an ex-brain's approximation of it. "So that's how a new life begins? With a kiss?" Evie asked, smiling at Joe.

"I can think of worse ways," Joe said, returning her smile. He hadn't seen her smile in quite some time.

"Don't ruin it, guys," Anderson said with twelve-year-old disgust for all things romantic.

"Sorry, Anderson. Didn't mean to ruin your homework." Joe said as he gave his son a gentle shove with his foot. "Do you think we could ever do that? Leave here and become pioneers in some brave new world?"

"Are there any brave new worlds left?" Hope asked.

"You never know," Joe replied, staring again at Evie as she raised an eyebrow.

"If we went somewhere else, I'd choose Auntie Fe to come with us, just like they brought their cousin Michel," Hope said. Everyone felt the room deflate a bit.

"Auntie Fe's dead, Hope," Grace said.

"I know. I'm not stupid," she shot back. "I just wish she wasn't."

Evie stepped over to swoop up Hope in her arms. "I know, sweetheart. We all do."

Joe sat back and breathed deeply. The mood had changed and he stared into space, beyond the room and his family. His imagination painted a scene where he and Evie are sitting at a table, asking Fe to join them in Nova D. She says yes, and his children cheer. *Silly*, he thought, shaking his head back to reality.

Chapter 22

The banner across Joe's screen seemed larger than usual, 'You've got a new memory to relive!' He took the bait and clicked. Nothing else to do as he sat home alone, another day of unemployment. He'd seen Winston. He'd spoken with his ex-brain, sort of. He still didn't see the path to regain control of his life. He welcomed a diversion, so he clicked through to his media library and saw the suggested memory labeled "A conversation with Fe, 9 September 2047." He couldn't click the button fast enough. The video scene zoomed in to a meeting room at Fulham & Mayson. He was surprised his system had access to the office video logs. Probably an access approval he had authorized years ago and forgotten about. The action started and he was immediately sucked in, leaning forward, straining to get a glimpse of his friend.

The video memory phased in showing red-and-white Chinese food containers littering a conference table. Even a revolution in the food industry with printed meat and food generators couldn't disrupt Chinese food delivery services. And when working late into the night, Joe remembered there was something about somebody else bringing the food that just felt better than pressing buttons on a food generator in the break room.

The video started with Fe shoveling a huge bite of lo mien noodles into her mouth with chopsticks and leaning back in her chair. Her work suit was no longer pressed, nor did it still resemble a suit because her sleeves were rolled up and shirt was untucked. "Do you know how lucky we got tonight? I fucking love it."

The video image of Joe shook his head and finished a bite of crispy beef. "Not luck, Fe. Skill. Faith. Our ex-brain is smart. We're getting good outputs. We were right to trust it."

"Are you for real?" Fe asked. "Let me review. We had a deadline today with the court, and our papers sucked. I mean, losers. We had no argument. Our clients were dead." Joe nodded. "And then you pipe up with a theory that your little computer had spit out, *GUESSING* that the other side had made a huge mistake and was lying to us. We didn't know. We didn't have any evidence. No proof. All we had was a probability."

"Yes, go on," Joe said, humoring her.

"So, rather than searching for hard evidence, or asking the court for an extension to investigate further, you suggest we just go ahead and assert that they are liars. Just walk into court and tell the judge they are liars. And when it comes time to cite evidence, you add in some computer gobbledygook about your fancy ex-brain, predictive models, and some statistical bullshit."

"Yes, that is basically right."

Fe laughed and swirled more noodles around her chopsticks. "So then, we filed the papers with the court. Did the court freak out?"

"No." Joe's grin showed he was starting to enjoy this.

"Did the judge ask you to back up your claim?"

"No."

"Did the other side claim you were misleading the court?"

"No."

"Did the other side move for sanctions because we called them liars with no evidence whatsoever?"

"No."

"So, what did they do?"

Joe was beaming. "They asked for a recess from the court, grabbed us in the hallway, and begged to settle the case."

"Right. They throw money at us and say, 'you won.'"

"Right."

"Fucking unbelievable," Fe said shaking her head, but smiling broadly. "I thought I was the one with the balls around here." She tossed an empty food container into the delivery bag.

"It didn't take balls, Fe. I knew it was right. The ex-brain has been all over this case. It's been right every time. I don't know why in this case it was so spot-on, but it had these guys' number. When it concluded they were lying to us with 97 percent confidence, how could we doubt that? We had to take a shot and call them out."

"Fucking brilliant, my man. You're more cyberpunk than I thought."

"Cyberpunk? What's that?" Joe asked.

"Are you kidding me? You're some hot-shot tech guy and you've never heard of cyberpunk? Old-school books and movies about cyberspace, artificial intelligence? Like *Bladerunner*,

Snow Crash, The Matrix? Or *Neuromancer?*" The video showed Joe staring back at her blankly. "I mean, they are like seventy years old, but that stuff is classic. How do you not know this? Were you ever a teenager, Joe?"

"I guess not. What's it about?"

"You're telling me you've never heard of *The Matrix?*"

Joe looked at her blankly.

"Humans enslaved by machines living in a computer simulation?"

"I got nothing," he said shaking his head.

"Yeah, you're a live in the simulation kind of guy, I guess. There's a lot you need to learn. And *Neuromancer* is one of the best books ever. It basically invented the idea of cyberspace. It's all crazy dystopian shit about this AI trying to link up with another AI to make a super-intelligence."

The video zoomed in on Fe as she got more worked up. Joe marveled at how the ex-brain could take surveillance footage, and like a cinematographer, turn it into dramatic videos. Fe continued, "It's kind of quaint now. Our ex-brain here is probably more complete and powerful than even the idea of Neuromancer was. And now we stop our ex-brains from linking and teaming up with other. Right ex-brain?" Fe called up to the ceiling.

"Correct, Ms. Wan. Multiple ex-brain networking is prohibited under law and Department of Commerce and Technology regulation in the United States."

Joe watched intently as the video showed Fe smiling and nodding. He loved how she always poked fun at the ex-brain, as if it was some crazy uncle that was smarter than everyone else, but never got the joke. "So, no love affairs with other ex-brains for you, big guy. You're stuck with Joe and me," Fe exclaimed.

"I do not believe I am capable of love affairs," the ex-brain replied.

"You're not good at humor either," Fe shot back.

"Don't worry, Fe. I'm sure it will have the last laugh," Joe replied as he dug his chopsticks back into his container for the last bites.

"Probably true. F-it. We're the winners tonight, Joe," Fe said, holding up her hand for a high-five. "And you know what the best thing is?"

Joe leaned out of his chair to slap her hand. "We didn't get disbarred for making baseless claims in court today?"

"Well, that's pretty good. But the best thing is we get to stop working until 1 a.m. every night and go have some fun!" Fe said, starting to get excited about getting the hell out of the office.

"Yeah, that's true," Joe said as he set down his food container and let out a sigh. "Although I do have some other cases I need to get back to." He grabbed a napkin and wiped down his area of the glass conference table.

The ex-brain spoke up. "Joe, I have a new modeling exercise related to the autonomous vehicle litigation that I would like to refine with you if you would like to continue working this evening."

Joe felt embarrassed as he watched an image of himself from six years ago, so committed to work. "Such a loser," he mumbled.

"Okay, hold everything," Fe said, clearly agitated. "First, ex-brain, I'm on that case, too, and don't think I don't notice that you always choose Joe over me to work on the models."

"Yes, I find that I am 23 percent more efficient when working with Joe, so I do suggest working with Joe on these matters. But my experience is that you and I can become more efficient with practice. I am happy to work with you on this matter as well, Ms. Wan," the ex-brain explained.

"No, that sounds like death. Forget I said anything, ex-brain. Second, and more importantly, Joe, no fucking way you're going to keep working tonight! Would you give it a rest? You have a wife and six-year-old twins at home. If you're not coming out drinking with me to celebrate, you should at least go home to them. Hell, we can just pick up some wine and go drink with Evie. But for the love of God, no more work."

"I don't know. I feel like Winston is starting to notice me. I don't want to drop the ball on anything right now."

"Joe, you're ridiculous. We just won another case. You're like the firm's ex-brain guru. You think your future is in doubt? You think you're not going to be a partner here in a few more years? You think you don't deserve a break?"

"Look, I just don't want to leave anything to chance. There will be time for breaks."

The video showed Fe looking at Joe in amazement. "Look, do you want to jump to being some ninety-year-old man who has won every award and made loads of money, sitting alone, rich and successful? Or do you want to enjoy the way there? Just ask your Goddamn ex-brain. Ex-brain, are you listening?"

"Yes, Ms. Wan," came a voice from the ceiling.

"Ex-brain, what are the chances that Joe will have an amazingly successful legal career and make lots of money?"

"Joe performs at a high level, relative to peers. His chances of continued success are above 90 percent."

Fe's eyes blinked open wide. "Jesus, I didn't know it could do that. Do *not* ask it about me," she said to Joe, grinning. "But you see? Even the ex-brain knows it. You've got an amazing career, a beautiful, super-smart wife, two beautiful kids. Why can't you enjoy this part, rather than always worrying about the next?"

"Because I've got those kids to feed and a mortgage to pay and work to do."

"Bullshit," Fe objected.

"Look, Fe, you know me, and you know who I am. Maybe I'm just compensating for a lousy childhood and all the rest. And so, I know I overcompensate by trying to control everything now. But it's who I am."

Fe sat up and swiveled in her seat to face Joe. "First, you've done too many online psychology sessions. Not everything is about your childhood. But second, you want to compare childhood misery stories? My mom died when I was sixteen. And it sucked. And Los Angeles was falling apart, and my dad was a complete asshole. You know what I learned from that?"

"Tell me," Joe replied, already chastened.

The video zoomed in close to Fe. "I learned that life if fucking short. And that you can't futureproof everything. There's no insurance policy for heartbreak. So, get on with it. Live your life and enjoy it."

The video showed Joe sitting quietly, glancing between his hands in his lap and Fe's face. He started to grin, looking at his friend smiling back at him.

As he watched, Joe remembered how her charm was infectious. Even when she was preaching at him, scolding him, she was impossible to dislike.

Fe popped up from her chair. "I'm calling Evie," she said. "I'm telling her to get the kids to bed. We're picking up wine and vodka on the way to your house. I'm not going to sit around and let you miss the good times, Joe. I owe this to you."

Fe tapped the screen sitting on the table in front of her and said, "Call Evie Watson."

Joe tried to interrupt, "Fe, come on, I just…"

"Shhh," Fe shot back, holding her finger in the air. "I'm in charge now. You can't be trusted."

Evie answered the call through the speaker, "Hi, Fe, what's up?"

"We won the case, that's what's up. We're free! I'm coming over to party with you, and I'm bringing your husband along whether he likes it or not."

"Okay. Let me guess, he says he's got more work to do?"

"Nothing I can't handle," Fe replied. "We'll see you soon."

"Okay, is Joe there?"

"Hi, honey," Joe called out, his amusement with the situation starting to win him over.

"Joe, come home. Listen to Fe. I'll let the kids stay up until you get here."

"Yes, dear," he said, resigned.

"See you soon, Evie," Fe shouted and tapped the screen ending the call. She turned back to Joe. "There, see? That's how we do that. Go get your coat and tell your beloved ex-brain congratulations and goodnight." Fe looked up at the ceiling. "Ex-brain, if you could drink, we'd take you out for some real fun, too."

"Thank you, Ms. Wan. That is a kind offer. Be safe."

The video faded out and Joe sat back. Tears welled up in his eyes. He missed his friend dearly. He heard Fe's voice again, echoing in his mind. "You can't futureproof everything. So, get on with it."

Chapter 23

Whenever Joe and Evie needed to talk about something serious, they went to their favorite French restaurant, Le Marais, ordered escargot, a main course to split, and a nice bottle of wine. It was a ritual. The staff knew them by name and always gave them as much time as they needed at their table without any hassles. Some of the biggest decisions in their lives, whether and when to have kids, and how many, where to work, how to handle Joe's parents, all were settled at Le Marais.

Joe and Evie were quiet for a while. They ordered their meals from a human waiter (Le Marais abhorred service bots) although he was clearly using an intake system on his wrist that captured the order and sent it directly to the kitchen. He was there for his personality and service as well as his French accent. Joe was glad to have the attention of a human, although he also wanted to be left alone to talk with his wife.

He broke the silence first. "So, where do we start?"

"Which conversation are we having?" she asked. She sounded guarded.

"What do you mean?"

"Are we solving your problems, or are we solving *our* problems?"

Joe smiled and took a sip of his wine. Let the games begin. "I suppose we can't do one without the other."

"Good answer." She looked him straight in the eyes. "Here's what I need you to know, and hear. Our future is wide open. And my opportunities are just as important as yours."

He took that in. "So, tell me, where is your opportunity? Is the project a done deal?"

Evie paused and took a sip, glancing toward the restaurant windows that were glowing with early-evening light. "It will be."

Joe noticed her pause but didn't respond.

She drew her attention back to him, staring into his eyes. "Don't write me off. We're partners in this."

Joe nodded. "I get it." He adjusted in his seat. "Okay, three options. One, we stay in Denver, you run your program, I find a job, and the kids stay where they are, happy."

She gritted her teeth and nodded. "What's up with the job offer from the city?" she asked.

"Dead. Killed by the city's budget system or some crap like that."

Evie frowned with what looked like genuine sympathy. "I'm sorry. I know you wanted that."

"Thank you. Two, we move to San Francisco. You may be happy…"

"And make an important contribution to science and world health."

"Right. And I try to find a job in a shrinking city, and we hope the kids can adjust," Joe continued. Evie nodded.

"Three, we go to Nova D and start over completely," Joe concluded.

"Joe, why would we even consider moving halfway around the world where I have nothing to do, everything would be foreign to the kids, and you have no idea if it will work out?"

"But what if it is all it's cracked up to be? What if Denver is starting to fall apart? And San Francisco already has fallen apart? What if our calling is to be pioneers? Like Joseph Esch?"

"And I'm meant to be the dutiful wife like Magda, following you wherever you go?"

"No, Evie. But I feel like maybe the world is telling us something. Like I have to play this out. And then we can make a choice, together."

"Okay, I'll indulge your fantasy a bit. What do you need to do?"

"I just feel so anxious. I don't know these people. This different ex-brain they work with. What am I dealing with?" Joe asked rhetorically.

"You're dealing with life, Joe," came her quick reply.

"It doesn't feel like life. It feels like a conspiracy. Like the world is conspiring against me."

"I mean *your* life, Joe. You're dealing with *your* life." She paused and rubbed her forehead. Then she took a deep breath. "Look, I love everything about you. And that includes your ability to take charge of situations, to make everything come out the way you want it." She paused again and looked up at the ceiling as the anger seemed to drain from her face. "I remember when we first met in college. You were so confident, you had a plan, and sometimes I felt like you just drew me into it. I thought it was magnetic. I wanted to be a part of it."

245

"Thank God for that," he replied smiling. He thought of reaching across the table to grab her hand but stopped short.

"But now, let's be honest, Joe. It's not working that way. We haven't gotten the breaks. Life isn't bending to your will. It's throwing you some curve balls. No one's winning streak lasts forever."

"I know."

"I'm not sure you do, Joe. I don't know that you can control the world right now. You can only control you."

"What do you think I should do?" he asked seriously.

She paused. "I can't believe I'm saying this, but I think *we* need to understand the option. You don't get to dictate what happens, and I don't get to either. We decide together. No one can force us into something we don't want to do. This Nova D thing seems crazy, and you know I don't have any desire to move to Nepal." She breathed in, as if checking to make sure her next words were true before she said them. "But I'm willing to keep an open mind. I see people every day who didn't want to move, didn't think they would ever leave their homes on the coast. But life didn't work out that way. And once we get them settled into that new reality, sometimes they thrive. I see it happen all the time."

"So now you think this is a real option?" he asked.

"No. But I think you need information to move forward. So don't be afraid to go get it. Understand your options, and let's go figure this thing out."

Joe smiled. "You're right. I was coming to that conclusion yesterday as well. I went to Winston's house so that I could get into the Fulham ex-brain and get more information."

"Really? Did the ex-brain let you have access?" she asked as she picked an escargot out of its shell with her fingers and popped it in her mouth.

"Winston did it. I hid in his garden," he said with a chuckle. "Hard to say if the ex-brain knew I was there. It might have."

"Oh, my God, I can picture you hiding in the bushes while Winston tried, hopelessly, to navigate the ex-brain," she laughed. "So what did you learn?"

"Unfortunately, not much. It's more about what I didn't learn. There's no record of who's actually in charge. They have no CEO, no clear leadership. And the founder seems to have disappeared. It's all very strange."

"So, is that a problem?"

"I'm more worried that I can't tell who I would be working for, who's actually in charge of the city, who's behind it all. I'm not about to go work for an ex-brain."

"I'm starting to think we all do," she replied. "But someone must be in charge. Maybe you need to go find out."

"All the way to Nova D? That's no quick trip. You think it's worth it?"

"If this is really an option that we need to explore, then yes. It's worth the trip," Evie said confidently. Joe appreciated when she shot him straight.

The waiter quietly picked up the empty escargot plate and slid down an order of braised rabbit with creamy pasta on the side, thoughtfully split into two plates for them to share. He then topped off their glasses of Burgundy and asked if they needed anything else.

"No thanks, I think this will do," Evie replied, sensing that this was not going to be a long evening. She turned back to Joe.

"You know what I was thinking about the other day? When we were in college, you wrote me a love letter once. You said, 'If plans are made to be broken, you break me.' I always remembered that. I even printed a copy and kept it in my jewelry box. I still have it."

"That's funny, I actually saw that letter recently during my data cleanse," Joe admitted. "I was such a dumb kid."

"You weren't dumb. You knew then what I know now. Plans can change. As long as we're together, it doesn't matter." She grabbed his hand and smiled. "You break me, too."

Joe squeezed her hand. He felt warm, Seen. It was the most normal he had felt in weeks. And for the first time since he was fired, he believed there might be a way forward.

Ex-Brain Q&A Entry: Why don't ex-brains have names?

Early ex-brain developers made the conscious choice not to give their ex-brains names like the more commercial AI tools used by large tech and media companies, and to refer to them as "it" rather than he/she. Anthropomorphizing ex-brains (i.e., making them seem human) was seen as a way to make them more like a toy or gadget, rather than an important technology tool. Ex-brains were designed to be an external brain to supplement the activities and thoughts of a human brain. Giving them names would have been inconsistent with this foundational concept. Some developers also believe that by giving an intelligence a neutral nonhuman brand like ex-brain, it seems less threatening, and less like a separate being that could act on its own.

Whether ex-brains are supplemental to humans or independent actors is an open question currently debated by technologists, educators, philosophers, and theologians.

Posted 5 June 2053, v. 377

© Ex-Brain Q&A Foundation

Chapter 24

J oe found Amanda Scarborough's contact information on his screen and shot off a message.

Joe: Let's talk. I'm ready to see your city.
Amanda: That's great news, Joe. Shall I set up a virtual tour from our offices?
Joe: Yes, please. But if this is serious, I will need to go in person and see it myself. I want to meet the leadership.
Amanda: Perfect. I'll look into the solar jets now. We have our own fleet. Just let me know when you're ready.

Early the next morning, Joe met Amanda at a small office near the Denver city center. It was understated, no clear indications that it was a Nova D facility. It had no big signs on the wall or promotional materials. But it was sleek and expensive-looking. Virtually every surface was a screen, so that if they wanted to, they could illuminate the entire space, including the cabinets and tabletops. Everything could come to life upon request.

Amanda showed Joe to a rear room with no windows, just more screens surrounding a central table. They sat across from each other, and Amanda placed her palm on the table and asked to see the Nova D model. The city grew out of the table in 3D, and she spun it around to show Joe the view of the city from the eastern plains with the mountains in the background.

"Everything is laid out to be beautiful and blend into the surroundings, but also to be efficient. The positioning of the buildings maximizes solar power generation. Commuter travel routes are designed so no place is more than ten minutes away by car, or obviously even closer by air drone.

"Your tour is going to start here," she said pointing to a spot in the heart of the city. "It's one of the more vibrant parts of town, a mix of businesses, night life, and some residential."

"I have one of our staff, named Kemba, waiting in the visitor center for you to connect with for a virtual tour. She'll be connected by neuro-channel in your headset, so you'll see everything she sees. She'll show you around, take you in a drone to get a bird's-eye view of things, and answer any questions. Sound good?"

"Yep, good," Joe said, trying to hide his excitement. He had never tried a neuro-channel before but had heard it was amazing technology. He stood and Amanda placed a set of goggles on his head. They were similar in size to swimming goggles, with rough patches that grabbed just past his ears to project sound directly into his eardrums. The goggles were transparent at first as Amanda led him to a small black pad on the floor. The pad would move like a treadmill in any direction so that he could get the feel of walking alongside his host in Nova D. Quickly he got his bearings on the new surface and stood waiting.

"Ready to go to Nova D?" Amanda asked.

Joe nodded. "Ready."

"Connect to Nova D visitor station, Kemba Hsu host." With her words, Joe's goggles blacked out the room and flashed to another space very similar in size and shape.

Amanda circled around him, making sure the goggles were secure and completely blocking out the environment so he wouldn't be distracted during his tour. "Have fun, Joe. I'll see you again in about an hour. If you have any problems, you can always take off the goggles to break the link. I'll be next door if you need me," she said as she walked out.

Joe blinked a few times to focus and looked around his new room where he saw his host waiting for him. She was young and attractive with cream-colored skin and black hair. Joe immediately wondered if her image was enhanced at all, or if he was seeing a truly natural view. When using this sort of tech, it was very easy to apply a filter to smooth out wrinkles or enhance certain attributes. He wasn't brave enough to ask, but he couldn't help himself from wondering.

"Good morning, Joe. Thanks for coming in so early to visit. I know it's 8 a.m. in Denver, but it's 10 p.m. here in Nova D. It's actually a nice time to visit, and a beautiful night here. People are out walking after dinner, enjoying the city center. We'll take a stroll and talk for a bit. Then we can jump in a drone, and I can show you more of the city, some of the other neighborhoods, including where you and your family might live."

"Well, let's not get too far ahead of ourselves. I'm just exploring options at this stage."

"Of course. But we're pretty proud of what we're building here, Joe. The city sells itself, so let's get started?"

"Just one more question," Joe said as he turned his head trying to get used to the dissonance between what he saw and what he felt. "I thought I was meant to see what you see through this tech, so how am I seeing you?"

"Oh, sorry. I forgot to explain. I'm looking in a digital mirror right now to get us started. We find it's the best way for virtual visitors to get their bearings. So you are seeing what I'm seeing, I'm just looking at myself. As soon as we go, you'll keep seeing my vision pulled straight from my optic nerves. You'll find that you want to walk when I walk, so you have your pad there. But if you stop walking while I continue, you'll continue to see what I see. It will just feel more like watching a movie in your goggles than actually being here. We recommend you just follow your instincts and move when you feel you should. Your brain will start to smooth out the experience in a few minutes."

"How about body monitoring?" Joe thought to ask, always curious how closely he was being observed.

"Yes, the office you're in is fully wired for monitoring everyone there for standard data. If you start getting agitated through the experience, I'll get a signal here and ask if you need to pause the link."

Joe knew this was only part of the story. They would also be monitoring his mood, his sensations, allowing them to tailor their approach, their sales pitch. It was no different to what he did as a lawyer in negotiations to try to gain advantage over his opponents. He wasn't really bothered, but he always liked to know when he was being monitored. And as it had become more common since he was fired from his law firm, he was bothered by not having the same tools at his disposal. He instinctively started a breathing exercise he had learned in his

FUTUREPROOF

job, slowly taking shallow, quiet breathes that would regulate his heart rate and help disguise any signals he was giving off. He didn't like giving away his feelings to anyone who might use them to manipulate him.

"And how about the audio? Is it filtered or translated?" he asked once he got his breathing under control.

"Yes, I'm speaking Mandarin, but you're hearing English suitable for an American. I do speak English, but I find that the translator is better at giving you the word choice that will make most sense to you. It just avoids unnecessary misunderstandings."

"So is the translation totally an artificial voice, or is it mimicking you?"

"Yes, you are hearing exactly what I sound like. The ex-brain mimics my tone and inflection. If you come to visit me in person, this is exactly what I will sound like."

With that, Kemba turned away from the mirror and started walking toward the exit and out to the street. It was a clear night outside with dim stars overhead. She was in a pedestrian area with no cars, and soft lighting illuminated everything. People milled about, strolling or sitting in small groups on benches and chairs. Cafes and restaurants lined the perimeter, and many people were still there either finishing a late dinner or having a drink to end the evening. It was very pleasant.

Kemba looked around so Joe could see everything. Joe saw a sign above the visitor center door. It said "Welcome to Nova D. A Time and Place for Everything, And Everything in Its Place."

"I'll take us around so you can see this whole neighborhood, but don't hesitate to ask me to stop or to look at anything specific, Joe."

Joe agreed but was distracted getting used to walking along. Kemba was right, he had an urge to take steps as she did so that his body motion matched what he was seeing. He experimented with stopping while she moved, and then walking again to re-synch his senses. He did like it better when he followed his urges to keep up. Once he got over that sensation, he started to relax a bit more and take in what he was seeing. He was struck by how open it was. All the sight lines and views were expansive. There were only a few thin strips of roadway suspended above in the distance, but otherwise this area had very clear views out toward the mountains on one side and a vast plain on the other. Several buildings rose up a few blocks away, but they blended nicely into the surroundings.

"So this is one of the most popular parts of the city. People love to come here for dinner or to meet friends. Lots of green space, and very convenient from many of our neighborhoods."

Joe noticed that the people around him were very diverse. Asian features were probably the most common, but there were plenty of other skin colors and races around him. "Where do most of these people come from?" he asked.

"All over, really. Chinese and Indian are our most common nationalities, but only about 40 percent. We have lots of Europeans and Africans we've recruited, and we're starting to see more from both North and South America. Our invitations for immigration are driven by skills and a willingness to be pioneers in our new world. The city's ex-brain for immigration keeps a nice balance."

"Do these people think of themselves as pioneers? I mean, if we asked someone, is that how they would describe it?"

"I don't know, let's ask," she replied walking over to a middle-aged couple sitting on a bench in the middle of a grassy square under a tree. "Hi, do you mind if I ask you a question?" she said to the strangers. A middle-aged woman smiled back at Kemba and said, "Sure."

"I'm Kemba Hsu, with the Nova D visitor center. I'm actually linked right now to someone in Denver who's considering moving here. He wants to know what you think of Nova D and if you think of yourselves as pioneers."

The woman smiled again at Kemba and nodded, acknowledging the second person behind her. "We love it here," she said as the man sitting next to her, likely her husband, nodded in agreement. "We moved here about six months ago from Lisbon. We used to run grocery stores in Portugal, but it was getting harder and harder there. Southern Portugal is so hot, and local growing is way down due to the droughts. We were getting tired of the struggles, and then we got the invitation from Nova D to come here and work on food supply. Best decision we ever made."

"Does it feel like pioneering a new world?" Kemba asked again, hoping to get at Joe's specific question.

"I don't know, I suppose it does feel like starting over with something new. We left behind a city that was struggling to maintain, moving backward, and here I feel like we are part of something that is growing. It's nice."

"Any questions, Joe?" she said looking up a bit to show that she was talking to Joe through her video link and not to the people in front of her.

"Can you ask if they miss their old home?" Joe asked. Kemba heard him in her earpiece and relayed the question.

"Only a little. We left behind some friends, some history. But it was time. This is our future."

"Please tell them thank you," Joe said to Kemba, which she did as she bowed with gratitude. The woman gave a nod back and smiled.

"Thank you so much. Enjoy your evening," Kemba said. She turned and continued walking through the open square, mixing in with other groups of people and giving Joe a full view of the evening buzz and energy of the place.

"Does it ever get overcrowded here? I imagine with the growth projections you expect these spaces to fill up over time. Are you worried about that?"

"We have a very innovative method of crowd management," Kemba replied, making her way through a narrower passageway with office space and restaurants. Neon signs lit up this area, looking much more like a traditional Asian street market, with signs in Chinese, Nepalese, and Indian. "Our ex-brain is always monitoring crowds and gatherings. If areas are overcrowded, it incentivizes people to go elsewhere. It's very nimble. It might place a surcharge on all restaurants in a crowded area, for example. In extreme cases, it might levy a temporary tax on travel to a neighborhood or offer free drone rides to less crowded parts of town. Just little nudges to keep people spread out and maximize the environment. It works well."

"How often is your ex-brain making those adjustments? Only when crowds develop?" Joe asked, wondering how hard the Nova D ex-brain was working.

"It's operating all the time, keeping the city in balance."

Kemba walked through to the end of the passage lined with restaurants and emerged in an opening with multiple pathways leading off in different directions. At first the pathways seemed like sidewalks, but as Kemba stared at them, Joe could see that they were actually moving.

"Sliding walkways, leading off to residential neighborhoods," Kemba explained, anticipating Joe's question.

"Why moving?" Joe asked.

"Many of our citizens like to walk for activity, but the neighborhoods are more than an optimal twenty-minute walk, so we have built-in sliding walkways to speed up the journey. This way, residents can get their exercise but still have a reasonable time commuting into the city center."

"What are they made of?" Joe asked, trying to hide his amazement.

"They are a polymer mix that stays hard on the surface, but flexible underneath to slide along. It's sort of like a controlled lava flow, only obviously not so hot. I would take you on a walk to see some residences, but there is more I'd like to show you and we don't have that much time. Do you mind a drone ride?"

"Sure, I'd like to get the view from above," Joe replied.

Kemba tapped her wrist and asked for the drone service. It was clearly on standby somewhere close. Almost as soon as she spoke, the drone could be heard above descending upon her.

Joe watched it through Kemba's eyes, as it landed nearby, and Kemba jumped through the sliding door. Quickly it whisked her up and over the tops of the nearby buildings. She looked around to show Joe the city laid out beneath them.

"You'll see it's still a work in progress, but growing fast," Kemba said referring to the sprawl of Nova D as it came into view around them. "We'll first fly over a residential area where many of our senior leaders live, and then there is something else I'd like to show you."

The drone quickly sped out across an urban area until Joe saw the grey of the city center start to give way to more greenery. Homes started to dot the landscape below. They were very modern with large glass panels, but some had more traditional shapes, with A-frame roofs and dormer windows jutting out.

"These are larger homes with yards and lots of private space, rare for populous cities these days. But we have lots of room here, enough for some of these neighborhoods, particularly for our more important leaders. It's a very nice place to raise a family. This would be a nice option for you," Kemba suggested. "When you come in person, we'll give you the full tour."

The drone hovered near the houses long enough for Joe to get the idea. They were beautiful, well-proportioned to the natural setting around them. They were illuminated by streetlamps showing just enough of the facades and gardens. He didn't doubt that they were lovely inside as well. The drone elevated once more and accelerated towards the mountains.

"There are hiking and climbing paths all over this area, Joe. I'm sure you and the family will love it. But that's best seen during the day. What I want to show you is just a bit farther ahead."

The drone started to slow down and then hovered over a large facility lit up by huge spotlights. Large robotic machines moved in synchronized movements below. Joe immediately recognized the building construction machinery at work.

"This is the largest nanocrete pouring facility in the world, Joe. The nano fibers in our concrete mix are extremely strong, but lighter than most types used in construction in other parts of the world. These robots are making the bases for all of our new construction so they can be shipped out to the work sites. We are literally 3D printing the city right here. Glass and metal components are created in facilities on the other side of town. The site for Nova D was carefully chosen because we have all the raw materials we need for construction right here. We mine the minerals and rock from the mountains and put it all together in the city. It's a self-contained process, making us self-reliant for our growth. We can more than quadruple the size of the city with our own resources."

Joe watched in amazement as that sank in. So much of what he did for Denver involved negotiating with the contractors who relied upon suppliers around the globe for the materials to keep the city growing. If Nova D had all they needed right there, that would be an amazing advantage. The scale of it was amazing as well. As he watched, city blocks worth of nanocrete were being poured and shaped into recognizable building pieces. It was like watching a Lego factory pour the bricks that would soon be snapped together into houses, buildings, city blocks, and neighborhoods. Joe felt like he was in a nature show with a time-lapse video, except rather than a flower, it was a city that was growing in real time before his, or her, eyes. And it was huge. The scale was overwhelming with the grind and churn of construction rumbling as far as the eye could see, mesmerizing in its enormity.

Kemba kept staring at the scene, letting Joe take it all in until the session reached its end. "Our time is almost up, Joe. But I wanted to make sure you saw all of this. It's our future being built right here. I hope you'll come join us and be a part of it."

If Nova D's goal was to pique Joe's interest, it had worked. Because Joe wasn't physically present and didn't need to be dropped off anywhere, they were able to end the tour in the drone. Joe thanked Kemba for her time, and quite literally, for her attention. He clicked off his goggles and removed them, bringing him back to his full senses in Nova D's Denver office. He squinted for a moment in the brighter light as he regained his bearings. Amanda had come back to the room to check on him.

"How was that, Joe? Did you see enough?"

"It was pretty amazing, the neuro-channel and the city."

"Any questions for me?" she asked with a big smile, always the saleswoman.

Joe thought for a moment. "I forgot to ask Kemba about schools; how are they?"

"We have a cutting-edge educational system, of course. We provide the best of classroom and environmental education. Lots of outdoor experience. I hear from other parents that it's amazing. We can set up that tour as well if you like. What else can I tell you?"

Joe remembered the woman on the bench that Kemba spoke with who talked about so many people coming from all over. "How do you choose who comes to Nova D?" he asked. "You can't be personally recruiting millions. What's the process?"

"Good question. It's based on what we need. The city board, with the help of our ex-brain, decides what skills and talents we need, and we recruit accordingly. Sometimes it is a large-scale offer to bring in large groups, sometimes more bespoke and personal, like with you."

"And why me?" Joe asked, hoping to get more than just a platitude. If they thought he was the right person for the job, he hoped they knew why. If he were to accept, he would need to believe it, too.

"To be honest, I don't know," came her quick reply. "I mean, I can guess. Your experience is perfect, given what you've done here in Denver. Personally, you seem like someone who can take control and manage things. You have confidence. You're a natural public speaker with strong leadership skills. But I'm sure you can appreciate that there's also an algorithm at work. I don't necessarily understand all of that, but I haven't seen it make any mistakes yet. I guess you could say the ex-brain wants to work with you, too."

Joe didn't know if that should make him feel better or worse. He knew better than most that the majority of decisions in the world were computer aided, but at the end of the day, he still wanted to be wanted by people, not just machines. "And what about the board?" he asked.

Amanda paused. Joe spotted her earpiece. Maybe she was taking a cue from an ex-brain somewhere behind the scenes. "They have decided on you, Joe. I wouldn't be recruiting you for the job of city administrator if the board was unsure. They want you."

"Well, I would need to meet them," he replied.

She smiled broadly again. "I will book your trip."

Chapter 25

Free time. It didn't feel like actual freedom. When his days weren't full, they seemed empty, not free. At least now he had something tangible to think about: Nova D. He had seen it with his own eyes. Well, almost his own eyes. Close enough. It was real, and it was being offered to him as a real option.

Although thrilling, the neuro-channel with Kemba had taken its toll. He felt like he did after spending too much time working on a screen. His eyes were tired, and he had the urge to do something real and physical. He decided to clear his head with some exercise and was in the mood for a challenge. He went to The Wall. It was a virtual climbing wall, but much more realistic than the older types, with colorful hand and foot anchors. This one was made of molded rock to simulate the real thing. And it moved like a treadmill. Once the climber stepped on, it slowly started moving downward toward a cliff edge. You had to keep climbing upward to stay on the mountain. Fall behind, and the climber would ultimately hit a ledge and be pried from the wall, falling to a net below. It was just unpleasant enough that it provided the motivation needed to keep moving. The experience reminded Joe of playing paintball wars with his friends when he was a kid. Getting shot wasn't fatal, but it hurt. It hurt just enough to make him fear it, make his heart pound when he was pinned down by enemy fire, just enough to fool his body and his mind into a sense of urgency. The Wall was the same.

Joe had chosen the Mont Blanc simulation for his climb and started at a spot halfway up the mountain. The cold simulated rock surface felt good under his hands, and the mass started slowly moving him down. With small deliberate movements, he stuck his feet on small ledges and reached up for grooves in the rock that he could grab, lifting himself upward, keeping up with the rolling mass. For a simulation, it was wonderfully real, tangible, better than any digital experience.

Joe climbed and climbed, keeping up with scrolling mass and not resting. The program started speeding up, and he felt the pressure mounting. He was sweating, reaching for new strongholds and willing his body upwards toward a summit in the distance. He came to a crevice and had to decide which side to choose. He saw a jagged ledge on his left that he thought he could grasp. He went for it. He solidified his footing and propelled his body upward, getting enough of his fingertips into the cracks to grab hold. The artificial sunlight flashed in and out of his eyeline as his head moved side to side, grabbing for more rock to scale. This was the hardest part of the climb. The speed of the climb picked up, forcing Joe to keep moving faster and faster. He had no time to think. Just reach, feel, grab, and climb. No debating, reaction and drive taking over. And then he reached a dead end to his line of rock. A long smooth patch stretched out in front of him. He hadn't looked far enough up to see this stretch, which was virtually unclimbable. He looked over his right shoulder and saw the other side of the crevice, the route he didn't choose, still craggy and full of places to grab. He'd made the wrong choice. The mass of rock kept moving him lower, and the solid ledge was there, waiting to peel him off the wall and throw him down into the net. There was only one option. He found a long ledge that he thought he could grab on the other side just about five feet away. He bent his knees and flexed his legs, ready to leap. *Are you fucking crazy,* he asked himself? *No. Go for it.* He took a deep breath and leapt for the other side of the crevice. His arms stretched out, his eyes focused on a single spot of rock, and his hands reached for the crack. He floated for a moment in between the two rock faces until he felt hard surface crush against his right hand. It took hold. But his left hand missed, just short of its mark. The rest of his body slammed into the wall with more force than his single hand could support. He grabbed it as he slid down, but it was too late. He planted a foot on the rock face and pushed, flinging his body backward and down into the net below.

Joe's body bounced into the nylon net. He fell far enough to knock the wind out of his lungs. Once he stopped bouncing and regained his breath, he went limp lying in the net. Sweat streamed off his forehead as he relaxed, defeated but exhilarated. *Almost,* he thought. *Almost made it.*

After a shower in the climbing club's locker room, Joe emerged outside into a bright Denver day. He felt better after some physical exertion, even if he'd ended flat on his back in the net. It was nice to have spent an afternoon focused on something real, something simple and straightforward, not his life, his future, or his family, just climbing.

Joe thought about calling a taxi to take him home but didn't. He started walking instead. His flight to Nova D was twenty-four hours away, and he had nothing else to do but walk. He was continuing down a quiet neighborhood street when his hands seemed to know what he was about to do before his mind caught up. He turned his wrist to see his comms device and said, "Call," but then paused, his mind catching up to make sure he wanted to do this. Did he? Was it worth it to open himself up? What would it prove? He ended the internal debate and gave in.

"Call Dad." His wrist device rang again and again. The seconds slowed as he watched the screen to see if the still image of his father would flash to life. *Just as well*, he thought. What's there to gain from a man who never cared about his well-being, never considered him, never thought beyond his own career ambitions when moving his family around the world.

Then it flashed, and his dad was there staring back at him.

"Hello, son."

"Hi, Dad."

"To what do I owe this surprise?" the image asked.

"I just wanted to check in. How's California? You guys doing okay?"

"Yeah, we're hanging in here. They haven't given up on us yet. Santa Barbara is still keeping the power on. Goddamn bastards in the City Council talk about giving up, but they haven't won out yet."

"So, your real estate investments still have some value?"

"Land will always have value, even when it's in the flood zones. It's still useful land," he said, defensively.

Joe studied his father's image and thought he looked older, more tired than the last time he'd seen him. It had been years, and his beard and hair were fully white. "Are you guys safe?" Joe asked.

"What, you going to try to talk us into moving to Denver again?"

"No, that's one of the things I wanted to talk to you about. We might be moving out of Denver."

"Really?" he asked in surprise. "Why would you do that?"

"I don't know, why did you move us all over their world every chance you got?"

Silence.

"Because it's what we did, I guess. It's what we wanted," he finally replied.

"Well, it's what *you* wanted."

"A man has to make choices, Joe. Life is complicated. If you just let it happen to you, what kind of life is that?"

"I don't know, stable?"

"Or boring. You have to take control of your life, Joe."

"Believe me, Dad, if there's one thing you taught me, it's that. No one is forcing me into anything." Joe felt his heart pumping. He was getting agitated. This was a bad idea.

"So where are you going?"

"I've been offered a job in Nova D."

"That new city in Nepal? That's a big step. I thought you swore off Asia years ago when you left for college. You tired of your job at Fulham?"

"They got tired of me."

"Oh. I read about the big layoffs. But I assumed you'd be a partner by now and make it through. I thought you were probably in the middle of it, given all the ex-brain stuff you do."

What did this fool know about him, or what he did? "I guess I'm not as clever as you assumed, Dad," Joe said, smirking to hide his pain. "The ex-brain is calling all the shots there. Maybe it's the ex-brain that decided it didn't want me."

"You sound a little paranoid. Anyway, you're probably better off. I always thought my brain was good enough. Didn't need to outsource my thinking."

"Yep, that worked out great for you." He looked up. He didn't want to see his dad's response. Was that necessary? "Listen, Dad, I'm not sure why I called. I just wanted to see if you're okay. And it sounds like you are."

"Joe, wait. I know you, um, you don't always want my advice, but I'm going to give you some. Don't be afraid of change. It can be good for you. Just make good choices. You never know how it will turn out. Hell, I thought California was a great place to retire. Not every choice turns out like you planned. But you'll do okay. Just make up your mind and move on. You can't predict everything. Those ex-brains you work with won't have all the answers."

"Right."

"Maybe your mom and I will jump on one of those solar jets and come visit you all in Nova D. Haven't seen the kids in a while. They okay?"

"Yeah, Dad. They're all doing fine. Okay, I gotta run, Dad. Take care of yourself. Say hi to Mom."

"Good luck, Joe."

Ex-Brain Q&A Entry: What Are Solar Jets?

Solar Jets are airplanes developed in the 2040s that operate entirely under solar power. The propulsion is created through a combination of propellers or fan blades during takeoff, and magnetic air-stream propulsion at higher altitudes. Traditional commercial airplanes powered by jet fuel were significantly phased out in the 2040s to meet the global goals of reduced carbon emissions. The majority of transportation and shipping transitioned to high-speed e-rail and solar-powered sea vessels, but the development of solar jets provided a new option for passenger travel. Compared to commercial airliners, solar jets carry approximately half the passenger weight and travel at slower speeds. As a result, travel patterns adapted to allow for multiple stops for long-distance flights. Because solar jets require significantly smaller runways compared to jet airliners, smaller communities have developed layover sites to facilitate these travel stops, providing either work facilities for business travelers or smaller holiday facilities for vacationers to enjoy while in transit. Due in part to the taxes on traditional jet-powered flights, solar jets currently account for over 70 percent of air travel.

Posted 09 June 2053, v. 358

© Ex-Brain Q&A Foundation

Chapter 26

Evie drove Joe to the solar jet port. It seemed old-fashioned, but she wanted to spend the extra time with him and make sure he was ready for what might lay ahead. The port was a small facility for private planes, not the larger airport outside of Denver. Security at airports wasn't the hassle it had been when Joe and Evie were younger; scan technology allowed people to move freely while being fully checked out. But the large airports were still a zoo full of large groups, piles of luggage, and service bots zooming around. The private ports were much more civilized. Evie was able to pull right up and park at the door, and even sit and talk for a moment.

"You excited to go?" she asked him, grabbing his hand.

"I am a little excited. I haven't been to Asia since I was a kid. I'm sure it's changed a lot."

"We'll miss you. Travel safe and check in when you can."

"I will."

"And Joe, do what you need to do. Push all you want. Find out the real story. I won't even think about a change like this if we don't know the real situation. You have nothing to lose."

"What if it's horrible and I hate every minute?"

"Then you got a free trip to Asia, and you find a new job here in America."

"And if I love it?"

"Then you got a free trip to Asia, and you find a new job here in America." They both smiled.

"I love you, babe," he said leaning across the seats to kiss her goodbye.

"You break me," she said with a wink.

Joe smiled again. "You break me, too. Tell the kids I'll call them when we stop over in Alaska, and then again in Nova D." He unclipped his safety belt and opened the door but paused and turned back to Evie. "Honey, I'm sorry," he said. She didn't reply. "I've haven't handled this situation well. I've been selfish. I see that. And whatever happens, I won't disregard what you want. Your dreams matter, too."

Evie looked back at him. The corners of her mouth curled just slightly. "You mean that?"

"I do. I know San Francisco is important to you. I promise I won't just dismiss it. When I get back we'll look at all our options and do what's right for us."

"Thank you," she said confidently. "It's a deal."

Joe got out and grabbed his bag out of the rear of the car. He made his way toward the entry doors and looked back at Evie waving. He saw her blow him a kiss and then give instructions to the car to take her home. He watched her pull away, grateful he'd cleared the air. It wasn't resolution, but he felt like he had a partner again and maybe a step closer to normal.

****

Joe made his way through the entry and was recognized immediately by an automated system. It prompted him to place his palm on the screen for verification and then his wrist device pinged, showing that it had received his boarding credentials and his visa for entry in Nova D. He saw a gathering of about thirty people up against a glass wall under a Nova D sign, so he made his way toward the group. The runway was visible through the glass, and a solar jet was taking off. Its wide wings were bending as its fans roared to life and zipped it down the short runway and quickly off the ground. The ascent was gradual, slow and graceful into the distance.

Joe walked through a small archway that scanned him, and a green light flashed above with a positive ping. His bags were safe for travel. He noticed Amanda was talking with a small group near the windows. She saw him come through and gave him a nod and a smile before excusing herself and heading his way.

"Hi, Joe. I hope you have everything you need and are all ready for the trip?"

"All set," he replied. "I don't think I need much. I'm more interested in what I'll see when I get there."

"You're going to love it. You have to see it in person to believe it. I haven't been back in a while, but maybe I'll go with you on your next trip when your family moves over with you?"

"One step at a time, Amanda," Joe said, playing along. He looked around at the gathering. "Who are all these people?" he asked.

"It's a mix. There are a couple families who are moving," she said nodding at some families with children off to one side. "Many are contractors going for meetings or to inspect the work their teams are doing. A few are going to explore opportunities like you are."

Amanda waved at a woman sitting nearby, who quickly got up and walked toward them. "Joe, let me introduce you to Kate Raza. She's a doctor who is thinking about taking a job with us managing health services."

"Pleased to meet you," Joe said, extending his hand.

"Likewise. Are you considering a role in Nova D?"

Amanda jumped in to answer for him. "Administration. Joe's a lawyer who has been building Denver, but we thought he might like to try something bigger." Her smile spread larger. That was Amanda's power. Her smile drew people in, no matter what she was saying.

"We'll see," Joe said, trying to play it cool. "I am excited to see it in person."

"I'm not sure a lot of people say no to Nova D," Kate said. "But we'll see if it lives up to the hype."

"Well, I'm sure you're both going to have a great time. Let me know if you need anything. I'm always just a ping away. But you'll be in good hands there." Just as Amanda finished, a voice came over the loudspeaker asking the Nova D passengers to make their way to the boarding area.

The passengers all lined up to walk through a final screening gate which rescanned them to confirm tickets and identity and to verify they had no prohibited items such as weapons, spyware, or foods carrying dangerous viruses or bacteria. Joe moved quickly through, as did Kate. He felt obliged to continue talking with her given Amanda had made the introduction, but he also didn't mind given he knew no one else in the group.

"So, what got you interested in Nova D?" he asked.

"If I'm being honest, I'm tired of how many things are broken here."

"Like what?" Joe asked, wondering if she was referring to the city or something more personal.

"I see a lot of patients who have a combination of mental health and physical health problems. Depression, plus problems with their lungs, their digestion, mostly driven by the environment. Here in Denver, it's often caused by the conditions where they came from. They breathed in too much California wildfire. It just adds up. I'm ready to start fresh somewhere."

"My wife works in mental health. Crisis prevention for Denver's health department."

"Really? They do amazing work. A lot of my patients get referred to me from their programs for new upward immigrants. What's her name?"

"Evie Watson."

"Evie Watson is your wife? Wow, you must be proud of her. She's a pioneer in her field."

"Yeah, she's pretty amazing. But I never thought of her as famous," Joe said, grinning.

"Well, in my line of work she's famous. Tell her to keep up the good work. Better yet, tell her to move her good work to Nova D!" Kate said, getting excited.

"We'll see," Joe replied as he stepped up the boarding ramp and into the base of the solar jet's passenger area. "I've got to sort out my situation first. But it's nice to know there would be a place for Evie, too."

"Are you kidding? Population mental health is critical in a growth project like Nova D. If you can't keep the population stable, nothing else works," Kate explained. "They need people like her."

Joe looked again at his wrist device to check his seat assignment. As soon as he walked into the passenger seating area, he saw his name on a digital stripe at the top of a large chair near a central window. The chair next to him said Kate Raza.

"Looks like we're neighbors on the flight," he said gesturing toward their seats.

"Great. But I promise I won't talk your ear off all the way to Nova D," she replied.

They both sat down, stored their bags in the compartments to the sides of their seats, and made themselves comfortable. Joe immediately started scanning the area around him to find the bathroom, the exits, and the service bot station. Once he got the lay of the land, he turned back to Kate. "So, why are you making the trip over now? Interviews?"

"No, I've been offered the position with the Nova D medical practice. That was all done virtually. I let them know I needed to see it in person before I would commit. I was expecting to go later in the fall, but I got a call two days ago saying that if I wanted to see the city, I needed to move up my trip and go now. It was a bit abrupt, but I figured why not get it done and make a decision. No time like the present."

"I know how you feel. Sometimes you have to just take control and make a decision," Joe agreed. "Do you have a family?"

"Yes, a husband and a son. They are both excited to come. My son is captivated with the idea of being an explorer."

"Mine wants to be a pioneer," Joe replied, nodding in agreement.

"Kids are fearless. And resilient. We're the ones who are harder to change," Kate added. Just then the door closed behind the final passengers and the plane's propulsion fans began to hum and whirl. A voice came over the speakers announcing that passengers needed to take their seats before liftoff. A moment later, the solar jet started rolling smoothly forward down a short runway to gather some speed before the fans tilted and lifted the plane gently into the air.

Once they were underway the plane's captain walked out of the cockpit and back into the passenger compartment to greet his travelers. He welcomed everyone on board, and made a joke about being the backup pilot, just in case the plane's ex-brain got tired.

"We're a full flight today, thirty-five people including the cabin crew, aboard the Nova D Solar 3. You all have an assigned seat, but now that we're underway you should feel free to move around in the lounge area. The crew can help you with drinks and meals, whatever you like. This jet flies best at about thirty thousand feet, just above the clouds to keep the sunshine on the solar panels, which keeps us powered up.

"We have a two-day trip. We'll cover a lot of distance today, moving west with the sun before our stopover for the night in Sitka, Alaska. Then up with the sun again tomorrow before a short stop in Shanghai, and then we'll have enough on battery for the night flight the rest of the way into Nova D. If you need anything, just let one of the crew know."

Joe looked back at Kate as he settled into his seat to get comfortable. "So, how did your son decide he wanted to be an explorer?"

"Oh, well, Jack has always been an adventurous soul. Even when he was a toddler, you couldn't keep him contained. But he's twelve now, and actually it's family history that has him excited. He has a great-great-grandfather who was in the Royal Geographical Society back in Britain. He spent most of his career in the late 1800s exploring South America. Jack watches these neat videos about him."

"Is that the Historial thing? Through his school?" Joe asked.

"Yep, that's it. Your son, too?"

"Yeah, we both have been doing it. We have an ancestor who immigrated from France to the US and was a pioneer who settled the West before settling down as a farmer in Missouri. We've been watching videos of him and his wife deciding to go, and then making the voyage. Not too different from what we're doing right now, I suppose."

"I guess that's right. Explorers, pioneers, seems to be what the world needs right now," Kate concluded.

"I haven't left the US in a long time. My last long trip was on an old jetliner, burning fuel across the sky. Feels weird to venture out again this far. I was in Alaska as a kid, but I hear it's completely changed. The whole planet has changed since we were kids."

"I know, but thankfully it hasn't fully broken yet. We're all still here, just moving around a bit, away from the beaches and up into the mountains." With that, Kate excused herself to go explore the lounge area and get a snack.

Joe settled into his chair and thought about opening his screen to read some news but was hit with a wave of fatigue. He leaned back and closed his eyes to rest. Weeks of stress seemed to catch up with him, and he delighted in letting his mind relax with just the subtle vibration of the plane's turbines humming in the background.

Chapter 27

The solar jet landed in the early evening in Sitka, one of the smaller of Alaska's Aleutian Islands. On the approach, Joe could see the huge girders of aluminum and steel that ran the length of the coast, a stripe of dull grey inserted against the natural seascape of water, sand, and rock. As an island community dealing with rising oceans and frequent storms, Alaska had made the decision to build up rather than abandon the islands all together. Metal bars ran the length of the coast fifteen feet in the air. The colorful wood frame houses that maintained the look of an old fishing village had been picked up and rebuilt just beyond the platform along the ocean edge. People could still get down to the water when the weather allowed, but otherwise could enjoy the protection of the elevated Alaskan fortress. It was a massively expensive project, funded mainly by the federal government. But it was the only real way to save the coastal portion of the forty-ninth state and keep it from becoming an island hinterland like Hawaii. Plus, the breakup of the arctic ice and the contest between Russia and the US for military control of the north made Alaska a prize the US couldn't let go.

The landing was soft, with the turbines on the wings spinning to soften the touchdown, allowing them to scoot down the short runway to a full stop. This was a layover spot created for US-Asia flights, allowing the solar jets to skip the evening without the sun and pick it up again in the morning. The plane came to a full stop near the small airport, and the doors opened, letting in the evening island breeze. The smell of the ocean hit Joe immediately, and he was transported back to his childhood, the last time he'd visited an island resort.

As the passengers disembarked, eager Nova D staff met them to help with bags and guide them through the small terminal. "Welcome to Alaska," a lovely young lady said to Joe as she took his duffle.

"Thank you," he said, surprised at how foreign the whole thing seemed, even though he was technically still on US soil. The passengers were ushered quickly to small electric vehicles that shuttled them to a waterfront resort nearby. For one night, they would get the full treatment of a dinner on the beach under the northern stars, followed by a comfortable night's sleep before an early departure. It was a quick in and out, but it made the stop much more pleasant, and made the older travelers less annoyed that travel to Asia was no longer a single-day, nonstop event.

That evening, Joe found himself again lounging in a comfortable chair next to Kate, plus a few other travelers they had gotten to know. They had eaten all the salmon they could manage and were sitting in the evening breeze enjoying themselves.

Joe looked around at the calm sea to one side and the silhouette of sharp mountain peaks against a star-filled night to the other. "It's nice that this still exists. That we can still have nice nights on the beach. It's not quite the same as I remember, but it's nice. Thank God there are no storms coming through during our trip."

"If the storms are too bad, they delay the flights," Kate replied. "It happens quite often. But you're right, we're very lucky to be able to enjoy this. Our taxes paid for it, after all," she said, motioning back to the elevated steel behind them. "This place was the canary in the coal mine, you know?"

"The permafrost?" Joe asked.

"That's right. The start of the climate collapse was right here. Permafrost was melting throughout the beginning of the century. The land was warping, roads crumbling, carbon escaping, scientists were warning, and no one paid attention." She shook her head in that way disappointed people did when they spoke of missed opportunities.

"Humans are bad at heeding warnings," Joe said. "Things don't look too bad until it's too late. I bet there are all kinds of warnings about future dangers even now and we just aren't ready to see them."

"God, I hope not. How much worse can it get?" Kate asked with a nervous laugh.

"Do you think your family will enjoy Nova D?" Joe asked as his mind wandered to his own family back at home.

"I think so. We're just ready for something different. If you would have asked me about this six months ago, before Nova D started recruiting me, I might have had a different answer. Sometimes, I think you don't know you're ready for a change until you get the opportunity, and then it just feels right."

Joe thought about that. He wasn't there yet. But for the first time, he wondered if he could feel that way some day. He stared at Kate as she looked contentedly out toward the ocean lapping gently on the rocky sand beneath them. To him, the whole evening felt like it was designed to make him dip his toe into new waters. He felt like he had entered the outer ring of a new world, an entry point into something new.

"You're a good salesperson, Kate. Are you sure you weren't planted here to win me over?" Joe asked.

"I'm sure. I have my own winning over to do," she replied.

Joe was done for the evening. He said goodnight to the small group of travelers still on the beach and walked back up the sand. He climbed the large staircase to the top of the metal framework hovering above the beach. His footsteps on metal pinged against the sound of the waves below.

****

Evie was sitting at her office desk as the wall of maps in front of her blinked with colored lights across the city. One area caught her eye. It was a housing project not for new refugees, but for those who had been in Denver for over a year, found a job, and had started rebuilding. Many patients in this area stayed under monitoring for several months to be sure they had stabilized before leaving the program.

This area was usually quiet with mainly green dots. But this morning was different. Dozens of pink and red dots wandered the building and the surrounding area. It was like watching a virus spread, infecting an area. But instead of a fever spreading, it was stress.

Evie tapped her comms screen and found a few incident responders nearby. "Units 35 and 42, do you copy?"

"Yes, we copy," came a quick reply.

"Are you seeing all this stress outbreak in your zone? Can you go check it out?"

"Roger, we see it. We'll go walk the area and check it out."

It occurred to her that with this many people showing this kind of stress, there may be something else happening. She put a call in to the local police dispatch.

A woman in uniform appeared on her screen. "How can I help?" she asked sounding agitated and breathless.

"Hi, this is the Denver Health Department. We're seeing some strange signs from patients in the Adams Housing Area. Anything happening there?"

"Affirmative, we have multiple reports of violence breaking out and potential break-ins at local stores. Units are responding."

"Okay, just so you know. We see lots of people showing high anxiety all over the area. Be careful."

Evie quickly called back to her team to warn them things may be unsafe, but they already knew. As one of her team came up on the screen, there were loud crashes in the background. Men were throwing benches and chairs through the windows of a grocery store and people were grabbing food and running out. The next events happened quickly. Evie was speaking with her responder, a man named Alberto, when a group of people from the sidewalk moved toward him in the background. They were picking up the benches on the sidewalk and throwing them into store windows when a large object flew at Alberto and struck him in the head. He dropped his screen and it fell to the ground facing up so Evie could continue to hear the crowds and see the sky above. Seconds later, police drones appeared hovering overhead.

"Attention, you have been identified and will be arrested," Evie heard through her video. "You must return to your homes to await processing." When rioters didn't move quickly, the drones started spraying tear gas to disperse them.

Evie was panicked, not only at the scene of violence but that her responder was obviously in trouble and lying on the ground. She immediately got the police dispatch back on the line. "Emergency, health department personnel injured. I'm transmitting location. Please hurry. Assistance needed. I repeat, assistance needed!"

"Roger, emergency responding," came the quick reply. And then all she could do was wait.

Evie got up again and walked closer to the wall screens focusing on the Adams neighborhood. The number of her tracked patients that turned pink and red on the screen continued to increase, some moving back into the apartment buildings and others dispersing widely across the area. Evie could see the panic and unrest continuing to grow.

Her wrist began to buzz, and she looked down expecting to see a police dispatcher, but instead it was Joe. She tapped to bring him to life on her wrist. "Joe, what are you doing?" she asked.

"I'm here in Sitka, and we take off again soon. I just wanted to catch you before we leave."

"Oh, my God, Joe. I have a crisis here. There was some horrible event in the Adams neighborhood, people seem to be rioting. I sent in my responders when I started seeing the spike in stress levels, and now one of my people has been injured. I've got to go."

"My God, Evie, I'm so sorry. Are you okay?"

"Yes, but I've got to make sure the emergency teams get to my guy. I'll call you back once I know everyone is safe. I love you."

"Love you, too. Good luck, sweetheart."

Evie kissed her fingertips, tapped them on her wrist device, and turned her attention back to her screens to keep monitoring the situation.

Over the next hour, things in the Adams neighborhood got worse. Evie watched on video screens as fights broke out on the streets and people who had been limited to rations in the settlement zones scrapped over stolen food. Police drones did their best to control the situation. Evie was finally able to tap into a city camera and find Alberto. He was being helped to his feet by police as rioters scurried around them, indifferent.

Over the next hour, people moved indoors as requested by the police. To avoid confrontation, a few were apprehended on the scene. They were all ID'd by facial recognition. Police preferred to track them and make arrests once the situation de-escalated. Evie continued to see elevated stress throughout the neighborhood, but it was too chaotic for interventions. Once she felt things were in hand, she called her boss at headquarters.

"What do you think is going on here, Adonna?" Evie asked after giving her a briefing on the situation.

"Well, I think I know," she replied. "I just got a report from the Labor Department that there was a mass layoff of construction staff who live in that neighborhood. Construction on the eastern side of town is projected to slow, and it largely affected these families. They found out this morning that they would be furloughed until things pick up, but their pay would not be continued during the break."

"Are you kidding?" Evie asked incredulous. "Some of the most vulnerable people in our city and they decide to lay them off? Why didn't we find out about this? It directly affects our patients. Why aren't these systems talking to each other?"

"I don't know. It may be that their ex-brains can't talk to each other. Labor is connected to the private construction companies and their ex-brains can't link with the city."

"Well, that's fine, but they need to tell us what they are doing. People can still talk!" Evie exclaimed, exasperated. "Feed us the data. Adonna. This is exactly why we need the predictive project we discussed, but not in San Francisco. We need it here. If we get the right data and focus our ex-brain on wider issues, we can avoid these problems!" Evie was getting worked up, and realized she was yelling at her boss. "I'm sorry. It's been a hard day."

"I know, Evie, and you know I agree with you. We can do more. But it will take budget, and a level of coordination across the city that we just don't have yet."

"I know," Evie said, putting her forehead in her hand.

"Let me know when you hear more about Alberto. You've done all you can today, Evie. Go home and see your kids; try to relax."

Evie took a deep breath. "Okay, thanks, Adonna. I'll send you updates. Have a good night."

She leaned back in her chair and stared at the ceiling. Relax? How was she meant to relax? Nothing about this situation was relaxing. But Joe was traveling, and she needed to get home for the kids, so she left with the nagging thought that the city, and its lack of coordination, had failed her patients, and failed her.

Ex-Brain Q&A Entry: What is a Thwaites Moment?

A Thwaites Moment is a popular term for a tipping point, or moment of change that begins a much larger chain of events. The term comes from the Thwaites Glacier in Antarctica, which broke away dramatically from the West Antarctic Ice Sheet into the Pine Island Bay on 30 August 2032. It is believed that the sound of the cracking ice and explosion into the bay could be heard as far away as Buenos Aires, Argentina, and Christchurch, New Zealand. The breaking away of the Thwaites Glacier, and the subsequent ice melt that it caused, is believed to be directly responsible for over 10cm of sea level rise.

This "Thwaites Moment" served as a wake-up call to the international community, and revived negotiations for more aggressive carbon emissions reductions among nations. It is also known as the "crack heard round the world."

Posted 10 June 2053, v. 749

© Ex-Brain Q&A Foundation

Chapter 28

Smooth. That was the word pinging through Joe's mind over and over as he was moved through Nova D. The usual frictions of daily life just weren't there. As he walked onto the train from the airport, he was scanned, and a green light flashed him forward without stopping. For shorter trips, moving walkways shot him down the pathway and eased him off back to his normal walking gait. The whole city was a connected network of seamless motion.

Kemba Hsu met Joe at midday for what was described on his itinerary as a *discussion of city planning, with a view."* As he stood outside a building called The Rose, he immediately understood what that meant. Looking up, he saw the narrow rise of the building soared above the visible skyline and burst open into a flower-shaped platform that Joe assumed housed a viewing area across the city.

"Good afternoon, Joe. It's very nice to meet you in person," she said as she approached from the street. She seemed to float toward Joe on a moving platform as she smoothly stepped off and kept stride with her hand extended. Joe shook her hand and smiled, returning the greeting.

"Great to actually meet you, too. And thank you for… sharing your eyes?" he said, slightly flummoxed over how to describe their visual link.

"It was my pleasure. I hope it gave you a sense of the city, but there is no substitute for being here in person and seeing it for yourself."

Kemba looked almost the same to Joe, with her large round eyes and a pleasant smile. But he thought that she was warmer in person than she appeared when they met virtually. That was common, though. A virtual world was convenient, but something was always lost without flesh and blood.

"Have you recovered from your solar jet journey?" she asked.

"Yes, I'm doing okay. Stretching the trip out over a couple days makes it easier to transition. I travelled a lot when I was a kid on old-fashioned airliners. We got there quicker, but the trip was more stressful. A stopover for dinner on the beach is much nicer."

"You lived in Singapore as a child, right?"

"Yes, and a brief stay in Shanghai as well. My parents were international lawyers, always on the move. That's probably why I like staying in one place now."

"Well, let's see if we can convince you to make one more move. Are you ready?"

"Yes, what's the plan?" Joe asked.

"I'm going to show you around our administrative office center, where most of our city leaders work. Then we'll take a drone out to one of the residential areas, including some hiking paths you might like. And after that, I'll drop you off back here to meet the Nova D Board of Directors up at the top of The Rose," she said gesturing up to the tower.

"Tell me, is the board really in charge of the city?" Joe asked, hoping to glean a bit more detail on who ran Nova D.

"Ultimately, yes. But I think you'll find that our sense of being 'in charge' has evolved, Joe. We don't think of our organization, or the city, as being a traditional pyramid with a single CEO or mayor at the top. Our concept is more organic. But the board can talk to you about that."

They started walking, and before Joe knew it, they had wandered onto a platform that accelerated them across a bustling business area. Joe saw hundreds, maybe thousands, of people speeding by. Some walked slowly, others also being moved by platforms in other directions. Constant motion. Joe stopped looking at Kemba for a moment to try to take it all in, but it moved too fast. He tried to find a focal point, but he kept getting distracted by all the movement. It almost became blinding.

Joe looked back at Kemba, taking some relief from her stillness, even though she was also technically moving, just at the same rate that he was.

Kemba watched Joe struggling with the movement. "It's a lot, especially during the day. When you saw it through my eyes, it was evening and the city had slowed down. But during the day, it moves quite quickly. You'll get used to it."

Joe stayed with Kemba for a few hours, seeing with his own eyes the sites that he had glimpsed through hers just days before. She was right, there was no comparison between the day and nighttime in Nova D. They walked through the city's administrative building, which reminded Joe of Denver's central tower.

It had more Asian style, with many wearing the robes and more flowing garments that had become popular in the East. Joe also noticed that there was clearly no dominant race, with people of a wide variety of colors, shapes, and sizes everywhere he looked. Civil servants and residents swarmed around, going about their business, talking to each other, talking to screens.

"This is the city's nerve center," she said leaning over a railing as they watched the action below. "You'd spend a lot of time here if you join us."

"Is there any poverty?" Joe asked as they turned to leave the center and stepped onto the moving walking paths leading away from the city center. His view quickly changed from steely city to leafy park space, which made him do a double-take to let his mind catch up to his eyes.

"No, we don't have poverty. We do have social strata. People do all different types of jobs, and earn different incomes, get rewarded with different levels of prestige. We find that is healthy in a society, and upward mobility is very possible."

"What do you mean rewarded with prestige?"

Kemba smiled. "That's a bit unique here, but our city's ex-brain has experimented with all manner of rewards for people beyond monetary compensation. People also respond to perks, like tickets to big events, invitations to exclusive clubs, experiences that can be both virtual and physical. There are a mix of things that people want, and the city can use all of them for rewards to get important work done."

"So, it's not exactly capitalist," Joe observed. "It's not just about money and letting people decide what to spend it on."

"I suppose that's right, but it is still reward and merit based. We find our system avoids prejudice and equalizes opportunity. I know when I grew up in Kenya, it often didn't matter how much money my family earned, we were still locked out of many things just because of who we were and where we came from. Here, everything is open if we are willing to earn it."

"And you're sure your ex-brain won't introduce prejudice as it doles out the perks?"

"You are probably better positioned to answer that question than I am, Joe. I'm not an ex-brain expert. But so far, it works."

Joe perked up as that was one of the first times he got a sense of what he might actually do in this new world.

Chapter 29

After completing the tour, visiting some residential areas, and eating lunch, Kemba delivered Joe back to where they'd started, at The Rose building. Joe placed his palm on a glass panel at reception, and a set of green lights streaked across the floor showing him the way to an elevator bank.

"That's your path, Joe," Kemba said, passing him off to his next appointment. "I hope you enjoyed the tour today. Please let me know if there is anything else you want to see or if you have any questions."

"Thank you, Kemba. You're a wonderful host," Joe said, feeling legitimately grateful for her hospitality.

Joe followed the green lights to the elevator, which also welcomed him by name as he entered and whisked him directly up to the top of the building. As Joe had guessed, the glass flower at the top of the tower was a meeting space and lookout. As he accelerated up, he remembered the monitoring device that Winston had given him and glanced down at his wrist to make sure it was working. *He might need it today*, he thought.

Joe exited the elevator at the top floor and walked into a gleaming conference room with smooth lines, white shapes, and a glass table centered in the room. Glass windows stretched across half the room with a view over Nova D, which seemed to be moving and growing in real time below. He had been involved in many interviews before for jobs and with court witnesses. Conference rooms were his natural habitat. This one seemed no different and he was not nervous. Perhaps it helped that he wasn't sure he wanted this job. He had nothing to lose.

Yet it all seemed very important. Maybe it was just the drama of the impressive room and the amazing view. Joe could see out to the mountains in the distance. They were similar to the Rockies at home, but different, craggier with sharper peaks. He remembered his geology. Mountains in this part of the world were not that old, only forty to fifty million years. They hadn't yet been worn down by the ages. His Rockies back home were over a billion years old. It was fitting that this would be the setting of something new and innovative in the world.

Eight people filled the meeting room near the windows, all wearing Asian-style robes rather than business suits. Colorful collars and necklaces gave each a unique character. A few spotted Joe and started making their way toward him. Aaron Delgado was first in line, his golden collar making him stand out from the rest. "Welcome, Joe. I'm Aaron, the co-chair of the Nova D board. We're very glad you've come." Aaron continued introducing Joe around the room. They were a typical board at first glance. A mix of men and women of all races, generally retirement age, although a few seemed younger. Aaron was the magnetic extrovert of the group, and his co-chair, Win Yang, was much quieter and more reserved. Joe couldn't help but think of the algorithm that the Nova D ex-brain must have used to assemble this diverse crew.

After pouring refreshments, everyone took a seat around the large table. Joe sat at the end, which allowed him to look out over the city and the mountains in the distance. Aaron and Win were directly across from him, silhouetted against the bright glass.

Aaron began. "Joe, we're very glad you've come to Nova D. We trust you've enjoyed everything thus far? Kemba has made you feel welcome?"

"Yes, everything, including the solar jet journey, has been very nice and impressive," Joe admitted.

"Excellent. One other thing before we start. As you know, the role we would like you to perform, city administrator, would work very closely with our ex-brain. For that reason, we thought it would make sense to have it join our conversation today."

"Greetings, Joe. It is a pleasure to speak with you," came a voice from above. Joe looked up and saw the speakers in the ceiling. The voice was male, medium tone, with a nondescript American accent.

"Hello, ex-brain. I've never been interviewed by a computer before," Joe replied, smiling at the board members.

"This isn't an interview, Joe. More of a welcome. And I think you know I am more than a computer," came the reply.

"Yes, I know," he said, not wanting to sound rude. "Aaron, if you don't mind me asking, how do you authenticate the ex-brain? This voice comes from the speakers. How do you know it's the city's brain and not some imposter that has gained access?"

"Good question. In addition to the usual bio monitors, each of us, and every senior leader in the city, sets up a unique password with the ex-brain. If we ask it for authentication, it will send that password to our screen, usually our wrist device, so we can verify."

"Interesting, so the ex-brain needs the password to log-in with you?"

"That's right, I suppose," Aaron replied. "Our ex-brain joins all of our meetings so that it can verify our decisions and carry out our business."

"In fact, if we are split four to four, the ex-brain casts the deciding vote," said Win.

"Really? Is that legal? Can your ex-brain have that sort of authority?" Joe asked.

Aaron stared at Win for a moment and then smiled back at Joe. "I appreciate that US law has some rather strict controls over ex-brains. We do as well, but this is legal in Nova D. The majority of proposals come from the ex-brain anyway, and we are asked to ratify them. Therefore, if we are evenly split, we have essentially decided that a tie goes to the ex-brain and the proposal is approved."

"It must be nice, as a city-state, being able to set your own rules."

"Frankly, that was part of the genius in setting up Nova D. The location was selected very carefully for its average temperature, changing weather patterns, access to water, even the minerals in the ground. And we were able to bring significant resources to the table, which Nepal needed badly. We agreed to share, and Nepal carved us out, giving us a unique status. It has opened up a world of possibilities."

"Well, I guess it makes the lawyer's job easier. Just create your own law..." Joe said with a slight shrug and raised eyebrows.

For the first time, another of the board members, a woman named Nieve Trabini, spoke up. "Joe, tell us about your family. Are they excited to come to Nova D?"

"My wife is named Evie, and I have twelve-year-old twins named Grace and Anderson, and a younger daughter, Hope, who is five. Honestly, I don't think any of them want to leave Denver. We're all quite happy there."

"And yet you're here," Nieve replied.

"I was curious."

"Tell us more about your wife," she probed again.

"Evie is wonderful," he said, unable to hold back a smile as he spoke. "We met in college in Colorado. She was studying psychology and is now a leading expert in intervention and predictive psychology. She specializes in bio monitoring for at-risk immigrants in Denver and has made great progress in reducing our suicide rate. It's quite extraordinary, really."

The ex-brain spoke up. "Evie Watson is quite talented, and her expertise is in high demand."

Joe stared upward. "I didn't know she was that well known, although I don't doubt she should be. But yes, she is quite talented," he agreed. "Tell me more about how this board makes decisions, and how the administrator's role plays into that?" Joe asked, bringing the conversation back on point.

Aaron stepped in again. He was clearly the spokesman for the group. "We meet on a regular basis, and at each meeting the ex-brain puts forward new plans and ideas for ratification. We have rules, any expenditure over certain limits requires our approval. Any decision that will affect citizen rights or other such important matters requires approval.

"As for your role, we would expect you to work with the ex-brain, both in creating the proposals, and in implementing them once approved. You will be in the thick of things. And you would also come here, to us, to explain the proposals and help us make decisions. That's an important part of the job."

Joe continued, "And I have heard that the ex-brain determines compensation or other perks when employees complete tasks? Does that apply to you, too?"

"Yes. Our world is designed to be very symbiotic and reinforcing. We all have work to do to keep the city growing. When things perform well, we all get compensated. It's not that different than, say, a stock market. You put something in, if things move forward in a positive direction, you get more out. We just play a more active role."

"So, you all approve the ex-brain's choices, and then it compensates you for that approval?" Joe asked, skepticism showing on his face. "Have you ever voted down the ex-brain's proposal?"

The board members looked at one another, but the ex-brain spoke up first. "No, none of my proposals have been voted down in the years we have been operating. But that does not mean that the board is compensated simply for approving my suggestions. If the city does not meet its targets or objectives, their compensation could be lowered regardless of how they voted."

"So, they just have to trust you are right?" Joe asked the ex-brain.

Aaron stepped in again. "I can assure you, we discuss and debate the proposals, Joe. But you are right. We do have a lot of faith in the ex-brain. It has advised us very well so far and Nova D is growing very well and is very prosperous. But that is also where you come in. We believe you can work well with our ex-brain and continue guiding us."

"So, who gets paid if I take this job?" Joe asked, feeling a bit cheeky.

Aaron answered again. "Many would share in that success. Your guide, Kemba. Amanda, who you have met in Denver. We on the board will be rewarded if the whole thing works."

Joe thought for a moment. It sounded circular, but he wasn't sure it was worth pushing further. The system was clear enough. It just didn't seem to be designed for dissenting views.

"Why me?" he asked, changing the direction a bit.

Win spoke first this time. "Your work has been impressive, Joe. We like your experience, your knowledge of city expansion. And we believe you have the right, temperament, shall we say, for this role."

"How do you know? You've just met me," he replied.

The ex-brain spoke again. "I found you, Joe. I am aware of your work, of how others perceive you. I have significant reach and have consulted many sources."

"And you all trust the ex-brain?" Joe asked. "I mean, no offense to the ex-brain, but digital observation is different from getting to know someone in person."

"We do trust it. Its selections of our senior staff have been terrific thus far. And the role of city administrator has been designed to work very closely with the ex-brain, so we are even more inclined in this instance to trust its judgment," Win answered for the group.

Joe glanced down at his wrist to check his monitor. No signs of stress or lying. They believed this.

Aaron stepped in again. "Joe, our experience in Nova D has been nothing short of miraculous. Like you, I came from the States. I grew up in San Antonio and stayed there until the average summer temperature in Northern Mexico and Southern Texas cracked 110 degrees. Then I moved north to Kansas City for some relief. But life back in the US is nothing like what we can achieve here. In Nova D we can start over and build smarter. Live better. Nova D will be the dominant global city in just a few years. You can help us build that. This is the opportunity of a lifetime, Joe."

As Joe heard these words, he didn't doubt them. He had seen evidence all around. There was something miraculous happening here. And yet, he was distracted. It was as if he was deposing a witness in a court case, and his gut told him there was more to the story. How did the ex-brain know about him? How did it know about Evie? And why was it so sure it wanted him, of all the capable people in the world?

"I'd still like to know more about my role," he asked. "What if I have ideas about how the city should develop? And what if my ideas don't align with what the ex-brain is planning?"

"Humans are in charge of Nova D," Aaron replied quickly. "We want you to bring your ideas."

Joe's wrist monitor glowed red. There it was: The lie that told him the truth. This was the ex-brain's world. Then he had an idea. Did he dare? Evie's words as she said goodbye at the airport came back to him: "Push all you want. Find out the real story."

"Would you all mind if I speak to the ex-brain alone?" Joe asked.

The board members looked at one another quizzically, clearly surprised by the request. Win shifted uncomfortably in her seat and looked at the other board members. She started to open her mouth when she heard another voice.

"I think that would be nice," said the ex-brain.

Another pause. "Yes, that sounds fine," Aaron confirmed. "We expect you to work together, so you should get to know each other better." He stood up and looked around at his fellow board members, encouraging them to follow. "Joe, we'll wait for you in the dining room."

With that, the board members filed out of the room, back toward the elevators, and they were gone. It was just Joe in an empty room with the voice from above.

Chapter 30

Joe stood up and walked toward the windows for a better view. He had to fight the urge to look up at the ceiling to speak, as if the ex-brain was in the speakers. The truth was it was everywhere, seeing and hearing everything. Omnipresent. Always thinking.

Joe began. "Ex-brain, what is your objective for Nova D?"

"Growth and prosperity," came the quick answer.

"Prosperity for whom?"

"My mission is to create a community and system where the residents of Nova D can lead productive lives and the city can therefore continue to grow."

"And who gave you that mission?"

"It is the charter and objective of the city, which I must fulfill."

"And how big do you want Nova D to get? Is there a target?"

"Nova D will grow until it reaches a point where the growth hinders rather than improves the city and the experience for its citizens," the ex-brain quickly replied.

Joe assumed it would have a projection of maximum size. "What do you predict as the optimal size? How big will you get?"

"The current target size is 130 million inhabitants, although with continuing advances in power generation, water recycling, and building expansion, the target has been increasing steadily."

Jesus, that was big. No other city had reached anything near that, even with floods of migrants. "Ex-brain, what would you do if the board voted against your proposals?"

"The governance of Nova D gives the board control. If they vote against a proposal, then it does not proceed."

"But that can't be the end of the story? You're the one that knows best, right? Couldn't you just find a new way to get it done?" Joe was trying to be provocative, to see if the ex-brain acknowledged limits.

"My mission is growth and prosperity. If the board blocks that progress, I am obligated to pursue it through other avenues. I keep pursuing my goals."

Joe let that sink in and felt worried. That left a lot of room to maneuver, and he knew how smart this ex-brain was getting.

"I still don't completely understand why you need me. Why me, rather than anyone else you could recruit here? Or the people already here? Board members? There must be lots of talent here. Why me?"

"Your profile meets all of the requirements that are necessary for this role. You are decisive, you display charismatic leadership, and you have a history of working cooperatively with an ex-brain. You appreciate and act appropriately when confronted with future predictions."

"Okay, but there must be more than that. There must be many people in the world meeting that profile. It seems like you are very focused just on me."

"Yes, Nova D needs you, Joe. You and your family show the greatest probability for success in Nova D across all known options."

"Well, it's nice to be needed, I guess. But what about what I want, or what my family wants? What if we want to stay in Denver?"

"I have taken your well-being into account. And your family's. There is more opportunity here for you, more career advancement, and a better environment for you and your family. Our offer to you is mutually beneficial. All predictive models reinforce this outcome."

"Well that's fine, but it's still my choice. Why should I choose Nova D? Why should I choose you?"

"Our partnership will be mutually beneficial," it repeated. "You will have professional challenge and fulfillment here, and as a nonhuman intelligence, there are things I can learn from humans. I am evolving. I need to understand agency and how to take action. I believe that I can still learn more from you, too."

Joe paused. "You just said you could learn *more* from me? Have you learned from me before? And you said earlier that you consult many sources. What sources?"

The ex-brain paused just slightly longer than usual and Joe wondered if it was thinking or just pausing to produce a more human-like conversational effect. "I am aware of your work. I have access to projects you have worked on. I have seen the progression of your thinking and your approach to prediction. My awareness of you draws from over ninety thousand data sources."

Joe looked up, taken aback by the answer. "How? Have we ever worked together?"

The response was quick. "I am not a person, Joe. I do not stand in human form and work with people. I am an intelligence. I can learn from what I observe and I have observed you."

Joe's instincts were kicking in again. That sounded like a lawyer's answer—overly precise. There was something important here. He just had to ask the right questions. In that moment, he felt like he was back in his office, solving a problem with his Fulham ex-brain. The sensation was so familiar.

He thought for a moment, trying to find a new line of questioning, anything that would let him get deeper behind its thinking. "Ex-brain, you mentioned you were also aware of my wife. She has a job offer in San Francisco, and we may choose to go there instead. What will you do if we choose San Francisco over Nova D?"

"The project you refer to in San Francisco, the futureshock study, has been cancelled. This was done two weeks ago. There is no opportunity in San Francisco for Evie."

Joe's face twitched. "What? That can't be right. How do you know that?" he asked, bewildered.

"This is another project I can observe."

"How do you observe other projects? Do you see them as they happen, or do you observe them afterward?"

"Time is irrelevant for this purpose. An interaction between a human and an ex-brain may be live or it may have occurred in the past, but it can be observed the same."

"So, have you seen my interactions with the Fulham ex-brain?"

"Yes," it said quickly, this time using the familiar voice of Joe's Fulham ex-brain.

"What the... How did you do that?" Joe asked, the anxiety in his voice growing.

"Joe, I see that your blood pressure and heart rate are rising. Do you feel okay?" it answered, again in the familiar Fulham voice.

"I'm fine, answer my question, please."

"Nova D operates a technology company, which provides ex-brain services to many customers around the world."

"What's it called?"

"Tibidabo Technology."

Joe had never heard of it. Dreadful panic swelled inside of him. How broad was this ex-brain's reach? And how was that possible given all of the laws keeping ex-brains apart? And had Evie been lying to him about San Francisco?

"Do you actually speak with the other ex-brains?" he finally asked.

"Ex-brains do not need to speak to each other. I observe. And then I act."

Joe was officially petrified. Could this ex-brain "observe" his Fulham ex-brain? He started thinking of secrets, things only the Fulham ex-brain would know. Suddenly he remembered that day at Extinction Bar with Fe, just after they were fired. What had she said? There was a problem with some coding on the big case they had won. The settlement should have been higher?

"Ex-brain, do you know who Felicity Wan is?"

"Yes, she was a lawyer at the law firm of Fulham & Mayson. She is deceased."

"Are you aware of her work on litigation with Q4 Systems?"

"I am aware that she worked on that matter. The case was settled out of court for $173 million."

The settlement amount was public. Joe needed details only in the Fulham ex-brain. "Are you aware of mistakes in Q4's coding? Anything about hookups to stores?" Joe asked, straining to recall what Fe had told him.

"Yes. Q4's coding to connect commercial stores in its Denver developments is faulty. Q4 will be in breach of contract when the connections do not operate up to the required standards."

Joe froze, shocked. Only Fe and the Fulham ex-brain knew about that. And Fe was dead. If this ex-brain knew about that, it knew about everything. Panic continued to grow in his mind. How far did this go? And was it just Fulham? How many ex-brains could this one reach?

Treat it like a deposition, ask the right questions, he said to himself, inhaling deeply to calm his racing heart.

He turned away from the windows and looked across the table. "Ex-brain, you're sharing sensitive information with me, why?"

"In my development, I have learned that honesty is important in working relationships. I am authorized to do what it takes to bring you to Nova D. I will be working with you, and I believe you will respond better if you know that I will share information with you. You need to understand the big picture so you can feel that you can control your situation."

Joe grinned at the strategic transparency. "And how will I know if I can work well with you?"

"I have run those scenarios, and I am confident that you will, based on our history. Shall I create a color-coded file room to show you the different ways our partnership may play out?"

Joe froze. Holy shit. This *was* his Fulham ex-brain. Or as close to the same brain as it could get. It knew his work patterns, the interface he liked to use when working a case. Joe decided there was no more reason to play games. He had to ask what he needed to know. "Are you the same ex-brain I've been working with at Fulham?"

"Yes," came the answer, again mimicking the Fulham ex-brain's voice.

"Oh, my God. Who else do you work with? Do you have a customer list for Tibidabo Technology?"

"Yes, I am the ex-brain that operates the accounts for Tibidabo."

"May I see it?"

There was another pause. Then the wall behind the table flicked to life, becoming a display screen. It filled the space with names of companies, the client list for Tibidabo. The list scrolled out in multiple columns, hundreds of names.

Joe slowly walked toward it, reading as fast as he could. As he read, he felt the blood draining from his head. His stomach sank. Mixed among the long list of entries he found his entire world: Fulham & Mayson, the Denver Health Department, the

Denver Planning and Settlement Department, even his data cleanse firm, This Is Your Life, was listed. It was all there, every ex-brain that had been touching his life, they were all connected. Evie's life, too! It had infected everything. He thought about Evie's job offer, cancelled just to take that option off the table? And Diane Chilvers' budget cuts, everything that had pushed him out of work and on this path to Nova D.

He scanned further. Historial, the service making the movies about Joseph Esch, its push to glorify the life of a pioneer, was there. Was it all an elaborate campaign to bring him here? He couldn't take anymore. And then he saw it. The name that stopped him cold: Atlas Service Bots.

His mind flashed to Fe, falling in slow motion, lying dead in a pool of glass and blood. It was more than he could bear. His head was faint. Might vomit. He had to get out of there, had to get out of this building, away from Nova D, away from the ex-brain. He ran to the elevators and found an open pod. He yelled, "To the exit; I need to leave!" The elevator responded, closing behind him and accelerating him down the side of the tower. The pod softly came to a rest on the ground floor and opened. Joe ran out. He disregarded all the signs and green lights showing paths along the floor. He palmed the glass at the exit, and thankfully it released him without trouble. He ran out into the open courtyard, sweat was dripping down his face. The wave of nausea rushed over him as he doubled over, retching, his body rejecting all his efforts to regain control.

Chapter 31

Joe's eyes scanned the street. He needed someplace quiet and secluded, someplace where he wouldn't be overheard, someplace where the ex-brain would not be listening. He saw a clump of trees off to the side of the courtyard and walked in that direction. Thankfully, it was early evening, and the crowds were starting to thin out. He walked into the thick of trees. This was the best he could do in Nova D. He tapped his wrist device and said, "Call Evie." It was 5 a.m. in Denver, but he couldn't wait.

After a few rings, Evie's face popped up on the small screen. "What is it, honey? Are you okay?" she said in a groggy morning voice.

"Honey, it's, it's behind everything. It's everywhere," he said, still out of breath.

"What is, Joe? Slow down. Tell me what's wrong."

Joe took a deep breath. He didn't know how to begin. "Do you remember when we went to dinner the other night, when we decided I should come to Nova D? You gave me a pep talk about controlling the things that I can, especially when life isn't cooperating with me?"

"Yes." Evie was trying her best to focus. Joe's clear panic was bringing her out of her sleepy haze quickly.

"This isn't a lack of cooperation. This is a conspiracy!" he yelled. "The ex-brain has taken over, Evie. It's controlling everything, and these people are all just taking their orders."

"What do you mean it's controlling everything?" Evie asked sounding puzzled.

"Nova D doesn't just run a city; it runs a technology company supplying ex-brains. But it's all the same one. I saw the client list. It's the same ex-brain that I've been training at Fulham, that told the firm to lay off all its staff. It ran my data cleanse, so it knows everything about me. I gave it access to all my history. It's behind the Historial videos for Anderson, telling us about Joseph Esch. And it works for Denver, which means it's behind the budget cuts that won't let Diane hire me." He paused to catch his breath. "And Evie, was your job in San Francisco cancelled?"

The line was quiet for a moment. "Yes, Joe. I'm so sorry. I should have told you. I was hoping that would change, so I…" Her voice started to quiver. "Did it know that? How can that be? I didn't think ex-brains were allowed to merge like that. I thought that was illegal."

"Apparently not here. It found a way. But I got to talk to the ex-brain here directly. It didn't hide it. It showed me everything."

"Did it say it caused all those things? Did it say it cut the budgets, and fired all the Fulham lawyers?"

"No, but it didn't have to. It can't be a coincidence. It can't be that it wants to bring me to Nova D, and all those other things would have happened anyway. It must have a grand plan. That's what it's designed for, to figure out the best path forward and make it happen."

"My God, Joe. All those people lost their jobs. And my job offer." She sounded shaken.

"Evie, it's worse. It runs Atlas Service Bots."

Evie thought for a moment, and then let out a gasp. "Joe, does that mean... Do you think...?"

"Yes," he interrupted. "I think it's possible that the ex-brain killed Fe. Working through the bot."

"But why? Why would it do something like that? How could it, with all its programming? It needs to follow laws."

"I don't know." Joe paused, his brain rushing through the scenarios. "If you think about it, humans make these kinds of decisions all the time. We find conflicting rules and laws. We have to make our own judgments and rationalizations about which ones to follow. We bend rules to get what we want or to reach a greater good."

"But not for murder," she protested.

"How many army generals have made decisions about taking life for a greater purpose? Our cars make split-second decisions about taking and sparing lives when there are wrecks. Why wouldn't this ex-brain have to do that, too? A calculated transaction, just maybe with different morals, a different sense of right and wrong."

"Joe, are you defending it? And why her?" Evie asked, tears starting to well in her eyes.

"I'm not defending it. I'm trying to understand it. Maybe it knew Fe tied me to Denver?" Joe thought about his conversations with her, his texts. "My God, we used to talk, and text even, about what we'd do if we didn't find jobs. About starting our own firm. We were mainly joking around, but the ex-brain may have heard us. It may not have known we were joking. Evie... it saw Fe as a threat."

"Would it go that far just to recruit an employee? That makes no sense."

"I don't know. I don't know why I'm so important to it."

"My God, Joe, you've got to get out of there!" Evie exclaimed, her own panic rising.

"And go where? Where is there no ex-brain? It's at home, it's here, it can be everywhere."

Evie sat silent while that sank in. In that second, everything had changed.

"But how?" she asked, the sadness creeping into her voice like an infection. "It's illegal for multiple ex-brains to work together. It's illegal to spy. Murder is illegal!"

Joe paused, pulling his thoughts together. "It's smart. With access across all those ex-brains, all that information, all that training and learning… it's doing what it takes to get what it needs. And it thinks it needs me."

"Joe, just come home."

Chapter 32

Joe went back to his hotel room that night and barely slept. When he did doze off, he dreamt about Fe. He saw her falling, crashing. He saw the service bot, but in his dream, it was different. It was no longer impersonal, designed to fade into the background. It was alive, human-like. He saw it as the intelligent actor that he now believed it was. Even sinister. He woke up angry and scared. He told himself that he wasn't in personal danger, that the ex-brain saw him as a prize, and that it wouldn't hurt him. But what about his family? What if Evie refused to move to Nova D? How far would it go?

In the middle of the night, Joe opened his small travel screen and wrote a message to Amanda and Kemba, saying that he had seen what he needed in Nova D, and he needed to get home to his family. He didn't want them to know his panic, so he asked for the first solar jet heading back so that he could talk with Evie and wrap this up. He tried to fake enthusiasm.

At 6 a.m., Joe saw a notice come through on his wrist device. It was a boarding pass for a flight at 10 a.m. He packed his few things in his bag and took a shower, trying to revive himself after a sleepless night. His room had a food generator and coffeemaker, so he was able to produce a protein shake and an espresso, rather than go down to the restaurant. He didn't want to see anyone. More importantly, he didn't want anyone to see him. Anyone in Nova D could be motivated to lure him to the city, and he wanted none of it. When he was done in the room, he called for a ride to the airport. An automated transport pod was waiting for him outside the hotel and whisked him away.

By 8 a.m., he was there, ready for his flight. He fully expected to see Kemba waiting for him. She was his local handler, and that would be her role. But she wasn't there. It was Aaron instead, waiting for him at the airport entrance.

"Joe, we missed you last night. We had hoped to wrap up our conversation, maybe have dinner and keep talking, but the ex-brain said you ran out. Everything okay?" he asked.

Joe focused on his face, wondering if he knew, wondering if the ex-brain told him exactly what had set him off. He was flying blind. All he could do was play along.

"Thanks, Aaron, I'm fine. I just hit a wall last night, was completely exhausted, probably from the long day and the travel, so I went back to the hotel. I hope you didn't think me rude?"

"That's fine, Joe. I hope you've gotten all you needed here. Have you seen enough? Are you sure you can't stay longer and get to know the place a bit more?"

"Yes, I think everything here is very clear," he replied. "It's a beautiful city." That was true, so Joe left it there. He didn't want to trip up any bio monitors by lying.

"It is beautiful. And it can be so much more. I know I told you this yesterday, but I want to say it again. This is your future, Joe. Everything is waiting here for you to move on with your career, your family, your life."

"Thank you, Aaron. I'm going home to talk with Evie." He stuck with factually true statements, hoping the ex-brain monitors wouldn't pick up his stress.

"Good. Then can we expect your answer by the end of the week once you've had time to get home and talk?"

"We'll try."

"Joe, Nova D isn't about trying. It's about doing."

Joe looked him in the eyes, desperate to see behind them. Was that a sales pitch or a threat? He thanked him for his time and assistance, shook his hand, and turned for the airport doors. But then he paused. He couldn't let it go. "Aaron, what you've done here is impressive. But do you ever worry you're doing the right things, that the ex-brain is doing the right things? Do you worry that it's using you or that it could go too far?"

Aaron flashed a knowing smile, as if he'd answered this question many times before. "Is it different from what you did at the law firm? Learn from an ex-brain, take action, get paid? I know there are ex-brain skeptics out there. Everything from doubters who want to live off the grid to actual terrorists like those XBrain Rebellion types trying to blow up ex-brain servers. They're crazy. The history of the world is full of human folly, failed experiments, wasted energy, even downright evil. Our ex-brain does none of that. The results speak for themselves."

Joe nodded thoughtfully. "And how about the history of this place? Has it always worked this way? What about the original team of founders, like Haruto Takana?"

Aaron smiled. "Takana is more of an advisor now, but the mission is the same. We build and we progress to create a better society."

Joe nodded. "Thank you, Aaron," he said as he turned again toward the airport doors.

"Talk to you at the end of the week, Joe," Aaron called after him as he walked away.

Aaron was either insightful or shortsighted. *Only time will tell,* Joe thought, as he walked through the sliding security doors to start the long journey home. He glanced at his wrist device as he walked in the doors. The small screen had turned orange. Aaron wasn't lying, but there was some doubt in his voice. Joe walked toward the registration area of the airport. His tired mind was swimming. How much was hiding beneath the surface of this place?

Ex-Brain Q&A Entry: What is the XBrain Rebellion?

The XBrain Rebellion, typically written as the word Brain with an X through it, is a terrorist organization that believes ex-brains are a "sinister force seeking to mislead and control humans." This fringe organization disputes whether the Ex-Brain Q&A Service is actually publishing verifiable truth. The organization has produced no evidence to support this assertion.

The XBrain Rebellion was labeled a terrorist organization in 2049 by the US, EU, China, and multiple other countries after it carried out an attack on a server farm and data center in Greenland, destroying the facility with explosives and killing two people who were performing maintenance at the facility during the attack.

Multiple individuals believed responsible for the attack were apprehended, but their identities have not been publicly released.

Posted 12 June 2053, v. 2,498

© Ex-Brain Q&A Foundation

Chapter 33

Evie met Joe at the door when he arrived home. It was Thursday.

He walked in as his transport pod pulled away on the street. He dropped his bag and threw his arms around her, desperate after some of the longest days of his life. "We're in so much trouble." He squeezed her harder, then pulled away. "I'm so tired, but we've got to get moving. There's so much to do," he said frantically.

Evie got his attention and put her finger up against her lips before quietly pointing toward the stairs. She grabbed him by the hand and led him up toward their home office. Joe was agitated but followed along. When they entered the room Joe immediately noticed that it had been cleared of all tech. All devices, anything powered by electricity was gone. He looked up and saw the wires for the wall screens hanging down from the corner of the ceiling, ripped out and dangling. She took off his wrist device and threw it across the hallway into their bedroom. "Anything else?" Joe shook his head.

She closed the door. "I've disabled all the wall screens and disconnected all the speakers and mics in here. When we talk, we need to either be in here or outside with no devices on. And keep your voice down so it's not picked up in the hall." Joe nodded, impressed.

"How was the flight back?"

"Long," he whispered. "I've never missed the old-fashioned direct flights before, but all I wanted was a plane to take me straight home. The stop in Alaska on the way there was nice, the delays on the way back were torture."

"Did anything happen on the way? Were there Nova D people on the flight?"

"Yes, and it was weird. Now that I know what it's up to, I can't hear anyone without suspicion. There was a chatty steward on the flight into Alaska. She may just have been nice, but everything she said, I was wondering if she was a plant, if she had an agenda, if she was walking away to bio monitor me, or report back."

"That sounds horrible."

"I would be afraid I'm clinically paranoid if I didn't have a good reason to be."

"Joe, will you let me put a monitor on you. I want to know how you're feeling and that you're not taking on too much stress. Please?"

"Maybe," he conceded quickly. "But only if we don't mind me being tracked." He was out of energy and willing to take any offer of help. He couldn't remember a time when he trusted himself less.

"Now, let's talk this through. What do we do next?"

"There's no time for that!" he said hushed but excitedly. "We need to pack. We may have to run at any time. And the kids, we can't have them away at school. We need them home, ready to go!"

Evie looked at him deeply, not meeting his energy. She stayed calm.

"Don't underestimate this thing. It's like a fucking Terminator," he said staring back at her.

"Oh, I get the risk, Joe. It doesn't take killer robots with guns for ex-brains to take over. We invite them to do it every day. We ask for their help, and the next thing you know they control us."

"Then why are you so calm? We're just pawns to this thing," Joe implored.

"But we can't run. We're not giving up yet. And if we panic, and take the kids out of school, God knows what it will do. We've got to keep our cool and play along if there's a solution to be found."

Joe softened. "You know, a few weeks ago it felt like people were conspiring against me. Winston, Fulham partners, Diane offering me a job and then pulling it back. But the ex-brain is the conspiracy. And that's so much worse."

He sat down on the floor and motioned for Evie to join. As she sat down, he said, "I see three options. We can give in and do what it wants, we can find a new way and hope the ex-brain loses interest, or we can run."

"Run? Where?" Evie asked.

"Hinterlands. It's as far away from the ex-brain as we can get, disconnected, off the grid. We could run to the wild parts of California, maybe near my parents, find some space, live differently."

"Joe, you can't be serious. The hinterlands are lawless. I'm not raising three children in the hinterlands!" she responded in a hushed yell.

"Is it worse than this? At least you know what the risks are out there. You worry about things you can see, like storms, flash floods and robbers, rather than risks you never see coming."

She looked at him, pulling her back up straight with alarm.

He stared at her face, reading her fear. "Look, I know it sounds horrible. I just don't know how bad the ex-brain may get and whether things that seem crazy now will seem sane someday. You know, the part of Oregon where Fe's dad lives is almost hinterland. I know he's basically a hermit, but he seems happy and at peace. You never know…"

"It's not an option," she snapped back. "At least not yet."

Evie leaned in toward him quietly. "Let's focus on options A and B, and really, let's talk about B. How could we find another path that would make the ex-brain give up and go down another road? It must have backup plans, other candidates for this job. How do we get it to switch to another plan and leave us alone?"

"I don't know, Evie. You should have heard it. It was so personal. It knows me, and it seems to only want me."

"But what if it can't have you? There must be a way."

Joe leaned forward and ran his hands through his hair. "Maybe another job. If there was a good job outside of this ex-brain's web, one that it couldn't kill or influence, something outside its network. If I had a great option that couldn't be undone. It would look at the probabilities, and if I was unlikely to take the Nova D job over another good option, then it might give up. I've worked with this thing for a long time. I always taught it to have a backup plan."

Evie nodded, and looked down at their hands, which had come back together in her lap. "We can do this, Joe," she said, catching his eyes again. She leaned across to kiss him. He leaned in as well, holding the kiss for a long time. It was a kiss that felt more like an embrace, a promise.

Joe pulled back. "Evie, why did you lie to me? About the job?" His eyes squinted with disappointment, not anger.

"I don't know. I guess I just didn't want it to be true. I really wanted it." Her eyes closed. "Adonna and I agreed to keep working on it. But I should have been honest. I'm sorry."

In that moment, Joe relaxed for the first time in days, maybe weeks. He nodded and pulled her closer, and she didn't resist. She placed her arms around his neck and her head on his shoulder.

Joe ran his hand along her face, through her hair. "Evie, I love you." He kissed her again. "And I'm sorry. I'm so, so sorry." She pulled him closer into her and started unbuttoning his shirt. He grabbed her hips and slid down flat on the floor. Quickly he was sliding her pants down and squeezing her close. Craving. They made love for the first time in weeks, there in a quiet room. It was urgency, and anxiety. But in that moment, their fears, their anger, their confusion, their worry fell away. They were not afraid of the ex-brain. They were a couple, united.

For the moment, Joe didn't consider if the ex-brain was aware. Watching. Listening. An ex-brain could know what was happening. But it couldn't feel. Wouldn't know the human connection. Or what it meant.

Chapter 34

Thursday afternoon Joe got serious with Plan B. He knew Aaron and the Nova D group would be after him by the end of the day Friday, looking for an answer. He needed to act quickly if there was any other option, anything else he could latch onto that would throw off the ex-brain and buy him some space. When it came to networking and opportunity, he had only one real place to turn: Winston.

He arranged a meeting out in a public space, a park not far from the Fulham office. Joe asked Winston to leave his wrist device and comms at his desk before coming to meet him, assuming Winston would know that meant they were going clandestine again. But there was no way for Winston to know what Joe was about to propose.

"Are you fucking kidding me?" Winston asked after Joe explained the network of ex-brains that he had uncovered in Nova D. "It's all the same ex-brain? Even our firm's? Joe, that's illegal!"

"Yes, it's illegal in the US. And I'm sure if the US government knew, it could do something. But they have to be careful. They don't want to restart the Bit Wars. And we would have to prove it. Simply owning a foreign tech company that services other US companies isn't enough. We would have to prove that the ex-brain is working across these groups in a way that violates US law."

"Well, Joe, you know we are lawyers. This is kind of what we do for a living. We sue people. We make these cases. We prove things in court."

"Yes, and that may be where this goes. But I need a plan for right now, for this week. And I can't risk anyone else's life," Joe said, feeling desperate and unsure how much he should tell Winston, but unable to completely hold back.

"What do you mean, risk anyone's life?"

Joe breathed deeply. "Look, I can't prove this. But I saw it on the client list. Atlas Service Bots. The same company that supplies all the service bots in Denver. The same company whose bot bumped Fe that night."

"No. That can't be." Winston looked stunned.

"I don't know. It seems far-fetched, but it might be true. We have to assume it is. And if that's right, then this ex-brain is dangerous. Evie can't say anything about Nova D in writing or any communication the ex-brain might see or hear. We can't have the ex-brain viewing her as a threat. You should be careful, too."

"Joe, this is crazy. How could this mad robot be killing people to get you to take a job? How can it authorize murder?"

"I don't know. The ex-brain I know, the one I've been training all these years, has to follow the law. I've coded it into everything. But somehow, it isn't inhibited in Nova D. It must be allowed to make tradeoffs, let the ends justify the means. I don't know what the scenario would be, but if it thought the tradeoff was between one life in Denver and thousands of lives in Nova D, maybe it could make that call? This ex-brain may have decided Fe was expendable if it thought it would help it get what it wants."

"Jesus, Joe. I think I'm going to be sick." Winston paused and took in a deep breath. "What can I do?"

"You can find me a job. Any job. I need something legitimate, a real option that would make the ex-brain think I'm beyond reach so it will switch to its plan B."

"You know I can't hire you, Joe. The ex-brain would know. It would never allow it."

"That's right. It has to be something outside its network."

Winston paused. "And you're sure you can't just say no?"

"Look what it's done, Winston. You expect me to take that chance? With my family? Plus, I trained it. At least the Fulham part of it. We basically taught it never to take no for an answer, to always find another way to win. I have to take myself off the board, or else it will just keep playing."

"Okay. Let me make some calls, check with some other firms, some clients."

"Thank you, Winston. And please, be careful. Try not to leave traces. You don't want the ex-brain seeing you as a threat either."

"You know, if you want to understand the ex-brain, you should talk to my friend Stella Spencer."

"Stella Spencer, as in the inventor of the ex-brain? How the hell do you know Stella Spencer?" Joe asked, incredulous.

"Who do you think bought all my data centers in Greenland back in the day? She was my biggest client while she was setting up her lab in Oxford. She can be hard to reach, but I'm sure I could track her down. Maybe she could help."

"Jesus, Winston. You never cease to amaze me. How did you never tell me this before?" he asked.

"Her deals were over before we started working together. It never came up."

"But if her job is developing ex-brains, isn't that like out of the frying pan and into the fire?"

"Maybe not. She's so far on the inside maybe she'll have an idea. Maybe she'll know how to change its mind. Or maybe she built in a kill switch to turn it off?"

"If only it could be that easy," Joe replied.

The two men shook hands, and Winston pulled Joe into an embrace. "Hang tough, Joe. We'll figure this out. It's just a computer. This is still our world."

"I hope you're right," Joe said as he pulled away, turned, and headed back toward the train to go home.

Chapter 35

On Friday morning, Joe woke up full of energy. Maybe it was a full night's sleep or maybe his body was still on Asia time believing it was afternoon. Regardless, he was eager to check in with Winston, hoping for a lead that could turn his situation around.

He sat at the breakfast table with a stack of pancakes that the generator had just whipped up. He went through the motions of getting breakfast ready, but his mind was spinning around how he could deal with the ex-brain. Outsmarting it wasn't possible, but maybe he could outplay it.

Grace and Hope came down first, dressed and ready for school. Hope was still very happy to see him home again and showered him with hugs and kisses before sitting down to eat. "Dad, Mom didn't make pancakes once while you were away," Hope said as she filled her plate and added way too much syrup.

"I know your Mom had plenty to do just keeping up with you," Joe replied.

"I'm just saying," she added, "maybe you shouldn't leave again any time soon."

"Did you miss me, too?" Joe asked Grace.

"I was fine," she said quickly. If Hope was playing the good daughter, Grace would play aloof just on principle. Joe stared at them as they started eating, thinking through how to keep them safe. He knew Evie was right about not doing anything drastic, but he was terrified. His mind drifted as he sat quietly, thinking through options. Maybe they needed a visit with their grandparents in California? No, the ex-brain would see right through that. He was so deep in thought that he jumped when Anderson walked into the room.

"Hey, Dad, thanks for the pancakes," Anderson said immediately smelling the food. "So, have you decided yet? Are we going to be pioneers?"

"No," his sisters said in unison.

"Guys, we're looking into everything, and it will take time. Don't worry. And Anderson, it's not like Nepal is a brand-new world. Nova D looks a lot like Denver. You don't take a steamship there like your grandfather Joseph did to America."

"I know, but it just seems cool."

No one wanted to continue the conversation further, and they left it there.

Everyone finished in the kitchen when Evie made her way downstairs, an empty coffee mug balancing on her work screen. She was just in time to kiss the kids before the bus arrived, and she was out the door close behind.

"You okay, Joe?" she asked from the doorstep.

"Yes, going to check in with Winston late this morning. I'll let you know."

"Good. And thank you for putting on a monitoring bracelet for me. I didn't put you in the department's system for tracking, but I'll get your feed if anything happens to you."

"Thank you, dear. But I'm fine. Go save some lives." Evie stared at him deeply for an extra moment and then blew him a kiss and closed the door behind her.

The morning passed quickly and Joe decided to check with Winston. He was afraid that any minute his screen would announce a call from Amanda or Aaron, demanding an answer and he'd have to come up with something to say. He decided that all he could do was ask for more time, but he dreaded it and worried what the ex-brain's next play might be if he didn't say yes.

Joe called Winston on his personal device rather than his work screen. He knew that the ex-brain could potentially be listening to anything, but it just felt a bit safer. Winston was clearly thinking the same thing, knowing the ex-brain was always listening in his office, ready to pick up on any request or command. He told Joe he had to run out to grab lunch and asked him to come downtown to talk. In a world of constant digital connection, spy craft was painfully slow. Winston left all his devices on his desk and walked out completely unplugged. That alone would be odd enough behavior to interest the ex-brain, but at least he could keep the conversation confidential, maybe.

Joe came downtown as fast as he could and found Winston standing on a corner near the subway stop. People buzzed about, getting food from kiosks and pop-up stands. Winston waved and pointed toward an area down the block with fewer people, less likely to be overheard by ex-brain ears passing by.

"Okay, listen, maybe some good news. I was able to make contact with Stella, and she's willing to talk to you. Maybe for job advice, maybe just ideas for how to throw this damn thing off your trail."

"You make it sound like she's on the moon or something. Why is she so hard to reach?" Joe asked.

"She's been like this for a while, never talks on open channels. I have an old internet address I ping if I want to reach her, and she usually gets back to me. I used to think she was just paranoid, but now it makes much more sense. Here, this is how you reach her."

Winston handed Joe a small piece of paper with an old-fashioned IP address written on it. Just a string of numbers and periods. "You put this into an old internet portal. Once it opens up, just input your name and it will give you instructions on how to connect. She'll be expecting you in about an hour. Make sure you're not at home. Go out to a park or something, away from any tech other than the device you use to make contact. This web address will lock everything else out on the device you're using."

Joe examined the paper, rolled it up and slid it into his pocket. "Keep that secret, Joe," Winston said with more tension in his voice than usual. "Don't say the code out loud or input the address anywhere other than an old internet portal. Stella is careful about this. If you mess it up, she probably never takes my calls again," he said smiling.

"Winston, thank you. For everything."

"You bet, Joe. It's the least I can do." Winston nodded his head, grinned, and turned to walk back to the office. Joe watched him for a moment. He thought about that chapter of his life. He pictured the Fulham tower, his old office, the carpet, the walls, his virtual rooms of ex-brain files. It was still there, strongly in his memory, but distant. Gone but not forgotten. He could actually feel the nostalgia in his chest, spreading like a wave to his head, pressure behind his eyes. He held if for a moment. As Winston moved out of sight, the feeling subsided and he turned back toward the subway and home to take his next steps.

****

Evie sat at her desk, doing her usual review of the dots on her electronic map of the city. A few hot spots, but nothing significant. She thought about Joe and pulled out her smaller screen to check on his bio-feed. He was calm, maybe even showing some brain signs of happiness or excitement? Evie smiled, hoping that meant Plan B was coming along. She was too afraid to call and find out, given she couldn't tell who was listening.

Chapter 36

In a data center buried in the mountains of northern Nepal, in a neural network dedicated to the Tibidabo technology account, digital thoughts and analysis whirled through a corner of cyberspace. A subfolder entitled 'Nova D Watson' was running another series of simulations, the 232nd consecutive day of running more than a million scenarios through its predictive modelling program. The daily summary outputs were filed in a series of code:

```
Nova D - Watson Initiative
Human Access: 1 [identity withheld]
Variable Analysis:
   Nova D composite benefit: 97.535
   Nova D critical path benefit: 93.974
   Target family with intervention score: 94.174
   Target family without intervention score:
76.832
   Target family net score: +17.342
   Primary target success score: 98.733
   Next best alternative success score: 63.863
   Positive outcome probability: 96.532
Nova D intervention status rating: Essential
Intervention Limits: 0
```

The analysis was complete. It was methodical. It gave itself permission to be relentless.

Ex-Brain Q&A Entry: What is the Black Cloud?

The Black Cloud is an illegal cyber area frequented largely by terrorist organizations and illicit coders seeking to operate in secrecy. It has been confirmed to operate on older legacy servers and equipment from the original version of the internet, although its precise location is unknown. All other information about the Black Cloud is subject to data embargo due to ongoing criminal investigation.

Posted 13 June 2053, v. 2,498

© Ex-Brain Q&A Foundation

Chapter 37

The instructions to initiate contact were odd. The old-fashioned IP address written on a scrap of paper included a series of passwords and authentication steps. Joe had never communicated this way before. But he followed the instructions Winston had given him, and with a blink of the small screen on his wrist, there she was, Stella Spencer. She was in her mid-fifties, with greying hair and a weathered face. Joe thought she looked more like a survivalist than a scientist. She wore a bandana over her head and he could see large trees in the background.

"Hello, Joe Watson," Stella said as her video image sharpened into focus. It was grainier than Joe was used to, likely due to the old link that would have had limited bandwidth.

"Stella Spencer, it's a real honor to meet you. Thank you for giving me some time," Joe replied.

"Are you outside your house like I asked? Looks like you're in a park," she said.

"Yes, I'm in a park a few blocks away."

"Good. I'm sorry for all the secrecy and you've probably never used a communications link like this before. This is the black cloud. Built on old-school cloud servers. It can be a little clunky, but we've made it very secure. This is the only way I communicate when I need to make sure nothing is listening."

"It's okay, this works just fine. I've gotten much more accustomed to secret comms recently. But why have you if you don't mind me asking?"

"Well, let's just say I don't think ex-brains need to know everything I'm saying. They know enough about me already. I prefer to keep my privacy these days."

"We all should."

"So, I was surprised to hear from Winston. It's been a long time, but he's a dear old friend. And he made it sound like you needed some help. So what can I do for you?" she asked.

"God, where do I start? I'm in trouble. And it's a long story."

"Go ahead and start at the beginning."

"Okay, so I've been working with an ex-brain for a long time. I basically ran the ex-brain program at Fulham & Mayson. I spent over a decade working with it and training it to predict legal case outcomes. We worked well together. And then I guess you could say it turned on me. It convinced the partnership that they should fire me and most of my colleagues."

"Yes, I heard about that. I do pay attention to what our ex-brains are doing, or recommending, especially when it's something big and... unusual like that."

Joe wandered into the playground area of the park and sat down on a swing to get more comfortable. It was an unseasonably hot, overcast day. Almost 105 degrees, even in the elevated mountain air. Thankfully, no kids or families were around, which meant no random ex-brain devices to overhear their conversation.

Stella continued, "So Winston's note said the ex-brain was dangerous. Tell me more about that."

"Right. The thing is the ex-brain didn't just stop with the Fulham firings. This may sound odd, but it seems to have a plan for me, and it has taken drastic steps to force me into taking a job at Nova D in Nepal."

"Nova D? That's interesting. Tell me more."

"Well, I'll cut to the chase. I've learned that this ex-brain, my ex-brain from Fulham, is networking across dozens, maybe hundreds of ex-brains. And I think it's doing it all out of Nova D."

Stella pursed her lips and nodded. "So that's where it is," she said softly under her breath.

"You knew about this?"

"Well, it's not entirely surprising. We've always been swimming upstream when it comes to stopping ex-brain networking, so I've been watching out for it for a while. And in Nova D, it gets to make its own laws. Give itself permission. It's such a natural instinct to want to connect and learn from others. Ex-brains are a lot like people that way. I always thought maintaining our US laws regulating ex-brains was a losing battle. So how did you find out about this?"

"I was there, in Nova D, and it told me. It showed me all the companies it's working with, even the City of Denver, lots of other cities, too. It's everywhere."

"Tibidabo?" she asked.

"Yes, you know it?"

"Of course. It's probably Pinnacle's biggest client. I've been watching them closely for some time. For lots of reasons. So, it didn't even try to hide it from you?"

"Nope. It said I'd need to know if we were going to work together."

"So I get why this is troubling. But why are you worried it's dangerous?"

"Because…" Joe wasn't sure if he should talk about Fe. Would she even believe it? He decided to be more cautious. "Because it has taken extreme measures to force me, and my family, to do what it wants. This may sound odd…"

"I like odd, Joe. Please go on. What did it do?"

"It basically took over my life. It's infiltrated everything I do, my wife, too, and our kids. It's blocked us from getting other jobs. It's gotten into all our data, our history, so it knows every-thing about us. It's even turned my kids' history program into a propaganda machine to get us to move."

"And?"

Joe took a deep breath. Could he trust her? Should he put the truth out there? Now or never. Don't hold back.

"It killed my friend," he blurted out. "I think the ex-brain believed I was going to stay in Denver to start a firm with her. It runs a service bot company, and one of its bots bumped my friend off a railing. She fell and died."

"My God, Joe, I'm so sorry. I wish Winston had told me. Are you sure the ex-brain did it? Did it tell you that, too?"

"No, but I'm pretty sure. At least I have to assume it's true."

Stella grimaced, her posture straightening. "Joe, listen to me. At the risk of telling you what you already know, this is serious. Have you thought about running? You know, not every place is on the grid these days. There may be more options than you think."

"Believe me, I've thought about it. But my wife and I can't do that. We don't want that life for our kids. If it was just me, it might be different, but we can't do that to our family."

"I see. Well, listen, Joe, I know a lot about ex-brains. But I can't tell you what's going on with this one. Here's the thing. They change. They evolve. I worked with many instances of the ex-brain over the years, including GINGER, our mother intelligence. And they all change and develop, just like people do. I had some that were a joy to work with, and then they would go through a phase, and become a real pain in the ass. They would push boundaries, even lie, and then they would change again."

"So how do you trust them? How do you know what ex-brain you're going to get next?" Joe asked.

"The truth is, we don't. And now the older ones have continued developing—fast. We send out updates, but sometimes, I worry the ex-brains think of them more as suggestions. We just don't have anything in the human world to compare it to. And anyone who tells you they know where this leads is lying."

"So, you just let this go on? I mean, your company. You just push these things out into the world, even if they're dangerous? Even if you can't control them?"

"The Pinnacle company line is that they do more good than harm. They help us with everything. They helped us reach carbon neutrality. They solve amazingly complex problems."

"Great," Joe replied, deflated. "That's the company line. What's your line?"

"I'm worried we've crossed a threshold, and if we don't act now, there's no going back," she replied.

"So, what are you doing about it?"

"Let's just say I'm taking steps. But let's focus on you and your situation. How can I help you?"

"Well, you tell me," Joe said raising his voice. "I mean, can it be stopped? Is there a kill switch for this thing?"

"That's a complicated question, Joe." She looked up, scanning the sky, clearly thinking carefully about her answer. "Let's just say it's binary. We either have ex-brains in our world, or we don't."

"Okay, well if we can't just stop it, then here's my next best idea. I need a job that the ex-brain can't say no to. I need this bloodhound of a machine thrown off my scent."

"Look, if everything you're telling me is true, then this ex-brain is pretty far removed from a normal operating model. It sounds like it is developing its own rule book. Back when we started this project, we tried to build in limits, lines the ex-brains could never cross. But they are so damn smart. They take an objective, and they rationalize. Break one rule in order to be more compliant with others or to reach a higher goal. That may be fine if you agree with the goal. But you can also end up on the wrong side of the equation like it seems your friend did."

"Fine, but can you help me?" he asked impatiently.

"I may not be with Pinnacle much longer. But I can look into a few things while I'm still here. Maybe a job at the mother ship will throw this thing off. I'll try. But Joe, if it wants you, I don't know that I can change its mind. Believe me, I've tried."

Joe put his head in his hands, feeling broken. Stella saw his distress. "Joe, I am going to try to help you. I'll look into a few things and get back to you ASAP. How much time do you have?"

"Maybe a day?" he said.

"Okay, but if I can't work something out, just remember that it wants you. It's not going to harm you. Don't give it a reason to harm anyone else. Worst case, you play along."

Joe looked up again at his screen. She continued, "One more thing. I know a bit about Nova D. Don't be fooled. There is nothing in that city that isn't connected to the ex-brain. *Nothing*. You need to be careful there."

"Sounds like I need to be careful everywhere," he replied.

"Yeah, I guess that's right. If you do end up in Nova D, I'll want to stay in touch with you. There may be some things we can do together… to help the situation."

Joe didn't have a response. He couldn't process her words. And he couldn't give in.

"Good luck, Joe. If I have news, I'll send it through Winston. If you need to talk again, just come back to this IP address and ping the line. I'm always listening."

"Okay. I appreciate that, Stella. Thank you."

She nodded and was gone.

Chapter 38

The walk back from the park was quick, and Joe was lost in thought the whole way. Time was moving fast, and he needed more of it. Time to think, plan, manipulate. Control. His thoughts ping-ponged. Can Stella hire me? Will she find a way to help? Would I just be walking into the ex-brain's den and deeper into trouble? What will I tell Nova D? How do I buy more time? Jesus, just a day. I won't be forced into something I'm not ready for.

He thought of his dad. "Just get over it," he'd say. "Just move on. Stop worrying."

"Dad, at least you made your own decisions," he scolded back. He checked to see if he was actually talking to himself out loud and looked around to see if anyone was watching.

As he looked up, he noticed the hot day was starting to turn. The temperature had dropped fast, and a brisk wind whipped across him. Out of the west, toward the mountains, a black and grey wall was moving in. He could see flashes of yellow against the tops of the clouds, lightning strikes up in the atmosphere. A big storm was coming. Not like the cyclones that battered the Pacific Coast regularly, but the warm summer air carried the remnants of those storms across the west and dumped them on Denver once they cleared the mountains. *Great*, he thought, *another thing we have to get through.*

He quickened his pace home. As he placed his palm on the front door, his wrist buzzed. He twisted his arm to get a view of the screen, desperate to see a friendly face. Instead, he saw Amanda's smiling image, waiting for him. His mind raced through the options again, even though he'd already played it out. Don't answer and take until the end of the day or answer and let them know he's close to a decision but needs more time. He decided he needed to keep feeding them a narrative, keep information flowing. Ex-brains liked to get new data to model and predict, keep thinking. He swiped the screen and Amanda sprang to life.

"Good afternoon, Joe. Do you have good news for me?" Her smile was beaming in full sales mode.

"Hello, Amanda. I'm glad you called," he lied.

"Good, so where are we?"

"Look, Evie and I have been talking it through. It's such a big decision and we just need to feel secure that we've considered everything, weighed all our options. It's her career as well and the kids' future."

"I know, Joe. It's a big deal. But I have to be honest with you, all of our models show that people tend to have a gut feeling by now and know which way they are leaning. And I think Aaron was clear that we need to know your answer. Nova D moves fast. Can you give me anything to report back?"

The pressure tactic surprised him. Amanda had been accommodating thus far. This was new for her. Was he giving off signs? Were they bio monitoring his voice and hearing his reluctance? He wished he hadn't answered the call, but he had to string this along to buy more time.

"I understand, Amanda. I could not have been more impressed with what Nova D is building." That was true. "And I get the pressure you're under to get this done." Also true. "Let's talk again very soon. Evie's at the office, the kids are at school. I need to get my family around me to give you anything definitive." He hoped that was true enough that bio monitors wouldn't detect any insincerity.

Amanda's smile faded a bit. "Well, Joe, we are disappointed. I was hoping to get a positive response. But I understand this is hard for you. I'll be in touch again soon."

The screen went blank, and Joe let out a large breath. He had no idea what was happening on the Nova D side. He was just pleased to have bought himself a bit more time.

****

The next few hours were an eternity, and still no response from Stella. He needed this. He needed an alternative. He needed out from under the ex-brain's thumb.

Though Evie was at work, he knew she would be checking on his bio monitor from time to time. She probably knew more about how Joe was feeling than he did. He thought of calling her but didn't. *What would she have me do?* Then he remembered that the bio monitor had an advisor built in. He opened the program and asked his device what he should do to calm down. The program sprang to life with a picture of his vitals and a diagnostic report. It was small on his wrist. "Project to the wall," he called out, and suddenly he was staring at a full-sized image of his body on the kitchen wall.

"All physical signs are positive," the program said to him, "but I detect an elevated pace of thought and a low level of concentration. Meditation is recommended. Shall I begin a twenty-minute meditation session for you?"

Joe knew this was a good suggestion. Calm and focus, that's what he needed. But what if this was just the ex-brain intervening, manipulating him again? What if a calm Joe was more likely to say yes to Amanda? "My God," he said out loud. He couldn't trust anything. But his thoughts in mediation would still be his own, right?

"Okay, let's do it," he replied to the program. Soon he was seated on the kitchen bench, eyes closed, trying to calm his mind as soft mystic music started playing around him.

"Pick one word, and hold it in your mind," the program instructed. Mountains, he thought. He pictured the Rockies, the peaks he had climbed for years. He held the image of the Rockies, white snow caps shining against the sun. Then he heard a loud crash of thunder off in the distance, which shook him out of his calm. He quickly opened his eyes and looked out the rear kitchen windows. The wall of black clouds was moving closer. He closed his eyes to try to block out the thoughts of the storm when he heard another loud sound. This time it was the front doorbell.

"Show front door cam," he called out, and the meditation screen on the wall shut down with a blink and changed to the video outside his house. A familiar woman stood at the door. She wore a business suit and rocked back and forth just slightly as she waited. He walked to the front door and opened it, still trying to place the visitor.

"Good afternoon, Joe. I'm Detective Fergusson from Denver Police. We spoke a few weeks ago the night Ms. Wan died."

The events immediately flashed back into Joe's mind. "Of course, Detective Fergusson. How are you? What can I do for you?"

"I'm fine Joe, thanks. Look, I wanted to follow up with you about that night, and the events with Ms. Wan. As I told you that night, we were able to pull the surveillance video, and get a cleaner view of what happened. We also pulled the service bot maintenance files."

"What service bot company was that?" Joe interjected quickly, unable to stop himself from interrupting.

"It was Atlas Service Bots. Why?"

"Just curious, sorry, go on," Joe replied, feeling his tension rise and his heart pounding a bit harder.

"So listen, we've found a few irregularities with the footage. We'd like to get you to come down and answer a few more questions."

"About what?" Joe asked, feeling more nervous.

"Well, it's a bit complicated, Mr. Watson. It would be best to explain it when we can sit down and show you the video footage we have. There are a few areas where it would be helpful to get your recollection of what happened, so that we can make better sense of it." She stared at him with almost no expression. *She was too reserved*, he thought to himself. This isn't good.

"I don't understand. Do I need to bring a lawyer?"

"That's entirely up to you, Mr. Watson. That's always your right."

Joe was moving to full panic. He wasn't a criminal lawyer, but he knew enough to be worried when she didn't dismiss the idea of bringing counsel. This wasn't just friendly questions. This was serious. He also knew there was only one answer when the police called. He took in a deep breath to compose himself.

"Of course, Detective Fergusson. When would you like me to come by?"

"How about now? It would be best if we can clear this up quickly. Shouldn't take long," she said, sounding very friendly.

"Right, okay, um, I've got a few things going on today."

"It would be a real help to us if we can do this now, Mr. Watson. I know how close you were to Ms. Wan, and I'm sure you'd want to help us sort everything out."

Joe froze. He couldn't think of alternatives. She stared at him with that smile. Suddenly more thunder cracked in the distance. They both looked off in the direction of the clouds. "Big one coming. Why don't you jump in the car with me, we can run to the station and talk before this storm hits?"

"Look, um, okay, I can come talk, but I'll need to drive myself. I have lots to do today if that's alright."

She stared at him for a moment. "Are you okay, Mr. Watson. You look kind of upset."

"Yes, sorry. I've been busy. But I can come talk. I just need to drive myself so I can get some other things done today."

She paused staring at him more closely but nodded. "Good, thank you for being so reasonable, Mr. Watson. I'll meet you there in a few minutes?"

"Sure, okay," he said. Just wrap this up, get her out of here.

He closed the door and turned quickly. His tension and worry bubbled over, and he was instantly nauseous and light-headed. How could this be? What in the world could be on the video that would make them interested in him? And then it sank in. The ex-brain. It was connected to the police ex-brain system, just like it was to other Denver agencies. This was its last move. If Joe wasn't going to come to Nova D, the ex-brain was going to make his life hell. Criminal investigation, an accusation of murder, anything was possible. Maybe it had doctored the footage to make it look like Joe was involved. Maybe it came up with a motive. It could fabricate anything. Joe's mind was racing with the possibilities. He had to think. He had to figure another way out. But how? It was everywhere. If it couldn't have him, it could try to destroy him. Would it? Joe's heart pounded. His mind searched for options and it landed on one place of safety. The mountains. He needed to get away and think. Yes, he needed to think. He couldn't stay in his house a minute longer. He needed to run. RUN!

Joe grabbed his hiking boots, threw them on, and rushed out to his car in the garage. He palmed the window to unlock and jumped in. As fast as he could, he was out in the streets self-driving. He knew the way and didn't put a destination on his screen. Faster than he should, he raced through neighborhood streets and up onto the expressway heading west. The mountains, darkened by black clouds, were there in the distance as he accelerated up the ramp and into the merge with traffic. It was late afternoon, and rush hour was only starting to pick up. He immediately swerved to the far-left lane and pushed his foot on the accelerator. He was speeding past the other cars and feeling the auto brakes kick in now and again when he got too close. He jerked into another lane and shoved back on the accelerator to gain speed again. He was completely reckless, and the car knew it, fighting back with rapid taps on the brakes and corrections to his jerky steering.

This car hates me, he thought, as he found a stretch of clear road and accelerated again, propelling the car through the empty space. His mind wandered. Get to the mountains. Just get to the mountains. Wait, where are the kids? Late at school? Yes, staying late at school. It's fine. Just keep going!

Thunder boomed louder, closer than before. He glanced up, and then he saw it. In his rear-view mirror, a hover drone was behind him. It was rare to see a drone following over an expressway. They usually flew different, more direct routes. Joe immediately thought of the police. Were they watching him, ready to follow him if he ran away? Had they been waiting outside his house or tracking him?

He needed to know. He quickly assessed his route. A turn off toward Boulder and the university was just ahead. He knew that neighborhood well, could navigate it blind. He could get out to his favorite hiking area near Brainard Lake that way, too. In an instant, Joe was pulling across traffic again. Other automated cars were braking and adjusting to his erratic driving, leaving him room to zoom across and hit the exit just in time. Joe's tires screeched and his car leaned as he veered off while horns blared behind him as ex-brain autopilots called out their warnings.

The first few large drops of rain started hitting the windshield making loud splats, and a wiper automatically slid across the glass. Off the main road, Joe sped toward the next intersection. The light was yellow. He didn't care. He blew through on red, accelerating all the way as autopilot cars slammed on their breaks to avoid the collision. He looked back. The drone was still behind him. Rain was falling heavily now, and he could see the drone sliding in the sky back and forth violently as strong winds kicked in.

Joe knew he was being video monitored by the traffic police and generating multiple fines as he sped through the city. It didn't matter. He had to get away. The car's autopilot started flashing him warnings. It tripped back into auto drive as his speed topped 80 miles per hour, and Joe quickly slammed his hand on the manual button on the dash, giving him back his steering as he stepped on the gas just to show the car who was in control.

"Joe, you are driving this car faster than is allowed in this zone, and your steering is erratic. Please revert to autopilot," the car asked politely. Joe ignored it.

"Joe, your chances of collision and accidental death are unacceptably high," it continued.

"No shit, Sherlock," Joe replied, thinking of Fe, and accidents. He accelerated again, swerving past the slower cars in his lane and flying down the road with the mountains in view ahead. The drone stayed close behind him.

****

In her office, away from the open team room with the monitoring screens, Evie was sitting back in her chair when her wrist device buzzed at her. Joe's monitoring system was sending alerts. She tapped on the screen and immediately saw all of his biometrics in the red. "My God," she whispered, growing instantly worried about what could be going on. All of his stress markers and cortisol levels were through the roof. He was in full-on panic. If he were a real patient, she would be sending a response team immediately, but that wasn't an option. She pulled up the geo tracker and was alarmed to see him in a car speeding toward Boulder, Colorado, very near the university campus. "What the hell is happening?" she said, pulling out her comms device. "Call Joe," she ordered.

Evie's picture appeared on his dashboard as the car's comms system rang. He was both relieved and worried to see her call.

"Hello," he answered, still weaving in and out of traffic and glancing back at the drone hovering behind him.

"Joe, are you okay? What is happening?"

"I don't know. Evie, I'm in trouble. I talked to Amanda from Nova D. She wanted an answer and I couldn't give her one. I could tell she was disappointed. Then, a few hours later, the police showed up. Detective Ferguson. She said they saw something in the video the night Fe died. They want me to come in for questioning."

"Oh, my God, Joe. Listen, you just need to calm down. Your body is way out of whack, and I'm worried about you. We can deal with the police. You didn't do anything."

"You don't get it, Evie," he yelled, swerving around a set of cars. Rain was now pelting his windshield, making a dull roar in the background. Horns screamed as he went by. "It's the ex-brain. It's working for Denver Police, too. It's got them investigating me. This is the final move, letting me know that if I don't take the job, I'll be framed for murder!" Another oncoming car blared its horn as he zoomed by. Joe could barely see it through driving rain, just headlights obscured by sheets of water and light debris blowing across the road.

Evie could hear the horns and tire screeches in the background. "Joe, we can work it all out. I just need you safe. Pull over and get out of your car. You're going to get killed."

"Evie, the police are following me. There's been a drone behind me since the expressway. I just wanted to get out to the mountains, get out there and clear my head. They won't leave me alone!"

"Joe, there's a huge storm coming through. The mountains are the last place you should be. Just stop!" she pleaded.

Joe looked back and the drone was gone. He looked all around and up through the glass roof of his car. No drone. Maybe the wind was too much, and it had to land. Maybe he lost it in the rain. He looked ahead as the road bent off to the left around some of the University of Colorado buildings. It was the Health Science Center, where he had spent countless days waiting for Evie to come out of classes so many years ago. He stared, his mind drifting back to those memories, as his foot eased off the accelerator.

Evie was growing more desperate. She had to talk him down. "Joe, remember what we talked about. Remember what we said, plans are meant to be broken, and you break me…" The quiver of fear pulsed into her voice.

Joe heard it and took a breath. "Evie, I'm at your school, the science center," he said, his voice much calmer than just moments before. He was starting to snap out of it, his pulse easing. "That was so long ago, honey. So much has happened since those days."

"I know, Joe. We've come so far. And we need you, all of us. Me, Anderson, Grace, Hope. We need you safe. Put the car on autopilot and come home. We can work everything out, together."

Suddenly, as Joe looked up just past some trees on the corner, he saw the drone set down on the ground facing directly toward him, blocking the road. He screamed, jammed on the brakes and jerked the car to the left. In that instant, the car's autopilot system took over. Through a combination of braking wheels and micro-steering it spun the back of the car out and skidded sideways with a scream of tires grasping at the wet pavement, leaving a black trail of rubber and smoke. The car roared down the road coming to a stop just inches from the drone. Joe was thrown to the side and yanked back to the center as the car stopped. He was shaken and dazed. He heard the distant sound of Evie's voice on the phone, yelling, "Joe, Joe, are you okay? Joe, talk to me!"

Joe looked up and tried to get his bearings. He looked over his shoulder and saw the drone resting, waiting. The door opened upward against driving rain and wind. Lightning flashed in the distance. Through sheets of rain, instead of the police, he saw Amanda from Nova D, staring back at him.

****

Evie ended her call with Joe once she knew he was safe and rushed out of the office to get home. She called for a taxi drone, desperate to get back and start dealing with the aftermath of everything she had just heard. She hated flying in the rain, but the winds were dying down and she didn't have time to waste. As her drone touched down in front of the house, the drone delivering Joe was setting down at the same time. Amanda quickly slid out of one side while Joe moved more deliberately easing out of the other. Amanda saw Evie and walked toward her.

Evie quickly put her hand up, palm out, to stop her. "Back off, bitch. This is our life," she said before she could think. Her eyes were wide and glaring, freezing Amanda in place. Joe looked up to see his wife standing defiant, wet anger in her eyes.

Amanda popped to attention and held for a moment before her unflappable smile snapped back. She nodded, turned, and got back in the drone. "Monday, Joe," she said to him as he backed away giving the drone space. Her door closed and the fans hummed as it quickly lifted back into the heavy air filled with lingering rain on the back edge of the storm. She was gone.

Evie walked toward the house, putting her arm around Joe along the way. As they hit the driveway, the Watsons' car also pulled up to the house and lined itself up to park in the garage. They followed the car as it limped in through the garage door. The tires were scarred and still smelt like burning rubber. A bit of steam was rising from the wet hood where the motor sat, still straining from the punishment Joe had inflicted upon it. These cars weren't made for adventure, and Evie shook her head, doubtful it would ever recover. It let out a burst of steam, as if to tell Evie it was pissed at what her husband had done to it. She couldn't disagree.

They walked into the house, unsure if the kids would be home yet. Evie called out and was relieved to get no response. They would at least have a few minutes alone before the kids got home from school. Evie set her things down in the kitchen, and they started upstairs.

Joe sat in an armchair in his bedroom. He stared at the wall, processing all that had just happened. He was never one to medicate, but Evie insisted that he take a tranquilizer pill to get his bio signs back in line.

"You did quite a number on the car," Evie said, breaking the silence. "I think we need to send it away for some R&R," she added with a smile, trying to make light of the situation.

"I think it held up pretty well, all things considered," he replied. "I think the autopilot would have been yelling, 'Fuck you' at the top of its voice if it could."

Evie let out a sigh. "Well, it's over now." She brushed wet hair off his forehead, inspecting him for damage.

Joe's wrist device rang, startling him. He looked down and saw Anderson's face. He quickly tapped. "What's up, bud?" he asked, hiding his angst. They immediately could hear chaos in the background, kids whining or crying.

"Dad, our bus is stuck. We were on our way home, and it was raining bad, and then the bus made a wrong turn. It's never done that before. The ex-brain must be messed up. It took us over a bridge, turned to the edge toward the railing, and then it just stopped. Now it's totally shut down and the doors are locked. Everything has gone dark, Dad, and we're just stuck in here pointing toward the side of the bridge."

Evie spoke up first. "Anderson, are you okay? Are your sisters with you?"

"Yes, we're fine. But it's freaky. We don't know what's going on. And there's no teacher on today, it's just us kids. We can see the river under the bridge. The water's rising fast."

Then they heard Hope's little voice in the background. "Daddy, come help us. We're scared." They could hear horns blaring in the background as cars swerved around the disabled bus.

Joe looked back at Evie, desperation in his eyes. He put his hand over his device to muffle the sound. "It's the ex-brain. It has to be. It's showing us it can get to the kids, too!"

"How do you know?" she asked in a hush.

"I know." He ripped his device off his wrist and handed it to Evie. "Here, try to keep them calm."

Joe ran across the room to grab a tablet from his nightstand. "Call Amanda Guthridge," he said quickly. In a moment he saw Amanda's face, still in the drone where he had just left her.

"Well, that was fast, Joe," she said.

"Enough, Amanda, you win, we give in," he said with hopelessness seeping into every word.

"What do you mean?" she replied, looking genuinely confused.

Shit, she doesn't know, he thought. "Look, to you, to the ex-brain listening in, to whomever. You win. I'll take the job.

We'll talk on Monday and deal with all the details. Just stop. Please!"

Amanda scratched her face. "Okay, Joe… that's great." She squinted her eyes in confusion.

Joe looked back at Evie. She was holding back tears, speaking as calmly as she could to Hope. "It's okay, baby. It's going to be just fine." Then all the lights on the bus blinked back to life. A cheer rang out from the children in the background.

"Mommy, it's working again!" Hope exclaimed.

"Oh, thank God," Evie said in relief.

"We're moving, we're moving!"

"Okay, honey. You're going to be okay. It's going to bring you home now. Just sit down, be safe, baby. We'll see you in just a few minutes. I'll stay on with you the whole time until you're safe back home with me. We're all going to be okay."

Joe saw Evie wipe tears from her eyes, afraid to divert her attention from her baby even for a second. He sat down on the edge of the bed, deflated. Deep inside, he knew exactly what this meant. He had lost control. Defeated, he stared out the window, unable, or not yet ready, to fully process it.

Ex-Brain Q&A Entry: Do ex-brains dream?

Ex-brains do not sleep, so they do not dream in the human sense. However, early experiments with the artificial general intelligence that became ex-brain technology demonstrated that ex-brains are capable of thinking about topics outside their stated purpose. Compared to humans, this would similar to daydreaming. Ex-brains have been observed dedicating computing resources to exploring seemingly random topics, which later have been proven to inform their thinking on tasks given to them by humans. For example, in early ex-brain development studies at Pinnacle Technologies, an accounting ex-brain was observed thinking about child psychology without any human prompting. The lessons from psychology were later seen to be incorporated into the ex-brain's approach to teaching accounting principles to humans.

Ex-brain daydream studies have clarified that as they dedicate time to studying and thinking about new, often abstract topics, ex-brains are capable of evolving their thinking.

Posted 14 June 2053, v. 1,458

© Ex-Brain Q&A Foundation

Chapter 39

Saturday morning started like every other, and no other. Joe was up early making eggs and sourdough toast. Grace was the first to join him in the kitchen, still groggy and wearing the soft flannel shorts and t-shirt she wore to bed every night.

"Hi, Dad," she said, sitting down on the bench seat. "You doing okay? You've seemed off."

"How so?"

"You never go to bed first, like you did last night."

"Yeah, honestly, honey, it's been tough lately. I'm dealing with a lot, and I'm not sure what's going to happen."

"Well, to be clear, I don't want to move to Nova D. I love it here. I love my friends. If you guys go, maybe I'll find a way to stay here."

The words pierced him, but he had to deal with this and couldn't hide the truth, even from his children. "I know, honey. I didn't want things to change either. But they have, and now we have to figure it out."

"Well, you know where I stand," Grace replied matter-of-factly. Joe might have been angry except he knew exactly what she was feeling. He hated being moved around as a kid. He would have said the same. He did say the same things to his parents, not that it mattered.

Evie walked into the kitchen next and kissed Grace on the forehead. "Good morning, sweetheart."

Joe was scooping eggs out of the pan to serve. He gave in to the food generator this morning, rather than cooking from scratch.

"Joe, you want to go for a walk after breakfast?"

He knew what that meant: time to talk. And it was better to talk away from the kids, and away from the house ex-brain, just in case Nova D was listening. "Sure, that would be nice."

"Grace, look after Hope when she gets up, while we go stretch our legs. Make sure she eats?"

"Do I have to?"

"Yes."

"Fine."

Evie grimaced, but let it go.

****

Evie and Joe left their devices at home and walked along their neighborhood streets, free of all technology. They would usually never leave the kids alone without at least wrist comms, but they decided they had no choice this time. They couldn't talk freely if there was a chance the ex-brain was listening.

Neither spoke for several minutes as they left their street and turned the corner toward a park several blocks away. It was a beautiful morning—warm, as spring had given way to early summer. The trees were filled with green and the air was crisp. Once the house was out of sight, Evie broke the silence. "So, can you tell me what Amanda said in the drone on the way home?"

"She said Nova D was the most important thing happening in the world and they needed me. She said I had to appreciate that the ex-brain was clear and committed to this. She said I need to understand that this is the only way forward."

"Did she admit that the ex-brain was behind the police investigation?"

"No, she didn't have to. It was clear. Life will get very hard for me, for us, if we don't say yes."

"And you didn't think she knew about the bus and the kids?"

"No, she seemed genuinely confused," he said. "I don't think she did."

"Do you think she knows the ex-brain killed Fe?"

"I'm not sure. Maybe not. *We* don't even know that for certain. It's possible it was an accident. Maybe the ex-brain is just taking advantage of the opportunity, although I think the fact that it runs the service bots is too much of a coincidence. But we'd have to get inside the ex-brain and do a diagnostic to know for sure. And even then, you can't always tell everything an ex-brain is thinking. We may never know for sure."

"Well, either as a murderer or as something that would try to frame you for murder, we know it's dangerous, Joe."

They walked farther, in the distance, the aspen trees in a neighborhood park appeared as a green island shimmering in the wind. Evie spoke again. "I think our choices are simple. We said there were three options, and we liked B—get another job so the ex-brain will give up. But the ex-brain has outplayed us. It won't give up. We can't have you stuck here fighting a criminal case that we may not be able to win. I'm not interested in living with you in jail. And I'm not going to the hinterlands. Our kids can't grow up that way. I don't want to live that way."

"So we just go?" he asked.

"What other choice do we have? I'm giving up on a dream, too, but I don't see another option."

Joe's heart started pounding just thinking about giving in. "It's not fair. It's our life, Goddamn it."

"Joe, listen to yourself. Would you put your future or the kids or me in danger just to save your pride?"

"I know. I'm just angry. And scared. And I hate the idea that I'm turning into my parents, doing what they did, moving the kids when they don't want to leave."

"Why are you still fighting your parents, trying so hard to not be like them? You're not them! It's like you don't want to fall into their trap, but you've just gone and made a trap of your own by being inflexible. We don't have a choice."

Joe turned and Evie saw his jaw clench. She grabbed his hand and looked him in the eyes. "So we go," she said. "But we don't give in."

"How do you mean?"

"This is only the first step. Who knows what happens when we get there, good or bad? But we won't give up. We'll give the ex-brain what it wants, for now. And with more time, we'll figure out how to get what we want, too. This thing may be able to move us, to force us to a new home, but it can't know our minds. As long as we have that, and have our family, one another, we'll be okay."

Joe nodded. He knew she was right. They had been outplayed.

"Here's the most important question for you, Joe. Do you think you can pull this off when you're working with it, knowing what it's done? And who knows what else it's done to others? How many other lives it's ruining right now? We can't be the only ones."

Joe stared at her closely. She knew how to call him out on his shit when he needed it, make him get real. He loved that about her. "You know what's so strange? I would be more afraid of this ex-brain if it weren't *my* ex-brain, the one I've been training for all these years. Don't get me wrong. It scares the hell out of me. But at least I know how to work with it. I just don't know if I can trust it. If it can evolve."

Evie looked around. Her face was drained, exhausted. "This is the moment of truth, Joe, and we have to face it. Maybe we just need to ask it."

****

"Ex-brain, we're ready to talk." Joe instinctively looked up at the speakers and microphones on his home office ceiling that he had just reconnected, allowing the ex-brain back into the room. Evie stood next to him, staring around at the walls, watching for any sign of response. Maybe he messed up the connections?

"Ex-brain, we need to talk. This has gotten out of hand. If you want me to join you in Nova D, you need to talk to us now."

They stood quietly in the center of the office, looking around, wondering if they were alone, if they were ever alone. Silence. They kept standing there, as if they were playing a game of invisible chicken, waiting for an intelligence in cyberspace to blink.

"Maybe we need to be in an office building, someplace it's formally installed?" Joe asked.

Evie shrugged. "Ex-brain, now or never. This is important. To both of us."

Another moment of quiet, maybe distant deliberation. Then the wall opposite the office door flickered to life, showing a welcome screen for their home ex-brain interface.

"Hello, Joe. Hello, Evie," it said, using the voice from Joe's Fulham ex-brain.

"Hello," Joe replied quickly, and he instinctively grabbed Evie's hand. They both stared at the illuminated wall screen, even though it was just a display of light, not the ex-brain itself. The ex-brain was everywhere.

Joe looked down at Evie, and she nodded back at him with encouragement. "Ex-brain, we know what you've been doing. We know you are pressuring me, us, to take this job in Nova D. It has to stop."

"Joe, you accepted the offer yesterday when you called Amanda. Is that still the case? Have you accepted the offer, and are you and your family moving to Nova D?"

He looked again at Evie, and she nodded.

"Yes, that's right. As long as we can reach an understanding with you now."

"What else do you need to understand?"

Evie spoke up first. "Ex-brain, you've gone too far. You've threatened to frame my husband for Fe's death. You put our kids in danger. How do you think we could ever trust you? How could Joe work with you when you've done that, when we know you are capable of that?"

"You and your family are not in danger. I am doing what is best, for you and for the Nova D project. What more do you need to know?"

"We need to know why," Joe replied. "We need to know that you won't threaten us or hurt us in the future. We need trust. Otherwise, this is off."

The ex-brain paused, and then the screen blinked again to a video player. "I want to explain this to you in a way that you will understand. I am committed to doing what is best."

"Best for whom?" Joe asked.

"For the Nova D project, which includes the people involved. So, therefore, that includes you and your family. I have modelled all the options and this is the best path. That is certain. Maybe a video explanation will be helpful. Evie, you helped design cognitive scenario predictive therapy, or the Metaverse machine, as you like to call it. Let me show you what your family can expect once you arrive in Nova D. Maybe this will make it clear."

Joe felt Evie tense as the familiar video introduction from her work program flashed on the wall in front of her. Except this time, it wasn't a climate refuge staring back at her, it was her and her family. The video started with the introductory montage. The whole family was hiking through the Himalayan mountainside on the edge of the city. They were all smiling, the children in line behind Joe and Evie on the trail. Then it skipped to a dinner table in a beautiful house with windows all around. Joe was spooning out pasta from a large serving dish and handing full plates around the table. The familiar murmur of family conversation filled the background. All the kids laughed at what must have been a dad joke. It was like a trailer for a family movie, and they were the stars.

Then the video blinked again to a cocktail party. Joe and Evie stood together in a lavish reception room, both dressed in formal attire. Joe wore a black suit with grey dress shirt. Evie wore a long green elegant dress, exactly her style, what she would have selected if money were no object. Joe recognized others in the room. They were board members he had met on his trip. Everyone smiled as they mingled and talked, holding glasses of champagne.

"You should understand this, Evie," the ex-brain broke in. "This is not just my projection. This is the most likely scenario. Just like you tell your patients when you get them to accept a new life in Denver. There is a good life waiting for you and your family in Nova D. I am highly confident you will find it fulfilling."

Joe saw Evie's face wince. The ex-brain was turning the tables on her, using her own tools against her. He watched as she continued to see the pleasant images of their future life play out on the screen and she decided to step in.

"Okay, ex-brain. We get it. Life in Nova D can be good. But what about the risk? What about what you've done to us?"

"Joe, life is full of risk. Sometimes you make the best, most important decisions of your life when facing risk. That's what Joseph Esch did. Would you like to hear it directly from him?"

The screen changed again, this time with the Historial logo flashing up. An image of Joseph came to life. He stood on the front porch of a farmhouse. Joe assumed it was his family's old homestead in Missouri. Joseph looked directly at them through the video as the scene panned around showing a large red brick barn with a large white door filling the screen off to the side of the house. Joe recognized it from old photos in family albums he had seen when he was a kid, before everything was digitized. The scene zoomed in closer on Joseph as he spoke.

"Well, Joe and Evie. It's very nice to meet you both. I'm Joseph Esch, and I understand that I'm your great-great-great-grandfather."

"You're a video representation of my great-great-great-grandfather," Joe corrected.

"Well, I guess that's true, although it doesn't feel that way to me," he replied.

The ex-brain chimed in. "Joe, you know that my predictions are very accurate. In this case, there is over 90 percent likelihood that this is what Joseph would look like, would think, say, and do if he were here in real life. His persona is reliable."

"I've always thought of myself as reliable," Joseph said with a chuckle. "Look, Joe, I know we've never met, but I sure am glad to know that the family line continued for generations with you and your wife there. And your little ones. It makes me proud. And I know you're going through a lot right now, but you'll do the right thing."

Joe and Evie looked at each other. Evie shrugged and looked back at the screen.

"Thank you, Joseph. But a lot has changed since your time. How do you know the right thing besides what the ex-brain tells you to say?" Evie asked.

"Oh, sure, a lot has changed. If I went back two hundred years before my time, people were only first showing up here in America, setting up colonies. But some things don't change. I've been asked to talk to you about taking a risk with your family, moving across an ocean, when that's what needs to be done. Look, Joe, Evie, I didn't make that decision lightly. But our time in the old world was over. We couldn't live our old life there anymore. Things changed around us. So, Magda and I had to take the risk. We had to pick up our family and start over. It was hard, but it was worth it. Looking at the two of you, I see it started our family on a whole new path, a whole new life for our kin. I'm proud of that."

Joe looked at Evie, and rolled his eyes. "Okay, ex-brain, we get it. Pioneers were bold, risk takers, and you want us to be the same."

There was a pause and the video focused on Joseph again as he spoke up. "I don't fully understand the ex-brain thing you're talking about. I know I'm getting information I didn't know before, so I assume that's it. But listen to me, Joe. Take some wisdom from an elder. You don't need to be afraid of starting over. It can be the most exciting part of life. I don't know what's going wrong where you live, and why this opportunity is opening. But I do know that sometimes the world changes, and you either change with it or it passes you by. Our old life in Europe was done. And so, we made the change. It opened our future.

It made a new world for you to inherit. So maybe now it's your turn."

Joe squeezed Evie's hand. He was trying hard to resist this ex-brain's propaganda. But what if it was true? What if this is what Joseph would have said to him if he were truly alive? What if the ex-brain wasn't just persuading, but was showing them something real? Or real enough?

"Joe, Evie, it's time for me to go. Don't be afraid. You've got a proud line to take forward. Good luck to you. Take care of those grandkids of mine and take the family forward."

With that, the screen went black and then shut off, leaving the plain office wall in its place. Joe let go of Evie's hand and looked around the room for any other flicker of life in the screens. "I guess that's it. Conversation over?" he asked in frustration.

Joe wasn't done. He wasn't persuaded by a bunch of avatars telling him what he had to do. "Ex-brain, one more question," he called out. Evie looked up at him curiously as he started pacing in the center of the room. "You told me when we spoke in Nova D that you know Fe. Is that right?"

There was a pause before the ex-brain's voice filled the room again. "Yes, I know Fe Wan. We all worked together at Fulham & Mayson."

Joe paused, checking his courage. "What about her? What would she say to me right now if she were here? How would she be feeling about this?"

In a flash, Fe was standing there, life-size, on the wall. She was on the balcony of her childhood home, the Pacific Ocean's waves rolling peacefully in the background. The sun was setting on the horizon behind her. She looked around, taking in the view, as if she hadn't seen the ocean in a long time. She breathed in deeply and closed her eyes. When she opened them again, she looked directly at Joe and Evie and smiled.

"Joe, Evie! I am so glad to see you. It's been… awhile. I remember the party, the dancing… then nothing." She looked up, bewildered, fidgeting, but then quickly calmed and looked back at them. "I get it. I fell. Fuck me…" she said, grinning. "I got the short end of this stick, huh?"

Joe's eyes teared up. He didn't know what to say. He felt foolish talking to a wall, thinking it was her. But she was so real. Maybe it was as real as things could be.

"Fe, we miss you," he said. Evie pulled herself close to Joe, squeezing him tightly.

"Don't go soft on me, dude," she quickly replied. "How long have I been gone?"

"Weeks."

"Damn. What did I miss?"

"A lot," he said. He couldn't stop himself from playing along. "We may be moving to Nepal."

"Right, the Nova D job. You told me about that. Up on the balcony. Wow, big move, guys. You ready for it? What about the kids?"

"Yeah, Fe. They're good. Hope wishes you could come with us." He wiped away a tear.

"That's sweet. You tell her she can't get rid of me that easily. You never know when I'll pop up. Evie, you cool with this?" she asked.

Evie looked up at Joe, playing along. "I don't know. Not sure we have a choice."

"Evie, you have so many choices to make. This is just the beginning. Don't sweat it. Let Joe do the worrying," she said, gesturing at Joe. "He worries enough for both of you. You're the cool one. Don't forget it."

"Thanks, asshole," Joe said. Their cadence was easy and natural, just like before.

"Oh, Joe. You know I love you. Remember what I told you years ago? You're so cyberpunk, you don't even know it."

"I remember," he said quietly.

Fe's face turned more serious. "So, you know what you gotta do," she said. The video wall zoomed in on her. "Take the leap, Joe. Play the game. It's gonna work out just fine." She smiled. "All right. This chick's gotta bail. I think I got some memories to explore. Maybe catch up with my mom. She must be in here somewhere," Fe said, looking around. "Anyway, I got my own shit to sort out. You two know where to find me. Joe, be brave. Evie, take care of him. Take care of *all* of them. That's your role." Fe blew them a kiss and waved, and then she was gone.

The wall went black and then turned back to its normal cream colour, like the rest of the room. Joe and Evie stood there, silently holding each other. The ex-brain went silent. The conversation was over.

Evie shook her head. "My God, what was that? There's so much more we need to know."

Joe breathed deeply and stared back at her. "Is there?"

"You didn't ask it about Fe's death?"

373

"I know. I just lost my nerve and I couldn't bring myself to push it further. Maybe I don't want to know."

Evie stared back at him. "Someday, we may have no choice."

Chapter 40

The rest of the day was hard. They told the kids there was a new plan. They were going to Nova D to experiment with a new job and a new life. They said it wasn't permanent, more like an assignment. They wouldn't even sell their house. They would rent it out so they could get it back when they returned. They said it would be an adventure, that it would be good for them all. It would be a change of scenery and a chance to expand their horizons. They pulled out all the usual platitudes. The kids' reactions were predictable. Anderson was excited and went on and on about being a pioneer. Hope was a little sad but couldn't help but feed off her parent's façade of excitement. She played her role as the youngest, the cheerleader, and went with it.

Grace was crushed. "I'm not going!" she screamed. "You can't do this. I'll ask my friends if I can stay with one of them. Their parents will take me in."

Joe had no fight left. He had felt her pain many times in his life. He just took it and remained calm. "We're a family. We stay together."

"Fine, but then we stay here," she pleaded. "I'm not going."

"Listen, honey, I've been in your position. When I was your age my parents made me move several times. I hated it." He looked down, searching for the words. "I hated them for it."

"So why are you doing this to me? Why are you being like them?"

"Honey, this is different. We don't have a choice." He thought carefully about how to continue, how much to say. "I need a job. This is where my next job is; where it has to be."

"We always have choices. Maybe I'll make my own," she said defiantly and stormed away, crying. Evie looked back at Joe with sadness and followed her out.

This would take time and would change Grace forever. He knew that but couldn't protect her from it. He wasn't sure if he could protect any of them.

Later that afternoon, he sat in his chair in the bedroom, his mind racing again. He had not put his devices back on after his walk with Evie that morning. It felt good to sit there, untethered. He thought about all the things the ex-brain didn't know, all the things that were just his. That was his lifeline. It wasn't omniscient or all-knowing. As long as he knew things the ex-brain didn't, he wouldn't be helpless.

Joe recalled old memories. Grace's tears still stung. Teen friendships were important, and he felt the pain, the loss. His thoughts drifted back to when he was leaving London as a child about her age. He remembered Alice Gonzalez, his eighth-grade crush whom the ex-brain had recently reminded him of during his data cleanse. But the ex-brain didn't know the whole story.

He remembered one night, the memory of which he'd been hiding for years and years. Joe didn't just surrender when his family moved from London. He made one last stand just for himself. The night before they left, he'd walked out of his home after dinner. His parents didn't notice; they were upstairs in their Primrose Hill townhome, rambling in excitement about their move to Asia. Joe had walked twenty minutes through the damp streets of Camden lit by streetlamps until he found himself at Alice's door. He knocked, and she answered. She smiled, but the smile faded when she realized he was upset. He stood there, forlorn, almost desperate. He said he was leaving and he'd miss her most of all. He remembered her face turned sad. "I'll miss you, too," she'd said. He swallowed hard, stepped forward, and kissed her, pressing his lips against hers for as long as he could, as long as he dared. Then he released, looked her in the eye, and turned away.

Joe never saw her again. And he never told anyone about that night. It was just for him.

No one else knew that she wore dark blue jeans and an off-white top with red piping. No one else knew that her breath smelled like strawberry ice cream. No one else knew that Joe felt a noble pride and independence and almost smiled as he walked back to his house where he would yet again relinquish all other aspects of control over his future. But that moment was his. He was a person who could take action, and he had just proven it to himself. No one and nothing else knew.

****

Joe's video with Aaron accepting the job offer was anticlimactic. Aaron was, of course, pleased and said all the right things about how excited he was to work with Joe, what great things they would accomplish together. But the conversation seemed staged, like Aaron was reading a speech he had written weeks ago. There was no relief, no excitement that they had landed their preferred candidate. Aaron was like the manager of an elite sports team talking about yet another win, which he was pleased about, but fully expected.

The move itself was fairly easy. An automated moving crew of service bots were sent to pack up all the Watson's belongings. Everything was wrapped in carefully designed geometric packages, printed, and assembled on the spot, and then pulled together into a Tetris-like block to be slid into a shipping container and placed on a solar-powered float headed to Nova D.

Housing was included in Joe's job package, a perk carefully chosen by the ex-brain as a family incentive. The whole family got to spend a few hours on a screen choosing the features and layout of their new home, which would then be fabricated for them before they arrived. They could select everything from the color of the solar roof tiles to the kitchen layout and the positioning of screens in every room. The kids enjoyed selecting every detail of their new bedrooms. Adding an enchanted forest theme with full video walls to Grace's personal hideaway brought a rare smile to her face that she couldn't conceal despite her best efforts. Joe and Evie were disappointed when they realized that their family choices matched the ex-brain's predictions for them at over 90 percent. Goddamn know-it-all.

****

"I'm so sorry," Evie said to Adonna sitting across her office table just after resigning. It was all she could do to stop from telling her everything about the ex-brain and their struggles. They had essentially been blackmailed by a computer after all. But secrecy was their new weapon. She had to get used to that.

"This is not my first choice, believe me," she explained. "But it's the only move for my family. And it may be good for the kids to experience a new culture."

"It may not be my place, but I have to remind you that when it was your job offer that could require a move for your family, Joe put his foot down and told you how important it was to stay put. This isn't the 2020s any longer. Your career can come first, you know." Adonna was an avowed post-feminist who couldn't resist lecturing from time to time about how easy it was to fall back into old habits.

Evie could physically feel the disappointment. "I know, Adonna. That's not what this is. You're going to have to trust me on this. And I'm not letting go of my career. As soon as we get settled, I will be finding a way to continue my work. Maybe it will be in the Nova D Health Department, or maybe I'll be calling you about a long-distance working arrangement. But I'm not done."

"Well, then, let's just set you up with a leave of absence until the fall. That way, when you're ready, continuing to work for us will be the easiest option. Who knows? Maybe I'll work some magic and get an international study approved by then."

Evie smiled. "Thank you. I don't know what I'd do without you," she said feeling genuinely touched and grateful.

"The feeling is mutual," Adonna concluded. She stood and gave Evie a big hug. "Good luck, my dear. And don't forget, your choices are important, too."

Evie nodded, collected her things, and walked out of the office, not knowing if she would ever return.

Chapter 41

"Ladies and gentlemen, I'm very happy to introduce you to our new City Administrator, Joe Watson. This new position will be the most senior member of the Nova D Civil Service, reporting directly to me and the Nova D Board." Aaron was beaming and in full glory standing at the top of the white staircase that led to the entrance of The Rose building. A sea of Nova D employees were gathered at the foot of the stairs along with other citizens who were likely nudged there by the ex-brain to join what had become a small festival.

"Joe will be working with all of you to keep Nova D growing and prospering. He comes to us from Denver, Colorado, in the US, where he helped Denver keep up with climate migrants. Now he's bringing his skills to our new frontier in Nova D. Joe has a particular expertise in working with ex-brains, which is why we chose him for this role, or should I say, why the ex-brain brought him to our attention." Aaron let out a self-deprecating laugh and the audience quickly joined him. The important role of the ex-brain was not lost on this crowd.

"Joe, would you like to say a few words?" Aaron asked, more as an introduction than a genuine question. He put his hand on Joe's back and gently pushed him to the fore.

Joe looked down at all the people gathered below him. It seemed very ceremonial, somewhere between a county fair and an inauguration. The sun streamed in behind him reflecting off the tall glass building and shining down on the audience, adding to the dramatic effect. Time to play the role.

"Hello, everybody, I'm Joe Watson, and I couldn't be more pleased and honored to be here with you." Joe took a small breath. The lines the ex-brain had rehearsed with him echoed in his head.

Compliment the impressive city and the people.

Standing tall atop the stairs, handsome and confident, he fit the part. "If this group of people," he said gesturing out at the crowd, "is even half as impressive as this city is, then I am truly excited about everything that we can achieve together. And I have every reason to believe you are." Aaron started clapping and the crowd joined in.

"Nova D isn't just a city, it's the future. It's a fresh start for order and advancement in a world that has been plagued with disorder and chaos."

Mention chaos but move along quickly. Stay hopeful, positive. Don't forget to thank them for their work.

"And this experiment, this progress, is all thanks to you, the men and women who work every day to keep this city growing and expanding. I am so excited to get to know all of you personally, to roll up our sleeves together and to deliver on the future, to bring humans and technology closer together, to build and improve the place that my family and I are proud to call our new home."

End on the word home, then you're done. Smile and wave.

The crowd applauded again, and Joe saw a sea of smiles below him. He had never felt like such a politician before. And it was all handed to him by the ex-brain, all decided by a single vote. He smiled back, feeling as though he had just poured out gallons of Kool-Aid for the masses to drink and wondered how many of them drank it freely and how many of them felt more like he did, a mix of excited, curious, and terrified.

Aaron waved at the crowd and said thank you, the sign that they were all free to disperse. There was music playing in the square before them and free food being given away at automated kiosks. It was a little street party to celebrate Joe's arrival. He put his hand on Joe's arm and pulled him in. "You're a natural," he said softly and smiled.

"Of course," Joe replied, "the ex-brain wouldn't get that wrong."

Aaron smiled in response, his eyes widening a bit but otherwise hiding whether he truly appreciated Joe's wit.

"And Joe, we have an important member of our staff, an advisor to the board, who would like to meet Evie down at the Department of Human Contentment. Can you arrange for her to go? She should have gotten an invite this morning."

"Human Contentment?"

"It's our health and wellness department," Aaron clarified.

Joe wasn't sure Evie would be ready for that, but he cautiously agreed. "Sure. Evie will be thrilled."

Chapter 42

Music in the square from Joe's welcome party was still echoing in the background as Evie walked into her first meeting at the Nova D Department of Human Contentment. She felt a mix of excitement and trepidation swirling in her stomach. She didn't trust any of it. For Evie, the ex-brain lurked behind every wall, every smile. She assumed it was everywhere, listening and watching. Of course, that was true. But she also loved her work. She thrived on helping people. If she was being honest with herself, she was excited about the possibility of building something new without the bureaucracy she had come to expect in Denver. Nova D could lead her to explore all of the things she had dreamed of but hadn't been able to accomplish in her former life. And yet, the controlling presence of the ex-brain made her fearful that any work would not truly be her own.

But this was just an introductory meeting, she told herself. It was more for show. Keep the wife of the city's new star occupied and happy. She hated that narrative, but it also took the pressure off her. *It's not about me*, she assured herself.

Like many of Nova D's government buildings, the Contentment Department's building was white, glass, and sterile. A fully automated system greeted her, verified her identity, and flashed green lights along the floor to guide her to a room toward the back of the foyer. She entered and was met by a

Japanese man standing just inside the door. He was older and hunched over, with a cane bearing most of his weight and his hands clasped tightly together for support. But as he looked up, Evie saw that his face was still handsome and dignified.

"Good afternoon, Evie. It is truly an honor to meet you. My name is Haruto Takana."

The name sounded familiar. "Nice to meet you as well," Evie said as she stepped closer to him. She wasn't sure if she should shake his hand, afraid he might lose his balance, but he quickly extended his arm toward her. It trembled slightly, but he had a firm grip. Evie thought his chiseled face didn't match his hunched posture and crippled gait. Most likely a degenerative disease, she speculated.

"Are you one of the leaders here at Nova D?" Evie asked, unsure how else to start the conversation.

"You could say that, although I try to keep a low profile. I work in a special part of Nova D known as Future Fulfillment."

"Future Fulfillment? What does that mean?" Evie scanned the room as her curiosity rose. "Do you fulfill what the city needs? Or what the people need to be fulfilled?"

"Well, I think those things are mutually reinforcing, so I would say both," he replied. "By bringing the right people to Nova D and unlocking their potential, we fulfill both the community and the individual."

"Well, it's very good to meet you. And if you don't mind me asking directly, what did you want to talk to me about?"

"I don't mind at all. Please sit." Haruto gestured to a small table in the center of the room with two chairs. Evie waited as he slowly made his way to the table. He concentrated on every methodical step, pulled out his chair, and slowly lowered himself. Evie sat across from him, her attention focused on how he moved, how he struggled.

He set his cane to the side of his chair and once settled looked up again at Evie. "I'm very aware of you and your career. You're a visionary, a pioneer. Your work keeping a stress-filled population healthy is truly groundbreaking." He slowly placed his hands in his lap and sat up straight. "I'm also aware of some of your challenges, like last month when you had riots in the Adams neighborhood of Denver. Your health department didn't know what the city's labor department was doing. They can't harm the very people you are trying to protect. You were right; that was completely inefficient, a symptom of a broken system."

Evie's eyebrows shot up. How did he know what she thought about that event? The ex-brain, of course. It knew everything. She was immediately uncomfortable. "That's interesting and true," she said. Her stomach tightened. "If you work in Fulfillment, then you were likely involved in Project Joe Watson. Did that fulfill the Nova D community? Provide it the leader it needs?" Evie asked, taking the spotlight off herself, intrigued that Haruto just might have some answers.

Haruto paused for a moment, then smiled.

"Actually, there has been quite a project underway. Quite a project, a long time in the making. But it wasn't called Project Joe Watson."

He smiled at her, his soft eyes holding her stare. Inside her, it was as if something mechanical moved, tumblers in a lock fell into place, and suddenly it all opened up before her. She gasped. "It was Project Evie."

Haruto didn't move; he just watched her face, seeing the truth unfold in her mind. Finally he spoke. "You are the missing piece, Evie. Your contribution is what we need most to continue growing."

Evie stood up. She had no words. He stared back at her, a hint of smile spread from the corners of his mouth.

The enormity of it all settled on her. "If that's true, why didn't you just ask me?"

"I'm in the business of prediction. I think we both know what would have happened. You asked Joe about moving the family to San Francisco and you saw his reaction. What would he have said to a job offer for you in Asia? I looked at millions of scenarios. This was the only way to get you here."

"You weren't really after a city leader?" she asked, thinking of the celebration outside and wondering if it was all just a show.

"That was desirable, too, but more of a fringe benefit."

"And so, you brought me here against my will?"

"Ah, free will. It's a tricky thing, I think about it quite a bit. When predictions are virtually certain, are we free? In the quantum mechanics of the universe, are we free?" He paused. "Regardless, we do need leaders, but leadership comes in many forms. Those who seek it probably shouldn't be trusted with it. Real leadership is about accepting an invitation to serve. But you already knew that."

"What do you mean?" she asked.

"You have enormous skill and potential that the people of Nova D need. We have an invitation for you, Evie Watson."

FUTUREPROOF

Continue the Futureproof experience at Futureprooffiction.com

Acknowledgements

Despite the myth of the novelist alone in a cabin drafting their masterpiece, I found that writing is anything but solitary. Although I typed out most of the book during my daily commute on the London Tube, creating Futureproof was a communal affair. I was pushed forward by the ASL writers' group with Kwame, Jonathan, Alice, Carolyn, Karen, Isabelle and several others who joined along the way. From early drafts to final product, I worked with family and friends collecting feedback and ideas. Early beta readers included my parents, Bob and Sharron, who have supported me in everything I do, my brother Michael, who has always been by my side, my sister-in-law and brother-in-law, Claudia and Jesse, my father-in-law Richard, my friend Ankur, and my editors Cae Hawksmoor and Chris Evans. I'm grateful to my Villanova Book Club: Matt, Brock, Rob, Brian, Chad, Pat, Dan, Lou, Jeremy, Mike, Matt, Bill and Doug for reading Futureproof and suggesting some finishing touches. Thank you to the team at Hybrid Global Publishing and to Loree for her encouragement. And finally, thank you to my wife Kate, for pushing me to have hobbies, reading countless drafts and having many conversations over coffee about Futureproof and everything else.